follow my lead

ADRIAN J. SMITH

EREKA PRESS

Copyright © 2024 by Adrian J. Smith

All rights reserved.

No part of this book may be reproduced in any form or by any electronic or mechanical means, including information storage and retrieval systems, without written permission from the author, except for the use of brief quotations in a book review.

Book Cover by Perrin of The Author Buddy

follow my lead

one

"I can do this."

Saylor dragged in a deep breath of the wet Seattle air. Her fingers trembled, her knees were jelly, but she was here for a reason. She needed friends. She needed a life. She needed to learn to love Seattle. That wasn't going to happen if she continued to hole herself up in the apartment and see no one.

"I can do *this*," she repeated to herself, but it didn't help the trembling in her hands.

Pushing open the door, Saylor stepped into the hallway of the building that held the dance studio. At least she hoped it did, because the sign outside said that *Follow My Lead* was inside. She'd triple checked the address already, memorized the directions her phone had given her. Saylor's heart thudded wildly, making it so hard to breathe.

Why was she doing this again?

She could be home on her couch, curled up under the blanket, and moping with the best of them. She hated it here. Who was she kidding? Seattle wasn't her cup of tea. She missed the open skies. She missed the cold temperatures of winter. She missed the people she knew and saw every day.

"You must be new."

The shock rang through her. Saylor wasn't sure she wanted to look up. But the redhead standing next to her was stunning. Her hair was in braids that moved down her back, tight braids and no flyaway hairs.

"I'm Jericho." The redhead put her hand out with a generous smile.

Saylor sucked in a breath. She had no choice now. She had to interact. Damn, she was so out of practice with this. She'd spent too many hours holed up in her apartment since moving here, and she'd completely forgotten how to interact with this thing called people. "I'm Saylor."

"Good to meet you." Jericho's eyes squinted, and her smile was genuine. "You're here for the dance class, right?"

"Uh..." Saylor stared at the door. Did she really want to do this?

"Oh, are you nervous? I was too when I first started here. Come on." Jericho slipped her hand into Saylor's and started toward the door.

Guess they were going in.

The studio entrance was a small area with chairs and cubbies where people could store their things. Jericho was already pulling off her jacket and switching out her shoes. Saylor stood next to her awkwardly. She'd bought the shoes, and she'd even tried them on, but that niggling voice in the back of her head still made it seem like she didn't want to be here. Maybe she would love dance as much as she loved figure skating. Maybe she would hate it with a fiery passion and never come back.

The website had said the first three classes were free, so the only money she was out were the shoes. Her fiancé had encouraged her to go even, so he wouldn't be upset about it if she lost out on the money. That was her own problem.

"You can use this hook. I don't think that Steven will be in today. I think he's still on his honeymoon."

Saylor wordlessly slipped her shoes out of her purse and hung up her coat. She mimicked everything that Jericho had done comfortably, while her nerves tried to force their way up and out of her body in a violent attack of the run-aways. Saylor slipped her second shoe on and stood up. Jericho immediately grabbed her hand and started toward the interior door where the studio was located.

"I know it's stupid to tell you not to be nervous because we all have our own shit, but I think you'll love it here. Everyone is welcome no matter who you are." Jericho stepped through the doorway first and half-dragged Saylor with her.

Her energy was contagious, and Saylor kind of loved it. The nerves eased a little, especially since she seemed to have found her new best friend. Maybe that's exactly what this was. Or maybe she and Jericho wouldn't hit it off. Either way, Saylor was going to stick as close as possible to Jericho tonight since she seemed like a safe person to be with.

"Tia!" Jericho called across the studio room.

The studio was larger than Saylor had expected. There were no windows, but the back wall was covered with mirrors from floor to ceiling. The floor was a stunning maple color, and Saylor's new shoes slid across it, making it so easy to move. This was why she'd needed them. Jericho practically dragged Saylor with her as she walked straight toward a small door off the side.

"Tia!" Jericho said again as soon as she reached the door. "We have a new student!"

"Oh!"

Saylor stepped closer, peeking into the office. The woman at the desk stole her breath away. Her dark hair was long and curly. It was in waves down her back. She had glasses perched on her nose as she stared at a computer screen before flicking her gaze up to meet Saylor's. Her eyes were so dark that they seemed like an abyss or void that Saylor could so easily fall into and get lost there, never to resurface.

"It's good to meet you." Tia stood up and pulled her glasses off, tossing them onto the desk covered in papers. She held out her hand and her lips curled up, her face open and soft.

"Y-you too." Saylor reached out and touched Tia's fingers, her hand sliding into Saylor's so smooth and strong at the same time. Her grip was firm. Saylor's stomach flipped with nerves, her heart racing again from the state it had calmed to.

"Thank you, Jer. Go ahead and get warmed up."

Saylor could feel Jericho leave the small office, her bubbly and warm presence gone in an instant. But that also left the full effect of Tia in her hand, literally. Because Saylor hadn't snatched her fingers back yet. She sucked in a breath, moving her hand away from Tia and sliding it along her side.

"So what's your name?"

"Saylor McGinnis."

"I'm Tatiana Schroeder, but everyone calls me Tia. I'm the owner of the studio, and the primary teacher here." Tia sat back in her chair, crossing her legs. The skintight leggings she wore had laces up the sides of her legs that ended at her hips. Her shirt was just as tight.

Saylor sucked in a sharp breath and held it.

"Sit on down. There's some paperwork you'll need to fill out to join us today, and if you choose to continue classes, we can register you then."

"Paperwork?" Saylor asked nervously, sitting down on the uncomfortable wooden chair.

"Just some liability waivers."

"Oh." Saylor rubbed her palms together. "I can do that."

"Good." Tia shuffled through the papers on the desk until she found the right one and then handed it over with a clipboard and a pen. "So tell me a little about yourself."

"Um…" Saylor stared at the paperwork, realizing quickly she wouldn't be able to fill it out and talk at the same time. She was too nervous to focus like that right now. "I just moved here to be with my fiancé. I thought dance would be a good way to meet people."

"It can be." Tia's eyes twinkled, and she pushed a strand of hair behind her ear. "So you're looking more for our noncompetitive class then?"

Saylor shrugged. "I'm not opposed to competition. I've done it before."

"What type of dance?" Tia seemed intrigued now. Her head canted to the side, and she leaned in closer.

Biting her lip, Saylor dropped her gaze from Tia's eyes to her full, full lips with a purple-red lipstick. "Not with dance. But I have taken a lot of dance."

Tia narrowed her gaze, as if even more intrigued now. "You've taken a lot of dance but haven't competed. Oh, color me curious." Tia grinned and leaned back in her chair, not taking her gaze from Saylor. "Tell me."

"I did figure skating."

"Oh." Tia smiled. "Why not continue that here? We have some great rinks."

Saylor shook her head. She had moved here to start new, and she didn't want to be stuck in the same ruts she'd gotten herself in back home. Dance was a close enough alternative, and it was easier on her body in the long run. But how could she explain that in a brief few seconds before Tia had to leave to teach?

"Wanted a clean break?" Tia asked.

"You could say that." Saylor put her pen to the paper and wrote her name in the box. She wasn't shaking anymore, so that was a good sign.

"So you took dance to help with skating, I assume."

Saylor nodded an answer, not sure she could trust her voice. Something about Tia seemed to leave her struck dumb.

"Well, let's spend today testing out where your skill levels are. We can pair you up with some people and figure out if this is the best class for you or if you need to be in a more advanced class."

Saylor gulped. She didn't need to be in a more advanced class. She'd studied the class levels for hours before she'd made the choice of which one would be the best fit for her. Tia couldn't mess with that. Saylor wasn't ready for it. She couldn't make herself speak either. She couldn't tell Tia that she was wrong and that this was a bad decision.

Maybe she should just leave and forget the whole thing.

"What type of dance did you take?" Tia rolled her ankle in a circle as if stretching it.

Saylor really didn't belong here. That's exactly what this conversation was telling her. She was a skater, not a dancer. She didn't belong in Seattle. She belonged back home in Denver. Saylor shuddered, her gaze dropping back to Tia's ankle as she continued to roll it.

No.

Saylor had to do better for herself. She was here to make friends, not to be perfect at something she was just starting. She had to lock that thought away if it was going to make a lick of difference for her in the long run.

"I did several kinds. Swing, hip-hop, salsa, a touch of ballroom." Saylor looked deep into Tia's eyes, looking for some kind of affirmation. "Oh yeah, and quite a bit of ballet."

"I see." Tia nodded slowly, her tone giving off a sense of disbelief.

Most people did that when she told them. But she'd been in competition skating, which was vastly different from hobby skating. She would skate in the morning before school, in the afternoon after school, and she'd take dance classes on the side when she could to increase her stamina, skills, and balance. It had been a second job on top of school, and when she'd graduated high school, she hadn't stopped.

Not until she moved here.

Her body was about to shake again, the trembling of nerves coming right back up and trying to take over her entire body. She was just about to get up and leave when Tia leaned in and covered her hand. Her fingers were so warm—so soft.

"I'm sure you'll fit right in. Jericho seems to like you already, and she's a fantastic person to get to know. We're working on the rumba this month, but we have improv nights on Tuesdays." Tia leaned back in her chair again. "This is a couples dance class, but you're not required to bring someone else to join."

"I primarily did singles skating."

"But you're well aware of how much trust it takes to work with a partner, how in sync you need to be with each other."

"Yes, ma'am," Saylor answered.

"Good." Tia looked through the doorway to the classroom. "Looks like warm-up is over. Fill out the form and come join us. We're working in lines today since no one has really danced the rumba before."

"Okay." Saylor let out a breath and gave Tia a small smile, though she worried it looked way more like a grimace than a smile.

Tia touched her hand again, and tingles rushed through Saylor's body. Her nerves were on overdrive today. She knew they would be bad coming here. She'd barely managed to get any work done on finding a job that day because she was so nervous about the class in the evening. She'd tried to tell Jameson about it, but he just hadn't understood what she was so worried about.

"See you on the dance floor in a bit." Tia walked right on by her.

Saylor had to close her eyes and do a centered breathing technique her therapist had taught her. She'd never managed her anxiety well. But when she was on the rink, it was like all of that vanished—if she could manage to block out the crowds, listen to the music, and force herself to ignore the world around her and the fact it was a competition.

It took her all of two minutes to fill out the waiver. But Saylor took an extra three minutes before she put the paper on Tia's desk and walked to the door. Now was the moment. Now was when she had to take a breath and listen to the music, focus on that and nothing else.

Tia had everyone in three rows. She stood at the front of the class, her back to the students and her front facing the mirrors. She could see everything from there, and she would make small corrections when she needed as she taught the moves. Jericho caught Saylor's eye and immediately walked over to her.

"Come on! Class doesn't last forever. Though I wish it would." She laughed lightly as she pulled Saylor into line next to her.

Saylor closed her eyes and focused on the music as best she could. She found the beat and let it into her soul. When she glanced up, Tia was staring at her in the mirror. Their eyes locked, and a rush ran through Saylor. Tia nodded firmly and led everyone into the next step.

By the time class ended, Saylor was sold. She hadn't moved like this in ages, and just getting exercise was amazing. But Tia's gentle way of teaching, her keen eye, and her way of paying attention to everyone and encouraging them was exactly what she needed. Jericho threaded her arm through Saylor's as they started toward the lobby area.

"So what do you think?"

"It felt so good to just move. I didn't realize how stationary I'd become since moving here."

Jericho grinned broadly. "So you'll be back?"

"Yes."

"I'm glad to hear that." Tia stepped closer to them, her long, lean legs strong. She didn't even have a sheen of sweat on her. "And you did well today, Saylor. I'm glad to see you haven't forgotten a lot of those dance moves."

Saylor shook her head, grinning genuinely. "Me either."

"Our class meets Monday, Wednesday, and Friday. But there are other classes if you want to check them out. I have one competition ballroom class, if you're interested."

The thrill that ran through Saylor was unmatched. *Competition?* She'd never thought she'd be back in that realm, but if this could just be something fun on the side? "I'll think about it and talk it over with Jameson."

Tia canted her head to the side as if confused.

Saylor added, "My fiancé. Since I'm not working yet..." she trailed off. How bad did that sound? That she had to check with him before doing anything? She'd never wanted to be that woman. But had she become the kept wife already?

"You just let me know what you're interested in. I have to set up for my next class." Tia walked away.

Jericho hummed, a sound of pleasure that was pure and sweet. "She's strict, but she loves every student that walks through these doors."

"Glad to hear it." Saylor struggled to drag her gaze away. Had she messed this up already?

"We should get drinks sometime!" Jericho pulled her jacket over her shoulders and buttoned the front of it. "Like after Wednesday's class."

"Sure." Saylor gave a little chuckle. She could manage that. And she wouldn't even ask Jameson about it. She could be a strong independent woman. She wasn't under his thumb at all. She could do this. She could make friends, she could build a life here, she could be exactly who she wanted to be. Whoever that was.

two

"Hey there, rat bastard."

Tia shoved her hands deep into the pockets of her wool jacket and kicked her boot against the wet grass. If only there were rocks, she'd gladly kick them all over the damn headstone. She hated him. So why was she even here?

Sighing heavily, Tia pinched her face and closed her eyes.

What was she doing here?

Her big brother's birthday was in two days, and for some damn reason, she hadn't been able to stop thinking about him in the last few months. So much so that she found herself standing over his grave when she hadn't been there in years.

Not since she'd come out here to rail at him for being such a rat bastard.

And again, and again, and again.

She would call him that every day she was alive. Because he was. He deserved to be six feet under in a grave of his own making. In fact, she'd pushed for him to be cremated so he could burn in the fiery inferno of hell he had caused.

So why was she here?

Tia cringed. This spiral wasn't new, but she hadn't been on the twirly ride in quite some time. So why now? Her niece was back in town. And staying in town for the most part. But more than that, her two nieces, Fallon and Monti, were talking. Probably for the first time in their entire lives, they were actually having conversations and being sisters.

The change left her in an odd in-between state.

And heaven and hell knew how much she hated change.

"Why am I here, you sick bastard?" She kicked the stone and dragged in a breath of cold, damp air. "You never did anything for me. You were the bane of my existence growing up, and I spent the last three decades cleaning up your mess. A huge one. And you know what? I'm kind of thankful for it."

Now why was she talking to his grave? He wasn't here, and she didn't need to justify anything to him. Yet she was drawn here. Her fiftieth birthday was looming and because of her brother's idiocy, she'd spent most of her good years raising his two kids instead of figuring out who she was. Now she just wanted to know who Tia was.

Who she wanted to be.

Other than mom to two adults who were severely traumatized. Other than the one who came in to clean up all her family messes.

She wanted freedom from those responsibilities.

It was time to take her clothes off, so to speak, and be completely bare. Tia was someone worth knowing, wasn't she? She just had to figure out who she was. Which was easier said than done. Pursing her lips, Tia shook her head.

"I hated you for so long, but you know what? I'm done hating you. I'm done letting you ruin my life."

Turning on her toes, Tia stomped back to her car. She slid behind the wheel and went straight to the studio. She wouldn't go back there. Something inside her clicked. This was the last time she was going to step foot near his grave, and she didn't even feel guilty about it. Blowing out a breath, Tia parked and walked into the studio.

This was her second home, though her first home was an apartment upstairs. It had been the best decision to move in there after the girls were grown and out of the house, after she'd really figured out that they wouldn't be coming back permanently. Tia smiled at that. They were both living their best life, and Tia was still doing the exact same thing that she had been doing for fifteen years.

Teaching.

Some competition.

Being alone.

It was time to change it up. She deserved love just like anyone else, and it was finally time for her to explore that. She deserved to have a life that was all her own and no one else's. Life wasn't all just about work. She needed more.

"Sorry if I'm early."

Tia jerked her head up, her heart in her throat as she spun around to face the door. She hadn't even realized someone was there. She didn't even remember leaving the main door unlocked.

"I thought I could sign up."

Tia searched for the woman's name. She wasn't prepared to entertain anyone just yet. She hadn't pulled herself together yet. She never forgot names, especially of someone so cute, adorable, and definitely anxious.

"Remind me of your name again. I'm sorry, my brain's not quite functioning up to par yet."

"Oh." The woman's cheeks tinged red, which matched perfectly with her auburn hair that was loose around her shoulders. The flush looked like it belonged there. "Saylor McGinnis."

"Oh! That's right!" Tia cringed. She should have been more careful, but she really wasn't in the right mindset to do this right now. "So you enjoyed the class you joined us for?"

"I did." Saylor's voice was so gentle and soft, as if she wasn't quite sure what she was saying or that she was confident in what she wanted. "I miss being active."

Tia's lips curled up. Perhaps Saylor was right and that was exactly what she needed too. A night out on the town, dancing into the wee hours of the morning. Maybe picking up a woman or two in the process. It had been a while since she'd allowed herself time to explore another person's body in just that way.

"Well, I'm glad you'll be joining us." Tia riffled through papers on her desk, finding the sheet with all the classes on it and then the paperwork to sign up for classes. "We have an improv group that meets on Tuesdays if you ever want to join. No requirement to participate, but it's always better to have someone in the audience to watch our fumbles."

"Do you dance for those?"

Tia twitched, making eye contact with Saylor. Saylor's light brown eyes were wide, as if she was asking something neither of them fully understood. Tia handed the papers over and sat down in her chair. Just what was she feeling? Because her foray to the cemetery earlier was still putting her on edge.

"I do dance for the improv nights when I'm not working the music."

Saylor nodded, her lips pulling tight and her cheeks still holding that nice rosy tint.

"Did you want to sign up for just the formal class?"

"If that's okay?"

"It is. There's room in every class, always. And if there isn't, well then, I make room." Tia winked, hoping that would ease some of Saylor's obvious anxiety. Except it seemed to have the opposite effect. Saylor tensed up, her lips pulled even tighter than before.

Tia really should be more careful, but there was something about Saylor that put her in an awkward spot. Neither one of her girls ever suffered from anxiety. Fallon was as bossy as they came, and Monti always had a quiet and calm confidence that couldn't be shaken. Tia had dealt with nerves before competitions but never as such a regular occurrence.

"You're welcome to any of the classes. When you register, it gives you access to all the classes I offer. And if you want to start with some competitions, you just need to let me know, and I'll start to pair you with other competitors. I also offer private classes, if you're interested in those."

Saylor shook her head. "I think just this class for now."

"All right." Tia tapped the papers. "Go ahead and fill out the registration forms, and I'll take your payment information. It'll come out the same day every month."

Tia did some extra work on the computer while Saylor did all the paperwork. By the time Saylor was done, Tia was expecting one of her smallest classes of the week to begin. She had the music already picked out, knowing they'd work on the same thing they had the week before. It was one of the classes she didn't enjoy because so many of them were inconsistent.

"Want to stay for this next class?" Tia asked.

Saylor paled. "Oh um...what class is it?"

"Just a basic introduction to ballroom. You're too advanced for it from what I saw, but you can stay for my secondary ballroom after this one."

"And dance the whole night away?"

Tia's lips twitched. Was Saylor finally finding her voice and comfort? "If you want, I'm sure that can be arranged." She added a wink just for fun. Saylor seemed like someone whose shell was thick and had a lot of layers she needed to pull back. Monti would tell her Saylor was like an onion.

"Oh. No. I shouldn't be out all night."

"Well, come on and join." Tia stood up and started toward the dance floor. "It'll be more fun with you than without."

Why was she being so flirtatious? Well, she was in general, but something about flirting with Saylor felt different. It felt intentional and purposeful. Tia almost held out her hand, waiting for Saylor to take it, but she resisted.

"But I haven't even paid yet." Saylor pointed to the computer.

Tia frowned. "It'll go through when it goes through. Besides, I enjoy your company. I think you have a few more surprises up your sleeve that you haven't shown me yet."

Saylor's jaw dropped. "What surprises?"

"Well, you said you did competitions for skating, so this timid act you've got going on now can't be all there is. I've been a competitor, and you have to be strong to do that."

"This isn't figure skating."

"It's not," Tia agreed, cocking her head to the side as she studied Saylor. "Are you saying if it was, then you would be a different person?"

"I *am* a different person on the ice."

"You'll have to show me sometime." Tia stood by the door. "Come on. I need to set up."

Tia walked out, anticipating that Saylor would follow her. She didn't strike Tia as someone who broke the rules ever. That could be fun to play with too. If she could ever get Saylor to an improv night, she'd have to make up the rules as she went, and it could be very interesting to see the results. Saylor finally joined her on the dance floor.

Tia started the music and then snagged Saylor's hand and spun her around, taking the lead role. Saylor furrowed her brow, but after a moment of tension, she relaxed slightly and looked Tia directly in the eye. This was who Tia saw underneath, just a glimpse of the confident, curious person that Saylor could be when she gave herself over to whatever she was doing.

"Ready?" Tia asked, her voice breathier than she expected. What was going on with her today? She was all over the map with her emotions. "We can get through the whole song before everyone shows up, I bet."

"I'll take you up on that." Saylor's jaw tightened, but her gaze was determined.

Tia raised her arms into position and held onto Saylor firmly. She could do this. As soon as the next beat hit, she pulled Saylor closer so their bodies pressed tightly together. This felt amazing. It had been a long time since Tia had danced like this with another woman. She'd taught, yes, but Saylor wasn't here to learn specifically.

As the music reached deep into her soul, swirling and capturing her in the moment, Tia moved. She slid her foot along the floor, letting the vibrations of the music come to life within her. She would have closed her eyes, let the energy flow through her, but the way Saylor was looking at her was filled with both trepidation and awe. Tia slid her fingers from Saylor's hand, trailing it up her arm to her shoulder and the back of her neck. It was almost as if they were in a lover's embrace, which was the exact intention of this song.

Tia slowed her breathing, easing into the moment as she took the first steps and spun around the dance floor. Saylor followed her lead perfectly. They pushed together and apart, Tia spun her around, caught her, pulled her close so their breasts smooshed together before sliding away again and stepping back. The music called for passion, for strength, for the tedious dance of romance. The fights, the tension, the worries and anxiety, but also the love, the flirting, the adoration built in.

As the song ended, Tia stepped back. Her eyes were locked on Saylor's amber brown ones, her auburn hair as it stuck to her slightly parted lips. Tia was about to speak, but she had no words. Something had happened in these few moments. Yet everything in Tia's body told her to run the opposite direction and create as much space between them as possible.

Clapping echoed through the classroom, and Saylor jerked with a start, the trance broken.

"I didn't expect a show when I came in!"

"Kirsten." Tia twitched, a cold shock running through her. She breathed out slowly. Of all people to show up first, it would be her, and it would ruin everything about this moment. Then again, maybe that was a good thing. Normally, Tia would provide introductions, but she didn't want Kirsten to get her claws into Saylor. Not now.

Not ever.

"What a show." Kirsten's voice grated on Tia's nerves. This woman never got over things, did she? To be fair, Tia should have known better. "And who is this?"

Tia looked Saylor directly in the eye, hoping that Saylor would understand. But the look she got back was filled with confusion. They didn't know each other well enough to have any kind of silent communication down yet. Then again—that dance certainly blasted that theory to hell.

"I'm Saylor." She plastered on an uneasy smile and leaned toward Kirsten, putting her hand out.

Kirsten looked Saylor over with a judgmental glance and then pinned Tia with a look that said *really?* Well, yes, really. Saylor was an adorable mess of anxiety and nerves that seemed to completely vanish when she was filled with music and in the moment, doing what her body did best.

Move.

"You're early for class," Tia said as she stepped toward the stereo system to turn the music off. They didn't need to listen to it on blast.

"Seems I'm missing the private lesson."

Tia bit back her retort. She didn't want Saylor to catch a whiff of just how mean she could actually be. Sighing, Tia held back her annoyance. "Saylor's a new student. I was testing her skill level."

"Seems she has skills for days."

Why wasn't Saylor saying anything? Nothing to defend herself. Tia managed to glance at her, and the look of horror on Saylor's face said everything. She was devastated. She was embarrassed. And she wanted to run away.

"Are we learning that little move you did at the end? That was sexy," Kirsten's voice dropped, as if she was making an innuendo where there was none.

"No," Tia answered sharply.

Saylor straightened her shoulders as if she had made a decision. She turned on her heel and started toward the door. Tia shot Kirsten a look of absolute disdain. She didn't bother telling Kirsten to fuck off. Instead, she followed Saylor toward the lobby and snagged her arm just as she was about to leave the studio.

"Don't leave on account of Kirsten." Tia rushed the words. "She's a brute."

"She's rude," Saylor responded, her lower lip quivering.

"She is," Tia agreed. "And I put up with it."

"Why?"

That was a really good question, and one that Tia wasn't ready to delve into. Not yet. Not today of all days when everything was so topsy-turvy and she was glad just to be standing on two feet right now. "Stay for class. Please."

Saylor held her breath, her lips pressed together in a thin line. All the ease they had gained before was gone, and Tia wanted it back. She wanted the closeness, the touches, the connection they'd had on the dance floor. "I'll be at class on Wednesday."

Tia released Saylor's arm as if she'd been burned. Her heart ramped up, forcing its way into her throat and clogging up everything she wanted to say. She nodded sharply. "Promise?" Why was she pressing so much? Tia had never been this concerned about a student returning for classes. At least not when they barely knew each other.

"I promise." Saylor's lips gave a small quirk until Kirsten's voice echoed through to them. Then Saylor's gaze faltered, and her face fell again.

"I'm looking forward to it." Tia took a deep breath and rolled her eyes when Kirsten called for her again. "Seems the devil waits for me."

"Me too," Saylor mumbled, but Tia wasn't sure she'd heard correctly. She was just about to speak up when Saylor slipped through the front door.

"You too?" Tia bit her lip and shook her head before turning on her toes. "Seems the devil's out for blood tonight."

"What was that?" Kirsten asked.

"Nothing."

three

"I'll get back late Sunday night." Jameson set another folded button-up into his small suitcase.

Saylor had seen him pack and unpack that thing a dozen times already for his various work trips. They had thought her moving here would make it so they could see each other more, but Saylor wasn't sure if that was actually the case or not.

Maybe it was just this soul-crushing loneliness.

Maybe it was the fact that in Seattle, Saylor had no one except Jameson.

Her entire life hinged on him.

She frowned and folded her hands together as she sat on the bed, half-reclined. She knew this was his job before she'd moved there, before she'd agreed to marry him even. It was how they'd met, during some of his travels, but that didn't make this easier.

"What's wrong?" Jameson closed up his suitcase and slid onto the bed next to her. He wrapped an arm over her shoulders and tugged Saylor into his side. "You seem down."

"I am down," she mumbled and tried to hold back the tears. "I've been here six weeks, and I don't have a job, I have no friends, and I don't know anyone. I mean. It's been six weeks, I'm not expecting a best friend to just pop up out of nowhere, but without even having work friends..."

"It's hard," Jameson murmured and dropped a kiss into her hair.

These were the moments she missed with him the most. She wanted more of this. Every day of this. Of feeling like she was so cared for and the center of his world. They'd gotten engaged as a way to make her parents happy about her moving so far away, but they planned on a long engagement. They hadn't even talked about wedding details or set a date yet. Maybe that's what she should focus on since she couldn't find a job.

"I miss home," Saylor whispered. She missed having things to do and people to see.

"Maybe you should call Callie." Jameson trailed his fingers through her hair, but it wasn't as comforting as she wanted it to be. She felt more distant from him now than ever. "She always cheers you up."

"Yeah, she does."

Jameson kissed her head again, hard enough to push her back a bit. Saylor would normally lean into him, accept the kisses and the touches, but she couldn't bring herself to do that this time. She couldn't force herself to turn to him for comfort, especially when he was leaving again. It wasn't because she was mad at him. In fact, it might simply be because she was jealous.

He had friends.

He had a life.

He had work.

She had him, and that was it.

"I've got to get going." Jameson took her chin and turned her face to kiss her lips swiftly. "I promise I'll call you when I land. Okay?"

"Okay."

He always did. Saylor wasn't worried about him. She was worried about herself. She needed to get out of this funk she was in. The door shut behind Jameson, and Saylor stayed exactly where he left her for another hour before she managed to drag herself to the bathroom for a hot shower.

When she got out, she had two texts from Jameson, explaining to her that it was normal to feel lonely after such a long-distance move, that she would find a job and make friends eventually, and that he wasn't stressed because she wasn't working yet. He really was trying to be sweet, but it seemed to land dully and wasn't much help. Saylor didn't even bother answering as she lay back on the bed with the towel wrapped around her middle.

She should go to class that night.

It would help, wouldn't it?

She'd promised Tia that she would be there after basically running out scared shitless when Kirsten had walked in. Why had she done that? Something about that entire interaction between Kirsten and Tia had seemed off, and it had set her on edge.

She really hoped that Kirsten wasn't part of this dance class, and that Jericho was there. God, she needed friends. Saylor was just about to start getting some dinner ready when her phone rang. She saw Callie's name on the screen and grinned broadly. Callie always knew when to call.

"Hey," Saylor said as she answered the video call and set her phone against a candle she'd placed on the table when she'd moved in.

"Hey!" Callie's smile was bright. Her face lit up the screen, and immediately Saylor relaxed. "Jameson texted."

"He's so sweet." Though Saylor wasn't sure she wanted him to be doing that. She wanted autonomy. But if her mood was bad enough that he was talking to Callie, then maybe it really was that bad.

"He is." Callie grinned. "You snagged yourself a good one there."

She had. But some days, well most days, she just felt like she wasn't giving him what he needed. She wasn't as compassionate toward him as she could be, she wasn't as interested in things like sex and kissing and touching. He wanted all those things all the time, and since moving in together, it was startlingly obvious that Saylor struggled with that.

"Saylor..." Callie trailed off. She looked over her shoulder and then clearly walked from one place to another. She settled onto her bed, and her joy from before was replaced with utter concern. "What's wrong?"

"I don't know how to explain it." Saylor bit her cheek. She played her fingers over the table and stared at the bowl of ramen she'd made. She hadn't even touched it, and her stomach wasn't even rumbling. She had no desire to eat, which really wasn't a good sign for where this was headed. She'd been here before.

"Just try. I'm here to listen."

Saylor sighed heavily, her shoulders slumping. She hadn't talked to anyone about this. She was barely even recognizing it within herself. She'd been so focused on finding a job and making friends, on attempting to make this entire move worth it in the end. She closed her eyes as tears formed on the brims and her nose stung.

She really didn't want to cry.

Not again.

"Oh my God, he *is* an asshole! I knew it!" Callie nearly shouted.

"No, no, it's not that." Saylor waved her hands before wiping her eyes. "I didn't realize how hard moving was going to be. And you know, when you go from a relationship that's only long-distance to suddenly living together, it's hard. I don't know what I'm doing half the time, and the other half, I'm just trying to stay out of his way."

"Out of his way?" Callie's brow furrowed, a deep line forming in the center. "He should be pampering you, taking you on dates, spending as much time with you as he can. He should be all over you right now."

And that was part of the problem, but how did Saylor even begin to put words to it? She didn't want him all over her. She valued her independence and the ability to do exactly what she wanted when she wanted. Not that she was particularly risky in her behavior, but she just wanted to be doing what she always did.

"Now you're scaring me. You're not usually this quiet."

"I know." Saylor brushed her fingers under her eyes again. "I'm starting to regret moving here."

Starting was wrong. She'd been regretting it the moment she'd stepped foot in Seattle. She wasn't built for this. She wasn't prepared for it. She didn't want to be here anymore.

"Oh babe." Callie's face fell. "You can always move home if it's that bad. I'll even fly out there and help you. Brady will help too. But you haven't been there that long, you know?"

"I know." Saylor bit the inside of her cheek. The apartment was silent, still, and claustrophobic. She'd never felt this stuck before. She was so used to being free in whatever she did, but now, she felt like she had to ask Jameson when she wanted to do anything since he was the one financially supporting her. She hated this. "I just need a job."

"You need anything to get you out of that apartment."

Saylor pressed her lips together hard.

"What's that look for?"

"Well, I did go to a dance studio and sign up for classes."

"See! That's a start!" Callie grinned again. She was always a perpetual well of joy. Saylor envied that. "When's the next class?"

Saylor glanced at the clock on the microwave. "In an hour."

"Are you going?"

"I hadn't decided yet." She'd actually decided not to go, despite promising Tia that she would. Something about that last exchange had her stomach fluttering like an idiot. She wasn't sure she wanted to throw herself back into that chaos so quickly without figuring it out first.

"You're going. What are you wearing? What kind of dance?"

The hundreds of questions flew in an instant. Saylor laughed lightly as she answered them all, still sitting at the small table Jameson had shoved against the wall in the kitchen area and not touching her dinner. It was a cheap meal, but she didn't want to burden Jameson any more than she already was.

"So go get dressed!" Callie squealed. "Come on, I want to see your outfit for the night."

"It's just leggings and a shirt." Saylor rolled her eyes.

"I want to see it!"

Groaning, Saylor walked to the bedroom and put the phone onto the nightstand, facing away from where she was changing. She'd never felt comfortable changing in front of people. Even when she was still skating, she'd always gone into a bathroom stall to get ready. She didn't want people to see her body or to leer. When she was all done, she popped back onto the screen and put her hands out to her side, spinning around so that Callie could see her outfit.

"Sexy lady!" Callie giggled.

Saylor laughed, a genuine smile on her lips for the first time in what felt like days. She rolled her shoulders and snagged the phone, flopping on her back onto the bed. It had never felt like her bed. Everything in this apartment was Jameson, and even the little touches she'd brought and the things from home weren't enough to make this her home.

"I can see you're still debating whether or not to go."

"I probably will until I walk into the studio."

"But you went to one class, right?"

"I did." Saylor sighed heavily, remembering Jericho who had been so warm and welcoming, along with Tia. But that dance with her, when it was just the two of them, that was something else. Saylor had never felt so alive before, so in tune with the vibrations and beat of the music, so in tune with another person's body and the way they moved. In skating, she'd never been interested in doubles. And maybe this was why. She didn't want to have to rely on someone else.

"So that went well?"

Saylor snapped back to the conversation, remembering all too late what had sent Callie on her tirade. "Yeah. It was fine. There was a woman there who was nice to me."

"Make friends with her. Or at least try."

"I will." Though the words slipped through her lips they felt like a lie. She had been trying, and was making no progress.

"It hasn't even been two months," Callie's voice sobered. "Give it some time. I read somewhere that it takes three years to really settle in when moving."

"Three years?" Saylor's eyebrows rose. "I can't do this for three years."

"Jameson's not any help?"

Saylor pursed her lips. "He's always working and on his trips. That's part of his job, and I get that, but he's not around as much as I thought he would be."

Callie frowned. "I'm sorry it's so hard, babe. I really wish I was there to help."

"But you have your own life." Which was exactly the problem. Callie was planning her wedding and Saylor wasn't there to help out with it. She'd left everyone behind, and it was so hard to keep those relationships going. It hadn't even been that long and they were already struggling. Saylor cringed. "I'll be out to visit soon, I promise."

"I know you will. I do miss you, Saylor."

"I miss you too." Those tears she'd narrowly avoided before were back. The conversation was ending, and she feared that the friendship was also coming to a close. She didn't want that. She needed Callie in her life.

"Go to your class, Saylor!" Callie demanded. "And then text me all about it when you get home."

"You'll be asleep."

"I don't care." Callie pointed her finger at Saylor. "If I don't wake up to texts, then it didn't happen, and I'll have to come out there and beat your ass to make you go."

"I don't think that's the exact threat you want to give me." Because if Callie could come out there, Saylor would do anything to make it happen.

After their conversation ended, Saylor stayed on the bed, staring up at the ceiling in the silence of the room. What was she doing here again? Jameson was gone all the time, and she was more lonely than ever. Turning on her side, Saylor curled into a little ball and let the warm tears slip from her eyes and fall onto her pillow. She wasn't sure how much longer she could do this.

Maybe she should get a cat.

Except Jameson was allergic.

She hated this.

Callie: Your ass better be out of that bed already.

Saylor stared at the text message. Callie knew her too well at this point. She took a couple more minutes before forcing her body to move. It was so hard just to get her arms and legs to do what she wanted them to do. She rolled her shoulders, filled her water bottle, and snagged her jacket.

She could do this.

She really could.

Maybe.

four

"That's a wrap for the day!" Tia clapped her hands together, her chest heaving from that last move.

Her students were all in just about the same state as she was, some more labored than others. Tia worked to slow her breathing, grabbing her water bottle and letting the cool liquid slide down her throat. Jericho grabbed Saylor's hands and spun her in a happy little circle.

Tia smiled at them. She had no doubt that Jericho had a bit of a crush on Saylor, but Jericho seemed to start with crushes and move to friendships later. The crush Jericho had on Tia had lasted a little longer than others, but it had eventually faded into a friendship that Tia could handle. Though the woman had an abundance of energy. Tia was certainly jealous of that.

Her students lingered for a little before snagging their jackets and bags and heading out. However, Saylor seemed to be talking to just about everyone, hanging out awkwardly as others finished conversations and disappeared out the door. Tia locked up the stereo equipment and held her water bottle close to her chest as she walked toward the lobby area.

Saylor didn't even have her jacket on.

Sliding her gaze down and up Saylor's body, her tight curves, her hips accentuated by the leggings she wore, her hair pulled back but with small strands flying around because of their exertion, Tia could imagine that look on her for an entirely different reason.

What?!

Tia straightened her back and frowned. She wasn't thinking about another student in that way. Kirsten was enough reason as to why. Not to mention, she was too old for young love and too young for a second chance at love. She sighed heavily. Her brother really had thrown her life for a loop, hadn't he?

Dating someone her age was next to impossible because they all had the experience of families and relationships that she didn't have. And yet, dating someone who didn't have those experiences left them too young to have a full understanding of the reality of the world. Tia had never been able to figure out how to navigate that, so she'd turned to short flings, no strings attached, and the unattached life she'd created for herself.

"Is everything okay?" Saylor asked, her cheeks still red from the workout. Her skin was so pale compared to what it probably should be, but Tia hadn't been able to put her finger on why.

"I was going to ask you the same question." Tia twisted the top off her water bottle and took a long sip before twisting the cap back on. "Want to help me clean up?"

"Sure." Saylor seemed to relax at the invitation.

Was this Saylor's way of avoiding going home? If it was, Tia could play into that for a while. She had more than enough work to do to prepare for her classes tomorrow, so she might as well get a hand while she was at it.

Tia set her water bottle down and went to the custodial closet to bring out the broom. She handed it over to Saylor while she took a cloth and spray to clean the mirrors. She'd done it a few days before, but she might as well do it again to keep herself busy. And this way, she could watch Saylor in the mirror to make sure everything was okay.

Something about Saylor's mood seemed off.

It had since the moment she'd stepped into the studio that night.

They worked in silence for close to an hour before the floor and mirrors were clean. Tia's skin had cooled and the glistening sweat had dried up. Putting everything away, Tia put her hands on her hips and narrowed her gaze at Saylor.

"So why are you avoiding going home?"

"What?" Saylor's head jerked back slightly.

But Tia wasn't going to repeat herself. She was pretty sure that Saylor had heard her, she was just surprised at being called out on it. When Saylor didn't say anything, Tia gave in and touched her arm lightly. "Want to get a drink?"

"I..." Saylor glanced toward the door. She sucked in a deep breath, her chest rising with the motion as she held it tightly before blowing out a puff of air. "Yes."

"Good. Let me grab my jacket and lock up." Tia wasn't sure what that whole conversation was about, but she for sure was going to find out. Rolling her shoulders, she changed her shoes and snagged her jacket before locking the office. "Ready?"

"Uh-huh." Saylor already had her jacket zipped up tight. She seemed suddenly nervous again. "I thought Jericho might want to go out."

"She has a big date with her boyfriend every two weeks."

"That's what she said." Saylor sounded disappointed as she stepped through the main door to the studio.

Tia locked up behind her and led the way out onto the street. "There's a bar a few blocks down. It's not posh and not grungy."

"Sounds perfect." Saylor couldn't even look Tia in the eye. She shoved her hands in her pockets, stared at her toes, and started walking in the direction Tia led.

They were nearly shoulder to shoulder, the dark sky surrounding them like a cocoon of damp, chilled air. But something about this felt warm and comforting. Tia wasn't sure what to say though. Saylor had to be handled with care, since she seemed skittish when they ran up against her anxieties.

"Here it is." Tia held the door open as they slipped inside. The damp air from the gentle rain was constant this time of year, and it clung to Tia's hair.

Saylor slipped past, her arm brushing against Tia's front in the tight confines of the doorway. It sent a ripple of pleasure through Tia's body, one that she readily schooled. She wasn't here for that. She was here to take care of a student who seemed lost, lonely, and scared to go home. She wouldn't ever let anyone have the same fate as her late sister-in-law and her nieces. She'd vowed to step in whenever she could.

Maybe that was all this was with Saylor.

They slipped into chairs at a small table in the corner. The table was worn down, the top sticky from years of use and spills, but it was clean. Tia ordered a beer, and Saylor mimicked the request. Shucking her jacket, Tia crossed her legs and eyed Saylor over again.

"You're staring at me like I'm a piece of meat." Saylor shut her mouth tightly, as if she hadn't quite been expecting herself to say that.

Tia's lips twitched upward. "I'm curious why you don't want to go home, but I'm not sure if you're ready to answer that question."

"Oh." Saylor frowned, her hands twisting together on the tabletop. "Jameson is away on business again."

"Again?" So it definitely hadn't been what Tia was thinking. Saylor wasn't afraid of being beaten—well, at least not that night.

"His work takes him all over the world, mostly within the US and Canada, but he's gone a lot."

"So you don't want to go home because..." Tia nodded to the waiter as their drinks were set in front of them. She took a long sip of her beer, but she didn't drag her eyes away from Saylor's face.

She wanted to know where all this pent-up emotion was coming from.

"Because I don't want to be alone."

"Ah." Tia set her pint onto the table a little harder than she'd intended. She was making up problems where there were none—another one of her issues any time she was in a relationship and why it was a very good reason to steer clear of them. "How long will he be gone?"

"A week and a half this time. He's gone more than he's home. I moved here to spend more time with him, you know."

"And that's not happening," Tia concluded. The conversation seemed to be flowing now, which was a good thing. Tia could hang onto this. She could figure out exactly what Saylor needed and move into how to help. Then Saylor could lean on Jericho when she was available instead of Tia.

"It's not. And I don't have a job. I spend so many hours holed up in that apartment on my own, and I just... can't stand to go back there. I hope that makes sense."

"It does." Tia smiled, knowing exactly what Saylor was talking about. "When my nieces moved out, finally, it was like the house was too quiet. I hated it. I had to move back into the city to get out of there."

"That's kind of you to let your nieces live with you. Were they in college at the time?"

"Uh...no." Tia needed to sidestep this conversation. Saylor wasn't ready to hear that story yet. Or perhaps it was more accurate to say that Tia wasn't ready to share it. She hated talking about her family and explaining just how screwed up her brother was. "But they're adults now and living on their own. Monti, my youngest niece, just moved back to town, actually."

"That must be nice to have family around."

"Some days." Then on other days she hated being so close to the memories of what her brother had done. That seemed to be coming up a lot lately. She needed to shift her thoughts in a different direction. "How long have you and Jameson been engaged?" Tia nodded toward Saylor's ring finger, where the diamond sat against her skin, encompassed by a silver metal.

"Oh, not very long." Saylor immediately started spinning the ring on her finger. "Couple months."

"When's the big day?"

"We haven't set a date." Saylor wouldn't look her in the eye, which seemed odd. Anyone Tia had met who had just gotten engaged usually wanted to talk all about the wedding and nothing else. Maybe something else was afoot.

"You haven't?"

Saylor shook her head. "We figured we'd have a long engagement since it happened so quickly."

"I feel like there's a story you're not sharing here."

"Not much of one. We met when he was in Denver for work about six months ago. But long-distance was hard, and we thought me moving here would help with that. So we got engaged, and I moved here."

Tia's face pinched. "Usually when people talk about being engaged, there's a lot of talk about love."

"Oh, I love him."

But Saylor's face remained passive.

"Of course I love him."

Why did Saylor sound like she was trying to convince herself? Tia kept quiet, drinking her beer as she listened for the different inflections in Saylor's tone, eyeing her mannerisms. "I've never been married. Or engaged."

"Do you want to get married?" Saylor's question was different from how people normally asked that.

And it was different enough that it didn't immediately put Tia's back up. "Not really, no."

"I never thought I wanted to get married either." Saylor spun her pint on the table. "But I guess I changed my mind."

She still sounded like she was trying to convince herself. Tia picked up on that tone from a mile away, and she was going to continue to look for it as much as possible. She finished her first drink and ordered a second one.

"I find dating at this stage of my life odd."

"Why's that?" Saylor's brow furrowed.

"Because I'm close to fifty years old, and most people my age have been married and divorced. Some of them were widowed. Most have kids, a lot of them have kids still in school."

"And you don't want those complications?" Saylor prompted.

"I don't understand them. Younger people tend to not have the worldly experiences I do. They're at the start of their careers. They want to have fun and then settle down."

"But you don't want to settle," Saylor concluded for her.

"Correct. Fun, I'll have. Settling... that's not for me." Tia smiled when her second drink was put in front of her. Considering how attracted she was to Saylor, she really should look into finding someone to help her expend some of that sexual energy she was carrying around. Someone who was free for the taking and who was interested in women. Though Saylor could be interested in women even though she was engaged to a man. Tia wouldn't shove her into the *straight* category just yet. They didn't know each other well enough.

"You're not afraid to be alone?" Saylor's voice was small, her shoulders collapsing in slightly as if to make herself take up even less space than she had been.

"No." Tia eyed Saylor over her pint. "Are you?"

"Yes."

"I love being alone. But I'm rarely lonely."

Saylor frowned, as if not quite understanding the difference.

"I suspect you're more lonely than you are alone."

"Maybe." Saylor finished her drink and pressed her hands into her lap, as if she was scared to say anything else.

"Do you want another one?" Tia pointed toward her drink.

Saylor stared at it, the debate in her eyes clear as day. "I shouldn't."

"That isn't what I asked." Tia leaned in a little, her hand flat on the tabletop. "Look, I'm not the police. If you want another beer, have another one. If you don't, then don't. Own your decisions, Saylor."

Saylor winced. "Yes."

"Good." Tia waved the waiter over and asked for another one. "Now, do you like Seattle?"

Saylor smiled. "I don't know."

Humming, Tia scooted from the chair she was in to the third chair at the table, sitting right next to Saylor. Maybe closeness would help loosen her up a bit. "Tell me about skating. I've only been once when I was a kid."

"Once?" Saylor's eyebrows rose in surprise. "I love it. It feels like flying."

"I get that from dancing."

"Maybe, but you can go faster when you're skating."

This had seemed like the safest bet for a topic. Saylor's entire face lit up at the conversation. "True. But I do love a slow dance." Fuck, that had sounded so flirtatious. Why couldn't she stop herself sometimes? Saylor was engaged. There was no reason Tia should be pushing this.

Saylor's cheeks pinked, clearly embarrassed by Tia's flirting. Tia cursed herself. She should know better. Saylor was fragile, and she didn't need an older woman coming on to her. Ever. Taking a long sip from her beer, Tia tried to find another topic of conversation.

"What do you do for work?"

Saylor bit her lip and shrugged. "I don't work right now. I've been trying to find a job since I moved here, but I haven't had any luck."

"It's not a great market for it." Tia played with the coaster on the table, forcing her fingers to think about something other than reaching over and touching Saylor's wrist for comfort. "What did you do in Denver?"

"Odd things here and there when I could. It's expensive to be on the competitors' circuit, so I coached a lot of kids, did some sewing projects here and there when I could, substitute teaching."

"Did you go to school for anything?"

Saylor shook her head. "No. My life was figure skating."

"And it's not now? Why stop just because you moved?" Tia looked directly into Saylor's beautiful brown eyes. If skating was that much a part of her life, why would she stop? Especially so suddenly. It seemed an odd turn of events, didn't it?

"It's just time to move on."

Well that was a nonanswer if Tia had ever heard one. But she obviously hadn't gained enough of Saylor's trust to talk about that yet. Just like Saylor hadn't earned enough of Tia's trust to talk about how fucked up her family was. Letting it drop, Tia ordered a third beer. What the hell did she care if she got drunk? Her home was two blocks away.

"Sometimes you have to break those ties," Tia mumbled into what was left of her beer before downing it.

"Yeah. Sometimes you do." Saylor sipped her new beer quietly, an elephant suddenly landed in the middle of the conversation, and Tia wasn't quite sure what to do with it. Not yet anyway.

"You know, if you need something to fill your time while you look for a job, I can always use help with some of my classes with kids. You're good enough and have the experience of working with kids that you could really help me out." Tia clenched her molars. What was she doing? She was so used to fixing everyone's problems that it came naturally to her. She'd just offered it up like it was nothing. Well, it was nothing. She really could use another adult to corral the kids, especially an adult she didn't have to pay.

"Really?" Saylor looked skeptical.

Tia could understand why. "Yeah. I'll need to run a background check, but having another adult who understands the basic principles of dance would be really helpful."

"I'll think about it." Saylor finished her second drink of the night. "I should really get home."

"Facing the fear?"

"It's not fear." Saylor looked Tia dead in the eye, confidence in her eyes. "I know what I'm facing."

"And what's that?" Enraptured, Tia couldn't look away.

"Failure."

five

"Saylor, stay a minute, would you?"

Saylor couldn't believe she was there.

Again and again she'd told herself she wouldn't show up, but something about the way Tia had eased her nerves when they'd gone out was enticing. She wanted to know if she could feel that calm again. Biting her lip, Saylor followed every step in the class as best as she could. But now as everyone filed out of the classroom and Saylor was stuck waiting for Tia to finish up her conversations, she wasn't sure what was right or what was wrong.

Or who she even was anymore.

Something about Tia was so easy. In a way she'd never experienced in her life before. Not with figure skating, not with friends. Jericho waved as she left, and Saylor gave her a small wave back. Maybe that was easier too. Was it possible that she was beginning to like Seattle?

Yet the thought of going back to her apartment filled her stomach with dread.

"I hope you consider competing."

"What?" Saylor jerked her head up and looked Tia directly in the eye. She worried her lip, folding her hands together and twisting them.

"Competing." Tia smiled as she pulled her hair out of the ponytail and redid it.

Saylor could barely take her eyes off the movement of Tia's hands, the tension of her fingers as she pulled the elastic, her hair as it fell against her back.

"Steven needs a partner for the next competition because Jericho is going to be on some cruise."

Saylor's ears stopped ringing. She wasn't tracking the conversation. "What?"

"Are you paying attention?" Tia chuckled, her voice low as she shook her head.

"Sorry." Saylor immediately looked down at the ground, her cheeks reddening. She'd been struggling to focus, because of the scent of Tia's body—sweat with something sweet—and because the warmth she brought each time she was in Saylor's presence was something Saylor found herself longing for.

"Don't be sorry." Tia laughed lightly again and put her hand on Saylor's arm. Her touch was firm, her grasp tight, and a shiver ran through Saylor's body. "We had an intense practice."

"Yeah..." Saylor trailed off. She kept her eyes locked on Tia's feet.

"Will you look at me?" Tia's question was so gentle, a beckoning.

Saylor pressed her lips together hard, dragging her gaze slowly up Tia's body, over the curves of her calves, the muscles in her thighs, her thin hips, to her waist. Her heart hammered, her breathing shallow as she reached Tia's breasts, tightly confined in her workout clothes, but straining against the material. Saylor struggled to pull her gaze away, but when Tia stepped in even closer, she had to—otherwise it would stay awkward.

"I meant my eyes," Tia murmured.

Saylor's mouth went dry.

But Tia looked amused, not offended.

"I'm so sorry."

"Don't be. I enjoy being admired, especially when it's not in a leering fashion." Tia reached out and put a hand on Saylor's arm. "I wanted to talk to you about competing with Steven in a few months."

"Months?" Saylor squeaked.

"Yes. I think you can be brought up to speed quickly, since you have more than the basics already down. It would be Steven's first competition, too. I'm not expecting much other than for you two to participate and get experience." Tia didn't move her hand. Instead, she squeezed tightly and moved her fingers up and down.

Saylor flicked her gaze to the touch before locking her eyes on Tia's. She had no idea what to say. Her heart was in her throat. "I don't know."

"Come on. You can do this."

"I..." Saylor swallowed down her fear. "I don't think I can."

"Let's try it then." Tia walked away, turning on the music and coming back. She didn't even take a breath to prepare as she snagged Saylor's hands and spun her into a circle.

It was exactly like before. Saylor moved against her, unable to force herself to stop as the music filled her soul and propelled her feet to follow Tia's lead. She moved her fingers lightly against Tia's body, sliding them when she was supposed to. She stepped closer into the circle of Tia's arms, pressing their chests together just like she'd done with Steven earlier when they'd practiced this very dance.

But it didn't feel the same.

This was so much more than a simple dance.

Saylor sucked in a staggering breath as she spun in a circle, landing right back into Tia's grasp. The music faded away to the point that Saylor barely even heard it. The only sound in her ears was her breath, a gentle ringing, and the sound of their feet against the floor. Tia held her so gingerly, guiding their movements as they spun around the dance floor from one step into the next. When she stopped, Saylor missed it.

"See?" Tia breathed. "You're a natural."

"I don't see," Saylor responded, more confident than ever in that simple phrase. She wasn't made for dancing. Not like Tia was.

"Then I guess you'll need a lot more private lessons."

"I—"

"I didn't realize you had private lessons scheduled." Kirsten stepped through the doorway and into the studio.

Saylor's cheeks burned. They were so hot, she wasn't sure she wanted to touch them, and she certainly couldn't turn to face Kirsten. What was it with that woman? Saylor hated her, but she was pretty sure it was only on principle. Tia tensed every second Kirsten was nearby, and that set Saylor off. She faced the ground again, worried that Kirsten would see her embarrassment.

"I didn't realize you kept tabs on my calendar," Tia fired back, an anger in her tone that Saylor hadn't witnessed before.

"I don't." Kirsten smiled and stepped in closer, moving right between them. She put her hand on Tia's arm.

Saylor instinctively stepped away, rolling her shoulders. She had to put some space between herself and the two of them. More than that, she needed to escape. Getting out of here would be the best thing possible.

"Why are you here again?" Tia asked, her voice louder.

Saylor risked a glance at her as she took a step back. She looked pissed, raging mad.

"I thought I'd catch you before you left for the night." Kirsten stepped in even closer to Tia, pressing against her arm as she wrapped their fingers together.

Tia extricated her hand and sent Saylor an apologetic look. "What did you need?"

Tia was annoyed now. Anyone within a mile radius should be able to see that. Saylor started toward the door, needing to leave the two of them to whatever argument was about to happen. She didn't want to see another fight. She had enough of that growing up. Biting the inside of her cheek, she slipped through the door into the lobby and snagged her jacket from the hook.

Tia's voice was sharp as she reprimanded Kirsten. Saylor had her jacket on and zipped up. She had her hand on the doorknob and was almost free.

"Wait." The word reverberated through the lobby. "Please just wait."

Saylor tensed, her shoulders sharp. She'd been so close. "I don't want to cause any drama."

Tia let out a wry laugh. "This isn't your drama."

Staying where she was, Saylor tried to convince herself to just leave. There was no reason she should be staying there. She cringed. She was such a pushover.

"Just stay. Let me get rid of her."

"And then what?" The words were biting. But she hadn't intended her tone to sound like that. Saylor winced. Her anxiety was getting the better of her already.

"And then we'll talk." Tia looked Saylor directly in the eye. "Please. Two minutes to get her out of here."

"I don't think this is a good idea."

"Saylor." Tia stepped in close, standing against Saylor's body as if they were back in their dance. "Please. Don't leave me alone with her."

Saylor's lips parted, suddenly the entire tone of the conversation changed. She wasn't escaping but helping Tia to escape. Saylor canted her head to the side, looking deep into Tia's eyes. She didn't want to have her leg pulled, and she didn't want to end up being walked all over again.

"I'll tell you all about it, but please don't leave me alone with her. Not right now." Tia moved in even closer, the warmth from her body seeping into Saylor's skin, taking root there. "Please," Tia whispered.

"Fine." Saylor stepped back toward the studio. She said nothing else.

Tia seemed at ease already, walking into the large studio with more confidence in her shoulders than she'd had before. Saylor noted it as she folded her hands in front of her body, trying to keep herself from wringing them together in her own nervous state.

"Kirsten, I'm busy." Tia moved to the stereo equipment, closing everything up and locking it. She kept her back to Kirsten, as if she was too scared to look at her.

"You don't look busy." Kirsten glared at Saylor and stepped between her and Tia, clearly a power move.

Just who was this woman?

On instinct, Saylor walked closer to Tia, leaning against the wall next to her, hands in her pockets, and she refused to look away from Kirsten. Something about this woman set her off. It had from the first moment they met, and Saylor was definitely not going to back down now.

"I'm closing up for the night. Unless there's something you need, I'm asking you to leave."

"She's not leaving."

"Saylor and I have some things to discuss." Tia flicked a glance in Saylor's direction, her lips pulling tight into an uncomfortable smile.

Kirsten snorted loudly. "You never change, do you?"

Tia cringed, openly.

"Always have one way to find them."

"That's not what's happening here." Tia spun around, cutting her hand across the air as if that would stop the conversation.

Saylor looked from Tia to Kirsten, wondering exactly what was going on that she was missing. Because there was a part of the conversation that she wasn't privy to. But if she had her guess, they had history—sexual history—and Kirsten wasn't taking the hint to leave well enough alone.

"Get out, Kirsten. Before I have to call someone to escort you out."

"You'll come back. You always do." Kirsten turned her gaze onto Saylor, the glare full force.

Perfect.

Now Saylor was the enemy when she didn't want to be.

Kirsten took one more step toward Tia. Saylor immediately moved in closer, almost between them. Kirsten lowered her voice, as if Saylor couldn't hear every word. "See you Monday."

A cold shiver ran through Saylor, one full of displeasure and worry. Tia said nothing as Kirsten flicked her hair over her shoulder and walked toward the lobby. When the door was shut, Tia let out a breath and relaxed. Saylor waited in silence, not sure what to say or do next.

"If you don't mind, I'm going to lock that just to make sure she doesn't come back." Tia walked away.

Cast into quiet, Saylor waited. She waited for everything. The explanation, the understanding, the reason why she was suddenly thrust into the middle of drama she had no part in. She crossed her arms and waited.

What now?

Tia stood in front of her, looking small for the first time since they'd met. This woman wasn't perfect. She wasn't strong. She had weaknesses and broken spots. Just like anyone else. But Saylor's were so much bigger, and she'd managed to hide them so far. That was the only reason Tia had let her stay to help, because if Tia knew the real her, she would understand in an instant how incapable Saylor was.

"Thank you," Tia murmured, already more relaxed than before. "Kirsten can be a handful."

Saylor wasn't sure what to say. She held the words deep inside her, knowing that anything she said would be the wrong thing in this moment. She was forced into silence by fear.

"I just wish she would move on. Sometimes I think she's about to, like last summer, but then she always comes crawling back here. I've tried so many times to convince her to check out different studios." Tia walked toward her office, locking up as if she didn't have a care in the world. She flicked the lights off as she went.

Saylor was three steps behind what was happening, because Tia waited for her in the doorway to the lobby, her hand on the light switch. Scrambling to catch up, Saylor strode directly toward Tia. But Tia stopped her with a hand to her arm as they stood in the entryway together.

"Come upstairs."

"Excuse me?" Shock ran through Saylor's body.

"I want to tell you what that was about."

"It doesn't matter what it was about," Saylor answered before she could think. The scent of Tia's body pulled her in. The warmth of her hands. The look in her eyes. They were right back to where they started that evening, and Saylor found herself slipping in closer.

Tia leaned against the doorframe, her gaze flicking down to Saylor's lips, lingering for seconds longer than she should have before she looked back into Saylor's eyes. "It does matter."

"No, it doesn't." Why was Saylor whispering?

God, if anyone saw them, they would think this was intimate. No wonder Kirsten had pushed those buttons. But nothing was going on between them. Saylor was engaged to Jameson. She wanted to be with him. Didn't she?

"I think for you it does." Tia trailed her hand down Saylor's arm to her hand, twining their fingers together in a tender grasp. "I want to tell you."

"I don't understand."

"I know you don't." Tia squared her shoulders, moving in even closer as if they were about to start a new dance. "This makes sense to me, which is probably all that matters right now. But I want to trust you, Saylor."

"Trust me?"

"Yeah." Tia's lips pulled upward at the sides, her smile almost freeing.

Saylor envied that. "Why would you want to trust me?"

"I haven't figured that one out yet."

"Okay?" Saylor asked, still not understanding what was happening. She shifted in closer, their bodies touching through their clothes. But this wasn't a dance. This wasn't purposeful in that way. This was pure intimacy. And Saylor longed for it. "I want to trust you, too."

"Then come upstairs with me. We can have a drink and talk. Get to know each other."

Warning bells went off in Saylor's head. This was crossing a line, wasn't it? This was a boundary she shouldn't be stepping over, and yet the pull to do it was more than she'd ever felt. Even with Jameson. He didn't understand why she was the way she was. He hadn't spent the time to learn about her family or her past.

But neither had Tia.

And yet this was an invitation to do just that, wasn't it?

"I don't know," Saylor mumbled, being as honest as she could in this moment.

"I get it." Tia didn't let go. She didn't move away. She didn't stand down. But neither did she push or coerce. "I like you, Saylor. Not just because you're cute and adorable, but because there's so much more to you than meets the eye. You intrigue me. And I want to know why."

"I'm not interesting."

"Says who?" Tia wrinkled her nose. "Because I think you're fascinating."

"Says anyone." Saylor looked down at Tia's parted lips, the fullness of them. Would kissing a woman be the same as kissing a man? She would like to know, just once, if it was the same. It'd satisfy this curiosity she'd had for years that she'd never been able to put into words.

"I'd tell you here, but I really just want to get out of this place.

I've been here all day, I want a drink, and I want to relax." Tia still hadn't moved.

Saylor looked her in the eye again and sighed. "I have to get home."

"Is Jameson back?"

Shaking her head, Saylor stepped out of the doorway. Whatever trance Tia had her in, she needed to break it. Kissing her dance teacher? What fantasy world had she jumped into? She'd never been interested in women. That thought had been crazy. Saylor shoved her hands into her pockets after opening the main door and holding it for Tia. She glanced up and down the hallway to make sure that Kirsten wasn't hiding out somewhere.

"So you can stay."

"No." Saylor knew she had to be firm in this. Because whatever was happening inside of her, it wasn't okay. She needed to stop it before she failed the one thing she knew she had to get right but swore up and down she'd ruin anyway. Saylor always messed everything up. She always failed when she should succeed. Watching Tia lock the door, Saylor took another step back. Distance. That was exactly what she needed right now. Jameson was her fiancé, and she needed to stick with that decision.

"I need to go home."

"Next time, then."

Saylor didn't answer her. Instead, she took another step back. "Stay safe, Tia."

"Thank you, Saylor." Tia ran her fingers through her hair. "Really. I mean that."

Without another word, Saylor broke the spell. She stepped out onto the street, the cold rain hitting her hot cheeks the perfect reminder of what would happen eventually. She always ruined a good thing, and she didn't want to lose the one place she might be making friends.

Six

"Well, shit."

Tia sat heavily in the chair at her desk, her phone next to her hand as she stared at the schedule and exactly what was happening in the next week. She hated this part of running a studio sometimes, but it was a necessary evil since she couldn't do it all by herself.

Jericho had called in sick.

For the entire week.

She had somehow managed to convince Saylor to come in for the day, and while that had been a fantastic decision, Saylor had made it clear this was a one-time thing. But Jericho was now sick for the week. Tia stared through the open doorway to her office and into the studio where Saylor led the last group of girls through their cooldown routine.

Tia finally pried herself from the desk, not knowing what was going to happen next, and helped Saylor usher the girls out to their parents. Once the last kid was gone, Tia crossed her arms and looked Saylor over and sighed heavily.

"Jericho called."

"That doesn't sound like good news." Saylor snagged her water bottle and twisted the cap open. Tia's eyes caught on her arm muscles, the pull of them as she moved, the easy way she seemed to go from one position to the next.

"It's not." Tia frowned at herself. She shouldn't be staring at Saylor like that. "Influenza A. She finally got the test results back."

"Wonderful." Saylor started cleaning up, putting things back in place. She bent down to grab the push broom and started going back and forth on the floor to pick up the dirt the girls had left.

"She's out for at least ten days now." Tia straightened her shoulders as she watched Saylor work, the line of her muscles, the confidence with which she moved as she put everything back the way it had been. Tia bit her lip. In another world at another time, she might have tried something with Saylor. Though Saylor really didn't strike her as someone who would be comfortable with no strings attached. And with the strong reminder of Kirsten just three nights ago coming into the studio when she and Saylor were there, Tia wouldn't make the same mistake twice.

"I'll have to make her some soup or something," Saylor said quietly.

"I bet she would love that." Tia stepped in closer, wanting to touch Saylor again, like the other night, but she resisted the temptation. Or at least she tried to. Her fingers had a mind of their own, though, and they flitted across Saylor's upper arm as she set the broom against the wall to store it for the next time in between classes.

"Will you stay?" Tia asked.

"I told you I'd be here all day."

"No, for the next ten days, while Jericho is out."

Saylor gnawed on her lower lip, her gaze flicking from Tia's eyes to her mouth and back again. "I don't know. I need to find an actual job that pays me actual money."

"I'll pay you while you work for me." Tia slid her hand up to Saylor's shoulder and stepped in closer. Her chest tightened, her entire body alight with anticipation, as if Saylor was going to touch her too. But that wasn't the case. They were simply getting to know each other.

"I'm not sure if that's a good idea."

"Why wouldn't it be? Mutually beneficial." Tia slid her hand down to Saylor's, twining their fingers together. She moved her other hand to the small of Saylor's waist and instinctively raised her elbows up as if she was about to start a dance.

What the hell was she doing?

There was no music.

There was no indication that Saylor even wanted to dance.

Giving into the instinct, Tia leaned forward and pressed her body against Saylor's, their eyes locking. In Saylor's brows, she saw the confusion swimming, the hesitation, and just an inkling of curiosity underneath. It was that curiosity that Tia snagged hold of, that she held onto and tried to pull out.

Tia stepped forward, guiding Saylor back. She would lead this dance if it was the last thing she did. But something magically happened to Saylor on the dance floor every time. It was as if she forgot all her worries. As if the world existed without them.

Was it the same when she was skating?

Tia took another step, Saylor's leg sliding between hers until she took a step back and righted her form. Tia's lips twitched upward in a smile, and Saylor moved her hand up to Tia's shoulder as if fully preparing herself for what was about to happen. Tia focused on the beating of her heart, the wild thudding that sped up and slowed down. It was a music unto its own.

She spun Saylor around, taking her toward the center of the studio floor. Bending, she slid her palms down Saylor's sides to her thighs, her knees almost touching the ground before she rebounded back up. Saylor raised an eyebrow at her in amusement. Tia grinned fully, taking Saylor on another spin before grabbing her and pulling her in close.

Their breath was the only sound in the room aside from their feet on the floor. Tia moved swiftly, pushing Saylor back again as they walked four steps before spinning. Tia held onto Saylor, dipping her back and over Tia's leg before pulling her up to wrap arms around her as if they were in a lover's embrace.

"You're built for improv," Tia murmured before splaying her fingers all along Saylor's back. "I'm finding that I enjoy dancing with you more and more each time we do it."

"Why are we dancing?" Saylor asked, her voice breathier than Tia had ever heard it.

Maybe Saylor wasn't as unaffected by Tia's presence as she'd originally thought. Tia didn't stop though. She moved into a slower spin as they trotted around the dance floor. She kept her hands on Saylor's body as much as she could, guiding them as they went.

"I love dancing."

"I never would have guessed." Saylor chuckled a little. "I think I'm learning to love it."

"Are you?" Tia's eyes lit up. This was most definitely flirting, and that was something Tia was very comfortable with. "There's something about dancing with someone else that's so intimate."

"Yeah." Saylor's voice caught on the sound. She rubbed her lips together as if she was going to say something else but couldn't find the words.

"Work with me while Jericho's out."

"Are you seducing me into a job?" Saylor straightened her back, taking a little more control of the dance than she had before.

Tia noted it and allowed it. She wanted to see just what Saylor could do, what she would willingly try if given the opportunity. Tia relaxed her body, giving in to the push that Saylor gave her to walk backward. She grinned when Saylor spun her and leaned against her back. Saylor's fingers dipped into the curves of her waist and over her hips before clasping on and twisting her back around in one quick movement, as if Tia had been thrown into the air on a spin.

"Is it working?" Tia asked, unable to wipe the smile from her lips. She was enjoying this tease too much. It'd been so long since she'd surrendered herself to the moment, letting her feelings and hopes and desires guide everything she did.

"Maybe." Saylor stepped forward, taking complete control of the dance.

Tia surrendered to the moment, letting Saylor take the lead as she followed. They moved swiftly in four spins around the dance floor, getting awfully close to the wall of mirrors. Tia had accidentally run into those mirrors so many times over the years, she wouldn't be surprised if Saylor was unaware of just how close they were getting.

One more spin and Tia's left shoulder hit the wall, her body jerking with a start. Saylor stumbled, falling into Tia to control herself and ultimately pressing Tia smartly between the wall and her body. Saylor sucked in a sharp breath, and Tia immediately wrapped her arms around Saylor's shoulders and flipped them.

With her thigh between Saylor's legs, her feet firmly planted, and a hand at the back of Saylor's neck, Tia tilted her head away enough to look directly into Saylor's eyes. Her chest rose and fell sharply as she tried to catch her breath. Tia couldn't stop herself when her gaze flicked down to Saylor's lips and lingered far longer than she should.

Tia wanted to kiss her.

She wanted to press their mouths and bodies together in a heated moment of passion and pleasure.

"I'm sorry," Saylor muttered, her voice back to that nervous wobble she typically had. "I didn't realize how close we were."

Tia had definitely noticed how close they were. She put her head on Saylor's shoulder and caught her breath. What the hell was she thinking? Saylor was engaged. She'd shown no interest in Tia. She'd shown no interest in any kind of relationship other than rudimentary friendship.

"Work for me. Just until Jericho comes back."

Saylor hummed, her hands still against Tia's back. If anyone were to walk in, they would think something else was happening. If Kirsten were to see them... Tia stopped that thought. She should never have let Kirsten get that close to her.

"What's wrong?" Saylor asked, her fingers falling to the small of Tia's back.

They were still wrapped up in each other, Tia pressed to Saylor, nose buried in her neck as she breathed in Saylor's scent. She dragged in a deep breath, her eyes fluttering shut as she spun through every way she could answer that question. Her initial response of *nothing* was bit back in favor of something closer to the truth.

Why?

Tia had no idea why.

"There are many things I regret in my life, Saylor." Tia pulled back, their hips pushing against each other, but this way Tia could see Saylor's eyes when she finished talking. She could know exactly what Saylor might be thinking or feeling when she dropped this bomb. "I don't want to regret anything else."

"Okay?" A line formed in the center of Saylor's brow, and Tia resisted the urge to smooth it out with her thumb. "What does that mean?"

"Today it means nothing." Tia stepped back, putting space and cool air between them.

"And tomorrow?" Saylor snagged Tia's hand and pulled her back so they were facing each other. But this was a much stronger Saylor than the one Tia had first met. This woman had questions and she wanted answers.

"I never know what tomorrow holds." Tia reached up and pushed a stray strand of hair behind Saylor's ear and then dropped her hand. The intimacy hadn't ended when it should have. "Think about helping me out with the kids' groups. I could really use it."

"I'll think about it." Saylor's lips pulled upward. "Jameson comes home tonight, though."

"I understand if you want to spend the time with him." Tia's shoulders tensed. There was something about Jameson that she didn't like, no matter how much she tried to push past it.

"Yeah..." Saylor trailed off. "Was there anything else I needed to do to help today?"

Tia shook her head and pressed her lips into a thin line. She needed to pull back. Maybe it would be a good thing if Saylor didn't help out with the kids' classes. Tia could use some space to get her head on straight again. Rolling her shoulders, she started for the stereo to find the music for the adult classes that night. She still had four hours of teaching to go before she could crawl into her bed and hide under the covers.

"I'm glad I came today," Saylor added, her voice softer than before. Was that acquiescence in her tone? Or was it honesty?

"Does that surprise you?" Tia asked as she opened the cabinet door.

"A little. Yeah." Saylor walked closer. Did she not want to leave? Was she avoiding going home despite saying that was exactly what she wanted?

"Why?" Tia faced Saylor. She couldn't figure her out. Did Saylor want to leave or stay? Was this that loneliness showing its face again? Or was it something else entirely?

Saylor's cheeks pinked. The sweet color brought life to her features, highlighting her youth and liveliness. Saylor glanced down and shook her head. "I needed to get out of my own head."

"I need to do that every day," Tia answered with a chuckle.

"This is more than that." Saylor stepped closer. "If I'm going to end up staying here in Seattle, then I need community. I feel like today was a step toward that."

Tia froze. She wanted to reach out and wrap Saylor up in a hug, push her against the mirrors again, but she couldn't. "Yeah. It probably is."

"Thank you for that." Saylor gave her a small wave before turning on her toes and heading toward the lobby.

Tia wanted to say something that would draw Saylor back. She wanted to encourage her to take up that extra time from Jericho being sick. She wanted to confess that she'd enjoyed Saylor's presence just as much, if not more. Saylor was such a breath of fresh air in her dingy and routine life. But she couldn't make the words leave her lips.

For the life of her, Tia was stuck.

And she hated it.

Seven

"You don't get it." Saylor crossed her arms, leaning against the counter in the kitchen.

Jameson's face went red. "What the hell are you saying?"

"I'm saying that you don't get it!" Her voice rose, a constriction in her chest tightening. He never seemed to understand anything she said, especially lately. "I sit in this apartment, day after day, alone. That's just it. Alone."

"I'm not going to quit my job for you."

"I'm not asking you to!" Saylor screeched. Her heart was in her throat and she wanted to cry. Desperate tears threatened to spill over her cheeks, but Saylor held them in. She just wanted him to understand. "I am so lonely."

"You're surrounded by people."

"People I don't know."

"So go get to know them."

They'd had this argument before, and it had gotten them exactly nowhere. But since he was finally back in town, since he was pushing her to make friends because he wanted to hang out with his friends and she had no one, because she couldn't—Saylor stopped. What was she even thinking?

"Look. I don't want you to give up your life just because I'm here now. I just want you to understand—"

"Understand what?" Jameson interrupted.

Why did he always do this? It wasn't like she was attacking him. She was just trying to explain to him what she was feeling, yet he always seemed to go on the offensive. Saylor clenched her jaw, not knowing what she was going to say or do next. If she could she'd walk out of the apartment and get a breather, but that wouldn't solve anything. In fact, it'd probably have the exact opposite effect from what she wanted.

"I'm lonely. That's all." Saylor's words were mumbled. She knew that would tick him off too because she wasn't just saying what she meant, but she was stuck between a rock and a hard place. Did she push to tell him more or did she step back and end the argument? Why was that always her choice? She never had another option, did she?

Because there was no winning this.

They were both going to lose in the end if she kept it up.

"Then you need to do something about it." Jameson's face hardened. His eyes were set right on her, the tension between them palpable. "Because I'm not going to be the only person you know out here."

"I don't want you to be." Saylor wrung her hands together, barely able to hold her own against him. She hated when they fought like this. She hated fighting in general, the conflict, the upheaval. It seemed as if they were more likely to argue lately, whether it was her isolation or him being fed up with being the sole provider, she wasn't sure. But it was intensifying.

"I can't be the center of your whole world."

When did he think he'd become that? Because he'd never been that for her. At least she didn't feel that way. Biting the inside of her cheek, Saylor held her ground. She didn't want to be a burden to him any more than she already was. "I'll find a job."

"When?" He fired back.

"As soon as I can. I'm already picking up some extra things this week for some income. You know, they always say it's easier to find a job when you have a job." She wasn't sure how that would work, but now she'd committed herself to working with Tia until Jericho came back. That hadn't exactly been how she wanted this to go, but here she was. She just hoped Tia hadn't found anyone else yet.

"What extra things?"

"Uh... I'm going to be helping with some kids' dance classes." Saylor bit her cheek harder. "At the dance studio I'm with."

"So they're charging you for your classes and paying you to help with kid classes?" Jameson snorted hard. "That makes no sense."

"It's just while someone is out sick. I imagine if I worked there more consistently there'd be no charge for classes I wanted to join." Saylor crossed her arms defensively. What did it matter anyway? She hadn't thought about the complications of pay, just that it was a way to meet people, make friends, and at least for the next ten days, get paid to be somewhere other than here.

Jameson eyed her suspiciously. "You're not a dancer."

"No. I'm not." Saylor's back went up instantly. What was he trying to imply? First he wanted her out of the apartment and now he didn't want her to leave it? "But I have taken dance classes in the past because of skating. And I've been in this class for a few weeks now."

"Weeks!" Jameson scoffed and shook his head slowly. "What makes you think that you're good enough to teach anyone?"

"It's kids! They're learning the basics. It's like toddlers who run around. The goal is just to keep them all focused and paying attention for forty-five minutes. Which is way easier said than done." Now she was the one who was defensive. She hated that he could make her like this, that if given long enough she'd feel like she had her back up against a wall.

"You're ridiculous. How is this going to help you find a job?"

"I don't know." Saylor was entering into desperation. She just wanted this argument to end. "But it's better than sitting around on my ass and doing nothing."

That was the nice way to put what she'd been doing these last few months. Because the depression and anxiety had fully set in, and even forcing herself out to the dance class three times a week was pushing the limits of what she could manage. Saylor tried to hold her own against him, but she felt her resolve wavering already.

"That's all you do, though!" Jameson threw his hands up in the air. "You sit around here, day after day, and do absolutely nothing."

"I'm trying my best." Tears welled up in Saylor's eyes. She hadn't anticipated this point of attack. She gripped onto the kitchen counter and held herself as tall as she could. "I gave up everything to move here. Do you understand that? I gave up my friends, my family, my job. And for what? For you to be gone more nights than not."

"You knew that when you came out here."

"Yeah. I did." Saylor nodded hard, finding her resolve. "That doesn't mean this is easy for me."

"For you?" Jameson took a step toward her.

Saylor's shoulders tightened, and she pushed back into the counter on instinct.

"This isn't easy for me. I'm the sole provider here. Not just financially, but I'm the only one you seem to cling to. What am I supposed to do with that? I need my freedom."

"I'm not telling you to stay home with me. I'm telling you that I'm having a hard time."

"You know what?" Jameson's hands clenched. "I can't do this right now."

"Can't do what?"

"You." He spun around on his heels, snagged his wallet and keys, and slammed the front door shut behind him.

Saylor let out a shuddering breath, collapsing against the counter. He'd never left during a fight before. Not like this. But she'd seen the escalation rising between them, and she wasn't surprised that they'd exploded like this.

Wiping the tears falling down her cheeks, Saylor stayed in the silence. This was so much like it was any time she was home without him. Silent tears. Absolutely alone. No sound at all. If she focused hard enough she could hear the television from the neighbor next door, the heater kicking on, the cars outside.

But none of that helped this oppressive loneliness that pushed down on her chest, crushing her.

What the hell was she supposed to do now? Wait for him to come home?

If he'd even do that?

Jameson had been going out with friends that night before their argument started, and Saylor was fairly sure that he wasn't going to be coming home to deal with her first. She walked to the front door and flipped the lock, a sense of security blanketing her as she stepped toward the window.

Seattle was so gloomy this time of year. Saylor wasn't prepared to be here. She hadn't done enough work before moving. She'd spent her entire life in the greater Denver area, building familial relationships and friendships. And while she'd traveled a lot, she'd never lived anywhere else. Crossing her arms, she stared out the window at the foreign city.

What had ever made her think she could do this?

Tears fell freely down her cheeks now that she was alone. Letting Jameson see how upset she really was would be too much for that day. She wasn't even going to have a chance to center herself before she was supposed to go to her class that night, and now she had to go. Because she needed to tell Tia that she was going to take the job for the next ten days, and somehow she really needed to find her own job.

Blowing out a breath, Saylor closed her eyes to center herself.

But it wasn't working.

That lick of anxiety had turned into full-on rage, and it swirled around her in her chest and belly, consuming every inch of her even when she tried to protect it. She should just move home at this rate. Maybe she could get some of her old skating clients back and go into coaching again. Maybe she could pick up subbing jobs again. Maybe she could just fail one more time at the one thing she wanted the most.

Marriage.

Because she did love Jameson, right?

He'd been so sweet to her when they'd met. But as their relationship had deepened, they'd found their struggles. And no amount of new-relationship bliss could cover them up. Saylor gnawed on her cheek until she tasted the iron tang of blood. Then she stopped. That was a bad habit she really didn't need to start up again.

Saylor's phone buzzed.

She headed for the bedroom, following the sound until she reached it and saw Callie's name lighting up the screen. Her head hovered over it, but she chose not to answer. She didn't have the capacity to even begin talking about this yet. She needed more time to come down from the high of the argument to put her head on straight.

When the call went to voicemail, she saw the texts from Jameson.

Again, Saylor hesitated before she picked up the phone and opened them to read.

Jameson: I won't be home until late.

Jameson: Callie will call you. I already told her what happened.

. . .

Saylor winced. What the hell had he told Callie? Not that it would make too much of a difference. Callie was her best friend from childhood. Surely Callie would take Saylor's side. Or was this all because he didn't want to put in the time and the effort to actually fix the problems between them? Did he want Callie to do it for him?

Cringing, Saylor set the phone down just as another text came through.

Jameson: We'll talk about this tomorrow.

Lovely. So he really was pushing this off until someone else could deal with her. Was she that bad a person that she needed a handler? Saylor left her phone on the nightstand and walked into the bathroom, stripping her clothes off. She'd take a hot shower, she'd get her head on straight, and she'd go to her dance class tonight.

At least there she could lose herself in the practice, in the repetition, in making her body move in the exact ways she wanted it to. It would be as close to skating as she could manage for now. But maybe she'd add that to her list too. Find a skating rink with open hours.

When the hot spray of water hit her skin, Saylor sighed.

This was exactly what she needed.

She'd deal with Jameson and their problems tomorrow. When they both had time to digest the argument and come at it with calmer heads. Until then, she'd try to find ways she could be a better fiancé and future wife. Because without more effort, their relationship would absolutely fail.

And she couldn't have another failure on her record.

eight

Saylor collapsed to the floor, her ankle turning as she tumbled down. Tia's heart clenched as she froze on the spot before rushing over to kneel next to her. That was a hard fall, and it had been a long time since she'd seen someone fall that painfully.

"Give yourself a second," Tia murmured, putting her hand on Saylor's arm and leg to keep her on the ground. Instinct would tell Saylor to get up immediately and walk it off, but if she'd done considerable damage, then she could make it worse by walking on it.

Saylor dragged in a sharp breath. Steven was on his knees next to her and the entire class was looking over them. Tia waved them off, hoping they'd start dancing again, but there were only five more minutes left in the class. She'd been watching Saylor all night, and it didn't surprise her that something like this had happened.

She'd been off her game.
Unable to focus.
All over the place.

"Take a few breaths."

Saylor's cheeks were red, but she looked pale under it all. *Forlorn*. That was the word. Tia wanted to wrap her in a tight hug and hold her for hours. But they were in a room full of other people, and something told her that Saylor wouldn't be comfortable with that.

"Steven, go get some ice."

"I'm fine," Saylor mumbled.

"You're not." Tia looked around to find the others already packing up their bags. They seemed satisfied that she had it under control.

"I'm really fine." Saylor sighed and pulled her foot up to press it into the floor. She didn't even hiss when she started to put some weight on it.

"Not yet." Tia made her voice as firm as she possibly could. She wouldn't have Saylor hurting herself, not when it could be avoided. She was worth so much more than an avoidable injury. "Stay here a second."

Steven arrived with ice, but Saylor waved it off. "I'm fine. Really."

She pulled her hands from Tia's and put them flat on the ground, pushing herself up. Tia wasn't going to let her get away with it, so she snagged Saylor's arm to help her up so she wouldn't immediately fall over again. Steven helped on the other side, and Tia sent him a smile of thanks. They both held on, not wanting Saylor to put her full weight on her foot yet.

"I'm fine. I promise."

"Just take it slowly," Tia ordered. She wrapped her arm around Saylor's back for added stability, and she wasn't about to let go any time soon.

As soon as she was upright, the rest of the class smiled and walked out of the studio into the lobby. Saylor cringed when she put weight on her foot, though she masked it well. The only reason Tia saw it was probably because she was so close.

"If it hurts, don't walk."

"It's not that," Saylor muttered and closed her eyes. "It really doesn't hurt that much."

"That much?"

Saylor shook her head. "It's just a twist. If I walk it off, it'll feel better."

"You good?" Steven asked.

Saylor glanced over her shoulder at him and nodded. "Yeah. Thanks. I think I've got it from here."

Like hell you do. Tia didn't say it out loud, though she was definitely thinking it. She held onto Saylor, unwilling to let her go. Tia tightened her grip to make her point.

"You sure?" Steven asked, checking in again like a champ.

He always was the sweetest no matter what.

"Yes." Saylor gave him a brilliant smile, but the look in her gaze was still so far away. Oh, she was the master at hiding. That's what all of this was about. Whether it was through her nerves or through her hard work, did anyone know the real Saylor?

"All right. You got her, Tia?"

Tia nodded. "Yeah."

"Good."

He started to walk away, and Tia held onto Saylor tightly. "Come sit in the office while I clean up, all right?"

"Sure."

The fact that Saylor was agreeing meant she was in a bit more pain than she wanted to admit. Tia helped her into the office, did a quick sweep of the floor and then locked up the stereo equipment. When she was done, she leaned against the doorframe and checked Saylor over with a fine eye. Saylor flinched.

"All right... I'll give you one chance to answer me because I don't want to pry if you don't want it, but this is more than a sprained ankle. What's going on?" Tia crossed her arms and stared, making her point clear. She wanted some kind of answer.

Saylor's eyes filled with water, her nose reddening in an instant. This was about so much more than a simple fall during class. Tia's heart broke, and she swooped in, wrapping her arms around Saylor's shoulders and pulling her head into her chest. She gave

Saylor the best, deepest hug she could possibly give because in this moment that was the only thing she knew she could offer.

Saylor grabbed onto Tia's arm with her hands, holding on and gripping as if Tia was her lifeline. The tears fell freely from Saylor's eyes, cascading down her cheeks and onto Tia's skin. Saylor's body racked with a sob, then another, before she finally shook her head.

"I swore to myself I wouldn't do this."

"Do what?"

"Let it affect me."

"What is it, Saylor?" Tia combed her fingers through Saylor's hair. She'd done this with so many people throughout the years—her friends, her family, her nieces. She was the bringer of comfort for everyone, and surely she could do this for Saylor.

"Jameson."

I knew I'd want to kill him. Tia kept her lips sealed shut on that one. It wouldn't help anything, but she hated seeing Saylor in such turmoil. Whatever Jameson had done, he had better be worth it in the end, and he had better start living up to this amazing woman he had. Because Tia had figured out pretty quickly that Saylor was hands down amazing.

"Want some liquid courage to tell me all about it?"

Saylor relaxed. She sucked in a sharp breath and pulled away, looking up at Tia. Their eyes met. Tia's breath caught in her lungs, pulling tightly to coil in the center of her chest before sliding its way down purposely. *Oh, now this is dangerous.* Tia was letting herself get too close to Saylor, too quickly. The only advantage to all of this was that Saylor was happily engaged—no, scratch that—engaged to a man.

Tia wouldn't stand a chance.

At least she better not.

"Yeah. I would."

Tia blinked hard, trying to remember what she'd even asked. Because without context, it was impossible to figure out what Saylor was saying. She dropped her gaze to Saylor's mouth, to her pink lips, the way she held them, the fullness of each one, just how damn kissable they would be. Tia tightened her shoulders and pulled away slightly.

Right. Liquid courage.

"Sure. We can go to that bar a few blocks over." She at least caught herself before she suggested her apartment which was in the upper floors of this building. Taking Saylor somewhere that private would make it impossible for Tia to avoid what she was feeling. She needed space and people surrounding them to keep her in line. "Think you can walk?"

"I know it."

They grabbed their jackets and locked up as they left. Tia kept her eye firmly on Saylor to make sure that she wasn't pushing herself too hard. She really didn't want someone injured on her watch. When they got to the table and had drinks ordered, Saylor's shoulders instantly relaxed.

"Um..." Saylor leaned in. "I can help out while Jericho is out."

"Oh! Good." Though now Tia wasn't entirely convinced *that* was a good thing. To be stuck day after day with Saylor when she was attracted to her was either going to break that attraction down or it was just going to build it right up. She really hoped it would be the former.

"If that's still okay."

Tia nodded sharply. "Yes, of course. I need all the help I can get."

"Perfect." Saylor wrapped her hands around the drink that was set in front of her. She didn't take a sip, but she did stare at Tia over the rim. "That was part of the issue tonight."

"Working for me?" Tia ordered two shots before the waiter left. If she was going to sit here all night, then she needed some liquid courage of her own.

"No." Saylor winced. "Well, kind of. Only because it's not a *real job*." Saylor said the last two words with a roll of her eyes. "Because it's temporary, not because it's unworthy."

"Right." Except Tia had heard that it was unworthy so many times over the years that she wouldn't have been surprised if Jameson meant it that way. It was meant as a diss because it wasn't a *real* job, meaning one with a regular paycheck that had normal nine-to-five hours. Tia held those comments in, though, because they were the last thing Saylor needed tonight.

"He's upset that I don't have a job or friends yet."

Tia frowned. "It takes time to make friends."

"That's what I told him! It's not easy to move. It's even harder to make friends when I don't have a job or someplace to actually meet people."

Tia took the tequila shot from the waiter and set it in front of Saylor, then she took her own. "Bottoms up."

She wasn't all that happy when the liquor slid down her throat and burned her tongue or when the salt and lime chased it down. She'd thought this would be a nice night out, but she was just getting angrier by the second at a man she'd never even met. Saylor set the shot glass down heavily, her cringe full-on now.

It was honestly adorable.

Tia reached up to wipe the drizzle of lime juice from Saylor's chin but she stopped herself just in time, handing a napkin over. "How does he expect you to have friends so quickly?"

"Probably because he makes friends everywhere he goes?"

"Friends or networking?"

Saylor shrugged. "Probably a little of both. He's really good at talking to people."

"Sounds like a classic extrovert who doesn't understand introverts." Tia spun her fingers in a circle on the table so she could stop looking at Saylor. The more she looked, the more she wanted to steal Saylor away from the big bad Jameson, and she really had to stop thinking like that.

She knew absolutely nothing about this man. And she only had one side of the argument, and everyone's position was always skewed. But there were things that stood out to her, that reminded her so much of her brother and sister-in-law, things that made her think she should say something now before it was too late.

"Yeah." Saylor frowned into her drink before taking a long sip of it. "We haven't finished our argument."

"So you're going home to it?"

She shook her head. "We'll finish in the morning. Hopefully."

"I thought you were excited about him coming back."

Saylor sighed heavily. "I was."

"And now?" Tia wanted to know, but she really shouldn't be prying like this. She should just let Saylor tell her what she wanted to share and leave it at that.

"I don't know," Saylor whispered. "Does that make me an awful person?"

"No." Tia reached for Saylor's hand, wrapping their fingers together in a tender touch. "You're not a bad person for having feelings."

"Then why do I feel so awful?"

Tia's heart broke a little more than it had before. She lifted Saylor's hand and pressed her lips to the soft skin before she realized what she was doing. Belatedly, she set Saylor's hand down but didn't pull away completely. "My guess is because it's still raw, and you're hurting, not just from the argument, but from everything you've experienced since moving here, and you haven't found a good place to find healing yet."

Saylor canted her head to the side and narrowed her eyes. "I don't need healing."

"We all need healing," Tia countered, dropping Saylor's hand and snagging her glass. This was getting way too personal. She wouldn't tell Saylor what had happened in her past. That would bring up way too much, and Tia wouldn't be able to control herself through it.

"Maybe you're right." Saylor reached for Tia's hand again, lacing their fingers and then dropping their joined hands into her lap. "But tonight I'm just hurting."

"I can see that." Tia squeezed Saylor's hand tightly, hoping it would be as much a show of support as possible.

"I don't think I'll ever measure up."

"Measure up to what?" The question was out of Tia's mouth before she could stop herself.

Saylor snorted lightly, blushing as she ducked her chin. "Expectations."

"Whose expectations?"

"Jameson's. Mine. Yours. Everyone's."

"Saylor." Tia let out a huge sigh and closed her eyes. This ran deep. Way deeper than she was going to be able to deal with in one night of liquid courage. "Expectations will steal your joy in life, you know that, right? They're always unmanageable."

"I know." Saylor looked Tia directly in the eye. "I've never managed to get rid of them."

"So what do you expect then?"

"I expect to get married. Have a baby or two. Live life like I'm supposed to do."

"What are you supposed to do?" Tia leaned in, wondering if this was the right direction to push or not.

Saylor shook her head slowly. "If you asked me that last year, I would have told you that I was going to coach. I was going to be one of the best damn coaches there was, and my kids would thrive in skating. They'd figure out exactly what they wanted to do and they would go for it."

"And now?" Tia rubbed her thumb lightly over the side of Saylor's hand, realizing far too late that Saylor was still clutching it in her lap.

Saylor opened her mouth like she was going to speak and then stopped. She waved at the waiter and smiled so sweetly. "I think we need another round of shots. Make it a double."

"Are you trying to get me drunk?" Tia laughed as soon as the waiter left.

"Nope." Saylor leaned back in her chair, still holding tightly to Tia's hand. "Just myself."

"Well, I think you'll succeed." Tia laughed and finished off her first full drink of the night. It had been a while since she'd gotten good and drunk, but she could at least still walk home. Then again, if Saylor was going to get sloshed, she'd have to take Saylor home first to make sure she was safe before heading home herself.

"We can only hope."

Tia held Saylor's gaze intently for a moment before breaking it. As much as she wanted to steal her hand back, she wasn't willing to break the sweetness that was coming between them yet. "So what are you supposed to do now?"

"Make friends I guess." Saylor rolled her eyes. "Find a *real* job."

"Whatever a real job is?"

"Yup. Whatever that is." She sighed heavily but grinned fully when the four shots were set in front of them. "Perfect."

Saylor let go of Tia's hand to set up for the next tequila shot. Tia took the chance and tried to put some more space between them. It really wouldn't do either of them any good if she got caught up in the fantasy that Saylor McGinnis could be. Because Tia would get caught up in it. Just like she'd gotten caught up in Kirsten. And they could all see what a disaster that was now.

She just had to keep her distance. Because she was way too old for this shit. No drama. No deep relationships. The last thing she needed was something complicated.

"Bottoms up," Tia said, smiling when Saylor tipped the shot glass upside down into her mouth.

"Bottoms up," Saylor responded, the first genuine smile of the night gracing her lips.

Tia loved seeing that.

That was perfect.

nine

Saylor moved into the office after the kids' class. They had quite a break before the adult class came in that day, and she needed it. The muscles in her legs were jelly. It had been so long since she'd used them this much, and it was damn near impossible to walk.

Still, she snagged the push broom to clean the floor while Tia did something over at the stereo. Saylor tried not to pay attention to Tia for the first hour she'd been there, but after that, she'd given up. Tia was something else entirely, and Saylor found herself riveted to every move that she made.

Saylor didn't want to be more than five feet away, which was ridiculous.

But their night out had put Saylor right. She'd needed that more than anything. And it wasn't about complaining about Jameson, it was just feeling like she'd found someone who cared. Saylor pushed the broom around the room, finishing up, and then grabbed the dustpan. She rolled her shoulders when she stood up again.

"How is your ankle holding up?" Tia asked, coming over to take the broom from Saylor's fingers.

"It's fine." Saylor gave her a smile, leaning in slightly. "I didn't twist it that hard."

"Uh-huh, sure. You didn't fall right on your ass either."

Laughing lightly, Saylor nodded. "Well, I did do that. Talk about embarrassed."

"So was it more hurt or embarrassment that made you close off that night?" Tia put the broom back in the small closet and closed it up, locking it. She pocketed the key into her leggings and turned around to face Saylor.

Saylor's breath caught. Tia truly was a magnificent human being. It wasn't just her kindness and caring nature with every single person who walked through the doors, it was also the fact that she was stunningly gorgeous. Saylor bit the inside of her cheek at that thought. Since when had she started thinking women were gorgeous?

Oh right, when she was about twelve and realized boobs were a thing.

Chuckling at herself, she shook her head and ended the internal conversation.

"Saylor?" Tia asked, coming a little closer. "What just went through your head?"

"Nothing." Saylor's cheeks were on fire. She would not, under any circumstances—or torture—admit to what she'd just thought about. Telling Tia that she'd thought about her breasts was a massive no. Saylor wiped her now sweaty palms along her hips and turned around to see if anyone else was coming in yet.

Except no one was.

Because they had two hours before the next class.

Right.

So what the hell was she supposed to do now?

"Jericho and I usually get dinner together on days like today, and we plan for the upcoming week." Tia caught Saylor's attention, and when Saylor's gaze reached her eyes, Tia's lips curled upward into a huge smile. "So do you want to get some dinner?"

"I..." Did she? Saylor's stomach clenched at the thought, but it wasn't because something bad was happening. Or was it? She couldn't quite tell. Something about spending so much time with Tia set her on edge, but it wasn't just the time, it was the fact that she felt close to Tia in such a short period of time. As if Tia understood exactly what she was going through.

"But if Jameson's home, then you're free to leave if you want."

"What?" Saylor blinked hard, trying to follow Tia's line of thought. Jameson was home, but she hadn't even thought about going to have a meal with him. She'd wanted to go out with Tia, she was just trying to figure out why exactly she wanted that. "No, we can go."

"Perfect. There's this little place just down the block from here that I love."

"Okay." Saylor smiled uneasily as they walked toward the office and grabbed their jackets. It seemed Tia walked just about everywhere in town. Saylor had yet to see her driving a car or calling a rideshare.

Once they were outside with the door locked, Saylor shoved her hands in her pockets and waited for Tia to take the lead. She had no idea where they were going, and she was determined to follow Tia as well as she had so far. Tia wrapped an arm through Saylor's and pulled her to the right.

So they were off that way.

Having Tia wrapped around her was a different experience altogether. It was so much like the other night when they'd been drinking and Saylor had held her hand for what seemed like hours. She hadn't wanted to give that up.

This was so much like that.

Comfortable.

Easy.

There was a closeness here that Saylor longed for. She closed her eyes as Tia walked, wondering if she could feel comfortable not knowing where she was going so long as Tia was in the lead, and sure enough, she didn't make one misstep along the way.

"We're here," Tia said as she held open the door for Saylor.

It was a quaint little place, barely big enough to hold fifty people.

"It's Italian food. I find on days like this that I need to load up on the carbs to push through the week."

Saylor laughed as she slid into the seat across from Tia. This was better. If she could look at Tia instead of reaching for her hand, that would be more professional, wouldn't it? Although, if she were being honest, nothing about her relationship with Tia had been professional. The woman didn't scream *boss*, and Saylor hadn't really screamed *employee*. It was much more like they were two friends working together to accomplish something.

Teaching kids to dance.

That's what they were supposed to be focused on.

Except Saylor had struggled all day with that. She'd been riveted to every move that Tia made. She hadn't wanted to let Tia get more than a few steps from her. What exactly did that mean?

"You ready to order?" Tia asked, the sweet scrawny waiter hovering over the side of the table.

"Oh. Um... I'll just have what she's having."

Tia gave Saylor a confused look before she ordered her own dinner and a glass of wine. Saylor hadn't expected to drink during this working dinner, but she would take the wine, she supposed.

"What's going on?" Tia leaned back in the chair and eyed Saylor.

There was no getting out of this one. Tia had her pinned with a look that meant business. Saylor had been on the receiving end of it before, but this time, a wave of pleasure ran through her. They weren't here because of drama. They were here simply to spend time together as friends.

"Nothing bad, I promise." Saylor folded her hands in her lap, leaning back in her own chair to mimic Tia.

"You've been pretty distracted today, which isn't like you."

Saylor pursed her lips, a shiver running through her. Jameson never would have noticed that. God, she really needed to stop doing that. What was that saying? Comparison is the thief of joy? Yeah, that's it. If she compared Tia to Jameson, it would only send her straight to ruin. Saylor folded her hands in her lap and twisted her fingers together.

"I guess I'm not used to working such long hours."

Tia squinted at her, as if not quite believing the words that came out of Saylor's mouth. Which was fine because Saylor wasn't sure she believed them either.

"Fine. It's not that."

"Much better," Tia answered, grinning when their glasses of wine were brought over. "I don't appreciate you not telling me the truth."

Duly noted. Saylor cringed. She did have to do better about that. She was so used to avoiding sharing what she was feeling because no one wanted to hear about it. No one wanted to know about the anxiety that raged within her. No one ever had.

"My friend, Callie, is talking about coming for a visit. Any good places I should take her?" Saylor fidgeted with her fingers in her lap, staring at the wine glass in front of her. She hadn't started drinking it yet, afraid that if she did, then she really wouldn't be able to hold her tongue.

"There's lots of places. Have you been to many of the tourist spots since moving here?"

Saylor shook her head. She'd barely left the apartment except for dance classes. Her heart sank. When had she become such a recluse? She sighed, knowing her face fell because Tia immediately leaned forward.

"What's wrong?"

"I just feel like I've been stuck in a rut. I can't get out of my own head. Have you ever felt like that?"

"All the time." Tia's lips quirked up slightly, and she leaned back again with her wine. "I got custody of my nieces when I was very young. Fallon was nine and Monti was barely two. And I raised them from there on, but there were so many times that I just felt like I was doing the same thing over and over again and it wasn't making a damn bit of difference. With each of them in different ways. And then there were other days when I was so exhausted and burned out and didn't know what to do next that I just wanted to lie in bed all day and never emerge." Tia gave a little nervous chuckle.

But Saylor had never felt more seen before.

She felt like that almost every day lately. She'd felt like that before, but it hadn't ever lasted this long. Saylor picked up her glass of wine and took a sip, debating about what to say next. She could confirm or she could deny. She could change the topic, too. But she didn't want to. Something about this felt right.

"I don't know what to do."

"About what?"

"Moving here." Saylor shrugged. "I can't find a job, I'm a strain on Jameson because I'm not contributing and I'm always home, and I'm just not myself anymore."

"Who are you?" Tia asked, and she seemed genuinely curious.

Saylor licked her lips, the bitter flavor from the wine lingering on the tip of her tongue. She shook her head slowly, tears nearly brimming in her eyes. "I don't know."

"Then we should probably start there."

We?

Never before had that sounded so good. Like someone was actually going to be there with her. Shouldn't it be Jameson who made her feel not alone? There she was again. Back to comparing. Cursing herself, Saylor bit the inside of her cheek.

"How did you do it?" Saylor finally asked.

"Do what?" Tia's eyes seemed to glitter with amusement at the obvious change in topic. But she didn't call Saylor out on it.

"How did you figure out who you were?"

"Oh." Tia took in a deep breath and let it out slowly. "I had a crash course. That's the flippant answer. Let me try again." Tia thought for a minute before starting again. "I don't think it's a one-time deal, figuring out who you are. When I got my nieces, I had to figure out who I was again. When they were grown up and moved out, then I had to do it again. Each time we enter a new phase in life, I think that's a process we go through."

"Maybe that's just what I'm doing then." Saylor's voice was soft, and she stared at the table as two heaping plates of food were set in front of them.

"Good. It takes practice." Tia immediately dove into her food. She took that first bite, moaning around the food in her mouth, her eyes rolling back into her head as she plopped her back into the seat and moaned again. "God, this place never does anything wrong."

Saylor's heart raced. Just hearing those sounds, so wild and erotic, her entire body was alight with something. She couldn't quite name what it was, but it made her incredibly uncomfortable. She was overheated. Her chest was tight and constricted. And she couldn't get the sound out of her head.

Is that what Tia sounded like in other situations?

Saylor had heard her groan like that when she was stretching before and after class, but it hadn't quite had the same effect as this time.

"Saylor?"

Snapping her gaze to Tia's, Saylor realized far too late that she'd become completely distracted and disarmed. "Yeah?"

"You're not eating."

"Oh." Saylor's cheeks burned. In fact, her entire body burned. She ducked her chin, refusing to look up at Tia, and shoved a forkful of food into her mouth. She didn't taste a damn thing. And she knew it wasn't because it wasn't good, or that it didn't have flavor, it was because her embarrassment over being caught in the spiral her thoughts had taken her down overwhelmed all of her other senses.

Finally convincing herself to look up at Tia, she found her dinner companion with a sly smile on her lips and amusement in her gaze.

"I like you, Saylor," Tia said, her tone light. "And I don't mean that in a mean way at all. You're interesting, and I want to get to know you better."

How had Tia known what to say? Saylor's shoulders tensed sharply. She shouldn't want to get to know her temporary boss or her dance instructor better, should she? Wasn't there supposed to be some kind of boundary there to protect each other? But this was so different from any other coaching relationship or boss relationship Saylor had in the past. Starting with the very fact that Tia was a woman, and Saylor had only ever related to men in those capacities.

"Just letting you know that," Tia said before finishing her glass of wine. She set it down on the table, looking Saylor directly in the eye. "In case you want to make a friend here instead of hiding away in your apartment all day every day."

Saylor choked back the worry that erupted in her throat. "Okay."

"Just okay?" Tia raised an eyebrow, sliding her finger along the curve of the wine glass and down the stem.

"No, you're probably right. I do need friends here." Saylor's lips pulled into a smile. "I definitely need friends here."

"Good." Tia grinned broadly. "The studio is a great place to start looking for that."

Saylor nodded, not quite sure what she'd agreed to. But it felt good and right, whatever it was. It settled deep into her chest, and she relaxed into the moment. Tia didn't want anything bad for her. In fact, it was the opposite. Tia just wanted her to thrive in Seattle. That's what a good friend would do, wasn't it?

"To friends?" Saylor picked up her fork with the pasta on it and held it toward Tia. "Since you don't have a drink."

Laughing, Tia followed Saylor's lead and twirled her food around her fork. They joined them in the middle of the table, a giggle erupting from Tia's lips. "To friends."

ten

Sweat dripped down the center of her back, pooling right at the top of Tia's ass. She breathed heavily as they finished up the last of the dance class that night, her heart still racing from the workout. Saylor looked alive with energy.

Tia had loved getting to know Saylor the last week, and with Jericho back in the reins now that she wasn't sick anymore, something had been missing. Tia wiped her hand over her forehead, clearing the droplets of sweat that had pooled there.

The class lingered around, grabbing water as the music continued into the next song on the track. No one was leaving quite yet. Which was interesting. Had they all found a second wave of energy? Tia walked over to the stereo and turned the music off, hoping to signify that the class had well and truly ended.

Laughter erupted from behind her as she locked up the equipment. Tia rolled her shoulders at the joyous sound. Saylor and Jericho chatted off to the side while some of her students finally started to leave. Steven touched Tia's arm.

"We're going to S-Club. You should come."

"Oh." Tia shifted her gaze around the room until it landed on Saylor. It had been a while since she'd gone dancing with her little crew. Saylor had a huge smile on her face, and immediately she looked up at Tia, their eyes meeting across the room. Tia overexaggerated her nod and kept her eyes on Saylor while she answered Steven. "Sure. That sounds fun."

"Perfect!" He squeezed her shoulder lightly and then ran off to invite someone else.

Jericho bounced into the lobby, and Saylor walked slowly toward Tia. The others were already scattering and preparing to leave. Tia's stomach tightened as Saylor came closer. Something about her put Tia on an edge she really didn't want to be on. But it was impossible to avoid her. It was as if Tia was drawn to her, pulled as if Saylor controlled every move she made.

"Good class," Saylor said, her eyes locked on Tia's face.

"Yeah. I think you're right on your way to being ready for the competition."

Saylor's smile, which had barely lit up her lips, faltered. "Uh... yeah."

"Are you worried about it?"

"I always worry." Saylor crossed her arms over her chest, which pushed her breasts up in her sports bra beautifully.

Tia flicked her gaze down and then back up, forcing herself to look away. Saylor wasn't interested in women. Saylor was an engaged woman. She was tangled up in a relationship already.

"Are you going dancing?" Saylor asked, so timidly.

Tia took a step in closer, wishing that Saylor would raise her head up and look directly at her. "I am. Are you?"

"I don't know." Saylor worried her lower lip. "I'm not exactly someone fun when it comes to going out."

"Oh, I don't know about that. I've enjoyed getting to know you these past few weeks. Besides, didn't you say you wanted to make more friends? Steven will be there."

"Jericho's going," Saylor supplied, looking up into Tia's eyes.

Saylor's amber eyes seemed to be filled with fear and something else. Tia held the moment, trying to figure out exactly what it was.

Did Saylor not want to be friends with Jericho? Tia hummed to herself. No, she did. But the only person Saylor might consider a friend in this room was her.

"You should come," Tia added, planting a smile on her face. "Unless Jameson is in town and you need to spend some time with him. It'll be good to get out, dance, burn some energy."

"Drink," Saylor supplied.

Tia laughed. "Yes, drink."

Saylor sucked in a sharp breath. "All right. Let's go."

"Jameson...?" Tia reached out for Saylor's elbow, holding onto it. She glanced down at her hand, realizing far too late she really needed to keep some distance between them.

"He's gone for the week. Florida and then North Carolina."

Nodding to no one but herself, Tia sucked in a sharp breath and let it out. "Then let's go."

"Shouldn't we clean up first?"

Tia looked around, finding the studio already empty. Saylor pointed toward the broom, but Tia shook her head. "I'll do it in the morning. I think we can ease off for one night to have a little fun, don't you?"

"Uh...sure." Saylor crossed her arms again.

Tia grinned and slid her hand into the crook of Saylor's arm, walking toward her office. "I just need to lock up."

With their jackets on, the studio locked up tight, Tia led Saylor arm-in-arm down the street. S-Club wasn't that far from the studio, which meant they could at least walk there. By the time they were drunk and it was after midnight, they'd probably want to get a ride home, but for now, Tia would take the walk to warm up her muscles.

"Jameson sure does travel a lot."

"He does," Saylor answered, tightening her grip on Tia's arm. "He enjoys it."

"Do you?"

Saylor sucked in a sharp breath. "I enjoy visiting new places. Though most I didn't get to properly visit when I was competing."

"Right. In and out, always busy practicing and winning." Tia bumped her shoulder against Saylor's.

"In a way, yes." Saylor looked down at the ground, her grasp tightening on Tia's. "I don't enjoy him being gone so much."

"I can see how that would be hard." Tia pointed up ahead. "We're almost there."

The building buzzed with noise already, even though it was early in the evening. Tia kept Saylor's arm in hers as they navigated through the people to find the rest of the dance class. Some people from other classes she taught had shown up as well.

Tia made nice small talk with all of them, cringing when she caught sight of Kirsten's blonde head off to the side. She had really hoped no one would invite her, but luck had never been on her side. Kirsten had woven herself into the fabric of the studio, and despite many attempts, Tia had never managed to get her out.

"Do me a favor," Tia whispered into Saylor's ear. She had to trust someone here, and so far, the others hadn't proven worthy to keep Kirsten away. "Don't leave me alone with Kirsten."

"With..." Saylor trailed off, her eyes landing on Kirsten. Saylor tightened her grasp on Tia's arm and turned to her with a smile. "Never."

"Dance?"

"Yes." Saylor started toward the main dance floor, dragging Tia behind her. They ditched their jackets on one of the small tables that their crew had claimed and immediately hit the floor.

Saylor took hold of Tia's hand and spun her around with a grin on her lips before stopping and swaying her hips side to side to the beat. Fuck, she was sexy when she did that. Did she even know it? Did she realize how attractive she was when she pushed aside the anxiety and worry and let her full personality shine?

Tia put her hands on Saylor's hips and pulled her closer, sliding a leg right along Saylor's and encouraging the grind. They'd likely move into more dancing later, but for right now, Tia wanted to center herself and lose herself in Saylor. She wanted to forget that she knew Kirsten was watching them, that she was likely getting more pissed off by the second.

Rolling herself up on her toes, Tia planted a hand on the small of Saylor's back. She slid her other one down her arm, lacing their fingers together. She was going to push thoughts of Kirsten as far back in her mind as possible.

"Are you ready?" Tia asked into Saylor's ear, making sure that she heard.

"Ready for what?" Saylor's chest rose up with her breath, and Tia found her gaze locked on her breasts. It really was impossible not to see how sexy she was. She should just give up on avoiding it already.

Tia grinned as she backed up slightly and positioned her hands out to her sides, Saylor's loosely in hers. "To improv."

"What?"

Tia didn't give her a chance to react as she spun Saylor around, leading her into a dance that neither of them knew the steps to. Saylor followed perfectly. Tia spun her around, caught her, and dipped her. She turned her back to Saylor's front, lowering her body in a shimmy before she slowly worked her way back up.

Saylor grabbed hold of her waist and pulled her along as they moved in steps forward and back and then shimmied together as the music reached its pinnacle. Saylor's lips were bursting with the biggest smile that Tia had ever seen. She didn't want the song to end, but she knew they were close. One more time around, Tia smoothed her hand down Saylor's side and pulled her in close, intimately, and then instantly regretted it.

Their bodies were pressed together, breath heaving from the exertion, skin warm from the movement. Tia gulped in air, her entire body on the edge of needing something else to happen, something else to push them together, something else—

"Hey. Mind if I have a dance?" Kirsten's smooth tones were a bucket of cold water over the both of them.

Saylor jerked back, looking from Kirsten to Tia and back again. "Actually, we're going to get a drink. Since we skipped that when we came in."

She grabbed hold of Tia's hand and dragged her off the dance floor forcibly. Tia couldn't catch her breath. She couldn't find words or anything. This little crush had become a snowball heading straight down the mountain and she couldn't stop it. She couldn't make herself put space between them again, to push Saylor toward a friendship with Jericho instead of her.

They got drinks and walked back to the tables with half the crew while the other half was on the dance floor. Kirsten, luckily, seemed to stay on the dance floor and wasn't bothering them. Tia took a sip of her cold cocktail.

"Thanks for the save."

"You asked me to save you." Saylor winked. "So I did what you asked."

"You seem to be really comfortable when you know exactly what you need to do."

"I am." Saylor shrugged a little. "I'm not a fan of the unknown."

"I don't think many people are." Tia fluttered her fingers over Saylor's hand, like she was going to grab on and hold it. But she stopped herself. The territory she was walking into was dangerous. That needed to stop. There were so many reasons she shouldn't, that they couldn't. She wasn't even sure if Saylor was interested in something like that. All she'd ever implied was that she wanted friendship.

"Come dance with me!" Jericho grabbed Saylor's hand and pulled her toward the dance floor.

"Go on," Tia encouraged. "I'll watch our drinks."

Tia stayed right where she was, watching Saylor as she and Jericho laughed and enjoyed their time on the dance floor. She made small talk with Steven, but as much of her attention as possible was focused on Saylor.

What was it about Saylor that intrigued her so much?

Because normally Saylor wouldn't be Tia's type, aside from her looks. Tia preferred confident women. Women who knew what they were doing, what they wanted and when they wanted it. Women who were queer, for starters. She really didn't want to be with anyone who had never done this before. She was good at teaching dance but not life. Not how to properly fuck a woman into oblivion.

"What's on your mind?" Kirsten. Again.

Tia tensed, looking directly at Saylor, but she was so distracted by Jericho that she didn't even notice. It wasn't her fault. She deserved to have fun and not be Tia's keeper for the evening. Tightening her shoulders even more, Tia straightened her back and slid over a little to put more physical space between them.

"I was thinking about the competition coming up." It was the biggest lie on the planet, but this was Kirsten. Who cared? Tia just wanted to keep everything as neutral as possible.

"How many do we have competing?"

We?

This was Tia's studio, not Kirsten's. The possessiveness was strong, and Tia wanted to give Kirsten a piece of her mind, but she held her tongue. It would only get her into trouble if she did that. She sucked down the rest of her drink and grabbed Saylor's. She wouldn't care, would she? Tia would buy her a new one. But she needed the alcohol to get her through tonight.

She should have just said no to coming out. She should have stuck to home. But she'd wanted to be free for a change. She wanted to spend more time with Saylor. Now that she was here, she could actually admit that to herself. It wasn't that she wanted to get out—it was all about Saylor.

Tia really needed to figure herself out.

This wasn't good for either of them. Tia sucked down Saylor's drink.

"How many are competing, Tia?"

Tia cringed. "We have four couples, so eight, and two singles."

"Wow. That's a lot."

Tia shrugged slightly. It was more than normal, but she was pushing competition a bit more than normal, especially for adults. It wasn't about earning titles. It was about challenging themselves. Kids were really good at doing that. Adults? Not so much, and they all needed challenges—Tia included.

"Why are you here, Kirsten?" Tia asked pointedly. She faced Kirsten fully, hoping to get an honest answer. "Because we broke up over a year ago."

Kirsten's lips parted in surprise before they curled up into a seductive smile. "I want to give our relationship another try."

"Absolutely not." Cold washed through Tia again. She couldn't help but glance at Saylor on the dance floor. They made eye contact, and Tia shook her head. She needed to deal with her own problems. She needed to grow up and face the consequences of her actions. "I have zero interest in starting anything back up with you."

"Why so adamant?" Kirsten trailed her fingers along Tia's bare arm. "Surely our relationship wasn't all bad."

"It wasn't. You're right about that." The sex had been insanely hot, though Tia wasn't ever going to mention that to anyone. But with the hot sex came the crazy woman. Tia would take boring sex over that any day. "But the bad far outweighed the good."

She stepped back slightly, locking her eyes on Saylor with a sharp nod.

"I'm going to get some drinks. I don't want to talk to you again. Stop whatever game you're playing because I'm not joining in."

Without another word, Tia walked away. She headed straight for the bar without even looking over her shoulder. She'd needed that. She'd needed to stand up for herself and make it understood that whatever was going on needed to stop immediately. When she got to the bar, she leaned against the counter and let out a sigh of relief.

This was true freedom.

eleven

Saylor paused her dance when Tia walked away from Kirsten. She really should have been there. She should have left Jericho on the dance floor and gone to save Tia from Kirsten so that she wasn't stuck on her own. Saylor's hand shook as she touched Jericho's arm.

"I'll be right back."

She had just reached the edge of the dance floor when Kirsten grabbed her arm and dragged her back. Saylor furrowed her brow at Kirsten, canting her head to the side and watching Tia's backside sway as she walked toward the bar.

"Let's dance," Kirsten murmured, her voice low and sultry.

"I..." Saylor straightened her shoulders. Keeping Kirsten on the dance floor would keep her away from Tia. "Sure."

They walked back to where Jericho was and started right back where Saylor had left off. But the tension was different. The mood had shifted. Jericho slid her gaze from Saylor to Kirsten, obviously at a loss for words and not sure what to say. Saylor didn't know what to say either, so she kept moving her body and her hips to the beat and tried to ignore the sense of unease in the pit of her stomach.

Kirsten stepped in closer to Saylor, effectively elbowing Jericho out of the picture. Saylor sent Jericho a plea for help, but she had her head turned down and missed it. Kirsten took Saylor's hips and started dancing against her. Their movements were clumsy and awkward. They had no feel for dancing together.

Saylor tensed again.

Something else was going on here. Something she didn't have the full details on. But did she need them to do this favor for Tia? Not really. Would it be helpful? Most definitely. Saylor tried to put more distance between them. Kirsten's perfume was heady, and it overwhelmed Saylor's senses, which was hard on a sweat-filled dance floor. Thank God they weren't in the same dance class together.

When the song quieted and started into another one, Saylor tried to step away. Kirsten took her hand. "Stay. We need to talk."

"About what?" Saylor hated that she'd asked that. She should have said they didn't have anything to talk about, that she didn't need to talk to Kirsten, that she needed to leave.

"Tia."

Saylor shuddered. The next song started up, but she didn't move as Kirsten held on to her hand tightly.

"You're just another notch in her proverbial belt."

"I'm sorry. But what?" Saylor cringed. "I'm hardly—"

"She does this with all the young cute women she finds in her studio. She has a *thing* for them. It's predatory, really." Kirsten's words wormed into Saylor's heart.

She was stunned into silence, not sure what to say or do next. She was frozen to the spot, people dancing all around her, moving as if there was nothing turning their worlds upside down. And there wasn't. Why was Saylor even letting Kirsten do that?

How could she?

It wasn't like Tia had shown any interest.

And Saylor was engaged.

There wasn't anything going on between them.

Saylor sucked in a breath, bolstering herself. "Tia and I aren't anything more than friends."

"That's how she always starts. Friends with the new dancers. Then she swoops in and pushes it beyond that." Kirsten stepped in closer, taking over the moment. "She especially likes first time lesbians."

"But I'm not... I'm not into women." But how much of that was the truth? Because Saylor had thought about women before. She'd thought about kissing them, touching them, going down on them. She never had. She'd never given into those temptations, and now more than ever since she was with Jameson, that couldn't happen.

"Sure you're not, honey." Kirsten's laugh was dry and humorless. "That's exactly why she wants to turn you."

"I don't think sexuality works like that." Saylor took a step backward. "But um... thank you for the advice." She turned around and took a deep breath.

The dance crowd was still milling around, dancing or drinking. But Tia was nowhere in sight. Saylor had to get out of there. She was in over her head. Tia would have to figure out handling Kirsten on her own. Saylor's heart raced, and she reached for her jacket, throwing it over her shoulders and zipping it up.

"Leaving already, Saylor?" Kirsten said, that drawl of satisfaction so strong that no one could miss it.

Saylor said nothing. She walked a couple steps backward, away from Kirsten, and then turned suddenly, running squarely into Tia. Words caught in Saylor's throat, and she couldn't force them out. Ducking her chin, she pushed past Tia and headed straight for the door. She'd walk a few blocks away and then call for a ride. She just needed to get the hell out of there.

"Saylor!" Tia's voice reached her ears, but Saylor ignored it.

She raced for the door. She needed the cold air on her cheeks. She needed to feel like she could breathe again.

"Saylor!" Tia grabbed her elbow and pulled her back just as she reached the middle of the stairs. "Stop."

"I've got to get home," Saylor said, her nerves ratcheting up again.

"Just stop a minute." Tia calmed her tone.

Saylor glanced down, finding Tia's jacket in her other hand. Saylor's heart raced, and she couldn't find the words again. What was happening? "It's fine. You go back and have fun."

"No. I'm not doing that." Tia blew out a breath. "What did Kirsten say to you?"

"Nothing." Saylor clenched her jaw hard.

"Don't lie to me." Tia eyed her.

The sound of the music filtered down the stairs, echoing softly through the doors they'd gone through. Saylor bit the inside of her cheek. Tia was standing so close to her. She had such concern crossing her features. She was worried.

"I'm fine," Saylor supplied. "I promise."

"Please," Tia begged. "Please don't ever lie to me."

That hit home. Tia's tone, her plea, her worry—it was all more than Saylor could defend against. Or perhaps she just didn't really want to. "I'll be fine."

"Good."

Just that small change in wording seemed to be enough. It seemed to ease some of what was bothering Tia, but she still didn't let go of Saylor's arm.

"What did she say to you?"

"It doesn't matter."

"Saylor…" Tia said in a warning.

"It doesn't matter," Saylor repeated. It didn't really. Saylor was with Jameson. At least she wanted to be, right? But she had been doubting their relationship more and more with each week that she lived there. He didn't make her feel good, not like he used to when they were just dating. They hardly ever saw each other. He stopped trying to take the time to spend with her. Saylor closed her eyes and loosed the words. "She said you wanted me to be another notch in your belt."

Tia sighed heavily, releasing Saylor's arm.

Saylor scrambled to say something else, to make Tia feel better, to stop hurting her. "For the record, I don't think that. I don't think you're just wanting that, or that you're even interested in that. I don't..."

"Just stop talking," Tia whispered. She stepped back and brushed her hands over her face. She glanced up the stairs toward S-Club and then back at Saylor. "She's not an idiot, Saylor."

"I'm sorry?" Confused, Saylor looked directly at Tia. "What do you mean she's not an idiot?"

"I mean she is because she won't just give up on me. I broke it off with her over a year ago, and she still clings to this idyllic relationship that we never had. We didn't even have a relationship, not really." Tia stopped. "I don't even know why I'm telling you this. It's not important. We're not together. But Kirsten isn't an idiot, and she's very sensitive to certain things."

"What things?" Was Saylor's voice wavering? She sucked in a sharp breath, still holding her ground. What was Tia saying that she wasn't actually saying? Was there something else going on? Did she want more than just friendship?

"That I'm attracted to you." Tia pressed her lips together in a thin line. "I'm not looking for anything, Saylor, I promise. You're engaged, and I'm not getting in the middle of that. I'm not looking to make you gay or anything."

Heat washed through Saylor. Tia found her attractive? How was that even possible? Saylor was anything but sexy. She had such a strong athletic build that most people were turned off by her muscles and the fact that she could outrun most guys on a good day.

"Are you okay with that?"

Saylor tuned back in to the moment, realizing far too late that Tia had continued talking and Saylor hadn't heard a single word.

She couldn't answer the question because she didn't even know what it was in reference to. Her heart raced, beating its way up into her throat and into her head. But it wasn't fear.

It was anticipation.

"Saylor?" Tia asked, that same concern from before back on her face. "I don't want Kirsten to make you think that there's anything else going on between us. I won't cross any lines."

But Saylor wanted to. She'd wanted to for weeks now. The more she got to know Tia, the more she couldn't stop thinking about her. She wanted to know what it would be like, to kiss a woman, to have Tia's body pressed against hers in more than just a dance.

Straightening her back, Saylor took a slow deep breath. She needed to get out of there.

She needed to figure out what was going on with her body, what was going on with her heart. She started down the last of the stairs, but Tia caught up with her as soon as she pushed out the main door. She hadn't said a single thing, and she should have known better. She should have known that Tia would follow her to make sure that she was okay.

She always did.

"Saylor, wait."

"Tia, I don't think this is a good idea." Saylor spun around, the rain falling on her face and chilling her burning cheeks.

"Don't just walk away. Talk to me, please."

"I can't..." Saylor stopped. She had no idea what to say. "What she said is true, right?"

"No. It's not. I promise you, it's not." Tia stood only a step apart from her.

"I just can't do this right now."

"Do what? All we're doing is talking." Tia's voice rose, getting louder by the second. She seemed desperate almost. "Please don't leave without us figuring this out."

"There's nothing to figure out!" Saylor raised her voice, stepping even closer when she wanted to step away. Something was always pulling her back toward Tia. She never could walk away freely, could she? "There's nothing between us."

"There's not," Tia agreed. "There's not, but I don't want you walking away thinking that I want more. I just want whatever friendship you have to offer. That's it."

"That's not it." Saylor bit her tongue. She couldn't stop the words from spilling. She'd tried so hard to keep it all in, but she couldn't. "It's more than that. It's so much more than that." Saylor took one more step.

"No, it's not. We're friends. I'm your dance instructor. That's all it is."

"It's not," Saylor reiterated, her eyes locked on Tia's as the rain fell on them. "Stop lying to yourself."

When had Saylor stopped doing that? When had she agreed to lean fully into the fact that whatever was between them was fraught with sexual tension? Because now wasn't the time to give into this. But fuck, she wanted to.

Tia looked at her surprised. Droplets of water trailed down her skin, over her cheeks and onto her chest. Her tank was drenched on the top, goosebumps ran along her skin. Saylor held her breath as she moved in and pressed their lips together.

Tia gasped.

Saylor pushed in even more.

She wrapped her arm around Tia's back and pulled her in close as warmth flooded her. It masked the chill air. It warmed the raindrops. Saylor closed her eyes, sliding her tongue out as she parted her lips. Tia hummed and then stepped forward, turning their bodies and pushing Saylor backward. Following each of Tia's steps, Saylor moved until her back pressed into the brick wall behind her.

Tia slid her knee between Saylor's legs just like she'd done on the dance floor, just like they were going to be locked together and never able to part ways. Saylor moved her hands up into Tia's hair, tangling the locks around her fingers as Tia tangled their tongues together in a dance of their own.

Saylor's entire body changed tune, moving from one of discord to one of harmony. It slid perfectly into place, highlighting the strength that Tia brought, the hope that she had, the softness they shared. Saylor melted into the wall behind her, dragging Tia even closer. She dropped her hips down, grinding against Tia's thigh, and pleasure shot through her instantly.

That had never happened before.

Tia's mouth was hot against hers. Saylor's entire body was ready for this, like she'd been waiting for a moment like this her entire life and she'd never found it before. Not until now. Not until she was in the arms of a woman. Saylor sucked Tia's lower lip into her mouth, scraping it lightly with her teeth as she dug her fingers into Tia's sides.

Her jacket was hot and constricting. She struggled to breathe with it on, and she wanted nothing more than to rip it off and feel Tia's entire body against hers. She knew what that would be like already. They'd danced that way. They'd stood together like that. Tia would be strong and firm against her, precise in each of her movements. Her curves would be a softness that Saylor had longed for.

Groaning, Saylor pushed her body against Tia's leg again, her clit throbbing at just the possibility that something more was going to happen. The anticipation she'd felt ever since meeting this woman reared its gorgeous head, blossoming into something wholly unlike anything Saylor had felt before.

Pure desire.

Tia slid her fingers up under the edge of Saylor's jacket, finding her skin with her frigid touch. The shock was strong, but Saylor didn't shy away from it. She leaned into it even more. She pulled Tia impossibly closer, not wanting even the smallest space between them. Tia wrapped her hand around Saylor's side, tickling her skin before she pulled back and closed her eyes with a heavy breath.

"Saylor..."

"I wanted that," Saylor said immediately. "I want you."

"We need to stop."

"I know," Saylor murmured, already regretting that she knew Tia would move away. "I know we do, but just know, I don't want to."

"We don't have a choice right now."

And that was what Saylor hated. All she wanted was to be right here, mouth against Tia's, bodies smooshed together, preferably naked. But there was so much else between them, and they couldn't do that. Saylor couldn't let it happen.

"I'm going to go home," Saylor whispered. She pulled away, tugging her jacket down and stepping backward, away from Tia. "I'll see you at class next week."

twelve

The silence was deafening.

Tia could barely stand it, but she had no idea what to text or what to say. She brushed her fingers over her lips as she sat in her office, secluded, confined, without anything to distract her except herself. That kiss had been everything and more.

But then Saylor had gone silent. Rightfully so.

She had so much to sort through, no doubt. Tia touched her lips again, remembering the way Saylor had moved against her, hot and ready, as if she hadn't been afraid of anything ever in her life. But it had taken Kirsten for them to get there, to push Saylor into acting. Tia cringed at that. She hated it.

They needed to talk.

But what was Tia supposed to say?

Hey, I really liked kissing you. I'd like to do it again.

Because Saylor was engaged to be married. She was in a committed relationship, and Tia was nothing more than a distraction for Saylor, who was having issues in her relationship, wasn't she? Or was it more than that? Hell, she hoped it was more than that.

But it couldn't be.

Tia just had to keep reminding herself of that.

The front door of the studio opened, the chime echoing through the empty dance room. Tia glanced at the clock, surprised to find that it was already time for the adult class to start. She needed to work with the couples that were going to be competing, help prepare them even more for what was swiftly coming up.

Tia walked out to get ready, although she already had everything planned. For the nights in between last Friday and today, she hadn't been able to sleep, so she'd thrown herself into work as best she could. Tia started some soft music for the warmup, letting her students join in as soon as they were ready.

Everyone trickled in slowly, but there was no sign of Saylor.

Surely she wouldn't skip just because they'd kissed. Would she?

Fear churned uncomfortably in Tia's stomach. She didn't want that to happen. No kiss was worth that. Saylor was making a name for herself here. She was starting to make friends and build the community that she really needed. Tia didn't want to mess that up for her. The door opened again.

Tia held her breath and glanced toward the lobby, hoping to see Saylor's brown head as she stepped inside. Instead, she was greeted with the always-present sneer on Kirsten's face. What the hell was she doing here?

"Hey," Kirsten said, coming straight up to Tia. "I thought I'd join in today. I want to do the competition."

Tia ground her molars together. "Who's your partner?"

Kirsten shook her head, her lips curling slightly. "I don't have one yet."

"You need to find someone."

"Can't you—"

"I'm the coach," Tia interrupted. No way in hell was she going to put herself in that position. "Find someone else."

Kirsten stood flabbergasted, but Tia didn't care. She deserved it after the shit she had pulled last weekend. Tia straightened her back, already feeling good about where she'd put Kirsten. Now, if only Saylor would show up.

Tia clapped her hands to get the class's attention when it was time to properly start. She paired everyone off, putting Steven with Kirsten since Saylor still hadn't showed. That would at least get Tia out of dancing with her, but Steven really needed to practice with Saylor if they—

Tia stopped.

The door rang. Only one person was missing from the class.

Saylor.

As soon as she stepped through the main door to the studio, Tia grinned. Everything in her body told her to walk right up to Saylor, wrap her in a hug and kiss her senseless. Tia froze. What the hell was she thinking?

Exactly that.

She wasn't.

Saylor barely made eye contact as she slid next to Steven and Kirsten stepped away, eyeing Tia over like she'd just won the lottery.

Damn it.

Tia told them all to start their routines. She walked by each partner as they practiced, Kirsten's gaze following her from the edge of the room. Tia took her sweet time, because she did not want to have to dance with Kirsten even though she knew that's what was going to happen.

It was hard to make it through the class. Every time Tia wanted to talk to Saylor, she knew she couldn't. By the time everyone was packing up to leave, Tia caught Saylor's attention. "Got a minute?"

Saylor worried her lower lip between her teeth.

"I promise nothing bad." Tia put her hands up in front of her.

"Sure, I guess." Saylor didn't seem like she was confident in that.

Kirsten lingered, but when Tia had ignored her long enough,

she finally disappeared into the lobby, and Tia gladly walked into her office, shutting the door behind her and Saylor. She breathed a sigh of relief as soon as it was closed.

But then she was left with the fact that she still didn't know where to start. Looking Saylor over, Tia could see the worry, the torment she must have put herself through over the weekend. They'd kissed. They'd crossed the boundary, and not only had it been a little kiss, it had been absolutely amazing.

"I don't know where to start," Tia said finally, sliding into the chair at her desk.

Saylor stood by the door still, her hands fidgeting in front of her. She couldn't even raise her gaze to meet Tia's eyes. Guilt slammed Tia hard. She didn't want Saylor to feel bad about what had happened.

"I almost didn't come tonight." Saylor's voice was so quiet, so reticent.

Tia hated it. Gone was the confident woman from before, replaced with this anxious one. And Tia completely understood why, as much as she hated it. Sighing, Tia waved to the seat Saylor had taken when they'd met. "Sit down. Please."

Saylor hesitated, but she did finally slide into the wooden chair. Her shoulders were stiff, she put her palms on the edge of the chair as if she was ready to get up any second. Tia watched her carefully, still trying to figure out what to say.

"I just want to be honest," Tia started, though words failed her again.

Saylor shook her head slowly, tears welling in her eyes. She closed her eyes and bowed her head, spreading her knees to rest her elbows on them. "I don't know if I can do this."

Tia's heart hammered. "Do what?"

"Whatever this is." Saylor wiped her fingers under her eyes.

"Jameson—"

"I want to be clear that I'm not asking you to do anything, Saylor. What happened the other night... that's all it ever has to be." Tia hated saying those words. As much as she believed them, as much as she would follow through with them, she hated that it had to be their reality.

Saylor shuddered, her entire body shivering. "Tia..." Her voice broke. "It's not *just* a kiss."

"No, it's not." Tia swallowed the lump in her throat, because she had to be the one to put Saylor out of her misery. She had to be the one to ease Saylor's distress as much as humanly possible. "It wasn't just a kiss. It's not *just* that. But it doesn't have to be anything else other than exactly what it is."

"I don't know what it is." Pain etched its way through Saylor's voice, breaking Tia's heart.

She just wanted to wrap Saylor in her arms and make everything better. She wanted Saylor not to be struggling, not to be questioning. But she couldn't. This was all part of the process of coming out. It was all part of working through your sexuality, and it sucked. Especially doing it while in a committed relationship. Especially doing it when you didn't have a support system.

"I want to kiss you again." Saylor's voice was so quiet that Tia swore she hadn't heard her correctly. But the redness in her cheeks gave her away.

"Does that embarrass you?" Tia waited on pins and needles for the answer.

Saylor shook her head. "No. But it should, shouldn't it?"

"Embarrass you?" Tia couldn't even fathom it. "No. Why would it?"

"Because Jameson..." Saylor trailed off.

Tia had to fill in so many blanks in this conversation because Saylor wasn't giving her all the words. "Because you're engaged?"

"Because you're a woman." Saylor winced.

"Right." Tia nodded to no one but herself. "You've never kissed a woman before, have you?"

Saylor shook her head. Tia's stomach swam. How could she have thought this was a good idea? Saylor was so far behind in everything. She didn't know what she wanted or how she wanted it. She was just figuring that out. Tia rubbed her palms along her thighs, working out the best way to say whatever had to happen next.

"It's okay to like women, Saylor. It's okay to like women and men at the same time. There's nothing wrong with you because you like someone, anyone."

Saylor whimpered a cry. "But there is!"

"There's not," Tia confirmed.

"There is! I'm twenty-eight! How could I have *not* known?" Her eyes were wide. She was so serious.

Tia's heart broke for her. She closed her eyes, digging deep within herself. Because she wanted to rant and rave. She wanted to yell at Saylor that there was absolutely nothing wrong with her. That she was made exactly as she was.

"I didn't know until I was nearly twenty." She hadn't told anyone this. Well, anyone except Monti because Monti had figured out her own sexuality when she was ten. Tia hated sharing this kind of stuff, but Saylor deserved to know she wasn't the only one oblivious to her own desires out there. "My oldest niece was just turning nine, and there was this mom of one of the kids in her class that came to her birthday party, and I literally couldn't get this woman out of my head. I couldn't." Tia chuckled wildly. "I wanted to do everything under the sun to her."

"Did you?" Saylor asked so innocently.

"No. She was married and so very straight." Tia snorted. "But it was the wake-up call I needed. I didn't start dating right away either because I had the girls, and I really needed to focus on them."

"It's hard to think of you as a mother."

"I'm not their mother." Tia raised her eyebrows. "I'm not. But I did raise them. I did parent them, and Monti especially turns to me as her mother." Tia swallowed the lump in her throat. "But not everyone just knows that they're queer. Sometimes it takes a while to figure it out."

"I feel so stupid. Like how could I have not known?"

"There are so many reasons that we're blind to it, Saylor. And I can't give you yours. I can only give you mine, which is that my parents weren't the most accepting people in the world, which is that my brother was...horrific. I was raising my nieces. Romance, sex, attraction—it was the furthest thing from my mind."

Saylor seemed to think about that one. She took a deep steadying breath. "I think... I think I just didn't think about it either."

"Then that's all there is to it, Saylor. There's no reason to blame yourself. This is exactly who you were made to be." Tia wanted so much to reach out to her, comfort her. But she couldn't force herself to do that. Touching Saylor would be such a bad idea, because she wanted so much more than to touch her. She wanted those heated kisses again. The desire pooling between them. The ache between her legs that only Saylor could satisfy.

"I don't know what to do."

"I can't tell you want to do." Tia hated this. She couldn't be the supportive friend and the love interest at the same time. It hurt so damn much. "Only you can decide where you want to go from here."

Tia let out a slow breath, hanging onto the silence as her lifesaver. If Saylor said nothing, there was still hope. Even if she didn't agree to leave Jameson and explore, there could still be hope that it might happen someday. Any day even if it wasn't today.

Hanging onto that was all Tia had in this moment, but she couldn't ask Saylor to make a decision now. That would be pure cruelty. She couldn't force Saylor to end her relationship, to jump into one with her, to completely turn away from everything she knew in the span of one weekend.

"Just take some time and think about everything. Okay?"

Saylor looked her directly in the eyes. Her lips were parted. The longing for Tia to lean in and capture those lips in another heated kiss, in passion, in the very hope that she wanted to find there—to make Saylor choose now would be the end to everything.

"Go home, Saylor. Think. Take time. I'll still be here whenever you figure it out or have more questions or just need some advice."

"Okay," Saylor answered meekly.

"I'm not going anywhere."

Nodding, Saylor gave a sweet smile. "I trust you."

thirteen

Saylor sat in the living room staring at the television for hours. Except it wasn't on. She hadn't even turned the lights on, and it was now light outside. The room was cast in the shadows of dawn, and she was just now noticing.

For as much as she had felt alive the other night, she'd been thrown into nothing but turmoil since then.

Saylor shuddered and checked her watch. Jameson was due home shortly, and she really needed to figure out what she was going to say to him. Confessing that she'd kissed her dance instructor probably wasn't the best way to start that conversation.

Telling him that she wanted to kiss Tia again would be worse.

Perhaps she should start with the fact that she wasn't sure she was as straight as she used to be. If she'd ever been that way. Saylor shivered. That wouldn't do either. She sighed heavily, still unable to force herself off the couch to turn the lights on or even prepare herself for her fiancé's homecoming. She should be doing something like that right? Play the dutiful housewife even though that wasn't her role yet?

The lock turned, and Saylor's eyes were riveted to the front door.

It was now or never.

Jameson stepped inside, looking ever the perfect businessman. The bag that he carted in was small even though he'd been gone longer than normal for this last trip. He looked her over, frowned, and then dropped his bag by the bedroom door before sitting next to her.

"What's wrong?"

She wasn't even trying to hide it. Saylor looked him over. He was a catch on any day. Handsome. Exactly what every mother probably dreamed of her daughter marrying. But that didn't mean her, did it? Saylor was about to speak when he jumped back in.

"Are you going to tell me?"

Saylor expected his voice to be piercing with anger, but it wasn't. Instead, he was soft in a way she hadn't seen from him in a long time. In a way she had longed for. It gave her hope that perhaps they could actually have this conversation and get somewhere with it. "I'm not happy."

Jameson sighed heavily and flopped back into the couch cushion next to her. "What are you going to do about it?"

Saylor tensed up. "I don't know what to do about it."

"You haven't been happy since you moved here."

"You're right about that." Saylor plucked at the blanket over her pajama-clad legs. She had stayed on that couch all night, sleeping on and off, barely able to think clearly. "I don't know how to be happy."

"Am I making you unhappy?"

"No." *But yes.* She thought those last two words but didn't add them. It wasn't him exactly. But that kiss with Tia had transformed her understanding of the world. It had changed how she thought about everything, and she just couldn't think straight.

"Then what is it?"

"It's so many things." Why was her voice so flat? Why did she sound like none of this was affecting her? Had she already given up? "I've told you not working has been hard. I just can't seem to find work out here."

"You can always try harder."

And there was the man she'd come to despise. Did he ever hear just how harsh his voice was? "I can," Saylor agreed. "But you're never home. And I don't expect you to find a new job, so don't hear that in what I'm saying. But I didn't anticipate how hard it would be to be so alone."

"Oh." Jameson ran his fingers through his hair, scuffing it up in a way that Saylor used to find adorable. "So what are you going to do about it?"

"I don't know," Saylor repeated with a sigh. Because that had been the question she was asking herself all week. "I don't know what I can do."

She couldn't do it. No matter if she wanted to, she couldn't force herself to bring up the fact that she'd kissed Tia or the fact that she had been so turned on by that simple kiss. Turned on in ways that she'd never been by him or any other man she'd dated. Because she still hadn't figured out what all of that meant.

And if it meant breaking off their engagement, then she wanted to be sure. She wanted to know without any hesitation or doubt that she was doing the right thing.

Saylor bit her lip. "I'm going to go to the studio, help with the kids' class today."

"Saylor." Jameson reached out, taking her hand and curling their fingers together. "I don't like seeing you like this."

That was at least some small consolation. He did still see her.

"I don't want you to be stuck in this apartment like it's your prison."

"That's what it's become." Saylor closed her eyes, feeling the weight and warmth of his hand on hers. Once, not long ago, she had taken such comfort in that touch. But she had betrayed him, and she knew it wouldn't last because of that. She'd already taken the step to walk away from him, and it was either come back with everything she had or continue to give up.

"Saylor..." Jameson trailed off, but he didn't say anything else.

Moving onto her knees, Saylor pecked his lips and headed for the bathroom. She needed to get out of there. She took a shower and got dressed as efficiently as possible. Jameson was already finishing his breakfast by the time she was ready to go.

"I'll be in the office late today."

"And leaving again tomorrow," Saylor finished for him. "I looked at the calendar."

"I wish I didn't have to. Not with you feeling this way."

Saylor gave him a small shrug. "It's no different than yesterday or the week before."

Except it was.

"I'll see you later." She kissed him again and grabbed her keys before she left.

The studio was alive even though no one was there but Tia. Saylor walked right in even though she wasn't scheduled that day. Jericho was back to work from her bout with the flu, which meant Saylor should be at home and looking for a job, not here wasting away her hours.

But she couldn't stay in that apartment any longer.

She needed to get out. Not just of the building but out of her own head.

"Tia!" Saylor called as she stepped into the main studio.

"What are you doing here?" Tia stood up and leaned against the doorway, her arms and legs crossed.

"I just..." Saylor blushed. Surely there was an easy way to say this that Tia would understand so she wouldn't have to break down in her office again. "I thought you could use some extra help."

Tia eyed her over, looking at her from head to toe. "Sure. If you want."

"Good." Saylor wiped her hands nervously over her thighs,

removing the clamminess from them. She pulled out everything they would need for that morning and got it ready. By the time Jericho arrived, they put on some music and started their own little warm-up fun that the kids joined in as they got there.

Tia didn't come out of the office.

Jericho started the class without missing a beat. Was this how it normally worked when Jericho was there? Had Tia taken over just because she didn't trust Saylor would be able to do it? The first day was understandable, but after that? Didn't she trust Saylor?

They were halfway through the class when Tia finally emerged from her office, working with the students that needed more help while Jericho and Saylor focused on the others. They were so close to their recital that most of what they were doing was memorizing the details of the routine.

It took until the end of the class for Saylor to really feel the difference. She was comfortable here. She was more comfortable here than she had been anywhere else in her life except maybe the ice rink. She found herself smiling, laughing, the weight that was on her shoulders all night and that morning gone in the blink of an eye. As soon as she stepped into this building, it was gone.

Why couldn't every day be like that?

Tia made eye contact with her, raising an eyebrow in question. "What do you think, Saylor?"

"What?" Saylor must have missed something, because the kids were all staring at her and so was Jericho. What question had she not heard in the midst of all her thoughts? Worry ate away at her stomach again, making it so hard to even figure out how to get that question back out again.

"Do you want to show them the spin with me?"

"Oh, um..." Saylor gnawed on her cheek and looked at Jericho. Why was Tia asking Saylor instead of Jericho, the one person who was actually paid to be a teacher there. "Sure?"

Tia narrowed her gaze but came around to the front of the class. She still had her thin jacket on, zipped up to the tops of her breasts. Saylor had been moving around so much that she'd discarded her jacket in favor of her workout clothes.

"All right, ladies. We start in position." Tia stepped up to Saylor and held her hand out. "Jericho, you take over explaining it."

Tia dragged in a deep breath. Saylor looked her directly in the eyes. She wasn't sure which spin they were doing, but she had no doubt that Tia was going to lead her right through everything. Tia raised her eyebrows and nodded.

"Just follow my lead."

"Got it," Saylor murmured. If there was one more thing she didn't have to think about, she would take it. She relaxed her shoulders and let the beats in her head take over.

Tia dropped down slightly, indicating they were about to move. Saylor took a step to follow. Tia turned to her left, taking Saylor with her and spinning her in a full circle before landing back almost right where they started. Then she stopped.

But Saylor didn't want to stop.

Turning to the class, Tia gave them a single look and indicated that she wanted them to try it. They all lined up and started the move over. Tia tossed Saylor a look and then went about correcting the students' form. Saylor did the same in the opposite direction. But the room faded. The kids' voices were there, but Saylor had eyes and ears for Tia and no one else.

They were twenty minutes deep into the second class of the day when the phone in the office rang. Tia pointed at Saylor, since she couldn't get Jericho's attention, and then pointed to the office. Saylor nodded in understanding and then pushed Tia from her mind. She was there to find focus, wasn't she?

Not to distract herself.

Not to find a way to avoid thinking about what she really needed to do.

Which was to make a decision about Jameson. To decide what exactly to tell him and how she wanted to do that. Or if she wanted to forget everything that had happened between her and Tia and throw herself fully into being the wife she'd already agreed to become.

Tia was gone for the rest of the class.

The kids waved at her as they left the room, and Tia nodded at them but put her finger over her lips to keep them quiet still. The phone was still pressed to her ear. Saylor started cleaning up and preparing for the next class when Jericho came over to her.

"Did you have fun last weekend?"

"What?" Saylor nearly froze, but she forced herself to keep moving.

"When we went dancing!" Jericho's laughter trilled through the room, like Saylor had missed the punch line of the joke. "You weren't there for very long."

"Oh, right. Um... Yeah I wasn't feeling as good as I thought, so I went home early."

Jericho frowned. "You didn't catch the flu, did you?"

"No, no, nothing like that. Just my nerves acting up." Saylor waved it off like it was nothing. "I'm not much of a people person. Sticking me in a room that's filled tries my anxiety."

"Oh, I totally get that."

Saylor doubted it, but she'd take the empathy even if Jericho really didn't truly understand. "But I did have fun while I was there."

"Good! We try to do that at least once a month. Just blow off some steam with our dance moves." Jericho laughed again, moving her arms and her hips in the cheesiest dance move on the planet.

Giggling, Saylor shook her head.

"What?!" Tia's voice boomed into the room.

Saylor jumped. Jericho turned toward the office, her eyebrows raised in confusion. She sent Saylor a side-long glance and shook her head. "That doesn't sound good."

"No, it doesn't." Saylor wanted to go see what was going on, what was wrong, but she held still. It wasn't her place. It wasn't her job. And while she might consider Tia one of her closest friends here in Seattle, that didn't mean she could go barging in there to figure out what might very well be a private matter.

"Should we—"

"No," Saylor said. "She'll come find us if she needs something."

fourteen

"What?!" Tia shouted loudly. Her heart thudded hard, and it was next to impossible to breathe. This couldn't be happening. There were ten days left until the recital, and the kids were expecting to be able to perform. She didn't have time for this nonsense. "Yes, yes, I understand."

She wanted to groan. She wanted to take the cell phone from her ear and throw it at the wall and watch it shatter. She wanted to crawl back into her bed, under the warm blankets, and go back in time and pretend this day never happened.

Maybe if she could groundhog this day like in the movie then it would go differently.

But it never worked in the movie, so why would she think it would now?

Sighing heavily, she ran her fingers through her hair and let out a whimper. "There's no way they can be made?" she asked, her last-ditch effort to get a different outcome.

But wasn't that the definition of insanity?

God, she *was* insane. In this moment and the next when she was going to have to find a new way to get costumes that fit all of her kids in just ten days. No one would be able to fulfill that order. She could just go with the standard practice uniform. Maybe? No, that would be awful. No parent would want to see their kid wearing that.

"What do you want me to do about it? It's not my fault that you contracted with an outside company who can't fulfill their responsibility." Now she was getting mad. This was exactly where she wanted to be. Feed that anger into the poor person on the other end of the line who had to make this call, and maybe, just maybe, she would feel a little better.

But she wouldn't.

She'd feel awful at the end of the day. Not just for being an asshole, but because she'd be no closer to a solution.

"I think if you don't find a way to refund the money that I already paid you in full, then I'm going to expose you to the media. This is ridiculous. And I won't be doing business with you again."

The apologies weren't getting anywhere with her. Tia wanted the money back. She wanted things to be made right. Or better yet, she wanted the costumes for the class! Growling, she said a few more choice words and then promptly slammed her phone onto the desk loudly in a fit of rage. It was the closest she could get to throwing it across the room.

"What's wrong?" Saylor's sweet voice filled her head, such a gentle balm to the raging inferno of irritation that Tia really wanted to experience in that moment.

Tia knew, without a doubt, that if she looked up into Saylor's eyes that she would never find a thread of that anger again. And for once, she just wanted to stay mad. So she ducked her chin, curled her fingers around the edge of the desk, and grunted. "The jerks at the manufacturer fucked up."

"They what?" Saylor was still all confusion and innocence.

How did she manage to do that? Tia had spent too many years exposed to the dark side of the world to ever carry that kind of sweetness inside her again. She cringed. What were they doing together? Anything Tia did with Saylor was going to ruin her. And no one deserved that. Tia was there for fun and partying. She liked her life exactly as it was, and she didn't want that to change. She didn't want Saylor to be caught up in fantasies. Saylor wanted something deep and meaningful. And she was engaged! Tia had to screw her head back on straight if she was going to keep herself together.

"The manufacturer." Tia clenched her molars tightly, the muscles straining in her jaw. "They sold the project to someone else, and *that* company was a scam. And then their equipment broke down. So I don't have costumes for the recital in ten days."

"Oh." Saylor stepped into the office, shutting the door behind her.

That was smart thinking. Tia didn't want the kids to get a whiff of this drama. They didn't need more stress while they were preparing. Some of them would take it so hard. If she could find a solution—who was she kidding? There was no solution. There was no alternative. She'd left herself wide open to this lunacy.

"I can make them." Saylor squeaked out the words.

Tia jerked her head up. Her eyes widened. She looked directly at Saylor as if she was an angel with wings. "What?"

"I can make them," Saylor repeated, this time a little more strongly than before, her near-constant anxiety not stepping one foot into this room. "I used to make all my own costumes for my skating competitions. I'm sure I can still whip out—what, twenty?—costumes for the girls."

"Twenty-seven," Tia corrected. "The younger kids can wear their practice uniforms. It's the older kids that need the design."

"I can do it." Saylor nodded sharply, as if fully confident in her ability to get this done.

"Are you kidding me?" Tia stepped in close and snagged Saylor's hands in her own. "You're amazing."

Tia almost cupped both of Saylor's cheeks and pulled her in for a kiss, but she stopped herself.

"Yeah. I just need to know the design, and we need to get the fabric."

"Can you do that?" Tia reached into her wallet and pulled out the business card. "Do you have a sewing machine? Because I don't have that. God, I have nothing for this. Sewing isn't my strength."

Saylor nodded. "Yeah, I do. It's a small one, but it should work."

Tia held out the card. Their fingers brushed. Tia held her breath, tingles erupting where their skin touched. Her stomach was in knots. They were going to have to be so close while Saylor worked this out. They were going to have to spend hours together in the same room. Tia sucked in a sharp breath.

Finding Saylor in her studio this morning had been one of the last things she expected, and yet, here they were. Still together, still in the same room, still staring at each other. Tia kept her grasp on the card.

"Saylor, why are you here this morning?"

Shaking her head, Saylor felt her eyes well with tears. Tia dropped all pretense and wrapped an arm around her shoulders and pulled her in for a hug. Saylor buried her face into the nook of Tia's neck. Silent tears fell onto Tia's skin. Something was going on with Saylor. Something far more serious than costumes for a dance recital.

"Saylor," Tia murmured, sliding her hands up and down Saylor's back. "What's wrong?"

"Just let me do this."

"Do what?" Tia looked out the window to the dance room as Jericho started the next class. Jericho frowned at them, but Tia gave her a subtle wave to tell her to ignore it.

"Let me fix this for you. It's something I can do. I promise you." Saylor straightened herself and wiped her cheeks. "I can do this."

Tia almost told her no, that it would be too much. She almost told Saylor to go home to Jameson, that they needed to stop this charade of a friendship, because it wasn't that. Saylor and Jericho were friends. But there was far more sizzling between the two of them.

"Here." Tia handed the card over. "If you need Jericho to help, grab her. Set up in my apartment." Tia rustled around in her desk for her keys. "It'll be quieter with fewer disruptions and you'll have more room to work."

"Your apartment?"

Tia nodded. "Fifth floor." She pointed above them. "It came with the studio rental. There's a spare room where we can set the costumes out and you can set up on the kitchen table. Just toss whatever on the floor and I'll deal with it when I'm done teaching tonight."

Saylor looked like she was going to object now. Tia held her breath, waiting for it to happen. But she wasn't sure she could stop this now that it was in motion. "It's not weird that I'll be in your apartment? I can do it here."

"No." Tia shook her head. "It'll be easier there. I'll pay you for doing all this work, of course." Because she would be getting her full refund for this fiasco. That she'd make sure, and if she could pay Saylor the same, then she absolutely would.

Saylor looked like she was about to object to that but stopped herself. At least Tia wasn't going to have to argue about that.

"Are you sure you want to do this?" Tia asked again.

"Yeah. I'll go get my machine right now and bring it upstairs. If you can have the rest of the information ready, I'll grab it on my way out to get the fabric." Saylor gave a small smile and nodded. She started to back out of the room and stumbled on the chair.

Tia immediately stepped forward to grab her arms and steady her. They were standing so close. Tia's grip was tight on Saylor's, holding her and not letting go. Despite the fact that she was trying desperately to make her hands listen to her brain, they just weren't cooperating. Saylor took in a shuddering breath, lifting her gaze to meet Tia's.

"I should get going."

"You should," Tia answered, but she still wasn't letting go. Right in this corner, no one out in the studio would be able to see them. Tia could lean in and press their mouths together and no one would be the wiser. But she couldn't do that. She couldn't make Saylor regret another kiss.

"Tia..."

"I'm moving." Tia winced and backed away, finally able to force her feet to move like they should. "Stop being so clumsy." She laughed lightly, but it sounded hollow. She failed to cover up the arousal in her own voice, and she was damn sure that Saylor heard it.

"I've always been clumsy," Saylor responded, her cheeks red. But was it with arousal, embarrassment, or something else entirely?

Tia held herself still. "You really should get going. Let me know if you need help dragging stuff up or even shopping. I can take over teaching and send Jericho with you."

"I'd rather you came with me," Saylor answered, as if confident for the first time ever.

"I think it's a better decision to send Jericho." Tia's shoulders tightened. She didn't want to have to explain to Saylor why. She hoped to death that Saylor just understood what she wasn't saying. Because to have to sit there and tell Saylor she was struggling with this would put so much on Saylor's shoulders that she didn't need. "I can teach the next class by myself without a problem."

Saylor frowned.

"Go on. I'll help you with cutting when I'm done teaching. I know that can take the longest. But don't put me in charge of the machine."

"Okay." Saylor put her hand on the doorknob and turned it, but she didn't open it. "I promise you I'll get this done."

"I trust you," Tia answered.

One more look, and Saylor was walking away. It was going to take everything in Tia to resist all the temptation she was going to face in the next ten days. Because being confined to a small room with Saylor was going to make it so hard. They were going to be pulling late nights. They were going to be working closely together. They were no doubt going to be spending all hours of the night together.

Tia tidied up in her office for another few minutes before joining Jericho outside. The girls were practicing their twists when Jericho sidled up next to her.

"What was that about?"

"A lot of different things," Tia mumbled. "Saylor's going to be busy the next couple of weeks. She might need your help carrying some things up to my apartment."

"Did she and Jameson break up?" Jericho's eyes went wide.

"What? No." Tia frowned, glancing at the kids to make sure they hadn't heard them. "Why would you think that?"

"You said she's moving things up to your apartment. You have that extra room. I just figured if she needed a place to stay that you'd offer it. You've done it before."

Tia frowned. She would have done that. It wouldn't be the first time her home had served as a refuge. But that wasn't the case at all. Tia crossed her arms and sent Jericho a firm look. "No, that's not what she's doing. I'll tell you during the break when the kids are gone."

"That bad, huh?"

"Focus, Jericho." Tia scolded, hoping it would be enough to get Jericho back into the lesson and away from the topic of Saylor.

It didn't take Saylor long to return with the sewing machine. Tia took her upstairs and grabbed the printed papers with the information Saylor would need from her office. Once again, she offered Jericho's help, but Saylor refused. Tia watched as Saylor left one more time.

She could do this.

She could be there as a support and not push Saylor into something she didn't want or wasn't ready for.

They could work this project together, because Tia desperately needed it, and then they could figure out the rest.

Right?

If only she could convince herself that would actually happen.

fifteen

Tia's apartment was quaint and warm. The colors were dark and unique with brick walls lining the outside walls of the building, and large open windows to allow light in during the day. Saylor sighed as she dropped the keys onto the kitchen counter and surveyed the room she'd essentially be living in for the next two weeks.

Jameson wouldn't be happy.

But this was giving her some kind of purpose, some difference that she could make, and Saylor had to cling to that. Because without it, she was afraid of what might happen to her. She started with the sewing machine. It had been far too long since she'd set it all up and turned it on.

Saylor used the guest bedroom to lay out the fabric and prepare it for cutting. She'd start with just making one, start to finish, make sure that everything looked right and worked correctly. Then she'd break it all down into a process.

She was just finishing cutting when Tia came in. The sun had already fallen, and darkness cast into the apartment. Saylor's brain was weary from figuring out pieces and sizes, from threading the needle to her machine and trying to calm her anxiety that she could actually get this done.

Because it was a big ask.

"I thought you could maybe use a break." Tia set two white take-out bags on the kitchen counter.

As if on cue, Saylor's stomach rumbled. When was the last time she'd eaten? She couldn't remember, and when she stayed up all night doing absolutely nothing because she couldn't sleep, she'd just stared at a wall. She hadn't even managed to make herself dinner the night before.

"Thanks."

"It's the same thing we got the other week. But I noticed you picked out all the mushrooms, so I asked Giordi to make one without them for you."

Saylor stopped the machine and looked up, directly into Tia's eyes. She had noticed Saylor didn't like mushrooms? Not only that but she'd gone to the extra length to actually order it in a way that Saylor might like?

"Thank you," Saylor said, her voice barely leaving her lips after that surprise.

Tia left the bags alone and moved to stand right behind Saylor, peering over her shoulder to look at what she was sewing. "How's it going?"

"It's going. I want to finish one before I head home tonight, if you don't mind me being here late."

"I don't mind." Tia's fingers tightened on Saylor's shoulders. "But take a break for some food."

As if on cue, Saylor's stomach grumbled loudly again.

Tia bubbled with laughter. "Exactly. Come on. Break time. Boss's orders."

A shiver ran through Saylor, one that was completely different from the one before. If Tia was her boss, that just added another layer to why they shouldn't have kissed. She finished the line she had been sewing and found a good place to stop while Tia made up a couple plates of food. She handed one to Saylor before moving to sit on the couch to eat.

Saylor followed, staying quiet.

She still couldn't figure out what she was feeling when it came to Tia. It seemed far more than just a passing physical attraction. She actually quite enjoyed spending time with Tia. But that didn't mean that it was right for them to do that. Guilt still ate away at her for that kiss.

"How did the rest of the classes go?"

"Good." Tia nodded, flicking her gaze over to Saylor. "Nothing unusual."

Saylor focused on her food, nervously taking a bite and still not really tasting what was so amazing about this meal. But she was pretty sure that again it was about her and not about the food. She could never quite get herself pulled together, could she?

"I can leave early if you need me to."

"Saylor, you act like I have some wild life and need the apartment for the party that I'm having tonight." Tia set her plate on her knees. "Trust me. I'm not that wild a person."

"I just meant if you needed me out, kick me out."

"I don't need you out." Tia sent her a sweet smile. "You're welcome to stay as late as you need."

"I don't want to overstay."

"Saylor..." Tia sounded exasperated now. That was something Saylor was so used to. Everyone ended up feeling that way about her. She was always too much for them. "I want you to trust what I say."

"What?"

"Trust me when I say you're not overstaying, you're welcome to work late. I can help you or I can stay out of your way. Whatever you need." Tia reached for Saylor's hand, hesitated, and then wrapped their fingers together.

"I..." Saylor's stomach was doing flip-flops again. Her entire body warmed at the touch, but her head and her heart were at war again. "Can we talk about it?"

"Talk about what?" Tia removed her hand and went back to eating. She didn't look back up at Saylor.

Was this the right decision to make?

Saylor worried at her lower lip, her stomach grumbling, but she couldn't force herself to eat either. She wasn't even sure what she wanted to talk about with the kiss. Or maybe it wasn't the kiss at all. Maybe it was just what everything meant.

But Tia couldn't help answer that, could she?

"Talk about the other night?" Tia asked, this time looking directly at Saylor. "When we kissed?"

"Kind of," Saylor mumbled. "I don't even know what to ask."

"What do you want to know?"

"Everything," Saylor whispered.

Tia laughed lightly, shifting and pulling her leg up onto the couch cushion next to Saylor. She dropped a hand onto Saylor's shoulder before trailing it down her arm, her gaze following. It was the sexiest look that Saylor had ever seen. She wanted to melt into Tia's arms, sink into her body and never look back.

"What is everything?"

Saylor's cheeks heated. The wave of embarrassment moved down her neck into her chest, making it harder to breathe. How the fuck was she supposed to ask what she'd been thinking? She'd spent all night trying to work it out and her brain was moving as slow as molasses already. "When you... when we were..." Saylor stuttered again.

"Just take a breath and say it. There's no judgment here. You can ask anything you want to know."

Right. Saylor had never felt judgment from Tia ever. Which was probably why she'd been so willing to even try to kiss her, especially after Tia told her that she was attractive. But that didn't mean Tia wanted anything else from her, did it? No, she'd said she did. She'd just said she wouldn't be the one to get in the way.

So if anything was going to happen, Saylor was going to have to be the one to initiate. Which she was already shit at doing. Jameson had told her that several times. But a niggling feeling told Saylor that sex with him would never compare to sex with Tia.

"It's happened several times, but when we were kissing, and you put your leg between mine..." *God, this is so embarrassing.* "It felt really good."

"So you like grinding." Tia's lips pulled up into a smile.

Saylor covered her face and shook her head. "I can't believe I just said that."

"Don't do that." Tia reached up and pulled Saylor's hands away. "Like I said before, there's nothing to be embarrassed about here. You're exploring and figuring this out. You should be able to do that without feeling bad."

Except Saylor was going to feel bad no matter what, because of Jameson. She had committed to marrying him, to being with him for the rest of her life, and now she was wondering if she was even interested in that. Was it just cold feet or was it something else entirely?

"When I was little, I used to grind on things because it felt good. My mom would yell at me and tell me it was disgusting." Saylor frowned. Where had that memory come from?

"What?" Tia's eyes widened. "That's awful. It's natural for children to figure out how their bodies work. She should have just told you to do it in another room."

Saylor shrugged slightly. "My parents are really conservative. There was a huge argument when I moved in with Jameson because, oh my God, we might be having premarital sex."

Tia stiffened even more.

Saylor did too. What would they say knowing that she'd kissed a woman? Knowing that she wanted to do so much more with the woman sitting right beside her. Saylor flicked her gaze over Tia, noting her reaction finally. "I'm sorry. What did I say?"

"My brother was very homophobic. In some ways, I'm glad

he's dead because the girls didn't have to grow up under his thumb like that. My younger niece, Monti, she's in a very loving relationship with a woman. I'd hate to see who she'd be had she grown up with him instead of me."

"It sounds like you were able to be exactly who she needed." Saylor rubbed her hand up and down Tia's thigh in comfort, realizing far too late that that was probably a bad idea. It was probably giving Tia an entirely different impression from what she intended.

"He never knew about me. I hadn't come out to him yet."

"And your parents? Were they just as bad?"

"No." Tia shook her head. "I think by the time I came out to them they were just so happy that I wasn't dead or crazy they didn't care much." Tia curled her hair behind her ear before moving her arm along the back of the couch and shifting even closer to Saylor. "They're a little upset that I haven't settled down yet. I think they wanted the girls to have two parents growing up, but I was honestly just in survival mode for twenty years and then it took another five just to get out of that."

"It makes sense." Saylor shifted a little closer, playing her fingers along Tia's knee. She was glad they'd moved off the topic of sex onto something a little more serious, but then again, she really wanted to know more. "Is grinding normal during lesbian sex?"

Tia burst out laughing, her eyes and face lighting up as the sound bubbled from her. "Oh my God."

"What?" Saylor's eyes widened. "You said I could ask anything."

"I did." Tia wiped her fingers under her eyes. "And it can be, depending on the couple. It's all about who's with who and what people like. In any relationship."

Saylor frowned slightly. Everything about her sex life with Jameson was mostly about what Jameson wanted. Not because he was opposed to what she wanted, but she just never knew what that was, and nothing had ever really felt right. But Tia's leg between hers had felt perfect.

And she wanted it again.

Saylor wanted to feel that pressure and know exactly what would happen if she didn't relieve it. Something clicked into place in Saylor's chest. She glanced at her cell phone that she'd set next to her plate. She'd seen the texts from Jameson come in all day and she hadn't answered them. She hadn't even known what to say.

She knew she was running from her problems.

But what was the problem even?

That she was a lesbian?

How was that a problem?

"Saylor?" Tia asked, reaching forward and touching Saylor's shoulder to get her attention. "Everything okay?"

"No, it's not," Saylor murmured. She closed her eyes, steadying her breath. She had no doubt in her mind that she really wanted this. Tia was so different from Jameson, and it wasn't just because Tia was a woman. She was open, calm, serene. She listened. She cared. She took time for Saylor when she didn't have to.

Saylor moved her gaze from her phone to Tia, to the openness she found there. She felt more connected to this woman she barely knew than she did to her own fiancé. All because Tia was willing to listen and Saylor was willing to talk. Why was this so much easier than any relationship Saylor had tried before?

"What's wrong?"

"I don't think anything is wrong," Saylor answered. Another click in her chest.

Had she already decided?

Yes.

Was she going to do this?

Without a doubt.

"I think for the first time ever, that nothing is wrong." Saylor stayed still, her gaze roving all over Tia's body. This time, she openly looked at what was right in front of her, accepting that she would find attraction here. That she would find something she liked, someone who liked her just for her and not who she should be.

"But you said everything wasn't okay." A line formed in the center of Tia's forehead, and it was adorable.

"That doesn't mean anything is wrong." Saylor trailed her fingers purposely up Tia's arm to her shoulder and down to her collarbone, tracing the lines of her body.

Tia stilled, her entire body going quiet.

"All it means is that I'm unsettled, that I know what's coming." Saylor slid her fingers up to Tia's neck, tracing the curve of her jaw and then her lips.

Tia stayed in place, but she parted her lips so her hot breath brushed across Saylor's fingers, sending a wave of pleasure through Saylor's body, ending right between her legs.

"All it means," Saylor started again, trying to get the words out that she wanted to share, "is that I'm glad I met you."

"Saylor, what about—"

"It doesn't matter right now, Tia." Saylor had already made the choice. She moved her hand behind Tia's neck and pulled her forward. Tia moved willingly. "I don't want to think about that tonight."

Saylor pressed their lips together in a soft kiss. This kiss was everything the last one wasn't.

Intentional.

Gentle.

Wanted.

Tia pulled away slightly, closing her eyes and ducking her chin. "I'm not sure we should be doing this."

Saylor kept her hand right in place. She slid her thumb against the soft, hot skin just under Tia's ear. She wanted to keep their physical connection as much as she could. Saylor did the only thing she could. She waited.

"What will happen when you go back to him?" Tia looked at her.

"I don't know that I will."

"Saylor..." Tia trailed off. "This isn't a good idea."

"I think it's a perfect idea." Saylor held her breath, finding the next words she wanted to say. "One, we're not committing to anything. Two, no idea is without the good and the bad. Three, I think we both want this."

Tia clenched her jaw. "Our first kiss, that was unexpected. It was feelings and nothing else. I've had time to think, and I don't want you doing this because you feel like you have to in order to know if you're queer."

"I didn't have to kiss you to know," Saylor answered, because it was true. And she'd never known something more true than that. "It helped me figure it out faster. It helped force me to think about it when I would have rather avoided it, and let's face it, I'm really good at avoiding things I don't want to think or talk about."

"Like Jameson?" Tia interrupted.

Saylor resisted the urge to glance at her phone, but barely. "Yes, like Jameson."

"You should talk to him."

"Not tonight." Saylor took a deep breath and dropped her hand into her lap. "Look, I'm not saying I'm in love with you. I'm not saying we're even going to be in a relationship together. But I don't think Kirsten was lying."

"Kirsten?" Tia tensed with a frown.

"I think—no, I know that you won't hurt me. I trust you to guide me through this."

Tia's frown deepened. "Through what?"

"My first time with a woman."

"Saylor." Tia sat back, her eyes wide and face filled with worry. "I thought we were just talking about kissing."

"No. I want..." Saylor had to get these words out. She had to make sure that Tia understood exactly what she was looking for. "I want to know what it feels like with you. Someone I trust. Someone I know."

Someone she felt closer to than her own fiancé.

"So you want one night? That's it?" Tia didn't get up and walk away, which was what Saylor expected her to do. After that bumbling ramble of an explanation, any sane person would, wouldn't they?

"I want tonight," Saylor answered, folding her hands together in her lap.

Tia sighed heavily and closed her eyes. "You have to promise that you won't hate me after."

"How could I ever hate you?"

"Oh, it's entirely possible." Tia looked her directly in the eye. "You have to promise me that you won't regret me."

"Never." Hope flared in Saylor's chest. Was this actually happening? Was she going to do this? "I don't think I could ever regret tonight or you."

"Never say never." Tia moved in, pressing their mouths together fully.

Saylor moaned instantly, pushing back and closing her eyes and just feeling. This kiss was free. This kiss was passionate. This kiss held every promise she hoped for.

sixteen

Tia couldn't believe she'd agreed to this.

She moved, pushing Saylor back into the couch and covering her. Their mouths remained pressed together, soft and sweet kisses exchanged. For the first time since they'd met, Tia felt as though Saylor truly knew what she wanted.

Because Saylor had mentioned she'd enjoyed it before, Tia planted her thigh right between Saylor's legs and pressed in. Saylor's resounding groan was music to her ears, but she still didn't want Saylor to regret this night.

"Saylor," Tia murmured, kissing across her jaw to her ear.

Turmoil in her stomach, wrapping and coiling around itself and growing. Tia dropped her head to Saylor's shoulder and took a long deep breath.

"Saylor, I don't know if I can do this."

"What? Why?" Saylor skimmed her hands down Tia's sides. She pressed down onto Tia's thigh hard, already grinding against her.

"Because I don't want you to hate me."

Saylor lifted her hand to Tia's hair, threading her fingers through the tangles. Tia didn't move. She stayed right where she was, trying to calm the raging arousal in her body, trying to find her brain in all of this.

"Will you look at me?" Saylor asked.

Tia had struggled all night to really look at Saylor. She'd avoided it. She knew that as soon as she did that she was going to have to face the music. This wasn't just about Saylor's first time. Tia didn't want Saylor to hate her because she wanted so much more than one time. She loved Saylor's quiet countenance, the fact that she was working on exploring who she was, how sweet she was, how caring.

"Tia," Saylor said, lifting her crotch again and pushing it down onto Tia's thigh, though this time it didn't seem intentional. "Tia, look at me."

"I'm afraid of what you'll see," Tia said into Saylor's shoulder.

"It's nothing I haven't already seen." Saylor continued to thread her fingers through Tia's hair in a soothing motion.

It felt so good. Tia shifted, pushing into Saylor's body. Sex she could do, but the emotions that were so tangled up in this moment tightened and made it hard to breathe.

"Tia, talk to me."

She had to find words. Saylor had been so honest in what she was thinking and feeling. Tia owed it to her to do the same. But it was so hard. "I want to be with you."

"So be with me."

Tia cringed. That hadn't been what she meant. "What I'm saying is that I'll give you tonight, if that's what you want." Raising her head, Tia looked at Saylor. She wanted to make sure that Saylor understood exactly what she was saying. "But I want to be with you beyond just tonight. And I know you can't decide that right now. I know you're not in a place to make that choice, and I'm not asking you to. But know that's what I want."

"Tia." Saylor's voice was so soft. She brushed her fingers over Tia's cheeks. She looked so lost. "Can we just start with tonight?"

"Yeah." Tia gave a gentle smile. "Yeah, we can."

Saylor pulled Tia's face toward, pressing their lips together tenderly. Tia shifted again, knowing exactly what she was doing to Saylor by increasing the pressure of her leg against Saylor's crotch. Saylor gasped and dropped her hands to her sides before reaching up for Tia's hips.

"Move against me if that's what you want to do," Tia whispered, pressing kisses against Saylor's cheek and neck again.

"You sure?"

"Yes." Tia scraped her teeth over Saylor's neck, moving down to her collar bone. She would love to have their clothes off. She would love to be pressed together in all heat and sweat and weird noises. She wanted Saylor to have every part of this experience. Every experience that she could get in this one night that they knew was going to happen.

Saylor moved. She lifted her hips up and then down, grinding hard against Tia's thigh. Tia leaned in, changing the angle slightly to give Saylor an even better ride. She peppered kisses all over Saylor's face and neck and chest where she could reach without moving. Saylor dug her fingers into Tia's sides, clenching tightly and holding on for dear life.

Tia started moving in counterpoint to Saylor. Saylor moved her hands up Tia's back, pulling down hard and digging her nails in. Tia growled into Saylor's ear. She nipped Saylor's neck, sucking. Saylor grunted. Her movements became jerky.

"It feels... it feels so good." Saylor clung to Tia, pulling Tia down hard.

"Then don't stop," Tia murmured.

Gasping, Saylor arched her back up, clenched her eyes tight, and her entire face became one of complete and total bliss. This was everything. Tia held her as she continued to rock through her orgasm, moving ever so slightly against Tia's leg as she kept the sensations up. Tia knew exactly what Saylor was doing. She didn't have to say it. She didn't have to ask.

Saylor turned her cheek slightly, seeking Tia's mouth for a

sloppy, satisfied kiss. Even if this was all they ended up doing tonight, it was perfect in Tia's eyes. Saylor had gotten what she needed.

"How do you feel?" Tia asked when Saylor seemed to come back to herself.

"Amazing," Saylor said with a grin, her eyes bright and her cheeks red with arousal. "Absolutely amazing."

"Good." Tia pecked Saylor's lips, waiting to see where Saylor would lead them next.

Sure enough, Saylor tugged at Tia's shirt, pulling it up her body to her shoulders. Tia moved slowly, leaning back on her knees so that she could pull her shirt and her sports bra the rest of the way off. Saylor stared at her breasts, at her hardened nipples. Tentatively, she reached up and brushed fingers across Tia's goose bumped skin.

"You're so beautiful." Saylor sounded completely entranced.

Tia sucked in a sharp breath and closed her eyes. It had been so long since anyone had called her that. "Are we doing this?"

"Yes," Saylor answered.

"Then come on." Tia stood up and pulled Saylor by the hand.

She walked directly into her messy bedroom, with the clothes still on the floor right next to the laundry basket and the bed completely unkempt. She didn't even bother to move things to the side as she pulled Saylor to her in a spin that any dancer would know, and planted their mouths together.

Taking Saylor's hands, Tia pressed them to her breasts before reaching for Saylor's shirt and pulling it off. Skin to skin was exactly what she was going to get. She teased Saylor's nipples as soon as they were free, bending down to cover one with her mouth and flicking her tongue hard over the tight little nub. Saylor moaned, fingers deep in Tia's hair.

Next, Tia stood and shimmied her leggings off until she had to sit on the bed and jerk them over her calves and feet. Tight clothes, while nice when form fitting on her body, weren't the easiest things to get out of on a good day. Though they were beyond necessary for work. Saylor finally started to pull her clothes off, though slower than Tia did and with a bit more hesitation in her moves.

She was still nervous.

Which Tia completely understood. She'd been nervous her first time with a woman too. Hell, she was nervous just about any first time with someone new. A good dose of nerves meant she'd always stop to talk before going any further. Scooting back on the bed, Tia spread her legs to sit comfortably while she waited for Saylor to join her.

Saylor moved in, sitting next to Tia, and waited.

Right. Tia had to lead this. Fair and square from beginning to end. Saylor wasn't someone who would lead on the first go-round. Skimming her hand down Saylor's arm, Tia kissed her gently.

"Tell me if you don't like something or if you want me to stop. Okay?"

"Yeah. Okay." Saylor kissed her back, clearly comfortable with that level of touching.

Centering herself, Tia deepened the kiss. She would start slowly, as if from the beginning. She parted her lips, bringing Saylor deeper into the moment. Tia moved her hand behind Saylor's neck, holding her firmly.

"Touch me any way you want," Tia murmured before kissing Saylor again. She needed to be firm and confident. She needed to be open to whatever was going to happen. "But I would love to take you again."

"Yes."

Tia moved down Saylor's body, planting kisses here and there. She cupped Saylor's breast, teasing her nipple with her thumb while she teased the other one with her mouth. Saylor moved under her, wiggling. The small noises that left her lips were adorable. They spurred Tia on.

As much as Tia wanted to speed up, get exactly where she

wanted to go, she knew she needed to keep things slow. She needed to take care of Saylor and not push her before she was ready. Saylor was so quiet. She wasn't saying anything, and that unnerved Tia. Though Saylor never seemed to be much of one for words.

"Saylor," Tia murmured against her skin. "Are you ready to continue?"

"Yes." Saylor pushed the top of Tia's head gently, encouraging her to move farther down Saylor's body.

Tia smiled, glad to see that Saylor was enjoying this, that she wasn't nervous or worried. Tia kissed past Saylor's hips and down the tops of her thighs to her knees. Her legs were smooth, and Tia sat up, lifting one of Saylor's legs to kiss on the inside of her thigh. She licked, moving closer to right between Saylor's legs before backing away.

Just the smallest whiff of Saylor's scent was exactly what Tia needed. Her body hummed. Pleasure coursed through her, and she had to close her eyes to center herself. Relax. Calm. Centered. Tia had to remind herself of that too often. Turning her cheek into Saylor's thigh, Tia opened her eyes and looked directly at Saylor.

"One last time, are you sure you want this?"

Saylor nodded, a smile playing at her lips. "If before was anything to write home about, this will blow that out of the water. I'm sure."

"Sure. No pressure, huh?" Tia chuckled quietly. She hummed and closed her eyes again. "You smell delicious."

"I do?"

"You do." Tia nodded and made eye contact. She wanted Saylor to be confident in what they were doing, in what direction this was going.

"I've never really thought about that." Saylor's cheeks darkened, the blush moving all the way down her chest to her breasts.

"So alluring." Tia kissed Saylor's thigh again, this time moving closer to right where she wanted to be. "So strong." Another kiss right on the crease between hip and pussy. "So enticing." One more kiss right on the dark brown hair. Tia couldn't help but suck in a sharp breath to get the fullness of Saylor's scent. "So wet."

Settling onto her belly, Tia slid her fingers along Saylor's outer lips. She was slick, her lips already swollen and parted from her first orgasm of the night, damp with the results from that. What would it be like to have Saylor grind against her naked? Tia stuck one finger in her mouth, wetting it and getting a small taste of Saylor's flavor.

Humming her pleasure, Tia rubbed circles right around Saylor's opening. Slow, deliberate circles. Saylor sucked in a sharp breath and let out a moan that told Tia everything she needed to know. Tia kissed her again, gently, right on the side, then again on the other side. Tia knew exactly what she was doing to Saylor, making her question when everything was going to happen, wondering when she'd get exactly what she wanted.

Tia slid her finger in slowly, feeling the stretch of Saylor's body around her, the tight circular tension as it pulled. Saylor sighed a hopeful sound that Tia held onto. Tia took a slow long lick, circling Saylor's clit fully as she scooted even closer. She settled in, sliding her finger in deeper and licking Saylor full up, adding a flick of her clit at the end.

God, she tastes amazing, Tia thought.

Unable to hold back any longer, Tia moved her tongue in full sweeps. If Saylor liked grinding, then perhaps she would like this as well. On cue, Saylor moved her hips up and put her pussy directly into Tia's mouth. Tia didn't stop. Saylor groaned. She threw her hands over her head, grasping onto the metal frame of Tia's bed.

Tia watched every move she could. Saylor was stunning. She wiggled and moaned. She didn't try to hold back at all. She cried out loudly, the sound warming Tia as soon as it hit her.

"St-stop," Saylor breathed out the word.

Tia pulled back, resting her cheek on Saylor's thigh while Saylor continued to take shaky quick breaths.

"What's wrong?" Tia asked, smoothing her hands up and down Saylor's legs.

Saylor shook her head and closed her eyes. "Too much. I just need... a minute."

Tia stayed right where she was, kissing Saylor's legs and letting Saylor have as much time as she needed. Saylor sat up, pulling Tia up with her into a deep kiss. Saylor wrapped her arms around Tia's shoulders and pulled her down onto the bed, swinging a leg over Tia's hips so she sat on top of her.

Saylor bent down and kissed Tia again, then traced a single finger around Tia's already hard nipple. "I can't believe I've never done this before."

"Why's that?" Tia moved her hands up and down Saylor's thighs.

"Because it feels amazing. You're amazing." Saylor grinned as she bent down and kissed Tia again. Her hair brushed against Tia's chest and face when Saylor moved down, following a similar path down Tia's body that Tia had made on Saylor's. She stopped at Tia's breasts, teasing, testing, tasting.

Tia moved Saylor's hair, wanting to see her face, needing to know what emotions were flashing through her. Tia spread her legs, encouraging Saylor to move wherever she wanted to go. Saylor went down lower, sliding into the same position that Tia had just vacated. Tia moved her fingers between her legs, teasing herself by rubbing back and forth in a steady pattern.

Saylor studied her, like she was analyzing the best way to get this done, the best way to start and then finish. "Is there something you like?" Saylor finally asked.

"I love oral," Tia answered, keeping her body warm and ready. "But I also love fingers. Toys too, but we can save that for another day when you're more comfortable."

Why had she said that?

This was one night and nothing more. They'd agreed to that despite the fact that Tia had told Saylor she wanted more. And here Tia was, stupidly asking for more than she knew Saylor could give her. Biting her lip, Tia widened her legs even more.

"Do whatever you want. There's nothing I've tried that I don't like, and I'm willing to try anything."

"I don't think I'm quite ready to get kinky."

Tia laughed lightly. "I'll keep that in mind." She left off the *for the future* that she wanted to say. She really needed to get her heart back in order with her brain. That, or she needed to let her body take over already. "Start with your fingers."

"Okay." Saylor slid her hands along Tia's legs and through the dark curls. She tugged lightly and grinned when Tia moaned. "Like that?"

"Yes." Tia gave her a big smile and raised her hands above her head to grab onto the bed. She'd be too tempted to take control if she didn't.

"Good." Saylor did it again before slipping her hand down. She pressed two fingers against Tia's clit, cold fingers to her hot pussy. The temperature difference was tantalizing in so many ways.

"Yes..." Tia dragged out the word.

Encouraged, Saylor moved her hand like Tia had just done, mimicking the pattern and rhythm almost perfectly.

"Faster," Tia begged.

She closed her eyes, blocked out all the sounds and distractions around her and focused solely on Saylor's fingers on her. The back-and-forth swish. The little offshoots of pleasure that wrapped around her. Tia loved when other people touched her like this. When they would beg for her body to respond to them.

"Push in more." Tia's voice was breathy, the sound hitching momentarily.

Tia gripped the bed harder. Saylor shifted, the mattress bending to her will as she moved to Tia's side. Her mouth instantly covered Tia's right breast, teasing and flicking her nipple just like Saylor had done before. Tia groaned loudly. Dropping her hand to the back of Saylor's head, she pulled her up so they could kiss. It was sloppy, messy. Tia could barely control herself.

She clamped her thighs together, around Saylor's wrist. "Keep going. I'm close."

Saylor picked up her speed and kissed Tia again, half-lying on top of Tia. Breathing heavily, Tia rutted her hips, trying to keep her focus on her body and all the sensations that flooded through her. Saylor nipped her lip as she crashed through her orgasm. Immediately, Tia flipped Saylor over onto her back, straddling her hips and kissed her deeply.

She couldn't have hoped for a better night than this.

"How are you doing?" Tia asked, kissing Saylor again.

Saylor answered with a grin. "Absolutely amazing."

"You ready for more?"

"More?"

"Oh yeah. We're just getting started."

Seventeen

Every muscle in Saylor's body ached. She stirred, the blankets tangled around her legs as she tried to figure out where she was. Heat overwhelmed her, and she needed to free herself from its confines. Pushing to the edge of the bed, she sat up and looked over her shoulder.

Tia was naked on the bed, splayed out and fast asleep. Her dark hair was spread over her face as she lay on her stomach, the smooth lines of her body curving as she drew in a deep breath.

Saylor pressed her lips together. It wasn't just a dream, not that she'd really thought that. Maybe she'd wanted it to be just to make what was going to happen now so much easier. Because now that they'd done this, Saylor couldn't escape it.

Tia stirred, shifting and turning onto her side before landing on her back. She pushed her hair out of the way and rubbed her eyes before looking at Saylor. They stayed in silence, Saylor on the edge of the bed as if she was ready to leave and Tia spread out like they were going to go for another never-ending round of sex.

Saylor had to say something.

She needed to be the one to break the silence and move the

conversation in some direction. But what the hell was she supposed to say? Then it clicked.

"I don't regret it."

Tia's lips curled up, a full smile blooming on her face as her eyes lit up. "I'm glad."

"I have to pee." Saylor laughed, the sound bubbling up from her in a burst of joy that she couldn't contain. It was the first time she had felt so much happiness since she'd moved there. And she didn't want it to end. "I'll be back."

Saylor raced to the bathroom after snagging her clothes from the floor. She took a few extra minutes to make herself look as nice as she could, and then she stepped out to find Tia wrapped in a robe and sipping a cup of coffee in her kitchen. Saylor's entire body propelled her toward the coffee.

She made herself a cup and then set it down on the counter. What the hell were they supposed to say now? This must be the post-sex awkwardness that she'd never experienced because she'd never had a one-night stand before. She'd also never had sex this amazing before.

"Will you be going home this morning?" Tia asked.

Saylor nodded. "I should probably change into fresh clothes and shower."

Except, Saylor knew what Tia was asking without saying the words. She'd been wondering the exact same thing, except she knew that Jameson would be gone by now. He was supposed to be in New York—or was it Houston?—for the next three days. She couldn't even remember.

"Will you be back to...work?" Tia glanced pointedly at her dining room table, where the sewing machine and the outfit Saylor hadn't finished was left.

"Yeah. Got to finish the costumes." Saylor picked up her coffee mug and brought it to her lips, but she didn't drink. Were they just going to have awkward conversations now? "I don't know what to say."

"You don't have to say anything," Tia responded, stiffening instantly.

"I want to." Saylor put her coffee down again and stepped closer. She touched Tia's hip, turning her so they could look into each other's eyes. "I don't regret last night. I'm not sure that I ever could."

"But now you have to face the music?"

"Something like that." Saylor took Tia's mug and set it on the counter along with hers. Moving in swiftly, she pressed their lips together and sank into the kiss. It wasn't deep or meant to arouse. This kiss was for comfort. It was slow, emotional, heavy. Saylor kept her hand on Tia's cheek when she pulled away and gave a soft smile. "I'll be back tomorrow for sure. I hope to be back later today."

"Okay."

Saylor grabbed her jacket and her wallet. She didn't say anything else before she left. What could she say? Because in this moment, she wanted to abandon Jameson and run straight back into Tia's arms. She wanted to fall back into the bed, naked, and not emerge until they absolutely had to.

But what she wanted didn't matter.

The walk to her apartment was long and wet. The rain soaked through her shoes into her socks and seeped up the hem of her pants to her shins. By the time she arrived, she was no further in the internal battle than she had been when she left. But she felt colder. She felt more distant. She also felt more sure than anything that whatever had happened with Tia wasn't something that was fleeting or passing.

Sliding her key into the lock, Saylor turned it. As soon as she stepped into the apartment, she stopped. Jameson sat on the couch, much in the same position she had been in the morning before when he'd returned. He leaned forward to grab the remote on the television and turn it off before crossing his ankle over his knee and giving her a hard stare.

"Where have you been?"

Saylor tensed. She hadn't been prepared for this. He was supposed to be out of the state, and she wasn't supposed to have to talk to him yet. There were supposed to be days before she had to face this.

"Saylor, I tried texting and calling you all night."

He sounded so worried. Which he shouldn't, should he? She'd left so disconcerted over life, ready to abandon everything and go back home where all of this would be easier.

"I even called Callie, and she hasn't heard from you in weeks. Do you know how worried she is?"

He called Callie? Saylor fidgeted with her hands before shutting the door and pulling off her jacket. She dropped it on the counter-height chair and walked to the couch. She plopped onto the opposite edge from him, keeping as much space between them as possible.

"What did she say?"

"That you've gone AWOL. She's texted and called, and you haven't responded. We're both worried. This isn't like you." Jameson stayed still.

Saylor couldn't tell if he was about to explode on her or crumble into tears. She'd never seen him like this. She glanced out the window, the gray skies her new best friend. "It is unlike me."

"So what's going on?"

"I tried to tell you, but you didn't listen. I can't keep doing this, Jameson. I'm not working, I sit in the apartment alone most days, and I'm such a burden to you that I know you resent me."

"I don't resent you."

"How can you not?" Saylor pulled her legs up on the couch, curling them under her body. "I don't contribute at all. I'm a bum, living off you."

"Saylor..." Jameson's frustration was clear. It was written all across his face. "I don't know why you think so badly about yourself. Moving someplace new isn't easy."

"I know it's not."

"Then why do you keep expecting it to look like Denver?" Jameson put his hand over the back of the couch and leaned in. "It takes time to make a life someplace new."

"I know it does."

"Then stop trying to make it happen in a few months."

Saylor sighed heavily. She lifted her hand to her temple, rubbing circles. "I hate it here."

"You haven't given it much of a chance."

He was right, of course. And she knew that. She'd tried. She'd put so much energy into trying to make her life here work, and she'd run flat out.

"I don't want you to hate it here. I don't want you to hate me because you hate it here."

"I don't hate you," Saylor mumbled. That much was true at least. She wanted to love him so much. She'd agreed to marry him. Her stomach churned at that thought, with the memory of Tia against her, inside her. The kisses and moments they'd shared. "But it's more than just our relationship."

"What do you mean?" Jameson clenched his teeth.

"Don't you have to be on a plane or something?"

Jameson raised an eyebrow at her. "I canceled the trip. Well, postponed it. I didn't know where you were or when you would be coming home. You can't just stay out all night and not tell me where you are."

Saylor clenched her hands into fists. What was she supposed to say to that? Saylor shook her head, tears welling up in her eyes. How was she supposed to navigate this?

"Saylor?" Jameson leaned in, dropping his hand to her knee. "I know it's been rough, that we've been having problems, but we'll get through this."

They wouldn't.

Saylor knew that deep down in her heart. They wouldn't get through this. Shaking her head, Saylor swiped the tears that fell from her eyes, and she bolstered her breath. "I've been questioning a lot of things lately. Moving here. Who I am. Who I want to be."

"That sounds normal with a major move and engagement." Jameson rubbed his thumb across Saylor's knee.

"Yeah, some of it. But I've also..." How was she supposed to say this? He'd be hurt no matter what. "I've also been having some feelings."

Jameson tensed.

"I've been wondering if I like women." Saylor whispered the words because she wasn't wondering anymore. She knew she did. "Actually, it's more than that. I... I know I like women."

"Oh." Jameson tensed.

She was sure he had no clue what to say. She barely had any idea what to say. Saylor ran her fingers through her hair, finding some tangles. A stark reminder of everything the last night had held for her.

"So where does that leave us?" he asked.

"I don't know." Saylor cringed. She was failing this conversation so hard.

Jameson blew out a breath. "Do you still like men?"

"I..." Saylor stopped. She hadn't actually considered the possibility. She hadn't even thought about the fact that she might. She'd been so focused on whether or not she was attracted to women that she hadn't even worked out whether she was attracted to men. She furrowed her brow. "I honestly don't know."

"Jesus, Saylor." Jameson dropped his head into his hands and roughly moved his hands over his face. "You're seriously telling me that you might be a lesbian and you haven't figured that out already?"

Saylor clenched her jaw, hard. She had no idea what to say to that, but the answer was that she didn't know. She hadn't spent the time to work it out. She hadn't even considered it a possibility. She stared at Jameson hard as he struggled with this just as much as she was.

"I'm so sorry," Saylor apologized. She couldn't even bring herself to tell him about Tia, not about the kiss, not about last night. That would devastate him even more.

"I'm going to need some time with this."

"I think we both are." Saylor winced. She wished she had more time to put words to what she was feeling, to how she was going to explain this to him, because this wasn't the right way to have the conversation. He deserved so much better than her.

"I do have to leave tomorrow." Jameson sat back on the couch heavily. "Let's spend today figuring some of this out. All right?"

"What does that mean?"

"It means we're spending the day together. Talking." Jameson stood up and started for the kitchen. "Want some breakfast?"

Saylor bit her lip, watching him move. This was the man she'd fallen in love with. The one who could take control, who had compassion. So where had he been the last few months since she moved here? Other than not here.

"Saylor?"

"Uh... yeah. Breakfast sounds great." Saylor didn't want to tell him that she had absolutely no appetite. That she could barely even stand to think about eating food. Without saying another word, she grabbed her phone and texted Tia. She wasn't going to make it back until tomorrow. She really needed to focus on Jameson, on her fiancé, and the relationship they were building together.

eighteen

Tia had read the text message more times than she cared to admit.

Saylor: I won't be back today. Sorry. I promise I'll get the costumes done.

Short, simple, to the point. But something gnawed at Tia's stomach, something that felt off. She wanted to see Saylor, know that she was okay, that she didn't regret—the bell chimed to the lobby. Tia dropped her cell phone onto her desk and forced herself to wait in her office to see who was coming in.

It would be early for class to start, but that didn't mean someone wasn't there to warm up. Swallowing the lump in her throat, Tia waited. It seemed like everything in her life lately was about waiting. The footsteps were soft. Tia scooted a little to the side to see through the window.

Saylor.

Tia couldn't stop the smile that lit up her face. She was all right. She was here at least. And before anyone else arrived, which meant they would be able to talk. Perfect. Saylor stepped up to the doorway to the office, wringing her hands together.

"I'm sorry I missed class last night."

That was the least of Tia's concerns. Something had come between them since Saylor had left her apartment two days ago, and Tia couldn't figure out what it was. She hated it though. The tentative friendship they'd formed hung in the balance, ready to snap at any minute.

"I'm more worried about you than class."

Saylor's cheeks pinked, and Tia loved seeing that. "It's been a rough few days."

"Care to share?" Tia crossed her legs and leaned back in her chair, ready to give Saylor her full attention.

"Jameson and I have been talking." Saylor didn't sit down. She stood, tense and fidgety. "I'll spend the next few days upstairs if you don't mind, working to finish those outfits."

"Sure, if that's what you want." Tia crossed her arms and then immediately uncrossed them. She didn't want Saylor to think that she was upset. But at the same time, she was. It swam in the pit of her belly.

"It is. I could use the extra time to think."

What Tia would give just to have a little insight into those thoughts. Did Jameson and Saylor break up? Did they have a huge argument? Saylor sighed, and finally came forward to sit in the chair opposite Tia's. She put her hands on her knees, and on the left shone the giant diamond Jameson had given Saylor. It winked at her—taunted her.

Saylor was still engaged.

Tia's heart sank. Had she really been hoping that Saylor would go home, break everything off with Jameson, and come running to her? It was outrageous, but still the thought niggled its way into her heart and took root. She wasn't lying when she'd said she wanted more, and the only thing Tia knew at this point was that she was going to end up heartbroken by the end of this.

"I'll give you the spare key." Tia reached into her desk and pulled out her extra set of keys. She untwisted the one for her apartment and reached over, holding it out of Saylor.

Reaching forward, Saylor's fingers brushed along Tia's. Heat and warmth washed through her, and she had to close her eyes against it. Saylor took the key and moved away quickly. That was as much answer as Tia needed. Saylor had chosen, hadn't she? Or at the very least she still had no idea what she was going to decide.

The lump in Tia's throat grew even bigger. She needed to get herself under control. It was one night, nothing else. They had agreed to that, made it very clear from the beginning. But Tia hadn't been able to get their one night out of her mind.

"I'll have them done. I promise."

"I trust you." Tia pressed her lips together hard.

"Thanks. Jameson is on his work trip now, so I'll have some extra time while he's gone."

Tia nodded, not saying a word because she couldn't trust her own voice.

"He and I had a long conversation the night...well, the morning I got home." Saylor's cheeks tinged pink again.

Was she embarrassed about what they'd done?

Or was it simply a reaction to the memory?

"It was a good conversation. Probably one of the deeper ones we've had in a long time." Saylor rubbed her palms against her thighs nervously.

Tia still remained quiet. It was next to impossible to be Saylor's confidante while also being so damn attracted to her. Tia wasn't without her own feelings. She wasn't cold and heartless. And she wanted Saylor to be able to make this decision as clearly and without complications as possible.

"I told him..." Saylor trailed off.

Tia's mind went into a tailspin. Saylor told him what? They'd kissed? They'd fucked? That Saylor had spent all night in bed with another woman? Bile rose in Tia's stomach and moved into the bottom of her throat.

"I told him that I was attracted to women. I didn't tell him about you. I didn't want…"

Curse Saylor and her inability to finish a sentence without pausing. She didn't want what? Jameson to come over here and rage at Tia? She didn't want Jameson to hit Saylor? She didn't want to put everything on the table and let them figure it out already?

"I didn't want him to get mad at you for something I chose to do."

"So you didn't tell him about the other night?"

Saylor shook her head and whispered, "I didn't know how to."

Well, that was the same for both of them. Tia had never cheated in her life, and she couldn't fathom how she would tell a long-term partner what had happened. Tia clenched her jaw tightly. They had made such a big mess of this. It wasn't just a kiss in the rain, heated and unprovoked, unexpected, with passions flying this way and that. They had both consciously made the decision to have sex, a full and wonderful night of it.

And now they were left trying to swim upstream in the river they'd both so willingly dived into. And Tia could tell there was a waterfall coming. Swiftly. Tia had inadvertently been the other woman twice, but she'd never knowingly stepped into that role. It felt so different this time. Dirty almost, but definitely twisted with far more heartache than the others.

"Do you regret it?" Tia hated that she'd asked that question. Because she didn't want the answer. She'd much rather live in ignorance for a little while longer if she could.

"I don't regret what we did." Saylor leaned forward and lowered her voice. "I'm not sure I could ever regret that."

"But you do regret something."

"I regret the circumstances surrounding the night."

Tia could understand that. Without complications, she'd love to see where they were going and what they could be together. But they weren't there. They hadn't started their relationship without this heavy weight on both of them. "I think that pretty accurately describes how I feel."

"Then it seems like we're in the same place."

"Maybe." It didn't feel that way. Tia was stuck in a holding pattern, waiting for something that would never happen. She ran her fingers through her hair as the doorbell in the lobby chimed again. The rest of the class was joining.

She escaped her office, needing the space between her and Saylor and a vat of emotions she couldn't get under control anytime the two of them were alone. She fiddled with the sound equipment and tried to settle herself to teach the class. It went off without a hitch.

Saylor disappeared upstairs to Tia's apartment afterward. Which meant Tia could join her and rehash those memories—and sleeping there the last two nights had been hard enough that she didn't need Saylor's presence to make it worse—or Tia could avoid her. And she didn't want to deal with any extra dreams or longings.

She went back to her office, surprised to find Jericho lingering. "Did you need something?"

"You're off tonight." Jericho pulled her hair over her shoulder and ran her fingers over the long braids.

"What do you mean?"

"I don't know. You're distracted." Jericho plopped down into the chair and crossed her legs. "New crush maybe?"

"Jericho..." Tia said in a warning. The last thing she wanted to do was start rumors and drama. Again. She'd accidentally done that more times than she cared to admit.

"I'm worried about you, that's all. You vanished from the club, and no one could find you." Jericho continued to play with her hair. "And now you're working late. Usually you're home by now."

"Saylor's upstairs working on the costumes for the girls."

"Ah. Saylor." Jericho waggled her eyebrows up and down. "What is it about Saylor that has you so tied up?"

Tia groaned. This was the last thing she wanted to talk about tonight.

"Oh God, you like her." Jericho lowered her voice conspiratorially.

"She's engaged to Jameson. Nothing is going to happen."

"You always fall for the unavailable ones, don't you?" Jericho's lips turned up into a smile, but she didn't look very happy about her statement. "Is that why you're avoiding home?"

Tia pressed her lips together hard.

"I see. You should come out Friday. Get out of your apartment for a bit, have some fun."

"I'm not sure that's a good idea." The last time she'd tried that, she'd ended up kissing Saylor. A memory she hadn't been able to wash away yet. Not that she'd really tried. It had been too amazing.

"Come on. I'm throwing a party at my place. Come and have some fun. Relax. Let loose a bit." Jericho gave Tia a pointed look. "I promise you that it'll be fun. You know I can throw a good party."

"That you can." Tia nodded and steepled her fingers. "I'll think about it."

"That's the best I can ask for."

Jericho stood up and said her goodbyes, leaving Tia alone in her office. She couldn't make herself go upstairs. At least not until she knew Saylor would be close to done for the night. After getting ahead on all of her monthly administration work, she finally shut down her computer when her stomach rumbled.

Tia walked into her apartment to find Saylor bent over the sewing machine. She glanced at Tia and gave a small smile before she pulled out the fabric and snipped the string.

"It's finished."

"Yeah?" Tia tentatively walked over to the table and bent over Saylor. "It looks good."

She never would have been able to do this. She took the outfit and held it out to get a good view of it. "You're amazing, you know that, right?"

"Those high school *home ec* classes are finally coming in handy."

Tia laughed. "Monti and Fallon both hated those. Me too, for that matter. I even went down and argued with the counselor that they should be exempt or they could take another science class just to get out of it."

"Didn't work, did it?" Saylor stood up and stretched her muscles.

"Nope. Not at all." Tia looked over, her gaze dropping to Saylor's breasts and then farther down her body. Fuck, she shouldn't have done that.

"I'll uh... be back first thing in the morning. Does seven sound good?"

"Sure." Tia swallowed hard. "I've got a family thing in the morning, so I'll be gone. Just let yourself in."

Thank God for Fallon. Tia hadn't known how much she needed the excuse to get out of the apartment and leave it to Saylor. She'd have to come back eventually, but at least she wouldn't be there all day.

"Sounds good. I'll let you have your space back. Thanks for letting me work here."

"Don't worry about it."

Saylor stepped by, grabbing her jacket and shucking it on. As soon as she was gone, the apartment was thrown into silence. Tia cursed. She'd screwed all of this up. And there was no going back now.

nineteen

"You should come out tonight."

"What?" Saylor furrowed her brow and stared up at Steven. "We went out last week."

"Yeah but this is a smaller gathering at Jericho's. She usually hosts them once a month, but since she was sick, we missed a month." Steven wrung his hands together. "It'll be fun. I promise. Low key. A few drinks."

Saylor flicked her gaze to Tia. Everything had been awkward since that night. She hated it, but it was mostly her own damn fault. She was more than halfway done with the outfits for the recital. She was making good progress, and Tia had stayed out of her way for the most part.

"I don't know." The last time they'd all gone out together, she had ended up making out with Tia, which had led to *that* night, and as much as Saylor didn't regret it, she wasn't ready for a repeat.

"Come on. It'll be fun. Just some people from the class."

Did that mean Tia wouldn't be there? Saylor hesitated again. She really did need to make friends, and since she'd screwed up the direction she was going with Tia, she needed to find those friends somewhere else. Homelife had been so tension-riddled anytime

Jameson had been there, that she needed the escape and someone to talk to. Because she still couldn't bring herself to call Callie and tell her what was going on.

"You coming?" Steven held the door open for Saylor. They were the last ones there.

"Sure." Saylor's stomach twisted sharply. She hated imposing on anyone, and that was exactly what this felt like.

"Do you need a ride?"

"Uh, yeah. I don't have a car."

"It's no problem." Steven led the way to his vehicle, and Saylor got into the passenger side.

The drive to Jericho's took about twenty minutes, but Steven parked and grinned as they walked into the building. Saylor walked slightly behind him, letting him take the lead like she always did. When they got into the small apartment, it was filled with people already. Jericho was setting out food and drinks on the small kitchen counter while people milled around the tiny living room.

The shrill laugh put Saylor on edge. She shut the door behind her, finding Kirsten near the couch. She immediately wanted to leave. She didn't want to betray Tia any more than she already had. She didn't want Tia to think that she was consorting with the enemy. That's who Kirsten was, right?

"Hey!" Tia said, opening the door without knocking.

Saylor's shoulders tensed immediately.

This couldn't honestly be worse. She really needed to get the hell out of here. Saylor swallowed the bile that rose up in her throat.

Tia nodded at Jericho and then moved to stand next to Saylor, touching Saylor's arm lightly. "You okay?"

"Fine," Saylor muttered, the word harsher than she intended.

She needed to put some space between them. Walking away without saying another word, Saylor made herself a drink in a red Solo cup and walked toward the sea of people in the living room.

This wasn't a small gathering. The tiny apartment was filled with people not just from their class but others as well.

Saylor had seen most of them at least once, but she struggled to put names to faces. She sipped her drink and winced. It was way stronger than she'd intended it to be. Steven laughed boisterously. Saylor huddled down into herself again, wanting to appear as small as humanly possible. Her anxiety was rearing its ugly head again, and she couldn't get it under control.

"Hey there." Kirsten slid next to her, her voice bubbly but in that fake way Saylor had come to hate.

Saylor clenched her jaw, not wanting to say anything. After the experience she'd had with Kirsten at the club, she definitely didn't want a repeat.

"Not talking much, I see," Kirsten taunted.

Saylor was going to have to figure out something to say. Because staying silent probably wouldn't get her out of this conversation. "Didn't have anything to say."

"Sure, but you never miss a beat when it comes to our effervescent dance instructor." Kirsten laughed low, sipping her drink and pointing to Saylor's. "What did you make?"

"Nothing special." Saylor couldn't help but find Tia across the room.

Tia stared at the two of them, her face taut with tension and worry. Anyone would be able to see it, really. But after the club, Saylor had no doubt that Tia was wondering exactly what was being discussed over here. Saylor nodded at her firmly, hoping that it would ease Tia's worry even if it didn't ease her own.

"So did you and Tia have your night together?"

Saylor furrowed her brow, whipping around to face Kirsten and look her full in the eye. "Excuse me?"

"Well, the tension between you is palpable. And that only happens when she's fucked someone."

"You know, you're a despicable person. I can't honestly see what Tia would ever find attractive in you since you're so ugly on the inside." Saylor lifted her cup to take a huge swig of her drink. She was going to need the added bolster of liquid courage to get through this conversation, that was for sure.

"Oh, I'm so wounded." Kirsten chuckled as if there was nothing mean about Saylor's statement.

"You really are a trip, that's for sure." Saylor tipped back her drink, which was way too strong, and sucked down as much of the liquid as possible. She held back her wince and splutter, but just barely.

"So you're telling me nothing has happened between the two of you?" Kirsten turned to face Saylor.

"I'm telling you nothing at all." Saylor pursed her lips, keeping her eyes on Tia. She didn't want to tip Tia off to the tense nature of the conversation, but she also didn't want Tia coming over to rescue her. That was the last thing they needed.

"Oh, I do think I like you."

"I think you like anyone you think you can stomp on." Saylor finished her drink. "I think I'm going to get another."

She walked away and didn't look back. Kirsten was a nasty person, someone who didn't deserve any of Saylor's time. But unlike the last time they'd all gathered, Saylor wasn't going to rescue Tia from her either. Tia had to figure her own shit out.

"Do you need any help?" Saylor asked Jericho, wanting to occupy her time with something better than the pissing match that Kirsten seemed to take everywhere.

"You any good at bartending?"

Saylor glanced down at her empty drink and shook her head. "Afraid not."

"Good. Because it's a self-serve kind of night, and I want you to have fun." Jericho wrapped her arm around Saylor's waist and spun her around in a half dance. "How is everything going, really?"

Saylor sighed. "It's been a rough week. Jameson and I are…

well, we're still together, but I'm not sure for how much longer. We're trying to figure that out."

"Saylor!" Jericho's face fell. "I'm so sorry."

"It's my fault."

"Somehow I doubt that."

"Nope. This is completely my fault." Saylor found Tia in the crowd again, their gazes meeting across the room, and her breath caught. This was so much more than just one night, and she hated that it was. Saylor had been exploring her sexuality, yes, but she could have done that without sex. She could have done that by simply thinking, and feeling her emotions.

"You shouldn't be so hard on yourself." Jericho pulled Saylor into a hug.

"For this one, it's deserved." Saylor extricated herself from the hug and started to make herself a new drink. If she was here, then she would imbibe. At least maybe then she'd say what she really thought to Kirsten if she showed up in her vicinity again.

Tia sidled on up next to Kirsten, engaging the conversation but keeping her gaze on Saylor through most of it. Saylor started on her second drink, trying to ignore the elephant in the room. She'd doomed both relationships. The one with Jameson because she'd cheated and the one with Tia because she hadn't given it the chance it deserved. She'd gone about everything wrong.

Fuck, she was such a failure at the basic things in life.

"Are you and Steven ready for the competition?"

Saylor looked at Jericho again. "We're getting there. We had some catching up to do that most of the other competitors didn't."

"I'm so mad that I'm going to miss it." Jericho turned around and pulled herself up backward onto the counter, making a moat of alcohol bottles around her. "But this cruise—"

"Sounds like a blast, honestly. I've never been on a cruise, so you'll have to tell me all about it when you get back."

"You've never been?" Jericho's eyes lit up.

"Nope." Saylor took another long sip of her drink. She was doing well with getting drunk. And it had been a long time since she'd been good and truly drunk.

The volume of the music turned up. Saylor looked over to find the people dancing. She was pretty sure that this group could always be found dancing somewhere. As much as she was pulled toward them, she didn't want to intrude. She wanted to watch from the sidelines and see what everyone else was going to do before she decided where she belonged.

Kirsten took Tia's arms and spun her around into a dance. Tia didn't look very happy about being in the middle of that, but again Saylor wasn't going to come to her rescue again. Saylor stayed in the kitchen with Jericho, observing from a distance as Kirsten moved in even closer.

"You should go. It's good to take vacations. You could do one for your honeymoon."

Saylor's stomach clenched. She didn't even know if there was going to be a honeymoon at this point. They hadn't talked about breaking up, but there was no doubt in Saylor's mind that her relationship with Jameson was teetering on the edge of disaster.

But she had nowhere to go without him.

She could move home, which was probably what she'd end up doing, but until then? She was left relying on him and living in an apartment that didn't feel like hers. Saylor worried her lip between her teeth. "That's not a bad idea."

Why did it feel like absolute shit to plan a honeymoon for a wedding she was pretty sure wasn't going to take place at this point? She really needed to focus on Jameson and figure out what the two of them were doing before she did anything else stupid. Then again, that would be a lot easier if he was even in the state to have a conversation with her.

Saylor pressed her lips together after finishing off her second drink. "Where would you go on a honeymoon?"

"Oh, Jamaica? Hawaii? Someplace warm with a beach for

sure." Jericho giggled. "But I'm nowhere near close to an engagement."

"You're not?"

Jericho shook her head. "Nope, not at all. We just started dating last summer. It hasn't even been a year yet."

Would Jericho be shocked to learn how short a time Saylor had known Jameson before getting engaged? Also, why did the conversation once engaged have to turn to wedding planning? They weren't even talking about a wedding and yet everyone around them wanted to know the details. Saylor's stomach twisted hard again.

A shiver ran down her spine at Kirsten's laugh, something that Tia had said. Was that...jealousy? God, she needed to get the hell out of there. She needed to get her shit together and focus on fixing whatever she'd broken between her and Jameson, which would mean a full telling of everything that had happened with Tia.

They hadn't even touched on those points yet. Saylor filled a cup with a third drink. She'd finish this one and then tell Jericho that she had to leave. That way, she'd stayed a requisite amount of time so it wouldn't seem like she was rude and begging off. Jericho turned around when everyone in the living room started clapping.

Tia grinned broadly when Steven pulled her in close and started a rambunctious dance. It would be amazing to be friends with them, without all the drama hanging over Saylor's head, without feeling like she was going to ruin everything they'd already built. It was stupid to think that she'd have that much power, but she knew she could do some damage, that was for sure.

Steven and Tia spun around on the dance floor, improvising to the music as the beat continued to blast throughout the room. Everyone was laughing and enjoying themselves, even Tia. Everyone except Saylor.

And why was that?

Because she'd been invited here. She'd agreed to come. She'd thought she could find her place here. But the longer she was there, the more time she spent with the dance crew and got to know them, the more she realized she would never belong to this group.

She would do what she always did.

She'd break them and ruin them.

twenty

"Dance with me," Kirsten snagged Tia's arm and spun her in a circle.

Tia immediately tensed. She didn't want to be here with Kirsten of all people. Why couldn't she just take the hint and the very blunt tellings-off? Not wanting to cause a scene in such a small place, Tia let Kirsten spin her around in a dance.

But she couldn't drag her gaze away from Saylor.

Saylor who stood next to Jericho. Who sucked down drink after drink. Who was riveted to every move that Tia made.

Did she know how she looked? Did Saylor know that she looked like she was going to kill Kirsten as soon as she had a chance? Tia shuddered. Oh, to have that gaze and intensity focused solely on her again. Tia was like a moth to a flame, Saylor being the flame she was so fucking drawn to.

"What do you think about Saylor?" Kirsten whispered into Tia's ear.

"I think she's a skilled dancer."

Kirsten's chuckle was low and dangerous. "Does that dancing involve time between the sheets?"

Tia cringed. She hadn't realized it was that obvious. Then

again, she should have guessed—Kirsten seemed to be so in tune with everything like that where Tia was concerned. "Saylor is my student."

"So was I."

"So are you." Tia stopped their dance. "But if you continue in this vein, I'll terminate your contract. I'm tired of it, Kirsten."

"Tired of me?" Kirsten's cheeks flushed.

"I'm tired of your attitude, your pushing. I'm not interested in a relationship with you. Just leave me alone already." Tia tried to walk past Kirsten, but Kirsten snagged her hand and turned her back. "Let go of me."

"I don't believe you."

"I don't know why. I've told you time and time again that I'm not interested." Tia ripped her hand from Kirsten's grasp. "Enough is enough already."

"Tia." Kirsten stood up, stunned as if Tia had slapped her across the face. "I thought you loved me."

"No. I don't. I never did." Tia squared her shoulders. "And you need to accept that."

"I don't accept it." Kirsten stepped in closer. She grasped Tia's cheek and pulled her in for a sharp kiss.

Bile swirled up in Tia's stomach. She pushed Kirsten away, shoving her back a step. "Come to the studio again, and I'll have you arrested for trespassing."

Tia spun around as soon as she knew that Kirsten had heard her. Saylor was gone. The spot next to Jericho was empty. Tia cursed. Everyone in the room was staring at her, and she just couldn't bring herself to care. She was tired of trying to keep this under wraps, tired of trying to keep the drama from leaching into her studio.

Nodding sharply at Jericho, Tia grabbed her jacket. "I'll see you Monday for class."

"Tia, don't leave because of this," Jericho said softly, her voice so full of sympathy that it made Tia's skin crawl.

"It doesn't matter if I stay or go. I need some space tonight." Tia put her jacket on, zipping it up. "I'll see you Monday," she repeated more firmly. "Where did Saylor go?"

"Saylor?" Jericho looked around the room wildly. "I have no idea."

"I'll find her."

Whatever game the two of them were playing was going too far. Tia was tired of chasing after Saylor time and again. They needed to talk. They had to stop pussyfooting around and just figure this out. As soon as Tia had the thought, she knew it was ridiculous. Saylor wasn't going to be able to make that decision yet.

Tia took the stairs down instead of the elevator. She needed the extra time to settle her mind. She was halfway down from the sixth floor when she stopped. Saylor sat on the bottom stair, her head in her hands.

Slipping onto the step next to Saylor, Tia pressed her lips together hard and knocked her shoulder lightly into Saylor's. "I keep having to chase after you, don't I?"

"You don't have to."

"True." Tia glanced up the stairs to make sure that Kirsten hadn't followed her out of the apartment. "Let's go."

"Go?" Saylor looked up at her. "Go where?"

"Anywhere but here." Standing up, Tia held her hand out for Saylor to take it.

"Where are we going?"

"My place or yours? I need a stiff drink, and I don't want to have to worry about getting home." Tia kept her hand out, still waiting for Saylor to take it.

Saylor bit her lip. "Yours. I don't think... I can't bring you back to mine."

"Sure." Tia still waited with her hand out, but when Saylor stood up without grasping hold of her, Tia shoved her hand into her pocket. "I'll get a ride for us."

They moved in silence down the stairs, and when they

reached the bottom floor, Tia waited just inside the lobby for the car to come and collect them. Saylor shoved her hands into her pockets and rocked up on her toes. Tia watched every move that she made.

"I don't know how much you heard in there."

"It doesn't matter," Saylor answered.

"It does." Tia sighed heavily. "It wasn't ever meant to be anything with her, and she's taken it too far. I told her if she shows up at the studio, I'll call the cops. I'm tired of the harassment."

"Tired of it now? But you weren't before?"

Tia wrinkled her nose. "I don't want her to turn that harassing energy onto you."

"Too late for that," Saylor mumbled.

"Here's the ride." Tia started toward the car, holding the lobby door open for Saylor to join her. "Come on."

"I'm not sure this is a good idea." Saylor's eyes widened, and she looked directly at Tia.

"Do you want the truth or something that'll make you feel better?" Fear ratcheted up a few notches. They were walking such a thin line. Saylor needed to make decisions. Tia needed to give her the space to be able to do that. But it was so hard to watch her continue to torture herself throughout the process. And that was exactly what Saylor was doing.

"I want the truth."

Tia nodded, but she chose her words carefully. "I'm not sure this is a good idea either. But I can't stop myself from wanting to be in your presence."

Saylor's lips parted in surprise. Her entire body listed forward, her fingers latching onto Tia's and lacing together. "I don't know what to say to that."

"Tell me you won't run away again."

"I don't know what else to do."

Lifting her hand, Tia curled a strand of hair behind Saylor's ear and cupped her cheek. "The driver is waiting."

"Right." Saylor blushed and looked down at her feet in embarrassment.

How the hell were they going to contend with that?

Fighting against her own shitty emotions was hard enough, but to stand in the space for Saylor to fight her own? That was impossible. Saylor was going to have to do it, but that didn't mean that Tia wouldn't also be there as a support when needed.

When they were settled into the car, Tia buckled her belt and glanced over Saylor. "How drunk are you?"

"Not drunk enough." Saylor buckled her own belt and closed her eyes, tilting her head onto the back of the seat. "I wish I was drunk."

"We can get drunk if you want."

Saylor shook her head, then nodded, then shook her head again.

"Well, let's figure it out when we get there." Tia's fingers itched to move closer to Saylor's, to clasp her hand in a sign of solidarity, but she resisted the temptation. Tia had no idea where they stood together, and she certainly didn't want to talk about it until they were alone. No one else needed to be privy to their fuckups already.

It didn't take long. Tia thanked the driver as she followed Saylor out of the car and stood right in front of the studio. "Do you still want to come up?"

"I don't know." Saylor didn't look at the building. She looked directly into Tia's eyes. She grasped onto Tia's hands and pulled Tia in closer. "I'm scared of what will happen if I say yes."

"Scared of what exactly?" Tia glanced down at their hands. Her eyes stung, but she wasn't sure what else to say.

"That I'm just buzzed enough to let it happen again."

Tia sucked in a sharp breath. She closed her eyes, the damp air kissing her cheeks in the way she wished Saylor would. There were so many things that Tia wanted to say. So many ways she wanted to push the conversation and their relationship into a different direction. But she couldn't make herself do it. She couldn't make Saylor do anything she wasn't ready for.

"I'm not going to tell you that I don't want that. Because I do. I told you I wanted more."

"I know." Saylor turned her face, nuzzling her nose into Tia's neck. "I know you did."

Tia couldn't stop herself. She pressed her lips against Saylor's, increasing the pressure and sliding her tongue out for just a taste. Her entire body went into overdrive in a second, needing touch, needing passion, needing Saylor to do exactly what they'd done before.

"Stop." Tia pulled back, wiping her hand over her mouth. "Stop, Saylor. I can't do this. I can't be this experiment for you."

"It's not an experiment," Saylor answered, straightening her shoulders and looking all the more confident with each passing second. "You're not an experiment."

"Then what am I?" Tia shoved her hands into her pockets again, needing to keep them away from Saylor, away from temptation. "Who am I to you?"

"I can't answer that."

Tia frowned. She'd known that. She shouldn't have asked that question. Tia knew better than to push them when they weren't ready.

"I'm sorry." She ran her fingers through her damp hair. "We shouldn't be doing this."

Walking toward the door to her apartment building, Tia turned her back on Saylor. They could figure this out later. Right now, she needed some time alone. She needed to know exactly what they were doing and why, and she wasn't going to get any kind of conclusion on that yet. Tia put her key into the lock and stepped inside the dry building.

"Tia, wait." Saylor rushed in after her.

"I don't think I can do this." Tia stopped walking. "I don't think I can keep going on with this back-and-forth."

"What back-and-forth? I told you from the start that it was only one night."

"And what would you call tonight?" Tia fired back. She knew her tone was sharp, that she couldn't keep the anger and frustration out of it. "What are we doing, Saylor?"

"I don't know." Saylor clenched her hands into fists. "I don't know what we're doing. I don't know what I'm doing. What I do know is that I want you, Tia. I want to spend more time with you. I want to have sex with you. I want to be near you all the time."

Everything about this moment was raw. Tia held her breath, her entire body ready to shake. "What are we doing tonight?"

"What do you want?" Saylor asked back.

"You don't want me to answer that question." Tia stepped backward, farther into the hallway. She was retreating, not just from this conversation, but from all that Saylor brought with her. "I can't answer that."

"I don't believe you." Saylor followed her. "What do you want from me, Tia? Because I need to know."

"You deserve to make these decisions, to figure this out on your own. Without any influence from me."

Saylor snorted. "I didn't realize that you thought so highly of yourself. Do you really think that your opinion will influence how I feel?"

"I..." Tia stopped. Had she? If she did believe that, then she was an idiot. She deserved to be called out on it. "I'm sorry. That was wrong of me."

Saylor stepped in closer. "Tell me it's over between you and Kirsten."

"It's over. It has been for a long time." Tia held her ground. This was a side of Saylor that she had only ever seen once before. "Can you say the same for you and Jameson?"

"No." Saylor still moved in closer. "Is that going to be an issue for you?"

It would be. Perhaps not tonight, not with the way that Saylor was looking at her. But it would be a problem tomorrow.

"Tia?"

"Not tonight."

"Good." Saylor crashed their mouths together. She wrapped her hands around Tia's back and walked, guiding Tia toward the stairs that would lead up to the apartment. Tia lost her breath. She clung onto Saylor with everything she had, waiting to see what she would do next, how Saylor would handle the situation.

Saylor turned their bodies. She pulled Tia along as she walked backward. Tia followed effortlessly. They'd done this dance before. They'd been here before. She wasn't going to stop them this time. Saylor deserved to take the lead.

When they reached her apartment door, Tia looked Saylor over again. "Are you sure?"

"More than ever. Are you?"

Tia hesitated. This was her out if she wanted one. Opening the door, she moved her hand out in front of her and pointed the way inside. "I'll follow you, Saylor."

twenty-one

Saylor's heart clenched at those words. She wasn't good at leading when it came to sex. She was always a follower, always doing what everyone else told her to do. But with Tia it was different. Saylor curled her fingers around Tia's cheek, staring into her dark eyes. She could feel every part of Tia's body. Her skin, the fabric of her clothes against it, the breath in her lungs each time she drew air in and expelled it. Her heart as it hammered against her ribcage almost to the point of pain.

She could lead this.

Tia trusted her to do it.

But it was so much more than that.

Saylor trusted herself.

This was more than one night of exploring her sexuality. She wanted Tia. Tia turned her on. Saylor was safe with her. They could talk and communicate. Tia lifted her up instead of tearing her down. Moving in slowly, Saylor pressed their lips together. This kiss was different. It was full of simmering passion, of unspoken words, of hopes that Saylor didn't even know she had.

Tia wrapped her arms around Saylor's back and pulled her in. Saylor pushed Tia against the door, covering her. Saylor slipped her hand down Tia's front, over her breast in one smooth movement, to her hip. Their tongues tangled. Tia cupped the back of Saylor's head while Saylor moved her hand to the line of fabric at Tia's hip.

"Are you wet for me?" Saylor breathed the question, not sure she wanted to know the answer. She'd been asked that question so many times by previous partners, and the answer was always no. Would it be different this time?

Tia touched Saylor's chin lightly and lifted her face so that they could look into each other's eyes again. "Why don't you find out?"

"Is that an invitation?"

"Absolutely." Tia leaned back into the door, pressing her shoulders against it to jut her hips out. Her look was direct and sure.

Saylor pushed her hand past the elastic waist of Tia's leggings and under the thong she wore. It wasn't long until she found the coarse hair between Tia's legs, the soft, swollen lips of her pussy, damp and dripping just like Tia had promised. Pulling that confidence into the center of her chest, Saylor moved her fingers down deeper and pushed them through Tia's folds.

Tia groaned, her eyes locking on Saylor's.

Saylor's heart hammered, excitement coursing through her. People liked her because of her body. That's what Jameson said, that she was sexy. But Tia hadn't made those lewd comments, not that she hadn't thought them. But this attraction was more than that.

Getting onto her knees, Saylor pulled Tia's leggings over her hips and down to her knees. Tia lifted her feet and slid off her flats before sliding her pants off completely. With her lips quirked upward, Tia lifted her shirt off and dropped it to the floor.

The scent of Tia's arousal hit Saylor hard. It was like a siren's call, beckoning her right where they both wanted her to be. If this was what sex was supposed to be like, she had never experienced it before now. Saylor trailed her fingers over the front of Tia's thighs. She traced Tia's hip bones. She breathed in that scent she never wanted to forget.

They were quiet.

The stillness a calm that Saylor had never experienced in her life before.

Why did this feel so right?

Leaning in, Saylor pressed kisses right where her fingers had been. She pressed the flat of her tongue against Tia's smooth skin and left wet trails as she tasted and teased. Tia groaned again, reaching up and cupping her left breast while teasing her nipple as she continued to watch every move Saylor made.

Saylor was in charge of this. She was the one leading tonight. Touching tentatively between Tia's legs, Saylor traced her swollen and damp lips. She dipped her finger between them and gathered Tia's juices, sliding them between Tia's slit all the while looking directly into Tia's eyes.

"This is for us," Saylor whispered.

"Who else would it be for?" Tia's lower lip trembled, her cheeks hollowed.

Was she worried about what they were doing? Saylor shook her head slowly. "No one but you and me."

"Not just you?"

"Us," Saylor repeated, answering the question succinctly. This wasn't an exploration of sexuality, or feelings. This was connection and intimacy exactly as they both needed. "This is for us."

"Then what are we waiting for?" Tia murmured.

Saylor's lips curled upward, the exact permission she'd needed to begin. She hadn't even known that was what she had been waiting for. Curling her finger, Saylor found Tia's tight circular opening. Instead of diving her finger straight in like she wanted to, she circled. Tia rocked her hips out, trying to get closer to Saylor, all the while keeping their gazes locked together.

"I'm not waiting." Saylor pushed her finger in to the first knuckle before pulling out immediately. "I'm teasing."

Tia wrinkled her nose, her chest rising and falling in quicker succession. "Tease away."

Saylor's cheeks warmed at the thought that Tia wanted her to do this. She wanted the experience as much as Saylor did. Pushing her finger in again, Saylor leaned in and touched her lips to the soft flesh low on Tia's abdomen. She trailed a path of kisses lower, hunching her shoulders slightly so she could peek her tongue out and find the little nub she wanted to taste.

Tia whimpered, pushing her hips closer into Saylor and silently asking for more. Giving in to what she really wanted, Saylor pressed her mouth over Tia's clit. She didn't suck right away. Instead, she flicked her tongue and listened to every sound that Tia made. The movement of her body as she shifted, the pull of her muscles, the increase in her breathing. This was everything for Saylor—everything she had been looking for and more.

Sliding in a second finger with her first, Saylor started a gentle pattern that she didn't want to give up. Tia slid fingers through her hair, occasionally holding onto the top of Saylor's head when she made a particularly pleasurable move. Saylor had never felt so alive during sex before. She'd always just wanted to get it done and over with as fast as possible, but this was so different. This was what she'd read about, heard about. This was what it was supposed to be, right?

Saylor increased her tempo and pressure. Tia keened into the apartment, her eyes fluttering shut. Saylor couldn't stop looking at her. She wanted to memorize everything about this moment. Not because it would be the last time. No, Saylor knew it wouldn't be, not after tonight. But because this was pure, untainted beauty. This was them being there for each other and themselves, showing up in ways they both wanted and could.

Tia gasped, her body twitching. Saylor was tempted to continue in the same way she had been, but she moved instead.

Sliding up Tia's body, she left her fingers planted deep inside her. Saylor pressed their mouths together, tangling their tongues as she thrust her fingers hard and ground the heel of her palm against Tia's wet and engorged clit.

The moan that escaped Tia's throat spurned Saylor on. She rocked her body for a strong emphasis of pleasure. She pushed and teased and pressed Tia into the door. Saylor kept their bodies as connected as she possibly could while Tia careened through her orgasm and gripped onto Saylor's shoulders to hold herself steady.

But Saylor didn't stop.

In fact, she barely slowed down.

Tia was all but clutching onto her for dear life, and Saylor kept the momentum going, now rapidly moving two fingers in and out of her as fast as she could and using the door to keep them both in place. Tia cried out again, her voice loud in Saylor's ears.

"Stop," Tia said, her voice breaking on the word. "Stop. I surrender." Tia laughed lightly as Saylor slowed her movements and then halted them all together.

The tight circle Saylor had teased before pulsed around Saylor's fingers, clenching and letting go. Tia's breathing was ragged, her body hot and sweaty. Saylor kept her hand in place, pressing sweet kisses to the side of Tia's face, her jaw, her neck and her shoulder. Every inch of skin was as gloriously supple as the next.

"Fuck," Tia whispered, finally dropping the back of her head into the door to look at Saylor with hooded eyes. "I can't remember the last time someone fucked me so thoroughly."

Saylor's cheeks warmed at the thought. Only her second time doing this with a woman, and she'd clearly done a good job. Tia skimmed her hands down Saylor's shoulders to her elbows before wrapping her arms around Saylor's neck and pulling her in for a deep kiss. Saylor still didn't remove her hand from between Tia's legs. Her fingers were soaked, Tia's juices spilling down her hand, but it felt so damn good and so damn right. The pulsing had slowed, but it was still there. Every few seconds, Tia's body reminded Saylor just how connected they were.

Saylor wanted to be cocky in response. She wanted to say something like *And we haven't even gotten started yet*. But she wasn't the arrogant asshole that she wanted to be sometimes. Instead, Saylor leaned in and kissed Tia again. She deepened the embrace, bringing them together as best she could, as close as possible.

A bubble of laughter erupted from Tia's lips. She wrapped her arms around Saylor's neck and rested her forehead on Saylor's shoulder. "My legs are jelly."

"I'm going to take that as a compliment."

"You better." Tia turned her head and kissed Saylor's neck. "Always a compliment."

Saylor tilted her head toward the ceiling, giving Tia as much space to kiss her neck as possible. The sweet, soft kisses were everything she wanted and more. They sent a trickle of pleasure and anticipation through her and filled the rest of her with warmth and comfort. Dragging in a deep breath, Saylor scraped her teeth against Tia's shoulder.

"Keep that up, and maybe we won't leave the front door." Tia's voice was low, a murmur into the room.

Saylor wasn't sure if she'd meant to say it out loud. Tia tangled her fingers into Saylor's hair, pulling her closer and up for another lengthy kiss.

"Saylor," Tia said again.

Stilling, Saylor looked deep into Tia's eyes. All the nerves she'd had before were gone. She was content, unexpectedly happy. With a new fervor, Saylor started a trail of kisses over Tia's chest. She sucked each one of her nipples, flicking her tongue over the hard nub in a tease before moving on to the next and then back again. Cupping Tia's breast, she gently massaged. She'd never get enough of Tia's body, would she?

The way she moved.

The sounds she let loose.

The sharp intake of breath when something felt good.

Saylor was pressing kisses to Tia's hip bone and moving closer to where she wanted to go when Tia tapped her palm against Saylor's forehead. "Sorry, Saylor. As much as I'd love for you to take me against the door again, I'm not sure that my legs will hold me up."

"Oh. Okay." Saylor stood up and awkwardly kissed Tia's cheek.

"Bedroom." Tia snagged Saylor's hand and walked on her toes toward the bedroom.

A new heat washed through Saylor, settling into the pit of her belly before slowly sliding lower to right between her legs. Her clothes were suddenly itchy and rough. She wanted to get them off, get naked and slide her skin against Tia's soft, gloriously warm flesh. As Tia backed onto the mattress, Saylor pulled her clothes off one by one, dropping them to the floor.

"Come up here," Tia beckoned.

Saylor climbed onto the mattress, moving on her knees. She followed Tia's directions until she straddled Tia's head. Saylor brushed her fingers through Tia's hair, staring down into those dark and expressive eyes. Could this ever work between them?

Tia turned her head, pressing her lips to the inside of Saylor's thigh.

Fuck, yes.

This could work.

Saylor closed her eyes and leaned back slightly. She waited with anticipation as Tia worked her way close to right between Saylor's legs, to the place where all her arousal was pooling and waiting for simple touch. For Tia's mouth. For Tia.

When Tia's tongue finally slid against Saylor's slick folds, she sighed on a moan. Trembles ran through her, from breast to clit and back again. Saylor shifted, angling her hips for more attention. Tia wrapped her arms around Saylor's hips, pulling her in closer—

tighter. Then she reached up and cupped Saylor's breasts, flicking her hard nipples with her thumbs.

Groaning, Saylor had to work hard to find her balance and control her body. Every part of her was focused on Tia and nothing else. Saylor didn't want to give this up. She'd longed for this, read about it, dreamed about it. She'd never thought it was possible. She'd thought what she'd found with Jameson had been it. But she had never been more wrong.

Saylor rocked her hips against Tia's mouth, straining when Tia pulled her down hard. Saylor cried out, bracing herself on the headboard. She was so close. Every part of her was tuned in to Tia and the swipe of her tongue, the flick against her clit, the sucking of her breath. Saylor crumbled. Her orgasm washed through her in never-ending waves as Tia continued to tease her body and keep the pleasure coursing through her.

Finally, Saylor collapsed onto the bed beside Tia, her legs still tangled by Tia's head. Tia ran soothing fingers and hands up and down Saylor's legs as Saylor caught her breath. She threw her hand over her eyes and calmed her racing heart.

She had no idea what she was doing.

But she wanted more.

She wanted so much more.

Tia shifted, turning on the mattress to sit up and touch Saylor's arm, her neck, her lips. Bending down, Tia pressed their mouths together, air exchanging between them. Saylor sighed, her eyes fluttering shut.

"Let me stay tonight," Saylor whispered.

"Of course," Tia murmured with another kiss. "Are we done for tonight?"

Saylor's mind spun with all the possibilities. Closing her eyes, she could imagine them. Every fantasy she hadn't allowed herself to admit or even let come to full fruition flashed in her mind in seconds. Saylor felt more like herself here than she'd ever felt anywhere else. Staring into Tia's eyes, she felt at home. Her lips curled up into a smile, and she purposely moved her hand down Tia's body. Hooking her leg around Tia's hip, Saylor flipped them over so Tia was underneath her again.

"Absolutely not."

"Saylor," Tia said on a laugh. "I need you to know something before we continue."

"Okay?" Saylor straightened her arms so she could look down into those expressive eyes. "What is it?"

"I'm not going to chase after you again."

Saylor furrowed her brow in confusion.

Tia ran fingers gently across Saylor's cheek, pushing strands of hair behind Saylor's ear. "I'm not going to make you do something you don't want. The ball is in your court. I'll follow your lead."

"Oh." Saylor bit her lip as the words sunk in. She couldn't imagine being anywhere else right now. But what did that mean for tomorrow? "Okay."

"I want you to know where I stand."

"Thanks." Saylor forced her lips into a smile. "I appreciate that."

Tia moved her hand purposely toward Saylor's breast, rubbing circles over her hard nipple. Saylor flicked her gaze to her chest and swallowed the lump of discomfort that had suddenly formed. Pushing that thought away, Saylor bent down and kissed Tia hard. She wasn't going to let tonight get away from them, especially if it might be their last night together.

twenty-two

Tia relaxed her body as she woke up, sunlight just brushing through the underside of the curtain. She threw her arm over her eyes, the ringing in her ears finally easing up. Glancing at the clock on the nightstand, she paused. She wasn't waking up that much earlier than normal.

Turning on her side, she smiled. Saylor was sprawled face first into the mattress, her long dark hair covering her face and her back rising and falling with each gentle breath. Last night had been amazing. Unexpected, but wonderful just the same. Something about it had broken barriers that Tia hadn't fully realized she'd been holding before.

Still, it would probably do her well to put some of those barriers back up.

Her body was sore in the perfect way. She'd expected it this time, but she was pretty sure that if she stood up her legs would still feel like jelly. Something about Saylor made her weak in the knees, and it wasn't just being fucked good and hard either. There was an innocence there, but it wasn't that simple either. Saylor was a curious person, and she wasn't afraid to explore or to push the bounds of what she knew and understood.

That was something Tia appreciated.

The connection between them was strong—stronger than Tia had ever felt before. Trailing her fingers along Saylor's arm, Tia waited to see what kind of reaction Saylor would give her. Was she awake? Asleep? Or somewhere in the in-between? Tia left Saylor alone when she didn't move, and slipped from the bed.

An hour later, she emerged from the bathroom showered and wrapped in a towel. Saylor was on the bed on her back, playing on her phone. Tia smiled when Saylor set her phone down and turned immediately toward her.

"Morning," Tia whispered, sliding onto the edge of the bed. She bent down and pressed her lips to Saylor's.

"Morning." Saylor made the kiss quick. "Your phone's been going off nonstop."

Frowning, Tia reached for it on the nightstand next to where Saylor had set hers.

"You left it by the door last night, but the sound was still on."

"Oh." Tia unlocked it, knowing without a doubt Saylor had seen the name on the calls and texts that had popped up repeatedly. Because she couldn't even count how many missed calls or texts she had. Sighing, Tia set the phone back down without reading or listening to any of the messages. "I have to go in early to set up for the recital tonight."

"Need some help?" Saylor shifted under the blankets, pulling them over her chest.

"I'll never turn you down for helping." Tia wanted to lean in and kiss Saylor again, but something in Saylor's eyes made her hesitate. There was a wall back up between them. Whether it was because of the texts and phone calls or because of something else, Tia had no idea. And again, was it really her place to find out? Saylor was still engaged. The ring was still on her finger.

Tia's phone buzzed again. She spared it a glance before focusing back on Saylor. Giving in to temptation, Tia leaned in and pressed their mouths together. This time, Saylor reached up, cupping Tia's cheeks and holding her still. Their lips touched, their tongues slid against each other, and Tia sighed into the embrace.

This was what she wanted.

But until Saylor made some decisions, they were still in this never-ending void of the unknown. Trying to ignore it, Tia pushed in more. She wanted to forget what that pain would feel like. She knew and understood it well. She was always the one left cleaning up the pieces of broken lives, and she hated playing that role some days.

Except this time it might be her life that she was left picking up the pieces of.

"Answer the phone before I kill her myself," Saylor mumbled with a half-hearted chuckle.

Tia looked at the phone again, shaking her head. "I'm not answering her."

She picked up the phone and sent the call straight to voicemail. Then she took it to her charger to plug it in after silencing it. She'd need to remember to bring the cord with her that day because she'd no doubt need a boost of charge later in the night when the kids were getting ready for the recital.

Tia pulled off her towel and rummaged through her dresser drawer for the clothes she wanted to wear that day. She'd need something she could get dirty before changing into something else for the evening recital. She jumped when Saylor touched her, sliding a hand around the side of her hip to her front, splaying her fingers across her belly.

"I'm more obsessed with touching you every day."

Tia laughed lightly. "The feeling is mutual."

Again, that pang of guilt hit hard. Saylor wasn't hers to touch freely. They weren't in a relationship. This could very well be the last time that they spent together like this. Saylor's hand dipped between Tia's legs, teasing and rubbing lightly. With a deep breath, Tia broke the touch and turned around.

"Not this morning, Saylor."

"Oh." Saylor frowned, her eyes downcast as if she'd been scolded.

"I have a lot to get done." Instinctively, Tia reached up and touched Saylor's cheek.

"Okay."

Tia applauded herself for successfully putting that barrier back up, but she hated herself all the more for it. She didn't want to hold back. She wanted to give Saylor everything she had and more. She wanted to be free together. But that was impossible considering the current state of their lives.

"Take a shower if you want. I need to leave in about an hour to head to the theater to set up the sets for tonight. Like I said before, you're more than welcome to join me if you want."

"Sure." Saylor backed away. She dragged her feet a little as she moved toward the bathroom.

Finally alone, Tia let out a breath of relief. She couldn't allow herself to get tangled in distractions, as much as she might want to. She needed to focus on her kids that day, and then tomorrow she could focus on what was going on between her and Saylor.

Within two hours, she was at the theater with the costumes Saylor had sewn and the rest of the supplies she needed to set up for that evening. The older girls would start arriving as soon as school was out, but the littles would come for their regular classes so they could do a proper rehearsal for that night.

Tia spread out the costumes on the clothing rack she found. She turned on some music and let it wash through her body. She needed to clear her head from last night. She needed to get Saylor out of it, in other words. Because everything she did, every move she made, she couldn't stop thinking about Saylor.

"Where do you want the girls to line up for tonight?" Saylor asked as she stepped inside.

Tia froze. She hadn't expected Saylor to show up, had she? Cringing, Tia should have known better. Saylor was always willing to help with anything that Tia needed, especially the more they got to know each other. Pulling herself together and putting her self-protections in place, Tia pointed to the left wing of the stage.

"There are a couple of rooms back there. We'll have the little ones go on first because they're the most rowdy. I have some moms who will help keep everyone in line while they wait their turn to begin."

"Sounds good." Saylor shoved her hands into the pockets of her jacket and rolled up on her toes. "What do you need me to do?"

"Can you sweep the stage? I don't know who was in here last, but there's glitter all over and I'd like to keep as much of it off the girls as possible."

"Sure." Saylor turned around slowly, looking for the broom.

"There's a closet stage right that has the push broom." Tia watched Saylor's ass as she walked away. She shook herself from her distraction and closed her eyes. She had to get better control of herself. Immediately.

"You didn't answer my calls or texts, so I wasn't sure if you needed me this morning."

Tia's spine straightened immediately. Turning to her left, she stared at Kirsten, beautiful as ever and annoying as ever. She clenched her jaw, forcing herself not to flick her gaze to where Saylor had just walked off.

"So you thought you'd just show up anyway?"

"Of course." Kirsten's lips curled up as she walked closer. "We didn't exactly get to discuss details of what was happening last night."

No, they hadn't. Because Tia hadn't wanted to discuss any details with Kirsten, and she certainly hadn't wanted Kirsten to hang out with her all morning. But she kept her mouth shut about that. The last thing she wanted was another confrontation that was going to cause a major upset.

Actually, perhaps now was the perfect time for an argument. It'd put this unsettled energy into something useful.

"Kirsten," Tia started, straightening her back as she faced down the woman who had quickly become her nemesis. "I actually don't need your help today. That's why I didn't answer any of your texts or calls."

The door stage right closed with a loud click. Saylor was sure to be able to hear the entire conversation from where she stood. Tia had no idea whether she'd come out and show her face or if she'd hide away unseen.

"So, you can go home."

"Tia." Kirsten scoffed. "You can't possibly set up all by yourself."

"I'm not." Tia planted her hands on her hips. "But I don't need your help to do it either. I'd rather do it by myself. We've talked about this, Kirsten. I don't want you coming around the studio anymore when you don't have a class. I don't need you stirring up drama, either."

"Drama?" Kirsten's low and offended tone was surely a warning.

Tia chose to ignore it. She'd been gearing up for this fight for months now, and she was tired of letting Kirsten annoy her. "Yes, drama."

"I'm not the one who causes drama." Kirsten stepped closer. "That would be you. Choosing a favorite student to dote on. That's drama."

Tia snorted. Kirsten had never been her favorite student. They'd been drunk the first time they'd had sex, and after that—well, anything after that had been a mistake. Tia should have taken better care. But even now she knew that Saylor was nothing like Kirsten. She wouldn't lord it over Tia that they'd had some kind of relationship.

"Kirsten, you need to leave, and if you don't leave, I have no issue calling the police for trespassing."

Kirsten furrowed her brow. "You wouldn't."

"I would." Tia held her ground. "You're the one whose behavior is crossing boundaries. I'm tired of it. Either you quit it, or I will ban you from the studio."

Kirsten actually looked surprised by that. Did she finally believe Tia would do something? That she'd stop just threatening it and actually make a call?

"What you did last night was crossing a lot of boundaries." Tia's back ached from being so tense, but she wasn't about to show an inch of relenting. Not yet. "And it won't happen again."

Kirsten shook her head and closed her eyes. "I see where I stand. Fine. Have fun with your new pet."

Tia had a sharp retort on the tip of her tongue, but she held it in. Antagonizing Kirsten would only continue the argument when she wanted it to end. And defending Saylor wasn't her goal. It was laying down some very firm boundaries of what behavior she found acceptable and what she didn't. Instead of retorting, Tia glared. She gave Kirsten one of the hardest looks she'd ever given someone and waited for Kirsten to make her next move.

"I should shut you down, you know." Kirsten stepped closer, but she didn't get into Tia's personal space yet. "You're a shitty business owner, running your mouth and sleeping with clients. Talk about ethical issues."

"The only one I've done that with is you."

"Liar."

"Get out, Kirsten." Tia clenched her fists hard, her nails digging into her palms. "You need to leave immediately."

"Fine. I'll see you later when you've cooled off."

"No, Kirsten. I'll see you during your class and that's it." Tia ground her molars together. "No other time."

Kirsten's lips parted like she was going to say something, but her gaze flicked over Tia's shoulder quickly. "I see where your loyalties lie."

"My loyalties?" Tia's voice rose. "My loyalty is to my dance students. It's to my studio. It's to my family. It's not to you or anyone else who feels like they're entitled to my time or my friendship. If you knew me at all, you would know that."

"I *am* your student."

"You lost my loyalty a long time ago." Tia dragged in a deep breath. "I have a lot of work to get done, Kirsten. You need to leave."

Kirsten snorted, once again flicking her gaze over Tia's shoulder. "Fine. We'll talk about this later."

"No. We won't. This is the last time I'm going to be discussing this with you." Tia stood her ground while the realization dawned on Kirsten. She wasn't going to let her get away with this any longer.

Kirsten shook her head, her lower lip quivering, but she said nothing else as she turned around and walked out. Tia closed her eyes, breathing slowly and deeply. She wanted to vent and scream and burn off some of the energy from that, but she had so much to get done today. Recital days were always insane, and she only had one more hour before her first class was due.

The sound of metal clicking reached her ears. Looking over, she found Saylor standing at the edge of the right wing with the push broom in her hand. They stared at each other. Tia longed to walk over and wrap herself in Saylor's comforting embrace, in the solace she knew she would find there, but she couldn't bring herself to do it. Some kind of chasm had formed between them and made it impossible to force herself to move.

Saylor nodded at her sharply and took a step forward, sweeping the stage.

Tia had to get herself together.

Now.

Tonight had to go off without another hitch. And even if they weren't completely in sync, Saylor would help her accomplish that. Running her fingers through her hair, Tia forced the argument to the back of her mind and started the next item on her checklist. Tonight would be wonderful—at least for her girls. Tomorrow would be a new day and Tia could go from there.

twenty-three

"We really need to talk."

Saylor tensed as soon as she heard Jameson's voice. She'd been avoiding him for the last week, which was easy since he'd been out of town, but now that he was home, she couldn't. Sighing, Saylor shut the door behind her after coming home late from rehearsal. She and Steven had stayed late to practice some of their moves with Tia. It had been so light and freeing to be there.

Here she couldn't ignore her demons anymore.

"Sure. What's up?" Saylor dropped her bag by the door and moved to sit next to him on the couch, keeping some distance between them. She curled one leg under her, the sore muscles begging her to sit in another position.

Jameson winced. He rubbed his palms over his thighs and pursed his lips. "Callie called me."

"What?" Saylor cringed. She hadn't spoken to Callie much lately either. Because she knew exactly what Callie would say.

Cheater.

Ruining her life.

Horrible person.

Because this was beyond exploring sexuality. It was a relationship. At least, Saylor wanted it to be. But she hadn't ended things with Jameson. She hadn't even figured out how to explain to him that she wasn't sure if she wanted to get married anymore.

"She's worried about you, so she called me."

Why did her best friend have to get along so well with her fiancé? Wasn't that supposed to be the dream? Saylor tried to hide the panic that swelled in her chest, but she wasn't sure how effectively she did it. "Why didn't she call me?"

"She said she's tried." Jameson gave her a hard look. "And when I told her you weren't answering my texts or calls either, she got even more worried."

"I'm sorry." Saylor clasped her hands together and wrung them tightly. She had been a horrible friend lately, and fiancé. Even aside from the cheating, she wasn't giving him the attention or the effort that he deserved. It was one more reason why they shouldn't be in a relationship together. Saylor was awful at them.

"What's going on, Saylor?" Jameson reached out, pressing his hand over hers and gripping her fingers tightly.

It was meant to be comforting, Saylor knew that. Yet it was anything but. He didn't deserve this. He didn't deserve what she was doing to him. But here they were, having this conversation and her knowing exactly what she'd done.

Tia.

Twice.

Gnawing on her lip, Saylor pulled her hand from his and leaned into the side of the couch cushion. The secrets were piling up on top of the depression, and her stomach had been in such tight knots that the pain was almost unbearable. If she told Jameson what happened, he'd kick her out. He'd throw her out the front door on her ass and leave her there to rot. And he'd be right.

She'd prove to him how awful a person she was.

Hell, she'd prove to herself how bad she was.

Jameson squinted and cocked his head to the side. "What are you thinking?"

"Nothing," she murmured, twisting her hands together.

"It's not nothing, and I'm so tired of that being your standard answer. What the hell is going on?"

Saylor winced at the sharp tone. But could she really blame him for it? She'd spent every day since she moved to Seattle avoiding him, hadn't she? She should have known better from the start, that as soon as they moved in together he would see the real her and he wouldn't want her anymore.

For that matter, why would Tia be any different?

Saylor bit down too hard on her lip, the coppery tang of blood hitting her tongue along with the wash of pain. She was near tears, but she couldn't let them spill over her cheeks. Then Jameson would really know that something was wrong. She'd made so many bad decisions in the last year. She wasn't worth anything to anyone, especially not to Jameson.

"Saylor!" He said again, his voice loud this time. "Quit this cycle of yours. What's going on?"

Sucking in a sharp breath, she forced her eyes open to him. "N-nothing."

"Jesus." Jameson pushed off the couch and shoved his hands through his hair, pulling on the strands like he was trying to rip them from his scalp.

Saylor tried to melt into the couch cushions, not wanting to face the full brunt of his frustration with her. Hell, she was frustrated with herself. If only she'd made better decisions, thought things through better, then they wouldn't be in this situation. If only she could live up to expectations—

"What's going on with you? In all seriousness, Saylor, because you haven't been the woman I fell in love with since you moved here."

Saylor stopped at that.

Love.

Did he truly love her?

How could he? She wasn't worth any kind of love or devotion.

Especially after everything that happened with Tia. That thought settled onto her heart, weighing it down and pushing on her chest so hard that it was nearly impossible to breathe. She would never get out of this unscathed, and unfortunately, all the pain was her fault.

"I don't know what you want me to say," Saylor finally murmured, hoping that would turn Jameson in one direction or another, something that would give her an inkling of which direction she needed to go to try and make this right—or at least as right as she possibly could.

Jameson sighed heavily and stared down at her from where he stood in the living room. "Stop lying to yourself."

Lying to herself? Was that what she was doing?

"I'm so sorry," she whispered. She would say anything at this point to make it better, to stop causing him pain, to put their relationship right again so she had a bit of a balance when it came to where she was and what she was doing.

"Sorry for what?"

"For not being who you expected." Saylor couldn't even look at him. The anxiety spun relentlessly inside her, stealing over her heart and soul and consuming it in a fit of convulsions that only she could feel.

Jameson groaned. "I'm going for a walk."

He didn't wait another second before he walked out of the small apartment, leaving her curled up on the couch in silence.

When had silence gotten so loud?

Saylor wished she could bring herself to cry. She longed for those hot tears to spill down her cheeks, to release the pent-up tension that she couldn't even begin to form into words of explanation. Why was he with her? She wasn't good at anything except ice skating, and she couldn't even do that now.

If she closed her eyes, she could still feel Tia against her. The warmth she gave to just about everyone. Well, actually, everyone. Even when she'd been reaming Kirsten again and telling her to fuck off, Tia had been warm and kind. Saylor closed her eyes and pressed her face into the couch cushion.

What was she thinking?

Cheating on Jameson? Was she a lesbian? Had she ever really loved him or had she just used him? Saylor clenched her eyes tight, hoping that those tears would spill, but they didn't. What was wrong with her?

She couldn't even call Callie because Callie would tell her she was being an absolute idiot with the choices she was making. She'd tell her to fix everything with Jameson and make it right. And the worst part was that Callie was right.

The sky had darkened by the time Jameson came back. He shut the door and locked it behind him as he stood and stared at her. Saylor had no clue how much time had passed. She'd been so frozen on the spot that she hadn't even moved except to adjust one of her legs to be more comfortable. She swallowed a lump in her throat.

"Did the walk help?"

"No." Jameson glared at her. "You need to tell me what's going on."

"I don't know what's going on."

"Between us, Saylor." He shoved his hands into his pockets and rolled up on his toes. "What's going on between us? We haven't had sex in months."

"I...I know." A cold washed through her. "I don't know what to say."

"Say anything! Anything that's the truth."

Saylor clenched her jaw, searching for words that would be the truth but wouldn't make the situation any worse than it already was. But she couldn't find any. She'd fucked this up beyond reparation, hadn't she? "I don't know if I can do this anymore."

"Do what? Us?"

"No." *Yes,* she thought but refused to say the word out loud. "Living here. I...I'm so lonely, Jameson."

"I thought you were making friends at that dance studio."

Saylor's nipples hardened at the same time as the gut punch rolled through her. She nodded slightly. "I—I am. I mean, I was. I don't know. It's weird now."

"Why is it weird?" He sighed again, coming around to sit next to her on the couch.

"I messed up." Saylor scrunched her face up. "I think I'm going to cut back on going there. Just meet with Steven to work on our routine for the competition."

Jameson tensed, his entire body going hard as a board. "You and Steven didn't...do anything, did you?"

"What? No." Saylor pulled a face of disgust. The thought hadn't even occurred to her. Not with him, anyway. But then there was Tia—that's who she was really avoiding. Tia brought with her a slew of emotions and feelings and sensations that Saylor had never experienced before. Ones she'd never even thought were possible or dreamed of having.

"Oh. Okay. Good then."

"You're not..." Saylor wasn't sure she could finish that sentence, but she had to. "You're not doing anything with anyone else, are you?"

"No." His answer was firm and final.

But it didn't settle well in Saylor's chest. She wouldn't blame him if he was. She wasn't exactly the perfect fiancée for him—or anyone for that matter.

"I..." Saylor's throat plugged up again. Fuck, she just needed to get words out. Her brain was spinning in every direction, but she just needed to say something meaningful. "Do you remember when I said I might like women?" Her voice was so quiet she wasn't sure if he heard her, but it had taken her this long to get those words out that she didn't want to repeat them.

"Yeah, I do." His voice softened immediately. "Did you figure that out yet?" This was the Jameson she remembered, the kind and caring one. The one who wasn't stressed out to the max, the one who wasn't financially responsible for two adults. She missed this Jameson.

But finding him again gave her courage.

"I haven't done anything with Steven." Saylor bit her lip, looking him directly in the eye before dropping her gaze to the spot between them on the couch. "In fact, being with a man—you included—has been the furthest thing from my mind."

"Saylor, I have no clue what you're talking about."

Sighing, Saylor winced. "I cheated on you." The words rushed out, stinging the air. "But not with Steven."

The tension in the room skyrocketed. It was so thick and suffocating. Saylor could barely breathe as she waited for any kind of response. Would he be mad? Pissed off? Compassionate? Would he understand that this wasn't about him and all about her finding herself? Discovering who she was made to be?

"Y-you cheated?" Jameson was so tense. His shoulders looked like they were going to break from how stiffly he was sitting.

Saylor barely managed to keep looking at him. The urge to jump up and run away was so strong, but at this point, she had to see this conversation out. It was the least she could do for him. Honesty. That was what they both needed from the start, wasn't it? That lump was back in her throat. "Twice. I swear it hasn't been more than that. The first time I was just trying to figure out who I was, if I liked women, but the second time—I was lying to myself."

The tension tightened in the center of Saylor's chest. She couldn't move because it had imprisoned her on that couch. She didn't want to give him more details than he wanted, but surely he had questions. Surely he was going to start yelling at her.

A thick line formed between Jameson's brows. "What are you saying?"

"I'm saying I cheated twice with a woman. I told you before that I was trying to figure out who I was, and I don't know, Jameson. I...I don't want to say we need to break up so I can figure this out, but if that's easier—"

"Break up?" Jameson's voice squeaked. "Saylor, you moved out here to be with me. We're getting married."

"I know. I know." She wanted to cry. She wanted to bury herself in the covers and never emerge. But she had to have this conversation with him. She had to tell him what was happening as best she could. "I know I should have figured this out before. I shouldn't be in my twenties and figuring out that I might not be as straight as I thought."

"Jesus." Jameson ran his hands through his hair again. "Is this why you don't like sex with me?"

Saylor cringed. "Maybe? I don't know. Honestly."

How was he faster to pick on that than she'd been? Oh right, because she'd flat out ignored every sign that this might be a possibility until now. Until she couldn't stop thinking about Tia, about doing *things* with her. Holding back her shudder, Saylor focused on Jameson.

"Probably."

Jameson blew out a breath and all that tension, the sharp pull of what-ifs and how he would react vanished. "Who?"

"I'm not sure it's a great idea to tell you that."

"Who, Saylor?" His voice was sharp, pained.

Saylor broke again. "Tia."

Jameson blew out a breath, his eyes closing as his cheeks relaxed. His shoulders crumbled. They sat there in silence, longer than Saylor wanted to, but she had no idea what to say now. Should she offer to leave the apartment? Get a hotel room until she figured out what she was doing with her life? Should she offer to break it off so he wouldn't have to make that decision? That would be the kind thing to do, wouldn't it?

"I need you to figure it out," Jameson finally said after minutes of silence.

"Figure what out?"

"What it is you want." Jameson rubbed his lips together hard. "Because I'm not going to be in a relationship with someone who is in a relationship with someone else. That isn't who I am." Jameson kept the distance between them. Saylor could see it widening and growing already. "I'm not going to be your arm candy while you spend every night with Tia."

"I..."

"Don't talk." Jameson cut her a sharp look. "I'm not telling you to go fuck every woman you meet on the street, but seriously, take a bit to figure it out. I don't want to marry you if you don't love me. And I don't want to marry you if it's not what you want."

"I do love you." Saylor's words were weak and barely audible to her own ears. Was it that she loved him or the idea of him? Or maybe it was because she thought she should love him. She couldn't bring herself to say it again or to explain what she'd meant by the comment.

"You know, we haven't set a date and maybe this is why. But I don't want to set a date until we're on the same page about everything." Jameson's face was flat, void of any deep emotion.

Saylor supposed he was still reeling from the revelation she'd given him. "I get that," Saylor answered. "Totally understandable."

Jameson pursed his lips and glanced out the window. "And I don't want you to see her again until you do figure this out."

Saylor's cheeks burned. "I can do that."

"Make friends, do dance class, but no extra time with her. I need to trust you again if this is going to work, and it's going to take a long time for that to happen." There was an edge of jealousy in his tone that Saylor hadn't expected. She should have, but she hadn't. "That other woman, what was her name?"

"Jericho."

"Yeah, her. Go hang out with her."

Saylor nodded slightly. "Do you want me to quit dance?"

Rubbing his hand up and down the back of his neck, Jameson eventually shook his head. "No. I'm not going to tell you what to do with your life."

"Okay." But the weight in Saylor's stomach hadn't grown any

lighter. She really needed to figure this out sooner rather than later. She needed to sort her life out immediately. Making friends wasn't a priority anymore. She had to save the relationships she had. "Okay. Are you willing to trust me again? If that's where we end up?"

Jameson shrugged nonchalantly. "Right now it's a maybe. I think I need more time to figure out everything."

"Well, you could have kicked me out. Yelled and screamed. Said a lot of mean and nasty things." All those scenarios had played out in her mind more than once, and Saylor hadn't been able to stop them from spinning with the possibility that they still might happen. She was glad to have been proven wrong so far, but that didn't negate the possibility that there was still time.

"Why would I do that?" Jameson cocked his head to the side again. "I love you."

Saylor drew in a ragged breath. She wanted nothing more than to wrap her arms around his shoulders and let him hold her and comfort her. She needed that reassurance right now. She needed to know that he would still be there for her.

Giving in to that temptation, Saylor pushed up on her knees and hugged him. She breathed in his musky scent from the deodorant he wore every day. She reveled in the familiarity of it. Holding back her tears again, Saylor held him awkwardly. She had to figure this out.

Now.

twenty-four

"Thanks, Jericho." Tia glanced toward the door, hoping that she wasn't going to run face first into Saylor. That was the entire point of tonight. Getting out of the way of Saylor, avoiding whatever drama was going to happen between them.

She clenched her jaw.

She just needed a night away to clear her head.

Usually her studio was the place she ran to for that, but it had Saylor's fingerprints all over it. She couldn't be here without thinking about Saylor and what they had done—what she wanted to continue to do. Tia ran her fingers through her hair.

"It's no problem. You really should take more nights off, you know. It's good for your soul."

"Yeah." Tia didn't want to agree with her, but she had to now. It had been weeks since she hadn't found herself in this room, since she'd taken a single night to herself. Rolling her shoulders, the hair on the back of her neck stood up.

People were coming.

She always felt the disturbance.

"I'll see you tomorrow."

"See you!" Jericho waved at her.

Tia stepped into her office, pulled her wool coat over her shoulders, and buttoned it up. She'd been up to her apartment and changed into a beautiful dress and heels already. She didn't want to disappoint Fallon. That, and she wanted to feel good about herself. And nothing made her feel better than spending a bit of time making herself look nice.

But she had to get out of there before Saylor showed up.

It felt like running. It was definitely avoiding. But what else could she do? They hadn't talked since their last night together, not really. The morning had been good, but also awkward. The day had been filled with stress as they prepared for the recital, which went off without a hitch. And then? Then Saylor had disappeared and Tia had looked over her shoulder every two seconds for her.

That had been enough to drive her nuts. She needed to get a grip on herself and her life.

She had to stop sleeping with students.

Kirsten was one thing, but Saylor?

The draw to Saylor was more than Tia had ever anticipated, and she couldn't stop thinking about her. It was ruining the vibe of the studio every time she spun around on the floors. She wanted to be dancing with Saylor instead of teaching her. She wanted to be twirling circles in a tango that was only for the two of them.

Tia swallowed hard as she stepped out into the light rain.

Right. Get a grip.

That's what she had to do. She stepped under an awning while she waited for Fallon to show up in her sleek black car. It didn't take long. Moving swiftly, Tia slid into the passenger seat and shut the door. She leaned over and kissed Fallon on the cheek with a brilliant smile on her face.

"We need to do this more often," Tia said.

"You say that every time we go out together."

Laughing lightly, Tia settled into the seat while Fallon drove. It had taken some getting used to, but Fallon was always responsible and careful to a T, which meant that she was a really good driver in the city. Whereas Tia hated driving in the city and avoided it at every turn. Though teaching Fallon to drive had been a trying experience for the both of them.

"How's everything at the studio going?"

"Good. We just finished the spring recital for the kids." Tia brushed her fingers over her thighs, trying not to think of Saylor and only coming up with answers that involved her. Biting her tongue and avoiding those thoughts, she focused only on what she wanted to share. "There was a hiccup with the costumes, but I got it sorted at the last minute. The hiccup was probably for the better. The outfits were stunning."

"Hiccup?" Fallon sent Tia a sidelong glance.

"Yeah. Long story. One of my new students sews, and she was able to whip up outfits for each of the kids."

"That's amazing."

"It really was." Tia smiled to herself, remembering how her apartment had been a disaster for days while Saylor had been deep in work, sewing and cutting and making everything work. The nimble way Saylor's fingers had worked—

Nope.

That had to stop.

Immediately.

Tia sucked in a sharp breath and tried to push all of those thoughts away. She could do this. She could focus on her niece and this dinner and not make it about herself.

They arrived at the restaurant and were seated quickly. Fallon always did have good taste. Her two nieces couldn't be more opposite. Fallon preferred wining and dining, and Monti preferred to live in her van and travel the world.

Fallon played with the stem of her wine glass, running her fingers up and down it. A sure sign that she had something on her mind but wasn't sure she wanted to share yet. Tia eyed her niece carefully, debating whether or not to push her.

"There's a competition in a month that several of my students have signed up for."

"That should be nice."

Well, that confirmed it. Fallon was barely paying attention. Tia finished her first glass of wine and flagged the waiter down for a second.

"What's going on, Fallon?"

"What are you talking about?"

Oh, so they were both avoiding tonight. Tia could play this game far better than Fallon could. "You're hedging."

"I'm not."

"Try again."

"Fine." Fallon put her hands flat on the table and looked around the room. Then she leaned in, her voice quiet so that no one would be able to hear her other than Tia. "I think my boss is cheating on her husband."

Tia blinked carefully. Then she cocked her head to the side. She leaned back in her chair and shook her head. "What do you care?"

"I..." Fallon halted. Tia could see the words written on her face like she had a transcript of every thought. "Because I care about her."

"How do you care about her? As a friend? As her employee?"

"She's fragile, Tia." Fallon pouted, her full lower lip sticking out like it used to when she was six and wanted another ice cream, before everything had come crumbling down around them.

Tia hummed. "You don't have a crush on her."

"I'm not a lesbian. I don't know how many times I have to tell you that."

Tia shrugged slightly. "I wasn't saying you were. But you can have a crush on someone even if you're not interested in a relationship. You can have a crush on their work ethic, on their personality, on how they hold themselves. If you admire her, it can be considered a crush."

"Of course I admire her," Fallon mumbled. "She's brilliant."

Tia didn't take her eyes off Fallon. "I wish you would allow yourself to be loved."

"What does that mean?"

"It means I worry about you. Being loved isn't a bad thing, you know."

"I've been loved." Now Fallon was really pouting.

"Yes, you have. That's not what I said. What I said was that you need to allow yourself to be loved. You need to let someone love you and stop rejecting it."

"You love me."

Tia rolled her eyes hard. Reaching over the table, she snagged Fallon's hand and squeezed it tight. "Yes, I love you, and yes, you let me love you. But I'm your aunt. I raised you. We've been to hell and back so many times over again that you know you can trust me. Look, I know what your dad did. I was there. You were there. But that doesn't mean every single relationship you start is going to turn out like your parents. You have to learn to trust yourself to trust someone else."

Fallon's eyes watered, tears threatening to spill over the brim, but she managed to keep it in. "I think you should listen to your own words of advice."

"What the hell are you talking about?" Tia accepted the second glass of wine from the waiter and took a long sip from it.

"Tia..." Fallon pursed her lips and straightened her shoulders. "When's the last time you were in a relationship?"

"I was focused on raising you girls."

"And now we're adults."

"So?" Tia took another long gulp of her wine. This conversation was more uncomfortable than the last. It was worse than sitting in her office and waiting for Saylor to walk in and take her against the mirror.

Fuck.

"So you should be dating someone already."

"Life isn't about finding the perfect match. I don't need someone in order to be happy."

"Oh, who's avoiding their own advice now?" Fallon laughed, her gaze never leaving Tia's face.

Fallon's tone definitely put her into her place. She'd preached to the girls for decades that they shouldn't think that their parents' relationship was the model relationship or that they would fall into the same bad decisions that their mother had. For years, she had pounded it into them.

But when had she taken her own advice?

"You're right." Tia put her wine glass down and relaxed. "I was scared for years that I was just like him, you know? We grew up in the same house. So what makes me so different? Raising you and Monti? I had to make sure that I wasn't going to be him."

"You're not," Fallon whispered.

"I know. But there were times when I was close." Tia remembered every incident. The times when she lost her temper, when she was too insistent on knowing where the girls were and thought about tracking them down, when she'd clench her fist so hard that her nails would draw blood if only to control herself. She had been so close to becoming her brother, more times than not.

"You're not him," Fallon reiterated.

"Some days I can be." Had she been that with Saylor? She'd avoided talking about emotions, she'd knowingly entered into a relationship with someone who was unavailable, and she continued to do things that walked the line of decorum. Maybe she was more like her brother than she thought.

Finishing her second glass of wine, Tia closed in on herself. This wasn't the conversation she'd wanted to have. They'd gotten together to catch up and spend some family time together, and now she was feeling even worse about the situation with Saylor than she had when she'd left the studio earlier.

"I think you deserve to be happy."

"Fallon," Tia said, a warning in her tone. "I don't want to talk about it."

"Why?" Fallon froze. "Wait. Is there someone already?"

"No." Tia regretted the decision to finish her wine already. How she wanted to be able to say that there was, that she'd found someone who might be a good match for her, but they weren't together. Saylor had made that very clear from the start. But their last night together? That had felt so different. It was like Saylor had given in to the fact that perhaps they were meant to be together, meant to explore more than just a sexual relationship.

"Tia?"

Shaking her head, Tia focused back on Fallon. "I promise you'll be the first to know if something in my life changes."

"Okay." Though Fallon didn't sound very satisfied with that response. "Have you seen Monti this time around?"

Tia nodded. "We did lunch a few weeks ago."

"That's it?"

"She's a free spirit, Fallon. Stop trying to tame her."

Fallon snorted. "I just want her to respect the relationship you two have, to be thankful for what you did for us."

"Oh, she is." Tia never had any doubts about that. "But she doesn't express it like you do."

"I wish she cared more."

"She does." Tia worried her lip. She hadn't realized how hung up Fallon was on her baby sister, how much thought she put into Monti's life and what she did and didn't do. She should have. But she'd thought with growing up and becoming adults that Fallon would stop trying to mother Monti and finally let her be the amazing woman she was. Unfortunately, that didn't seem to be the case. "I think you two should start to figure out who you are now. Get to know each other again."

"She never wants to see me."

"Hmm, I don't believe that. I think you put expectations on each other that neither of you can live up to."

Fallon narrowed her eyes, clearly not happy with Tia's response. "That's ridiculous."

"Is it, though?" Tia did push now. She wanted to make Fallon think about it in a new and different way, and sometimes forcing Fallon to do it was the only way. "But enough about Monti. What are you doing when you're not at work? What new hobby have you picked up this month?"

Fallon winced. "Who says I picked up a new one?"

"I do. Because I know you that well."

Rolling her eyes, Fallon sighed heavily. "Fine. You're right."

Hours later, Fallon dropped Tia off at her building, stomach full, a light buzz from all the wine and the wonderful conversation. She missed these times together, and she longed to have the three of them in a room again. Maybe someday that would be possible. But until then, she would take what she could get.

twenty-five

Saylor's muscles were sore, but the rehearsal had been good. She'd met up with Steven at a local park instead of at the studio. Walking back into that place after her conversation with Jameson the other week wouldn't do anyone any good.

But she couldn't let Steven down.

Not after Jericho had to bail on him for the competition and Saylor was the backup plan already. If she pulled out now then she was sure no one would ever like her again. And she just needed a friend. Whether it was Steven or Jericho or anyone else. And they were the two closest that she could bet might work.

So for the last week and a half, she'd skipped the evening classes, telling Steven she'd gotten a new job and the times didn't work out right, and she'd met with him in the park on different nights so they could get their practice in on their routine.

Was it ideal?

Absolutely not.

But she couldn't bring him to the apartment. Not after her conversation with Jameson. Everything had been on edge since then. He was looking for things everywhere that she'd done wrong.

He was suspicious at every turn. And Saylor couldn't blame him. She'd been the one to break the trust they had been building.

"That was good," Steven said, slightly out of breath. His face was damp from the rain and sweat, though it had calmed down a whole lot since they'd started. Thankfully they were having a few good days, weatherwise.

"Yeah?" Saylor bent down and stretched her back out. "Think we can actually win?"

"No!" Steven laughed sharply. "But it'll be fun either way."

"Party pooper." Saylor rolled her eyes and straightened up. She did appreciate his honesty. She wasn't doing this for medals. She'd had that in her life before, and in some ways, it had sucked the joy right out of anything she had done.

But she really didn't want to go home. Not with Jameson there. Not with the way they'd left off the conversation they were no longer having. Not with the confession she'd given him still stinging in the air. But Steven had to leave. He'd given her a hard time about when they needed to be finished, and they were there.

"Thanks for practicing outside of the studio. I really appreciate it."

"Yeah, no problem." He picked up the portable speaker he'd brought and shoved it into his pocket. "Sorry your work schedule keeps you from coming to rehearsals. Tia's such a good coach, and she'd be helpful in perfecting our steps."

"Yeah." Saylor shoved her hands in her pockets. "It's going to be hard convincing my new boss for the time off to go to the competition anyway."

"I get that." Steven scratched the back of his head and grinned brightly at her. "Thursday?"

"Yup. I'll be here." Saylor shivered in the chill air but nodded at him.

"Good. See you around, Saylor."

He started walking back toward his car. Saylor, however, couldn't bring herself to go home. Jameson was there. And everything had been awful since she'd told him she and Tia had sex. Standing in the middle of the park, Saylor waffled.

What was she supposed to do?

A decision needed to be made.

And not just about whether or not she was going home.

The rain started in harder. Her hair was damp by the time she forced her legs to move toward the shops and restaurants. Had she really even taken the time to explore downtown Seattle yet? Or had she just assumed that would happen with time?

Was she really putting in an effort to make a life here?

Or just on the path toward destruction?

"Fuck." Saylor shoved her hand into her phone and called the only person she knew who could give her some help. She pressed her phone to her ear as she walked. "Hey, I know this is random and we haven't done this before, but I could really use a friend."

"Oh, absolutely! Is this a drink or a dinner kind of thing?" Jericho's ever cheerful and supportive tones washed warmth over Saylor.

Holding her breath, Saylor looked around. "Alcohol, but I'm going to need some food."

"Where are you at?"

"Um." Saylor looked around. How would she admit this?

"You know what. Ping me your location, and I'll be there in a minute. I've got the perfect place for this."

Saylor hung up and did as asked. Though she walked a bit away from the park and toward a small cafe first. She didn't want Jericho to know where she was at. Rubbing her lips together, she waited anxiously. This could either go really well or really bad. Jericho worked with Tia. She would have an insight to her that Saylor didn't, and they were friends.

Saylor didn't want to ruin that relationship too.

She should never have moved here. She wouldn't have ruined Jameson's life that way, and she definitely wouldn't have ruined

Tia's. She just kept making missteps in every direction she tried to go. Biting her lip, Saylor closed her eyes.

The car horn blared.

She jerked with a start to find Jericho staring at her with a window rolled down. "Get in, bitch!"

Grinning, Saylor jogged forward and slid into the passenger seat of the car. She missed this. Callie would have said the exact same thing if she'd been caught wallowing. Maybe it had been a good idea to call Jericho.

"Where are we going?"

"A little place just down the road from my apartment. That way, when we're toasted, we can walk back." Jericho giggled and drove.

The streets in Seattle had a steep incline in this part of the city. Saylor hadn't quite gotten used to it, but now it felt far more like the story of her time here than anything. Hard upward climbs and sharp drops when it felt like the floor was going to fall out from under her. Twisting her hands in her lap, Saylor waited for Jericho to take the lead in the conversation.

She didn't have the energy to figure out where to begin.

"We've missed you at class."

Saylor nearly groaned. That lie wasn't something she wanted to talk about. "Yeah, I got a new job, so I haven't been able to come."

Her new job? Yeah, that hadn't happened yet. But Jameson had been so wary about her being around Tia, especially alone, and Saylor couldn't blame him. She had fucked that up every which way.

"That's what Steven said."

Saylor pressed her lips together hard. They were talking about her when she wasn't there. She wasn't sure she liked how that felt. What exactly were they saying?

"Tia's worried about the competition."

"It'll be fine. Steven and I are still practicing."

"But without her."

"What? Is she some kind of control freak?" The bitterness in Saylor's words was unexpected. The look Jericho shifted her was enough to affirm that conclusion. Saylor clenched her jaw, no clue how to pull back from that one. She held her breath.

"Tia likes to make sure her students are as prepared as possible."

Saylor didn't respond to that. The bitterness was still swirling in her chest, and she hadn't figured out where it was coming from yet. "Tell me about your cruise. When do you leave?"

"Sure. We'll come back to talking about Tia." Jericho pushed her lips out and turned into a small parking lot. Turning the engine off, she faced Saylor. "Because you're not getting out of whatever is bugging you."

Of course she wouldn't. That had been why she'd called Jericho to begin with, wasn't it? "Okay."

"I leave the morning of the competition. It's why I couldn't do this one."

"A cruise sounds fun." Anything to escape the mess she'd made.

"It is." Jericho got out of the car, and Saylor struggled to keep up and follow. She wasn't ready for this. Calling Jericho had been a bad idea. She wasn't ready for a new friend, and she certainly wasn't ready to confess everything she'd been doing at Tia's apartment.

Jericho looped her arm through Saylor's. Saylor relaxed into that touch. Maybe it wouldn't be as bad as she thought it would be. They slid into a small booth in the corner and waited for the waitress to come over. After drinks were ordered, Saylor stared down at the tabletop. She so wasn't ready for these confessions to run wild.

"So why the panicked emergency call?"

Saylor sighed. Diving in it was. "It's been a rough time since moving here."

"Yeah. I get that. Moving is hard. But these last few weeks you've been...not yourself." Jericho eyed her carefully.

Saylor wished she could avoid, but hadn't that been why she'd called Jericho to begin with? So she couldn't avoid anymore. It was now or never. "You're right."

"What's going on? Do I need to beat Jameson up for you?"

Snorting, Saylor shook her head. She couldn't help the smile that graced her lips briefly. But it also felt so damn good to be able to do that. "No. I'm probably the one who needs a beating."

Jericho's face pinched. "You don't strike me as someone who would fuck up."

"Well, I did. Massively." Saylor sighed heavily. "I shouldn't have ever agreed to move here. I shouldn't have ever gotten engaged and thought we could make this work."

"What are you talking about?" Jericho's voice softened immediately. She reached across the table and stilled Saylor's hands just as their drinks were placed in front of them.

"We're having some problems, and they're all my fault."

"They can't all be your fault. And every relationship has problems."

Saylor flicked her gaze up to Jericho before taking a long drink. The alcohol slid down her throat and warmed her belly. How was she supposed to even begin to confess this? It had been hard enough to tell Jameson. Saylor set her glass down and drew in a deep breath.

"I cheated."

The words were out there.

They stung the air.

Jericho's eyes widened, her jaw dropped, and her cheeks paled. "You what?"

"I cheated on him. I mean, we had problems before that, of course, but I'm the one who pushed it and took that step. Not him."

"Saylor..." Jericho's voice broke. "I don't even know what to say."

"Neither do I." Saylor's eyes welled up, the tears stinging her eyes. Why was this so hard? It wasn't getting any easier each time she said it. It was supposed to do that, wasn't it? Instead, she was weighed down even heavier with the reality of what she'd done. She'd known that first night with Tia that it was more than just exploring herself. That was a huge part of it, but she didn't need sex to confirm that she liked women. That had just been the excuse she'd used to convince herself it was okay.

But it wasn't.

"Saylor," Jericho said again, this time softer and with pity. "What happened?"

"I don't know." Reaching up, Jericho wiped her cheeks. "I thought it was just one thing and it wasn't. It turned into something more, and I just couldn't bring myself to stop myself from being so fucking stupid."

"Hold on. Start from the beginning. Who...?"

Saylor shook her head sharply. "I'm not going to share that, okay?"

"Yeah. Sure." Concern flashed through Jericho's gaze. "So how did it start?"

"I don't know. I was trying to make friends, right? And we just kept getting closer, and then..." Saylor groaned. She had to be honest and stop trying to cover everything up. This wasn't the time to avoid anymore. "Then it became more than that."

"And you told Jameson?"

Saylor nodded. "I ruin everything, you know. Any friendship or relationship. I'm always the one that messes it up to the point where it can't be repaired."

"Well, I for one don't believe that for a second."

"You don't know me well enough." Saylor knocked back the rest of her drink and waved down the waiter for another. She was going to get drunk tonight. With Jericho she felt at least somewhat safe to be able to do that.

"Then let's change that." Jericho finished off her drink and ordered them two shots each.

Well, Saylor was going to get shit-faced then. Hopefully she'd be able to stumble home in the morning to take a long shower for recovery. As soon as the shots of tequila were delivered, Saylor held hers up and chinked glasses with Jericho.

"Bottoms up!" Jericho said.

Grinning, Saylor did as she was told. Wincing, she gasped as the alcohol burned down her throat. "God, that tastes awful."

"Well, I'm not springing for the good stuff if the goal is to get drunk."

Laughing, Saylor shook her head. "Don't blame you on that one."

They took the second shot, and Saylor relaxed. Her shoulders dropped, the tension crawling up her neck eased just a little. Enough that she felt like she had possibly found a true friend here. Or was that just the stress, emotions, and alcohol talking? Saylor picked up her drink and sipped it, still feeling the burning from the shots sloshing through her chest and belly.

"I can't remember the last time I took shots." Oh right, it had been with Tia. Saylor pursed her lips at the memory.

"Then it's been too long," Jericho answered. "So you slept with someone else, told Jameson, and now what?"

"I don't know." Saylor gnawed on her lip and stared at the tabletop. "I just don't know."

"Jameson didn't break up with you?"

"No." Tears stung Saylor's eyes. "But he probably should have. I expected him to, honestly. But he says he wants to see if we can work it out."

"Is that what you want?"

Silence stung through the air. Saylor hadn't fully considered that possibility. She was primarily just going through the motions and the fuckups that she'd already created. Her heart ached now, in a way it hadn't before. Had she really ever loved Jameson? Or had she just been caught up in the whirlwind that was their relationship?

"I don't know," Saylor whispered.

"Then I strongly suggest you figure that out first. If you don't want to be with Jameson, no amount of repair is going to keep you from repeating bad behaviors."

Saylor held still. She already knew what she wanted. And it wasn't Jameson. Something about their relationship hadn't been right since they'd gotten engaged, since she'd moved out there. It wasn't just him, either. It wasn't the travel or the fact that he was never home. It was her, and her commitment to what they were planning.

"Yeah. You're probably right."

"I know I am." Jericho giggled wildly. "Now, I think we need more shots."

twenty-six

"Steven, got a second?" Tia tried not to bite the inside of her cheek, but she had to in order to keep the worry from her voice.

"Yeah."

Tia snagged her water bottle and took a long sip while Steven walked toward her. She put it down and straightened her shoulders. She hadn't wanted to ask him, but she hadn't heard from Saylor in over a week. Hadn't seen Saylor since that night. Hadn't felt her skin—nope. Stop that.

"Any idea where Saylor is?" Tia asked as casually as possible. "She's missed a week and a half of class."

Steven frowned at her. "She didn't talk to you?"

"No?" Tia said as a question, concerned. Had Saylor moved back home? Had she broken up with Jameson and left him completely? Or, perhaps worse, was she staying with him and forgetting everything they had together?

"She got a new job. It conflicts with class time."

"Oh." Relief washed through her, a cool balm to the fiery anxiety that had taken root just under her ribs. Why couldn't Saylor have just told her that? Right. Because they weren't dating.

They weren't in a relationship. Tia was just her dance instructor and an experiment.

Nothing more.

"We've been practicing three times a week outside of class."

"Oh?" Tia raised her eyebrows at him. "So, she's still competing."

"Yeah." Steven had a shit-eating grin on his face. "She picks things up so quickly."

Tia couldn't agree more. Saylor really only needed to be shown things once or twice and then she took over, stubbornly determined to figure out how things worked. Dragging in a deep breath, Tia let it out slowly. "If you want to record it so I can watch and give some tips, we could do that."

"Good idea!" He laughed. "I'll see if Saylor has a tripod for a phone or something."

"Jericho has one. I'm sure she'd let you borrow it."

"Perfect. I'll catch you next week."

Tia nodded at him as he left. She closed up the studio for the night, sweeping the floor and locking everything up behind her. But she couldn't stop wondering.

Why hadn't Saylor told her about the job?

Because they weren't in a relationship. Still, Saylor had shared things with her before, that excitement, that hope when an interview had been set up. They were friends at the very least, weren't they? Tia couldn't let that go to waste.

Going back into her office, Tia snagged Saylor's address from her file and put it into her phone. She didn't live all that far. Dragging her wool coat around her shoulders and buttoning it up, Tia set out. They needed to talk this over. Even if she wasn't there tonight, Tia could find her tomorrow when she wasn't at work.

It took her ten minutes to walk to the apartment. As soon as she stepped into the building, a cold washed through her. Something didn't feel right, as though she was intruding on something that she didn't have permission to. Tia clenched her jaw and stopped at the bottom of the stairs, looking up at them.

What was she doing here?

This was Saylor's private sphere, and Tia had never been welcomed or even invited into it. Gnawing on her cheek again, Tia took one step forward. She needed to know for sure what was happening. Enough with the waffling and floundering. It was time to put an end to what was happening or not happening.

Taking the stairs one at a time, Tia made her way up to Saylor's floor and walked down the long hallway to find the right apartment number. She pocketed her phone. Her stomach twisted in knots, tightening with every breath she took and constricting her entire body into an impossible tension.

Her hand shook as she raised it.

Tia knocked.

The sound reverberated down the hallway and into her chest, reminding her once again why she shouldn't be here. She waited patiently for the door to open, but she didn't have the gumption to knock again. When there was no sign anyone was home, Tia turned on her toes and started back the way she'd come.

"Who are you?"

The masculine voice rolled through Tia and covered her with a cold, clammy sweat. What had she been thinking? Jameson was home. Fear followed that clammy sensation, and she almost didn't turn back around. Except there was no one else in the hallway, and it was very clear that she'd been the one to knock.

Turning on her toes, every muscle in her body preparing to run if she needed to, Tia looked Jameson straight in the eye. He was a handsome young man. She could see why Saylor would be attracted to him. He had shaving cream on his neck still from what she'd obviously interrupted, but he took care of himself. His hair was slicked back, wet from a recent shower, his eyes bright brown and curious as he stared at her.

"Did you need something?" He prompted, his tone still edging on annoyance.

Was that always how he sounded?

Tia wasn't sure she'd ever be able to handle that. Tia nodded. "Sorry, I was looking for Saylor."

"She's not here."

A second shudder ran down Tia's spine. "Oh. Um... I was just wondering if she'd finished the costumes for the kids' recital."

"And you couldn't call her?"

"She... hasn't answered." Tia clenched her fists and then forced her fingers loose. She needed to keep her cool when she was confronting him. "How's her new job going?"

"What new job?" Jameson's face pulled tight, clear confusion crossing his features.

"Steven said she had a new job. That's why she hasn't come to dance class."

"You're Tia." Jameson went white as a sheet.

Tia sucked in a sharp breath, noting every change in his features as that information sank in. She hadn't realized that she'd neatly avoided telling him her name until then. What exactly had Saylor told him? Had she told him everything? If that was the case, then Tia really shouldn't be there looking for her.

"I was worried..."

"I can't believe you'd show up here." Jameson stepped out of the doorway and toward her.

Tia backed up immediately. Jameson halted and shook his head. "I just wanted to know about the costumes. If Saylor isn't here, I'll try to call her again."

She turned around to rush down the hallway and race away, but Jameson's voice stopped her again.

"She won't answer your call."

"What?" Tia stopped and faced him again.

"She won't answer you."

Tia wanted to ask why. She wanted to pry and find out more

information, but it really wasn't her place. She couldn't make herself suddenly be in a role that she hadn't been given. And it was clear that Saylor was trying to put some distance between them. She should have just accepted that from the beginning instead of trying to track her down.

"Come inside, will you? I don't need the neighbors prying any more than they have."

Tia's lips parted in surprise. She shook her head slowly and pointed toward the door. "I'm not sure that's a good idea."

Jameson shrugged slightly as he backed into the doorway and disappeared into the apartment. He left the door wide open, as if expecting that she would follow him.

What was she supposed to do now?

Tia stepped forward tentatively. She caught sight of Jameson snagging a towel and wiping the small bits of shaving cream from his neck. He tossed it over the bar-height chair in the small kitchen. The apartment looked pristine and modern, so unlike her own. She drew in a deep breath, catching both his scent and Saylor's.

This was Saylor's home.

A place Tia had never been welcomed before.

"She told me about you."

"She did?" Tia raised an eyebrow, not shutting the door behind her as she stopped. "What did she say?"

"She likes you. A lot. I think that dance class is the one thing that's made her happy since she moved here."

"Including you?" Tia bit the inside of her cheek. She shouldn't have asked that. But she felt so backed into a corner that her defenses were coming out in droves, threatening to make a mess of the entire situation and never be able to put the cat back in the bag.

Jameson let out a wry laugh. "Yes, including me. It's no secret she's been struggling."

"No, it's not." Tia folded her hands together, trying to get herself under control. Jameson hadn't done anything to threaten her. She really needed to keep her cool. "So where is she?"

"She's out for yet another after-hours drinking session with Jericho. They've been out almost every night this week." Jameson sighed heavily and sat down on the bar stool.

The energy in the room changed instantly. Tia felt far more comfortable than before, though the discomfort was still present. She didn't feel as though she needed to run for her life. Staying in place, she looked him over again. He was exhausted. The dark circles under his eyes, the puffiness of his face. This wasn't easy for him either.

"She needs friends," Jameson muttered.

"We all need friends," Tia answered. "I'm glad she and Jericho are getting closer. Jericho is a good person."

Jameson shrugged slightly. He raised his gaze looking directly at Tia. "And what about you two?"

"What about us?" Had her voice just wavered? Those defenses were pulling tight again.

"Are you two still...friends?"

"I haven't talked with Saylor in a couple weeks. And she hasn't been to class."

"So you're really here for the costumes?"

"Y-yes..." Tia lied again. It had been the easiest excuse she could come up with as to why she was there even though the recital was done already. Maybe Saylor wouldn't have told him that.

Jameson nodded slowly. "I'll have her text you about them."

"Thank you." Tia's shoulders tightened. "I guess I should get going." Tia shifted her weight to leave the apartment.

"Is it really that hard to figure out?"

She froze. "Is what hard to figure out?"

"If you like women or not." Jameson's stare was undefinable. But it kept her locked in place. She couldn't force herself to move even if she wanted to. There was something so broken about the way he asked that question, as if his whole world was going to shatter in an instant.

"It can be," Tia answered carefully. "Some people take longer to figure it out than others."

"How long did it take you?"

The pit in her stomach opened wider, and Tia wished she could be swallowed by it. Tia sucked in a sharp breath and let it out slowly. "I knew when I was young, but I didn't tell anyone until after my brother died."

Jameson whipped his head up, eyes narrowed in confusion.

"I was young when he killed himself, barely twenty. He was... not a nice guy, to put it bluntly. My childhood was overshadowed by our parents trying to control him and their negative talk about anything that didn't fall in line with their views. My brother married young and had kids young. Two girls. And he hit a breaking point in his violence and not living up to the standards he thought others were setting for him. He killed his wife and himself, leaving the two girls alone."

"Jesus," Jameson muttered.

Tia shrugged slightly. She had shared this story so many times in so many different ways, it shouldn't be affecting her like it was. But it was. She was nearly in tears because she'd never quite connected this as the reason why she waited so long to truly live her life authentically. "I ended up with custody of my nieces. I fought hard for them. I couldn't let them grow up in the home that created my brother. So I raised them, and it wasn't until Monti was in college that I really started to step out into the world as a woman."

"But you knew before then?"

"Yes. I knew I was a lesbian when I was in middle school. But I never had a real, deep and meaningful relationship until..." Tia stopped. Because she'd never done that before. Not romantically. But she could see that happening with Saylor. She could imagine their relationship deepening to the point that she couldn't live without her.

"Until now," Jameson finished for her.

Tia refused to answer him. "Everyone works out their sexuality in their own time. Some people figure out when they're young, others older. There's so many things that can affect it, that it's impossible to know how and when a person will uncover their own sexuality."

Jameson pursed his lips and stared at her. "I've never questioned mine."

"That's a privilege not everyone has been given."

He hummed, nodded, and leaned back in his chair. "I'll let Saylor know you stopped by."

"Don't worry about it." Tia folded her hands together. "She'll figure out who she is eventually. I promise you."

Without saying another word, Tia walked out of the apartment. She didn't relax until she was outside with the cold air brushing her cheeks and filling her lungs. She should have never gone to the apartment. It was so inappropriate to do that.

And yet...

Now she knew why she'd been so compelled. Saylor was more than a quick and easy relationship. She'd known that, intuitively, but to be able to put words to it was something else entirely. Tia blew out a breath and settled herself.

What was she supposed to do now?

Saylor had lied about the job to so many people. She still wasn't living openly and willingly admitting the struggle she was going through. She had so much growing up to do still. Tia shoved her hands in her pockets and fingered her cell phone. It would be so easy to text Jericho or Saylor to check in. And she normally would. She'd normally want to make sure that all of her students were doing well mentally and physically. But this was so much more complicated than that.

Walking away from Saylor's, Tia headed for her studio.

They both needed the space to figure this out. And Tia was going to give each of them what they needed. Because who else would be able to do that?

twenty-seven

"You were out late."

Saylor froze as soon as she stepped into the apartment. Jameson was in the kitchen sipping coffee and looking her over like she was a child sneaking in after massively missing curfew.

Saylor wasn't drunk anymore.

Yet she didn't feel good.

The alcohol had taken over her system, dehydrating her and making her sick. She'd spent a lot of the night in Jericho's bathroom. She'd gotten a ride as early as she could. She just wanted to be home, in her own bed and bathroom. And she had to do exactly what she'd figured out before Jameson left for his next trip.

"I didn't think coming home so drunk I couldn't stay upright was a good idea."

"Probably right," Jameson answered. He poured her a mug of coffee, adding a touch of milk before sliding it over the countertop for her to take.

"Thank you," Saylor murmured as she took it and sipped. The drink did nothing for her stomach but did wonders for her mind. She couldn't decide which was better or worse. "I hope you weren't worried."

"I knew you were with Jericho." Jameson shrugged. "I hope it was helpful."

"It was." Saylor sucked in a sharp breath and let it out slowly. "When do you need to leave?"

"I have a couple hours."

She nodded to herself, trying to map out how this conversation should go, but she couldn't figure it out. Not with the way her head was hurting and stomach churning. She wished she could take a shower and clear her head a bit more, but she didn't feel comfortable walking into their bedroom.

Because it wasn't *their* bedroom anymore.

Since when had she decided that this was the direction their relationship was going? Since when had she answered Jericho's questions about whether or not she had wanted him to break it off with her? Saylor stared at the countertop like it was her lifeline. How was she supposed to even say those words?

"Tia stopped by last night."

"What?" Shock rang through Saylor's shoulders and down into her chest. "What did she want?"

"It seems you've been avoiding her." Jameson shrugged again and settled his mug onto the countertop. "It's comforting to know it's not just me that you do that with. Don't know why though." He muttered the last part softly before sighing heavily. "She said she'd tried to text and call and you hadn't answered."

"I haven't," Saylor said quickly, wanting to make it clear that she hadn't broken her promise to him.

"I know you haven't," he reiterated. "But you probably should."

"Excuse me?" Saylor frowned into her coffee, shook her head, and then looked up at him. "You want me to talk to her?"

Jameson groaned. "I think she can help you."

"Help me? With what?"

"Figure out what it is you want." Jameson threw his hands up in the air. "I don't know, but avoiding her isn't the way to get through this."

"I'm not... avoiding," Saylor ground out. She leaned back in the chair, wishing she felt good enough to stand up and pace, but that would be a really bad decision right now.

"Then what are you doing, Saylor?"

"I'm trying to figure this out."

"Figure what out? Us or you?"

That stopped Saylor. She stared at him with wide and curious eyes, her heart in her throat. When had they come to this? She couldn't even remember the last time they had enjoyed each other. And she'd only managed to push him further away each day. She was the one who had screwed this up, not him. And she needed to give him an out.

"No," Saylor stated firmly. "No, I figured it out."

"Did you?" Jameson raised an eyebrow.

"I can't keep doing this. I can't keep making you do this."

"Making me do what?"

"Be with me." Her voice dropped at the end of the statement. For the first time since she'd moved out there, this felt right. She wasn't going to be a burden on him any longer. She would figure out if she was still going to live in the Seattle area or if she was going to move back home to Denver. But she couldn't keep forcing them to live in the trauma of her own stupid mistakes.

"You've never *made* me be with you."

Saylor knocked her head to the side, not convinced by his opposition to her statement. "I haven't given you the time, the effort, the love, the energy, the loyalty that you deserve."

"You're right. You haven't."

That stung. Saylor winced even though she knew what she'd said was true and that his response was only upholding her mistakes of the past. She sucked in a breath, holding it in her lungs for a count of three before she continued. "I can't keep treating you like that. You deserve better."

"What're you saying, Saylor? Spell it out plainly."

"I'm saying I'm calling off our engagement. I'm saying that I'm breaking up with you." Saylor curled her fingers around the mug in front of her, burning her palms on the ceramic as it heated her skin. But she couldn't force herself to look away from his eyes.

Would he be angry?

Relieved?

Somewhere in the middle of the two?

Jameson swallowed hard, his Adam's apple bobbing up and down several times before his shoulders dropped. He wasn't going to yell. He wasn't going to scream at her. Saylor gnawed on her lip and pulled her hands away from the mug, staring at the red skin.

"I can't say I'm surprised," Jameson finally said. "Though I didn't think you would be the one to say those words first."

"Someone had to," she responded.

"Yeah, someone did."

Saylor's cheeks heated, and tears stung her eyes. She shouldn't be the one crying. She was the one doing the breaking up, the one making the hard decisions. Wasn't this supposed to make her feel better?

Why couldn't it be you?

The question died in her throat. Jameson had never made things easier for her. He always challenged her to think outside of the box she'd put herself in. It had been one of the reasons she'd liked being with him. He was so different from everyone else in her life who placated her inane whims.

"Where does that leave us?" Saylor asked. Though the words didn't quite match what she was meaning. Everything she had in Seattle relied on him. Her income, where she lived, her safety net. She had no one else here to help her. So it was either stay here and figure herself out or move home.

"What do you mean?"

"When do you want me to move out?" She finally asked, determined to have more agency in her life from here on out. She was tired of just letting life happen to her. She needed to be someone who did something, and it started now.

"I leave for a trip this morning. I can extend my visit and not come back for ten days."

"I don't want to kick you out of your own apartment." Saylor chewed on her lip.

Jameson gave her a hard look. "Right now it's still our apartment. And I'm not going to have you living on the streets. Take your time to move out. I'm gone a lot anyway."

"Are you sure?" Saylor couldn't imagine trying to stay in the apartment for longer than necessary. It would be so hard to live there, especially after everything she had done to cause the end of their relationship.

"Yes. I'm sure." Jameson poured himself a second cup of coffee. "We'll figure it out."

Saylor breathed relief. So much tension had been piled up in her chest, and immediately it released. Had that really been what was holding her back from this tough conversation? Had it held Jameson back any?

"Just do me a favor..." Jameson trailed off.

"Sure. Anything."

"Don't bring her here."

Saylor jerked her chin up in surprise. She shook her head in confusion before it dawned on her. "Tia?"

"I don't think I could handle that."

"Yeah. Sure. No problem. I don't even know if I'm going to see her again."

A tightness pulled in her chest. She knew that wasn't true, but she meant it in terms of a romantic relationship. She still had her competition with Steven next week, and Tia would be there as their coach. They would see each other at least one more time before Saylor made a final decision on her life and where she was going to live next.

"I'm pretty sure you will." Jameson walked around the kitchen counter and into the bedroom. He came back with his small suitcase and his work briefcase. "Stay as long as you need, Saylor. There's only one way to go from here."

"Which way?" She was desperate for an answer. Plotting this part of her life hadn't been in her plan for the future. She was supposed to have already done this.

"Whatever way is the best way for you." He smiled at her, setting his things by the door before standing next to her chair. "I'll be honest, I'm a bit relieved by all of this."

"Relieved?"

"Yeah. I think it'll be for the best." Jameson cupped her cheek lightly and kissed the top of her head. "I'm not mad."

"But you're hurt."

"So are you," Jameson responded.

Why was he being so cool with this? She'd expected anger and distrust, and to be kicked out on her ass. But this? Compassion? Understanding? They hadn't had that since she'd moved here, had they? Or had she just told herself that Jameson had become someone different than she knew before? Had she ignored all the signs of compassion he'd given her? Like being patient with her finding a job. Like encouraging her to go out and make friends. Like sitting down and truly listening to what she was struggling with.

Saylor pressed her lips together hard. It had all been there. She just hadn't seen it—or wanted to see it. Her anxiety made that difficult on a good day and impossible on a bad day. And she'd had a lot of bad days since moving there.

"We'll get through this," he said.

"Yeah, I think we will," Saylor answered, though she didn't believe it fully. She wanted to. She really did. But history told her that hoping for something better was pointless in her case because it would never happen.

"And I think you need to talk to Tia. I think she's worried about you."

Saylor frowned. "I don't think that's a good idea."

"She showed up here trying to find the costumes for some recital. Did you tell her you were making them?"

"Weeks ago, yeah." Saylor squinted. Tia had lied to him? What did she really want?

"Then she's probably trying to figure out where they are. If there's one thing you're not, it's flakey. You always follow through with your commitments. So if you promised her costumes, you better get sewing."

"Uh...yeah." Saylor stretched out the words, still not quite sure what to say. "Jericho did say she might have a connection to get me a job."

"Oh?" Jameson stepped back and finished his coffee. He rinsed out the cup in the sink. "Where would it be at?"

"Some call center." Last night when Jericho had suggested it, the idea hadn't sat well with Saylor. But today, in the light of being sober and newly single, it didn't sound awful. She'd probably still need a roommate to be able to afford any apartment in the city though. And the idea of living with a roommate didn't sit well with her.

"Sounds like a promising possibility."

Saylor looked Jameson over, then glanced down at her hand. The ring with the diamond glinted at her, as if mocking her. Instantly, she wanted it off and gone as quickly as possible. But she took her time. There was a finality to sliding the ring from her finger, to setting it on the counter in front of Jameson where he could take it if he wanted.

They both looked at it.

Silence rang through the kitchen, etching its way around Saylor's soul. She firmly believed that this wouldn't be the last time she had a ring on her finger. She still had hope that she would find love someday. But it just wasn't right with Jameson.

"I'm so sorry," she whispered. "I wish I'd figured myself out sooner."

"Yeah, that would have been nice."

Saylor glanced up to find him smiling at her.

"But we can't all figure ourselves out on our eighteenth birthday. Can we?"

"Guess not." She gave a wry smile.

"I'll text you to let you know that I got into Atlanta."

"Thanks." She was glad they wouldn't be forgoing those things. Whatever their relationship was now might fizzle later, but at least there wouldn't be a sudden cold cutoff of friendship. Because they had been friends before they'd dated. They had liked each other at some point. Perhaps they could simply get back to that.

"See you around, Saylor." Jameson walked around the kitchen counter and to the front door. He left the ring in plain sight in front of her.

"Have a safe trip."

And then he was gone.

Saylor found herself in the deafening silence again, except this time it wasn't oppressive or overwhelming. This time it was comforting. Picking up the ring, she took it to the bedroom and slid it into the box. She put it onto Jameson's nightstand and then stripped and headed into the shower.

It was time she started to figure out her life.

It was time she took control.

It was time.

twenty-eight

The competition hall was filled with a clutter of noise. Tia had come to expect it after all the years she'd taught and participated. It warmed her heart to see so many people clamoring together to elevate each other in dance.

Tia smoothed her hands down the sides of her dress as she stepped into the main hall. She checked her watch before looking around to see if she could find Saylor and Steven. They should be arriving soon. Tia had come down the day before to stay the night and visit with some friends, trying to clear her head from the rollercoaster she'd been on lately.

Portland had always been a nice escape, so when the chance to come down for a competition had happened, Tia had jumped at it. She would use it as a much-needed break. And with Saylor in the mix—well, it was a break for sure.

After doing three circles of the room and still not finding them, Tia's stomach twisted with worry. They only had fifteen more minutes to register before the event would close and the first dancers would start. Worrying her fingers together, Tia reached for her phone and stopped.

Should she even try to call Saylor?

Would she answer?

"Tia." Saylor's voice reached her ears, but it had such an anxious tone to it.

"Saylor." Tia breathed out her name, relief flooding her chest when her eyes landed on Saylor, dressed to the nines in a beautiful gown with her hair curled and plastered with hairspray just like Jericho must have taught her.

"Steven's not going to make it."

"What?" Tia's eyes widened, the anxiety Saylor must have been feeling settling deep into her stomach.

"There was an accident on the highway, and he's stuck behind it. I must have slid through right after it happened. They've completely shut down and even with a detour, he's not going to make it in time for registration and—"

"Saylor," Tia interrupted the rant. She took a deep breath and snagged Saylor's fingers, curling their hands together. "You can't compete without a partner."

"I know. But I don't know what to do."

The idea edged its way into the forefront of Tia's mind, but she didn't want to say it. Being that close to Saylor wouldn't do her any good. And she was there to coach, not participate. Tia looked around the room, dancers stretching and preparing for their routines. The noise of voices and music overwhelmed her now, a panic setting into her chest.

"Dance with me," Saylor whispered.

"What?" Tia spun around and faced Saylor full-on.

Saylor stepped closer, a hand on Tia's waist sliding around to the small of her back. It was an intimate move, one that spoke of a closeness they hadn't had in weeks now. Saylor's breath was hot against Tia's ear, sliding down her neck and below the line of her dress. Their chests brushed with each erratic breath, and Tia's entire body was on fire already.

"Dance with me," Saylor whispered again, this time with a

seductive quality to her tone. "You know the routine, there's no rule against two women dancing together—Steven checked."

"Saylor..." Tia trailed off. She drew in a breath and got nothing but the scent of Saylor, pure and simple. Tia closed her eyes, trying to block that scent from her body, but it was already too late. "I don't think this is a good idea."

"It's the only way I'll compete tonight."

"We don't have to do this..." Tia turned her cheek, pressing it into Saylor's, her eyes still closed as thoughts raced through her brain and sensations swept through her body.

"I think we do."

Humming, Tia held still. "Are you sure about this?"

"More than ever."

Pulling back, Tia looked Saylor in the eye, judging whether or not Saylor was telling the truth. Something had changed in Saylor's gaze, something confident bubbling to the surface in ways it hadn't before. Nodding slowly, Tia steadied herself. "All right. Let's do this."

"Are you sure?" Saylor's eyes widened with curiosity.

"No." Tia's lips curled upward. "But let's try it."

Were they even talking about the competition?

Not hesitating again, Tia tightened her grasp on Saylor's hand and pulled her toward the registration table to get into the line. They would need to run through the routine up until they were called just to make sure they didn't miss any steps and had all of the moves down.

It wasn't long until they were out in an empty hallway, spinning and dipping. Tia's heart raced as she held Saylor close to her before pushing her away just like the steps told her to. Saylor stumbled and nearly fell, but Tia caught her just in time.

"I think we should take a break," Tia murmured, holding onto Saylor's waist to make sure she didn't fall again. "Get some water. We're almost up anyway."

"Yeah. Sure." Saylor's cheeks were red when she turned away and snagged the water bottle from the floor near the wall.

"We're not going to perfect the routine in the next five minutes."

"I know," Saylor answered, that whine back in her tone. "But I think we can still be better."

Tia's stomach twisted at that thought. Was this Saylor in full competitive mode? If it was, then no wonder she'd been a force to be reckoned with on the ice. Tia cooled her throat with her own bottle of water and closed her eyes. She needed to calm her nerves and let herself focus on what needed to happen.

"Is this you trying to get out the last-minute jitters?"

Saylor's voice startled her. Tia cut her a sharp look and nodded. "Of course. Do you just barrel through them?"

"Of course." Saylor winked and grinned broadly as she stared at the door that would lead them into the competition hall.

Was this fake bravado?

Or was it full-on confidence in a way that Tia had never seen from her student before?

Either way, it was unnerving, especially coming from a woman who usually couldn't see through the fog of her anxiety. They stepped into the hall together, side by side, and ready to face whatever was going to happen next. They weren't likely to win, but they would compete and they would complete the routine one way or another.

"Next time, I want to be able to watch everyone else."

"Next time?" Tia parroted.

"Oh yes. You didn't think one competition was going to be it for me, did you?"

"I didn't think you were coming back to the studio," Tia answered honestly. She'd waited for a call or a text and had all but given up on it happening. Since Saylor and Steven had been practicing outside of the class, Tia had all but written Saylor off. She'd had to in order to protect her heart.

And this little bit of hope wasn't doing anything to help her put up those barriers.

Neither was dancing with Saylor again.

All it was doing was bringing up feelings that Tia had taken great pains to settle and push down. It would take twice as long now to get back into the same headspace she'd been in before.

"Tatiana Schroeder and Saylor McGinnis from Follow My Lead in Seattle."

"That's us," Tia whispered.

She bent to set her water bottle down next to Saylor's and then took Saylor's hand, wrapping their fingers together tightly. Tia led them onto the dance floor, playing the role necessary to get through the next four minutes and twenty-eight seconds.

She slowed her breathing.

Saylor's scent surrounded her, along with the feel of her skin against Tia's hand, the warmth of her body from the workout they'd already managed to sweat up in the hallway. Tia's muscles were going to ache by midday tomorrow in the sweet way they always did after the stress, anxiety, and wonder of a competition.

"Ready?" she murmured into Saylor's ear as she took up her position.

"Yes," Saylor whispered back.

The music reverberated through the dance hall. Tia sucked in a sharp breath and blew it out slowly as the fourth beat hit and slid her hand down Saylor's arm to grab hold of her fingers. She pulled Saylor's hand toward her face, pretending as though she was going to kiss her knuckles.

And she stopped.

There was no ring.

No diamond winking back.

No possession that she couldn't have.

Tia raised her gaze, looking directly up into Saylor's eyes. Was she single or did she just take it off for the competition?

How had she not even noticed before?

Tia stepped in close, the routine calling for them to hold onto each other and they spun gently in a circle first. She wanted desperately to ask Saylor, to get an answer, to know what the hell was going on. The flirting. The touching. The confident streak that Saylor suddenly had.

They spun in a circle slowly, then quickly. Tia locked her gaze on Saylor's, holding steady. They needed to look completely into each other, as if they were each other's worlds. That had been what was wrong during their practices. They weren't tuned in to each other, and it hadn't been Saylor's fault either.

Tia refused to break eye contact. She followed her instincts, she let Saylor lead as much as she was. They moved together, sliding their bodies across the floor as the music demanded. Tia kept her breathing even as she twirled Saylor out then tugged her back in.

Saylor's shoulder rested against Tia's chest. Tia dropped her chin, that scent overwhelming her completely now. She had so much she wanted to say, so much she wanted to ask, but she couldn't do it. Her arms around Saylor felt perfect, the way they were wrapped together, sliding against each other, moving to the beat that was solely for them even if it hadn't been at first.

They desperately needed to talk.

Tia brought her hand up to touch Saylor's cheek as the song ended. She held still, waiting for the dance to officially be over, but holding Saylor's gaze, hoping the look said more than words could for right now. She wanted her look to say so much.

Curiosity.

Compassion.

Love.

Tia's breath came in short rasps as she lowered her hands to her sides and stepped away. Saylor didn't break eye contact. Not until they had to. Tia curtsied toward the judges and took Saylor's hand immediately, dragging her out into the hallway.

She wasn't going to stay and wait for answers.

Not now.

Not ever again.

"Tia, they haven't announced the score yet."

"We didn't win," Tia mumbled as she pushed her way through the double doors and into the hallway they'd practiced in earlier.

"You don't know that."

"Yes. I do." Tia tugged Saylor's hand, trying to find someplace more private. This conversation didn't need to be broadcast throughout the dancing community.

"Tia!" Saylor's voice was sharp. She ripped her hand from Tia's and halted any forward movement. "I want to know our score."

Tia shook her head. "I'm not coming after you again."

"You won't have to."

Saylor's lips curled up in a gentle, serene smile. It suited her so well. Tia wanted to dive right into that feeling and bathe in it. But she hadn't found it in ages. And yet Saylor had. Somehow in the last few weeks, she'd managed to come into her own in a way Tia hadn't thought was possible. Definitely not that quickly.

"Do you trust me?" Saylor asked.

"Yes." Tia could answer that one. Not once had Saylor lied about her intentions, her curiosities, or what was going on in her life. She'd held back. She'd avoided. But she'd never lied.

"Then let's go see the score." Saylor took Tia's hand again, lacing their fingers together. They walked side by side back into the competition room.

The screen on the far side of the wall displayed their score. It was a good score, considering they'd never done the dance together before. But it wasn't a winning score either. Tia leaned in and pressed her lips to Saylor's cheek.

"I hope that's okay." Tia kept her voice quiet.

"More than—"

"Tia!" The voice was shrill, but Tia recognized it instantly. Abigail Benson.

"Abigail." Tia gripped hard onto Saylor's hand, refusing to let go. She knew exactly where this conversation was headed before it even happened.

"I haven't seen you compete in what, twenty years?"

Saylor's head jerked up at that.

"Just about." Tia ground out the word and tightened her grasp on Saylor. "How have you been?"

"Good. Good." Abigail dropped her gaze to Tia and Saylor's joined hands and then looked back at Tia. "You didn't do half bad for a veteran who hasn't been around."

"I've been around, just teaching instead of competing."

"Of course." Abigail locked her eyes on Saylor. "You must be Saylor."

"Yes, I am." Saylor stepped forward, holding her hand out for Abigail to take.

"Will you be doing the circuit now, Tia?" Abigail raised an eyebrow. "It'd be nice to see you competing again."

"Oh, I don't think so. This was a special occasion." Tia glanced at Saylor, making eye contact briefly before focusing on Abigail again. "Call it a happy accident."

"All right." Abigail didn't look convinced. "Oh, I've got to go. Those are my students."

Abigail flounced away just like she'd come in.

"You haven't competed in twenty years?"

"Since my brother..." Tia trailed off. She sucked in a sharp breath and bit her lip. "We have a lot we need to talk about."

"Yes, we do." Saylor brushed her shoulder against Tia's. "Where should we start?"

"How about with this?" Tia lifted Saylor's hand, her decidedly naked hand with no ring on a finger. "What about Jameson?"

"I broke it off." Saylor's cheeks hollowed and her lips thinned. "I cheated on him, and I couldn't keep hurting him while I figured myself out."

"And have you... figured yourself out?"

"I don't know." Saylor brushed her thumb steadily over the back of Tia's hand. "And for right now, I'm okay with that."

"Good."

"Who's Abigail?"

Tia groaned and rolled her eyes. "Let's just say that I've made a lot of stupid mistakes in my past and leave it at that."

"How many students have you had relationships with?" Saylor giggled.

"One. Well, two including you. Abigail wasn't my student."

"Right, just your competition."

"In more ways than one," Tia muttered. "Do we really have to stay here?"

"Fuck no." Saylor laughed. "I just wanted to see how well we did."

"Pretty damn well for a duo who hasn't really danced together." Tia pulled her lip between her teeth. The sudden rush of energy she had after the competition had calmed, but she still wanted to lean down and capture Saylor's lips. Yet Saylor hadn't given her permission for that. Saylor hadn't even said it was something she wanted.

"I think we should work on changing that, don't you?"

Tia frowned, a line forming in the center of her forehead. "Saylor…"

"Come on. Let's get out of here."

twenty-nine

"Is there someplace private you know where we can go to talk?" Saylor hadn't removed her hand from Tia's grasp, and she was holding onto Tia's fingers like her lifeline. She wanted desperately to pull Tia to her, kiss her, forget that they had to talk about anything tonight, and deal with the hard stuff later.

But that was avoiding.

And she was tired of being called out on it. She was tired of being the reason nothing moved forward in her life anymore.

"I have a hotel room." Tia stopped short in the hallway just before the outer doors. "If that's okay with you."

"It is." Saylor's stomach did a pleasant flip. This day hadn't gone as planned. Moving to Seattle hadn't either. But it was time for her to give up the plans and learn how to go with the flow a bit more. None of what had happened so far was for the worse.

"Then let's walk." Tia led the way, and Saylor followed dutifully.

Finally outside, the warmth in the air on the first spring-like day Saylor had experienced since moving up there brushed against her skin in a tender touch. She missed days like these back home, and was glad that she'd finally found one out here. It gave her hope.

"I told Jameson about us before you came over to see me."

Tia stiffened visibly. "I figured that out."

"I couldn't keep lying to him. He deserved better from me." Saylor rubbed her lips together and stared in front of them. It was so hard for her to even look at Tia. But the hand in hers never left, and that at least gave her some semblance of comfort. "I ended up breaking up with him because I needed to."

"Where are you living then?"

Saylor sighed heavily. "Still at the apartment for now. I'm working on an alternative, but it's slow moving."

Tia wasn't going to ask her to move in, was she? That was a thing lesbians did from Saylor's recollection, but she really hadn't expected Tia to move that quickly, especially when they hadn't discussed their relationship.

"I need to apologize." The words slipped from Saylor's lips suddenly.

They stopped walking and faced each other. Tia had a curious look on her face, the sun catching on her skin in a golden brush of paint. Saylor's breath caught in her throat, and she had to stop to breathe properly.

"What for?"

"Everything." The word flew between them on the air. Saylor took both of Tia's hands and brought them up to her lips, kissing Tia's knuckles gingerly. "Everything, Tia. I've been such an idiot in so many ways. I spent most of my life following the path that was set before me, and at the first deviation from it, I couldn't handle myself. I worked for decades to become the best skater out there, and when I met Jameson, I thought I'd found the out I'd been longing for."

"But you didn't," Tia filled in for her.

"I didn't. What I found was that I had no clue who I am."

"And have you figured that out now?"

Saylor snorted and shook her head. "No, not at all. But I think I'm working on it now instead of avoiding."

There was that word again.

Saylor sighed heavily and closed her eyes. She sucked in a sharp breath and took a sudden step forward into Tia's space. She pressed their cheeks together and slid her hand along Tia's side and back. The sequins and beads on her dress were rough against Saylor's fingers. Saylor turned her cheek and pressed a kiss to Tia's jawline.

"I thought you were bringing me into that hall to ravish me," Saylor murmured.

"I probably would have if you hadn't stopped me." Tia nipped Saylor's earlobe, pulling it between her teeth and flicking the edge with her tongue. "We still have so much to get to know about each other."

"Yeah, we do." Saylor pulled Tia closer, sliding one leg between Tia's as if they were preparing to dance again. "But right now, I don't want to talk."

Tia chuckled low. "I could take you back to that hallway."

"I think right here will be perfect." Moving her hand down Tia's side, Saylor found the edge of Tia's dress and slid her hand between it and Tia's skin.

"Saylor..." Her name was a prayer on Tia's lips.

"I'm done running from you." Saylor touched the edge of Tia's underwear. She fingered the line of it, rough against her fingertips, hot from Tia's skin and arousal. Would it be damp if Saylor moved her fingers over slightly? Would Tia moan loudly in her ear on the streets of Portland?

People walked by them, barely paying any attention. Saylor had an inkling of glances thrown in their direction, but she ignored them. She was tired of listening to the world around her and what they told her she should and shouldn't do. Right now, all she wanted was to bury herself between Tia's legs and forget that anything other than this stunning woman existed.

"Saylor..." Tia said again, arousal coiling around the two syllables.

Saylor found Tia's lips, pressing their mouths together passionately. Flicking her fingers, Saylor moved against Tia's pussy, the barrier of fabric dampening instantly. Tia groaned, nipping Saylor's lip as she rutted against Saylor's hand.

"We're..." Tia swallowed and tried again. "We're on the street."

"Yes, we are." Saylor said the words into the soft skin of Tia's neck as she pressed kisses in a trail downward. She hooked two fingers under the edge of Tia's underwear, brushing the backs of her knuckles against Tia's swollen lips in a slow back and forth.

Tia gasped. "Nope. Stop."

Stepping back, Tia put her hand up in front of Saylor. Her chest heaved as she caught her breath, her eyes wild with desire. Saylor wanted her even more now than before. She wanted to wrap herself around Tia's body and lose herself in the wonder that was flesh against flesh, heat against heat.

Tia said nothing as she shuffled forward just as quickly and snagged Saylor's hand, dragging her down the sidewalk. Saylor stumbled in her heels, trying to catch herself but Tia managed to help her upright first.

"I'm going to strip you down and lick you from top to bottom." Tia's voice was deep, wrapped tight with desire. "You're going to beg me to stop."

A shudder ran through Saylor, peaking her nipples and moistening her panties. Her lips parted as she tried to come up with a response, but she couldn't think of anything to say. She was stunned into silence by her own desire to have Tia do exactly that.

Saylor managed to keep her hands off Tia until they got to the hotel. But as soon as they were in the elevator, all bets were off. She pulled Tia against her, sliding hands up and down her back, her fingers tracing the lines of her fabric, the edges of it as she slipped to hot, soft skin. She couldn't get enough of Tia. She needed all of her right this instant.

The elevator dinged, and Tia again broke contact and dragged Saylor through the doors and down the hall. Tia fumbled with the small purse attached to her wrist until she found the key card to let them in. Before the door was closed, Saylor grabbed Tia by the cheeks and pulled her in for a brutal kiss.

Saylor started toward the bed, but Tia spun them around and started pushing Saylor backward.

"Shower first." Tia said through kisses.

They got to the bathroom, and Tia spun Saylor again, pressing her front into the countertop. Saylor watched in the mirror as Tia found the tiny zipper at the back of her dress and pulled it down. She jerked the fabric off Saylor's body, sliding it over her hips to pool at her feet. Saylor was about to move, but Tia put hands on her hips and held her still.

"Not yet."

This directly demanding side of Tia wasn't new, but Saylor had never seen it in this scenario before. She sucked in a sharp breath as Tia decisively moved her hand down the curve of Saylor's back and cupped her ass.

"I'm still waiting for my licking," Saylor teased, though she wasn't sure she was ready for whatever might come. A wave of pleasure washed through her at that thought. How many times would she succumb to pleasure tonight? How many times would Tia *lick her from top to bottom*? Saylor gasped.

Two of Tia's fingers were planted firmly inside her, a slow and delicate pulse in and out. Saylor closed her eyes, focusing on the sensations running through her. She was never going to run again, not from this, not from hope for what the future might hold. Saylor locked her eyes on Tia's in the mirror, watching with rapt attention as her pleasure built up one second after the other.

Tia reached around, their bodies pressing together. Saylor arched back as Tia cupped Saylor's breast and tweaked her nipple, teasing the peak. Saylor gasped and closed her eyes. She was on the brink of falling apart in Tia's arms, which was exactly where she wanted to be.

"Come for me." Tia's hot breath trickled down Saylor's neck, across her chest. "Come on, Saylor. You can do this."

Saylor clutched the edge of the counter, her fingers straining as she closed her eyes and concentrated. She was safe and whole here. She would be taken care of and loved. That last thought was her undoing. Saylor pulsed against Tia's fingers, the pull of her pleasure continuing as she rocked her hips into Tia's hand.

"Get in the shower. We need to clean off first." Tia hadn't moved her hand yet, fingers still pressed deep inside Saylor as if they were joined together forever.

"I'm not sure I can walk yet."

"Sure you can." Tia scraped her teeth along Saylor's shoulder to her back. "You just don't want to."

"I'd rather keep you inside me."

Tia chuckled. Saylor's cheeks heated with embarrassment before she closed herself off to it. There was nothing to be ashamed about. They both wanted to be here, and in Saylor's case, she desperately wanted to be in Tia's presence. As often as possible.

Tia stepped away, leaving Saylor warm and tingly. Tia pulled the tendrils of her hair up and showed her back to Saylor. "Help me with this, will you?"

Saylor's lips curled upward in a satisfied smirk. "Absolutely."

The zipper snagged only once as Saylor pulled it down. There was a trail of freckles along Tia's back that Saylor hadn't noticed before. Dipping lower, Saylor pressed a kiss to the first one, then the second. Tia's rough breathing spurred her on.

"Get in the shower, Saylor."

Stopping her forward movement, Saylor stood up and looked Tia in the eye. In silence, she pulled her heels off and dropped them onto the floor, shimmying out of her underwear and starting to pull the pins from her hair.

Tia mimed her movements, grinning the entire time as they

plopped the bobby pins onto the counter. Saylor eyed the ever-growing pile, the tendrils of hair as they brushed the tops of Tia's breasts. When she couldn't find any more pins in her hair, Saylor stepped into the small shower, immediately changing the temperature of the water and lowering it.

She was already overheated. She didn't need to add to that. She slid her fingers between her legs, cleaning the sticky wetness from her lips and avoiding her sensitive clit. She didn't want to touch herself. She wanted Tia to do it for her.

Coming into the shower, Tia grinned broadly at Saylor. "Have you ever done this before?"

"Had sex in the shower?" Saylor paled. Was Tia expecting her to know more than she did?

"Yes." Tia pushed Saylor's shoulders, moving her under the spray.

The chilled water hit Saylor's skin, cooling her instantly. Her nipples pulled tight, hardening into tight little nubs. Tia touched the back of Saylor's head, running her fingers through her long hair and pulling at the tangles as she wetted it. Saylor's skin was chilled, but her entire body was on fire. When she was thoroughly soaked, Saylor took Tia by the shoulders and switched positions.

If Saylor needed to be cleaned, then Tia deserved the same treatment. Saylor grabbed the bottle of body wash that Tia had clearly brought from home and squirted a dollop onto the palm of her hand. Without asking, she started to rub her hands all over Tia's shoulders and arms, her ribs and stomach, her back. Saylor stepped in closer, capturing Tia's lips in a gentle kiss as she cupped Tia's breast and flicked her thumb over her nipple. Tia gasped, arching back.

It was exactly what Saylor had been looking for. Keeping their lips locked, Saylor used both hands to tease Tia's nipples. The soap disappeared with the water, leaving Tia's skin shining and damp. Bending her head, Saylor captured Tia's breast with her mouth, flicking her tongue in the same way she had flicked her thumb.

Saylor couldn't wait. She wanted to be inside Tia. She wanted Tia to pulse around her fingers in the same way that she had pulsed around Tia's. Diving two fingers between Tia's legs, Saylor slid them against the rough texture inside. She pushed hard and then relaxed. Tia groaned, the noise filling the small shower and drowning out the sound of the spray.

Tia wrapped her arms around Saylor's shoulders, holding on tightly as she ground down into Saylor's hand. They weren't leaving there until they were both satisfied, until they were clean and ready to move to the next step. Saylor pressed her palm into Tia's back to hold her and bent her head. She couldn't get enough of Tia's breasts. She wanted them in her mouth at every available opportunity.

Where had that thought come from?

Saylor brushed it to the side when she scraped her teeth lightly, but she was drawn back to it. There was a reason she couldn't get Tia out of her mind, and it wasn't just sex. Whatever was between them was so much more than sex.

It was attraction.

Lust, yes.

But it was deep, romantic, tangible in ways it had never been with Jameson or any other boyfriend that she'd had in the past.

Tia grunted, her body jerking as if out of control. Saylor didn't stop. She wanted to watch Tia come apart around her, naked, unafraid, finally completely in the open together. Saylor had no more need to hide. She knew what she wanted, and Tia was right in her arms.

"Saylor..." Tia keened, digging her nails into Saylor's back as she crumbled in Saylor's arms.

Their chests heaved together as they caught their breath, Tia finally coming back to herself. She dipped her head under the water with a wickedly satisfied smirk on her lips. "Let's wash our hair and start again."

"I'll follow you... this time," Saylor added at the last minute.

Tia's eyes lighting up with mischief and pleasure was all she needed—she knew she'd done something right. For the first time in her entire life, everything felt right. She might not have a job or know where she was going to live, her life might still be in chaos with no answers in sight. But she had found herself in Tia's arms.

Saylor pressed their lips together in another kiss. "I'm all yours."

thirty

Tia's cheeks were warm.

She turned on her side, finding even more warmth than before. Sucking in a breath, she was filled with the scent of her shampoo, but there was something else underneath it. Reveling in it, smiling, blushing, Tia shifted on the bed so she could be closer to the body that warmed her soul.

She didn't want to leave this magical moment. She wanted to stay here for as long as humanly possible, exploring everything that they had yet to find in each other. Tia ran her fingers along Saylor's arm, from her shoulder to her wrist, as lightly as possible. She touched gently, not wanting to wake her up yet and just wanting Saylor's sun-kissed skin to be imprinted in her memory for the rest of her life.

Biting her lip, Tia spun that thought around. In all her years, she'd never thought she'd find something like this. All her relationships had been easy, quick, and surface level. She'd been scared to let anyone have any kind of control over her heart, scared of what she would allow to happen if that person couldn't be trusted.

But she could trust Saylor.

Even if their road had been bumpy to begin with, something

last night had changed for them. It had shifted them from being mere acquaintances and friends to being interconnected and entwined. Tia pressed a kiss to Saylor's shoulder and slipped from the covers. She walked on the balls of her feet to the bathroom, still trying to keep as quiet as possible.

The lights were harsh in here, but Tia couldn't help but grin at the mess they'd left. She'd never left her dance costumes on the floor in a damp heap like this before. She'd always taken the best care of her things. But Saylor was more important than clothing or hair pins.

Washing her face and freshening up, Tia debated what to do next. She heard nothing from the other room, so she assumed Saylor was still asleep. They'd had a late night after the competition, so she imagined Saylor would sleep half the morning away.

"Are you done yet?"

"Jesus!" Tia jumped a foot backward, her hand over her heart as she stared with wide eyes at Saylor, peeking her head in the doorway.

"I'm going to burst."

Laughing, Tia shook her head before gesturing to the bathroom. They stepped around each other, Saylor stopping for a very quick kiss before shutting the door on Tia. Laughing to herself, Tia made her way back to the bed and propped up pillows against the headboard to lean as she waited.

Saylor emerged, naked as the day she was born, auburn hair around her shoulders and a mischievous look on her lips. Her eyes glittered as she crawled onto the bed, moving on her hands and knees to Tia. She said nothing as she pressed their lips together, the mint from toothpaste biting Tia's lips and tongue as she pulled Saylor in to deepen the embrace.

Humming, Tia threaded her fingers through Saylor's hair. She ignored the tangles, her body right back to where it was the night before. She nipped Saylor's lower lip and pulled back slightly. "I'm not sure I'll ever get enough of you."

Saylor's cheeks reddened. "I feel the same."

"Good." Tia skimmed her hand down Saylor's side, tickling her skin until she reached Saylor's hip. "We still have a few hours before we need to check out."

"Did you have something in mind?" Saylor asked, her tone teasing. She fluttered her eyes shut and pressed delicate kisses to Tia's cheek, along her jawline, and down her neck.

"Many things." Tia's voice was husky, full of arousal. Bringing up one knee, she moved her foot to the other side of Saylor's hips, effectively positioning Saylor right between her thighs. She brought Saylor's mouth back to hers and put everything she had into this kiss.

Would Saylor know that this was different for her?

That Tia had never allowed someone in this deep before?

That she was one step away from falling wholly in love?

Saylor broke their kiss and moved down to Tia's chest, pushing her lips against Tia's skin, scraping her teeth, and moving the flat of her tongue along Tia's smooth skin. Tia hissed when Saylor reached her breasts one nipple at a time as she teased. They so needed to talk more about what this meant, about what the future might hold for them together. But with Saylor between her legs, warm, teasing, and in charge, Tia didn't have the heart to make it stop just to talk.

Saylor moved lower, a kiss to Tia's hip bone, her inner thigh. Tia couldn't drag her eyes away from Saylor, who seemed to have come into her own since the last time they'd seen each other. Saylor pressed her mouth against Tia, sucking on her clit and burying her face between Tia's folds. A wild sound escaped Tia's lips as she dug her heels into the mattress and pushed up into Saylor's waiting mouth.

"Yes," Tia murmured.

Her eyes fluttered shut as sensations overwhelmed her. She wasn't going to forget today. She wasn't going to forget last night either. Tia cried out, bucking her hips up against Saylor as she completely let herself go. She had nothing to hold back on anymore. Her head spun, overwhelmed with the feelings Saylor was causing but also with the realization that this was all for them. It was for no one but each other.

Tia pulled her knees up to her chest, grabbing hold of her shins and digging her nails in. It was as if the world was tilting obnoxiously to the right and she had to move to the left to keep herself from falling. Saylor's hands clamped around her sides, pressing her deeper into the soft mattress as she held on tightly.

With a rough voice, Tia tried to sound out words, to say something, anything that would help Saylor know what was going on. But she couldn't figure out how to speak. She was overwhelmed completely. Pleasure washed through her slowly at first. Tia almost missed it, except that Saylor didn't stop, so with each passing second it intensified even more, building and building until Tia couldn't deny that her body had already reached its pinnacle.

While her head still spun, Tia closed her eyes and tapped the top of Saylor's forehead with her wrist twice. She needed a break to catch her breath and find her balance again. She pressed her head into the pillow and slowed her breathing.

"You're amazing at that," Tia murmured, still keeping her eyes closed.

Saylor crawled up next to her, laying one leg over hers and wrapping an arm around Tia's waist. "Am I?"

Tia would have laughed, except she heard the uneasiness and the worry in Saylor's tone.

"Oh yes." Tia turned her cheek and pressed a kiss to Saylor's lips. "Definitely amazing at that."

"Are you okay?" Saylor asked, running her fingers gently across Tia's ribs.

"Yes." Tia smiled, kissing Saylor again. Quickly this time. She finally pried her eyes open and looked into Saylor's. "I just got dizzy there for a minute."

"Did I do something wrong?"

"No. Not at all." Tia turned on her side, capturing Saylor's hip with her leg and pulling her in closer. "I just lost myself in you."

"That's... unexpectedly romantic." Saylor traced soft patterns against the small of Tia's back.

"I can be romantic." Tia kissed Saylor's jaw and then her neck. Saylor's skin was so soft here, so warm and ready to be touched. She didn't want to leave any place untouched. Tia moved the tip of her tongue against Saylor's skin, not solely for teasing and inciting pleasure, but because she just wanted a taste. "We haven't exactly been at a place in a relationship to allow romanticism."

"Are we there now?" Saylor asked, her voice wavering a bit.

"I'd like to be." Tia pulled back so she could look directly at Saylor. She wanted to know what Saylor was thinking and feeling, and she wanted Saylor to understand how truthful she was being. "I want more than what we've had so far."

"What does *more* mean?"

Tia's lips quirked upward. "A relationship."

"I just broke up with Jameson."

"I'm not asking you to marry me." Tia moved in and kissed Saylor's nose lightly. "Not yet anyway."

"But you want to?"

"I want to find out if I want to." Tia moved her hand up, threading her fingers through Saylor's very tangled hair. They were going to take hours brushing the knots out, along with the ones in Tia's own hair. It was all worth it in the end, though. "Is that what you want?"

Saylor nodded slowly, her cheeks pink with arousal. "Yes. I want to figure out who we are together."

"Then let's do that." Tia pressed their lips together. She didn't move to deepen the kiss until Saylor tilted her chin up and parted her lips. Tia slid her tongue out, swiping it across Saylor's plump lips and tasting the lingering flavor of the mint again. "There's no need to rush into anything."

Saylor hummed and took Tia's lips again. Tia rolled on top of

Saylor, settling with their legs tangled and their lips touching. She lost herself in the kiss, unrestrained. This was the first time she could truly say that, where she could feel the difference from all the times before.

She'd never expected to find someone like this.

She'd never expected to find someone ever.

Maybe it was love or maybe it was just a serious case of like and lust completely entangled. Either way, Tia wasn't going to let it go any time soon. She wanted to explore. She wanted to settle. Pushing her knee between Saylor's legs, Tia rocked her thigh against Saylor.

Saylor gasped, her chest heaving with quick breaths. "That feels so good."

"Then don't stop." Tia angled her hips to get Saylor a better position to grind. "I know how much you like to do this."

"That's true."

Tia wrapped her arms under Saylor's shoulders, keeping a tight grasp on her. She buried her face in Saylor's neck, wanting this to be as fast and hard as Saylor wanted. Tia grabbed hold of the back of Saylor's hair, adding even more touch and pressure to what was already happening. Saylor didn't stop. She undulated against Tia, the wetness from her pussy sliding along Tia's smooth skin.

"Keep going, Saylor," Tia encouraged. She couldn't ever make herself stop doing that. Saylor had her heart in so many ways, far more than just romantic. "Don't stop until you want to."

Saylor grunted, her eyes clenching closed before flying open. She stared up at Tia, her lips parted, her cheeks red with arousal, and the biggest grin on her face possible. Tia's smile widened in response and she bent in to kiss her quickly. Words of love were on the tip of her tongue, threatening to spill and enter the room, but she held them back.

It wouldn't be fair to say those words without knowing each other better, without Saylor understanding everything that made Tia tick. Moving her head to the side to hide her face, Tia buried her lips against Saylor's neck as she rutted. She would stay right here, safe and protected in Saylor's arms while Saylor found herself.

It wasn't going to be easy.

Hell, it hadn't been so far.

But Tia wasn't going to leave Saylor to figure this out on her own, not when she felt so complete with Saylor in her arms. Saylor's movements became unpatterned, jerky, and stiff. Tia held on, holding in perfect place until Saylor finally cried out as she was washed with her orgasm.

Kissing Saylor's neck, her collar bone, the tops of her breasts, Tia cared for her as she continued to move in slow deliberate slides. Tia wasn't going to force Saylor to stop before she was ready. She was going to let Saylor get every last ounce of pleasure that she could. And then they were going to do it again and again.

They had three more hours before checkout, and Tia wanted to make sure that they were wrapped up in each other for as long as possible. She soothed Saylor's body with caresses and kisses. And finally Saylor started laughing, the giggles rumbling up from her chest and through her lips. She tossed her head back and shook it side to side.

"What?" Tia asked.

"I think we're going to need another shower."

Tia snorted. "You're definitely right."

thirty-one

"I'm a lesbian."

Saylor's voice was barely above a whisper. She sat cross-legged on the floor in the bedroom she'd once shared with Jameson. But since their last conversation, she'd slept on the couch. Still in a one-bedroom apartment, she had to come in here. All her stuff was in here.

"I *am* a lesbian."

Saylor pursed her lips. This time was louder, but it still didn't quite feel right. Never before had a word felt so odd on her tongue. This was stupid anyway. She used to give herself pep talks like this before competitions or big events, but to do it for this? Nope. This was ridiculous.

"I'm a *lesbian*."

She let out a deep, slow breath. *That* one felt right. It settled into the top of her chest, not like a weight, but like the foundation of her life was finally stable, as if it'd moved into a place where it wasn't going to shake or rattle or even crumble.

Which was the oddest sensation of all.

Saylor had found herself. And it was crazy to think that all it took was a woman, and admitting it to herself out loud, but here she was, looking at herself in a mirror, her hair loose around her shoulders, her eyes no longer giving that dead stare but a look full of life and confidence.

"I'm a *lesbian*," Saylor repeated, this time her lips curling upward into a smile.

Then a grin.

Then her cheeks heated with joy as tears raced to her eyes.

Who the hell would have thought that it'd be this simple?

Sucking in a sharp breath, Saylor reached her hands up and covered her face. No, she wouldn't do that. Pushing her hands back into her lap, she stared at herself in all her wounded mendedness and lifted the corners of her mouth again.

This is who I am, she thought.

"A lesbian."

God, who would have thought it would have been this easy. Saylor rolled her shoulders and rolled back on her butt, rocking in glee. She'd finally found herself. It *really* was that simple. Giddily, she pushed herself upward into a standing position and put her hands on her hips, surveying the bedroom.

This had never been her bedroom, and it had never been her apartment. She'd never felt like this was home, not that any home had felt like hers. But she well and truly felt that now. It wasn't a place that made her happy. It was finally accepting who she was and who she wanted to be. It wasn't because of Tia, necessarily, although having Tia and being attracted to her definitely helped in her self-discovery.

But that left her exactly where she had been two hours ago.

Packing.

Saylor snagged another box from the living room and started with the baubles she'd brought from home, the few she'd managed to find places for in the bedroom. Oh, and that candle on the kitchen counter that she'd never lit. She really should have done this before now, but she didn't have the courage until she had some place to go.

She finished with the bedroom first and the bathroom last. By the time she had all the boxes stacked in a corner and waiting for the car she'd requested, she was worn out and tired. Except she had an eventful night planned, so she needed to save her energy.

Nothing would have been possible without Jericho. And for that friendship, Saylor would be forever grateful. By the time she finished unloading the boxes into Jericho's small apartment, Saylor plopped her ass on the couch and closed her eyes. Jericho would be gone for quite a bit longer, since she was covering the evening classes so Tia could have the night off.

Which meant Saylor had to get the apartment organized enough that they could at least have a path to walk through. She dragged boxes around and stacked them where she saw fit. It would be a tight squeeze for a while, until she and Jericho could really make it their own, but this was only temporary. Saylor had to keep reminding herself that.

Just until she could get a job and find somewhere else to live, whether that was with a roommate or on her own. But one thing was for certain. She didn't want to go back to Denver. She was finally finding herself without the overtures of her family and friends, and she wanted to explore what that meant. Was she actually the figure skater they'd all told her to be?

Or was she just that because she was told she was?

Saylor had so many questions and absolutely no answers.

And for now, that was plenty.

Saylor dug through her small suitcase and found the clothes and items she wanted to bring on the adventure she'd planned that night. Despite being comfortable calling herself a lesbian, she still wasn't sold on calling whatever was happening that night a date. She wasn't quite ready for that, and Tia might not be either.

So an adventure it was.

Saylor arrived at Tia's apartment, nerves swirling in the pit of her stomach. Something had shifted in Portland, and it wasn't something she was ready to forget. *I'm a lesbian,* she repeated in her thoughts. Maybe if she kept that in mind, then she wouldn't have to worry about the rest. It would all fall into place.

Knocking four times, Saylor held her breath.

Why was she nervous?

She shouldn't be.

They'd had sex multiple times, and yet this was something so much deeper than that. Saylor bit her lip when Tia opened the door. Heat hit Saylor's cheeks, but this time it wasn't embarrassment or nerves. It was pure arousal. Tia was dressed in a windbreaker and leggings that were molded to her body. Saylor licked her lips as her gaze dropped down Tia's body salaciously.

"You said to dress for a workout. Is this good?"

"Absolutely." Saylor moved in and pressed her lips to Tia's. It would be so easy to lean in, deepen the embrace, and end up never leaving Tia's apartment. They'd done it a few times in the last week when they'd planned outings. But this time, Saylor wanted to get where they were going. "You look stunning, as always."

Tia's dark cheeks reddened slightly before she shut the door behind her and locked it. "So where are we going on this big date of ours?"

Date.

They were back to that word. Saylor might as well just admit it to herself, but at the same time, that hesitation came right back up. She couldn't do it. Taking Tia's hand, Saylor adjusted the bag on her shoulder and walked toward the stairs. She wasn't going to pass up this opportunity. It was hard enough to get Tia away from the studio for a few hours, and Tia had willingly agreed to tonight.

They needed tonight.

They had to figure out who they were together, now that Saylor was unencumbered by her engagement. Now that she was single and no longer chained to her former self. They got into the rideshare, and Saylor directed them to where they were going.

"Seriously, can't you tell me yet?"

"No, not yet," Saylor whispered to Tia, kissing just behind her ear. She really needed to figure out a way to be in Tia's presence without wanting just sex. But now that the walls were torn down, Saylor wanted nothing other than that. She wanted to be with Tia at all times and with her in all ways every moment of the day.

Tia groaned in mock frustration. She settled her head on Saylor's shoulder, snagging her hand and entwining their fingers. "I'm glad we were able to make tonight work."

"Me too. Though I have to say, I'm rather sore."

"From moving?"

"Yeah." Saylor brushed a kiss into Tia's hair. "But I did get everything over to Jericho's apartment." She didn't have the courage to even say Jameson's name around Tia. Not yet anyway. Maybe she would get there one day, but she knew what an awful mistake—well, multiple mistakes—she'd made when it came to both Jameson and Tia. She was just lucky that Tia was still even willing to talk to her at this point. She'd never imagined that Tia would actually want to have a relationship with her.

But that's where they were.

Relationship.

Tia was her girlfriend.

Or at least that was the direction that this was strongly heading. And it was the right direction, the one that Saylor wanted it to go. They arrived at the mall just as they were supposed to. Tia gave Saylor a confused expression before reaching for the handle on the door.

"The mall?"

"Let's go to the mall...today," Saylor singsonged it like Robin Scherbatsky.

Tia's brow furrowed, and she cocked her head to the side. "What?"

"Forget it. If you haven't seen the show, you won't understand."

"All right..." Tia dragged out the words as Saylor came to stand next to her, bag in hand and arm wrapped around Tia's waist.

They were here. Their date was about to begin. Saylor could admit that now. She'd wanted to surprise Tia, she'd wanted to impress her, and she'd wanted to have fun. It wasn't simply an adventure, although that was part of it—it *was* a date.

"Let's go." Saylor took Tia's hand and led the way inside.

They walked around the long hall of the mall until they found the ice rink. Saylor breathed in deeply, the scents of rubber and cold hitting her nose first. It was so familiar. She'd almost forgotten what it smelled like, or the comforting feeling that the odd scent brought her every time it reached her nose. Her shoulders instantly relaxed.

"You brought me ice skating?"

"You show me your moves every day. Why can't I show you mine?"

"You definitely can. But I hope you're not expecting much out of me." Tia raised her eyebrows, her eyes wide, and a tinge of fear settling into her gaze. "I'm not exactly known for being good at this."

"Have you done it before?"

"Once, when I was a kid."

"Then you're in for a treat. I'm a very good coach. Or so I've heard."

After they'd rented ice skates for Tia, and Saylor showed her how to properly tie them up, they moved toward the rink. There weren't a lot of people there that day, which was good. Because if Tia truly couldn't balance well, then Saylor was going to have to stay next to her the entire time.

"Just pretend you're walking."

"It's on ice." Tia gave her a doubtful expression. "I've walked on ice before, and it's not always gone well. In fact, most of the time it doesn't go well."

Saylor snorted lightly. "I've got you."

Saylor stepped backward onto the ice rink and held her hands out for Tia to take. Still dubious, Tia hesitated before grasping onto Saylor and letting Saylor drag her forward. She gasped and cried out in a laugh as they moved quickly along the rink, Saylor propelling herself backward with a saucy side-to-side.

The ice wasn't as smooth as she was used to, but this was a public rink, so she couldn't have as many standards as usual. Still when Tia looked up at her, with a grin on her face, Saylor knew she'd done well. They went around the rink twice, Saylor giving Tia small tips about pushing her foot away from her body, one after the other, to gain momentum.

Finally, Tia stopped and waved her hand out in front of her. "Show me what you got."

"What?"

"Show me. I want to be impressed, Saylor. So impress me."

Saylor's heart jumped into her throat, her nerves kicking into full gear before she quickly silenced them. Ice skating was something she could do. Even though it had been months since she'd been on the ice, she couldn't ever forget the moves. Nodding silently to Tia, Saylor pushed away from her after making sure she had a good, solid hold of the wall.

Saylor did two turns about the rink, gaining speed before she moved to the middle and flipped around so she was skating backward. Digging her toe into the ice, she lifted her body into the air and spun in a tight circle, her hands pressed against her chest before her other foot landed sturdily on the ground and she lifted her arms up to balance herself. Without waiting a beat, she moved into another spin.

She kept going and going until her muscles ached anew, in ways they hadn't hurt in ages. She was definitely out of practice, but the excitement and joy that bubbled within her from flying through the air took all of that away. At least it would for a little bit. Saylor rolled her shoulders as she eased her way back toward Tia, unable to tame the grin on her lips.

Claps erupted from around the rink, people who had stopped skating to watch her, those on the ice and off it. Saylor resisted the urge to bow as her cheeks burned with slight embarrassment but mostly exertion. When she reached Tia, she shook her head in disbelief. She couldn't believe this was becoming her life. It was exactly what she wanted it to be.

"You're amazing at that. I had no idea…"

Saylor shook her head and snagged Tia's hands, bringing her back out onto the ice. "I'm not that good."

"Quit being humble. You're fucking amazing."

Saylor bit her lip. "Well, years of practice."

"Stop it! Just take the compliment. If I'd known you were this good at skating, I never would've let you take up dance. You should be here, on the ice."

Shrugging, Saylor stopped that right where it started. "I didn't want to skate when I moved here. I wanted to figure out who I was."

"And have you?"

"Yeah, I think I have." Saylor jerked on Tia's arms, tugging her in tightly so their lips could touch. She took control of their movement, sliding them around the rink in a circle once more. Tia completely relaxed against her, giving complete control to Saylor and trusting where her skates were going to take them.

"Good, because we need to talk." Tia's voice dropped at the end.

Saylor's stomach plummeted right along with it. "Talk?"

"Yeah." Tia sighed heavily. "I think it's time we do that."

thirty-two

Tia's heart raced. She'd never sat down with someone this directly before to explain everything that had gone on in her early adulthood, but Saylor was different. This was more than a simple surface-level relationship. Taking Saylor's hand in hers calmed her significantly, but this was still going to be difficult.

Wrapping her arms around Saylor on the ice rink, Tia held on tightly. Warmth seeped from Saylor's body into her own. Tia relaxed instantly into the touch. She had seen Saylor's defenses go up instantly, coming in to protect her. Tia really should have chosen different words, but what other words were there?

"I'm not ending this," Tia whispered into Saylor's neck, followed by a sweet kiss against her skin. She hadn't realized just how much this simple physical contact would be a comfort to her. It had never done that before, not in the romantic sense. No one she'd dated or been with had been anywhere near this close to her.

"Okay," Saylor murmured back. Her arms came up around Tia's back and wrapped tightly. "So what are we talking about?"

"My brother." Tia lifted her chin, tears already welling in her eyes. She didn't want to cry. She really didn't. But she wasn't sure she was going to get through the story without it.

"Let's sit down." Saylor pulled Tia toward the little door on the side of the rink. She held Tia's arm as they stepped onto the plastic squares and Tia bumbled her way toward the bench.

Sitting down heavily, she closed her eyes. Her mind spun. Where was she even supposed to start with all of this? It wasn't just taking in her nieces. The conversation about her brother ran so much deeper than that.

"I have... had..." Tia corrected herself. "An older brother."

Why was this embarrassing?

Why was she suddenly filled with shame?

She should be over this by now, shouldn't she?

Tia wrapped her fingers around the edge of the bench and looked over at Saylor. "You're going to have to bear with me. It's been a long time since I've told this story from start to finish."

"I'm here for as long as it takes." Saylor covered Tia's hand.

Taking a risk, Tia flipped her palm up and laced their fingers together. Now, this was right. She smiled at the soft touch and relaxed. "My brother was nine years older than me, and he was an absolute terror growing up. Asshole through and through, and nothing our parents did changed it. Not that they did much proactively. Everything was done in response to the shit he pulled."

"Shit like what?"

"Drugs. Alcohol. Sex. He'd beat people up, skip class. If you think of it, he probably did it."

"And that left you where?" Saylor asked, definitely as a way to draw them back around to the point of the conversation. Tia was thankful for that. She needed the recentering. Focusing on the crap her brother pulled wouldn't get her anywhere.

"Decidedly in the background and avoiding him as much as humanly possible. He got his girlfriend pregnant when he was twenty. She was seventeen."

Saylor sucked in a sharp breath.

"Yeah, really tells you what kind of guy he was."

"That's brutal."

"Uh-huh." Tia tightened her grasp on Saylor's fingers. "They got married as soon as she turned eighteen. Fallon arrived about three months later."

"Your oldest niece?" Saylor asked for clarification.

"Yeah." Tia smiled fondly. She'd always loved Fallon, from the moment she was born. But she hadn't been around much when Fallon was a baby, fearing her brother and knowing exactly what was happening in that house and not being able to stop it. "Fallon is fiercely bossy, and loyal to a fault."

"That's an interesting combination."

"It's a winning one, if you ask me." Tia smiled again. "We can go to dinner with her sometime soon. I think you'll like her."

"Hopefully." Saylor rubbed her lips together nervously. Tia could already see the thoughts running across her head, the worry, the fear, the inability to tamp it back down. Would that anxiety ever go away? Probably not. But perhaps they could tame it a little.

"When you're ready." Tia lifted Saylor's hand to her mouth and brushed her lips across her knuckles. "Monti was born eight years later when the abuse going on in that house was at an all-time high. My sister-in-law threatened to leave, would leave, and then go crawling right back to him. I love her dearly, but God, she frustrated the hell out of me. I wish I'd been stronger to offer her support, to keep her out of that house, to protect her." Tia's voice broke on that last word.

"You can't control what other people choose." Saylor bumped her shoulder against Tia's. "And it doesn't do you much good to feel guilty over something you can't change."

"I know." Tia snorted. "But it's moments like this, I just let myself feel that." She sucked in a sharp breath, moving through the decades-old pain and letting herself calm down. "When Monti was two, my brother got really angry one night. And he took his handgun, shot my sister-in-law, and then killed himself. Fallon's the one who found them. Monti was lying in the pool of blood screaming."

Saylor reached up, brushing fingers across Tia's face, the hot tears streaming down Tia's cheeks and her nose clogging up with snot.

"I refused to let them be buried next to each other. I refused to let our parents raise Fallon and Monti. And so at twenty-one and two days, I gained custody of the girls."

"And they were yours from then on."

"Yeah." Tia looked up into Saylor's amber eyes. "Yeah, they're mine. And I just focused on them after that. So much legal crap, so much therapy for both of them—and me—and so much I wasn't ready to handle."

"I don't know them, but from what I can tell, I think you handled it well."

Tia laughed bitterly. "Eventually, I did. There wasn't a choice. I had to."

"You made your life your own. You took a crappy situation, and you made the best of it."

"I did," Tia agreed. She straightened her shoulders and looked back into Saylor's eyes. "But it meant that I gave up a lot of myself in the process."

"What do you mean?"

Tia sighed heavily. This was the part that no one understood, the part that she'd given up even trying to explain to others. So it was huge that she wanted Saylor to understand it. "I hope you know I've given up telling people this."

"Why would you do that?" Saylor's eyebrows moved together, concern etching her features.

"Because no one gets it."

"So why tell me now?"

"Because I think I'm in love with you." The words were quiet, but the meaning of them had so much weight that Tia couldn't take them back. She hated that it hadn't been that long that they'd been together, but the only thing she had been more sure of was taking the girls under her roof and fighting for custody. "I really do."

"Tia..." Saylor trailed off, her eyes downcast, her cheeks hollow.

"I get it. I really do, Saylor. It hasn't been very long, and you just broke off your engagement."

"That's not what I was going to say."

Tia closed her mouth, clenching her jaw tight so she wouldn't say anything else stupid. She couldn't let this moment fade away, not without coming to some kind of conclusion. Whether it was to wait longer, or whether Saylor's feelings weren't reciprocated.

Then again, Saylor had ended it with Jameson and—

"I love you, too," Saylor responded, her lips bowing upward. "I've known that for a while, but I just wasn't sure how to deal with it all."

Heat rushed through Tia, taking away the cold fingers of doubt that had crept along her skin and threatened to steal any of the joy that she might find in this moment. She didn't want to lose it. Smiling, Tia swiftly took Saylor's lips and pulled her in for a deep embrace. She held the back of Saylor's head, tangling her fingers in Saylor's locks and holding on tightly.

Was this even possible?

After all these years?

Saylor reciprocated, their tongues sliding against each other, chests heaving as they gasped for breath. But Tia didn't want to slow this down. She wanted to keep everything going as much as humanly possible, and for as long as possible.

The throat clearing broke them apart. Tia's cheeks burned with arousal, not embarrassment, as she pulled away from Saylor and turned to face the woman staring them down. She had an amused expression on her face, one that didn't quite say annoyance, but more entertainment? Confused, Tia kept Saylor's hand in her own.

"I assume congratulations are in order. Are you engaged?"

Tia furrowed her brow, but Saylor squeezed her hand tightly. "Uh...yeah. Sorry. We got carried away in the excitement."

"Oh yay!" The woman clapped her hands. "I took some pictures. I thought you might like them. If you give me your number, I can text them to you."

"Oh." Saylor blinked wildly and took the offered phone. She typed her number in quickly and handed it back.

Tia sat there dumbfounded the entire time. She'd never had this happen before. In fact, it was the oddest way to be interrupted making out. Being told off was one thing. But this? And neither one of them had proposed.

"Thanks so much. I really appreciate it." Saylor added sunshine to her tone, sunshine that sounded so fake Tia could smell it from a mile away.

"You're welcome! Your name is Saylor?" The woman's eyes lit up as she glanced at her phone. "It popped up since we both have iPhones."

"Uh... yeah. Saylor."

"Saylor McGinnis." The woman narrowed her eyes at her and then stuck her hand out. "Savannah Logan. It's good to meet you."

"You too..." Saylor didn't seem certain about any of this anymore.

"Well, I'll leave you two to it." She walked away with a chuckle and a wave.

Tia glanced down at Saylor's phone and saw the text messages come through with the pictures. "That was weird."

"So weird," Saylor echoed with a giggle. "But I'm kind of glad. It's good to have pictures to remember this moment by."

"Yeah." Tia moved in and kissed Saylor again quickly. "What I was trying to tell you is that since my brother, I haven't wanted to be in a relationship with anyone. I've been so afraid to fall into the same traps he set for me, to end up in a relationship that was abusive and harmful for me and the girls. I couldn't bring myself to even think about doing that."

"But they're grown."

"Yeah, well, then everything was just out of sorts. I didn't have a lot of experience with relationships, and anyone my age had tons of experience. Nothing ever really meshed well."

"How hard did you try?" Saylor raised an eyebrow at her. "Because my guess is you had your studio and your life, and that was enough for you."

"You're right. It was. I didn't try very hard. But I want to."

"You want to?"

"Yes. With you, to be very clear about where this conversation is going. I want to be with you, dating, girlfriends, in a committed relationship. That's what I want."

"Good." Saylor settled her head on Tia's shoulder. "Because that's what I want."

"Perfect." Tia settled in, calming herself down. She hadn't quite expected the conversation to go this easily, for it to end up with this much exchanged between them. They were quiet for some time, just enjoying each other. Finally, Tia shifted on the bench and took a deep breath. "We're done skating, right?"

Saylor laughed. "Didn't like it?"

"I think I'll stick to dancing."

"You do know there's dancing on ice, right?" Saylor touched Tia's chin and lifted her face to press their lips tighter. "I'm betting I can get you in on that."

"You'll have to try very, very hard." Tia kissed her back. "I would, however, love to see what moves you've got. What you did before was damn impressive."

"Are you sure?"

"Very."

Saylor kissed her again before making her way back out onto the rink. Tia walked to the edge of the wall and leaned on it. A lot of the people had cleared out, so Saylor had more free space to do exactly what she wanted. Saylor moved gently at first, probably warming up her muscles like any good athlete would do. Then she sped up, her skates scraping against the ice as she went from one end to the other, propelling herself forward and upward.

Tia held her breath as Saylor soared through the air, spinning in tight circles, landing with sure feet and legs. Saylor didn't even pause. She went around and skated again, this time doing a double something. If Saylor was going to keep this up, then Tia was going to have to learn the proper verbiage for all the moves so they could have actual conversations about what was going on.

Eventually Saylor came back over and held out her hands. Tia hesitated before she took them. She had a feeling she knew exactly where this was going.

"Join me."

"I'm really not built for this."

"No one is ever built for anything. We learn it all, and we learn it all through failure."

Tia sighed heavily. "You know, you're built for teaching."

Saylor laughed and shook her head. "Do I need to repeat what I just said?"

"Nope! No, you don't." Tia stepped around the side of the doorway and back onto the ice, nearly falling flat on her ass as if to prove her point. She grasped onto Saylor's arms, gave her a hard look. "This better be worth it."

"It'll always be worth it." Saylor kissed her quickly.

"Reward me with that, and maybe I'll stay out a bit longer."

"Good to know how to motivate you," Saylor said as she pulled Tia farther onto the ice.

"I'm not that hard to please."

Saylor's laugh filled her with hope, the hope that she'd been missing and searching for for so long.

thirty-three

The distinct beeping of the video call reached Saylor's ears, and she grinned wildly. She snagged her phone and hit the accept button, flopping onto her back on the bed. Giddiness bubbled up within her chest, and she didn't want to let it go. This had been what she'd needed to feel with Jameson, and she'd never quite gotten there.

"Do you know how hard it is to get you to answer a phone call lately?"

"I know, I'm so bad at it." Saylor brushed her fingers over her face and stared up at Callie's face. She should be better about talking to her, but she'd been so caught up in Tia and everything going on that she hadn't had time to sit down and explain it all to Callie.

"You are. What's going on? I'm worried." Callie's lips formed into a slight pout.

"You shouldn't be worried."

"Jameson said you two broke up."

Cold rushed through Saylor's body. Why was he still talking to Callie? She'd be tempted to think something else was going on, except Callie was very much in love with Brady. In fact, Saylor was supposed to fly back home in two months for their wedding. "We did."

"What happened?" Callie plopped down at her kitchen counter, propping her phone up so she could eat her dinner while they talked.

"A lot happened." Saylor sighed heavily and rubbed her hands over her face. "Why did he talk to you?"

"He was upset."

"But shouldn't he talk to his own friends?"

Callie shrugged slightly and dropped her shoulder. "I don't think he has very many. At least ones that aren't also business partners, and he doesn't want to talk to them about personal stuff."

"So instead he co-opted my best friend?" That didn't sit right with Saylor. For a man who was always telling her that she needed to get her own friends, wasn't this something like the pot calling the kettle black?

"I don't know. We didn't talk much, and he didn't share much. Just said you two had broken up and you were looking for a new place to live out there. You're not moving home?"

"I'm not. And I'm in my new place." Saylor lifted the phone up to show Callie the bedroom she was in. "I'm crashing with a friend, Jericho, for a little bit. She also helped me get an interview for a job at a call center. Hopefully, I can rent my own apartment in a few months."

"Who are you?"

"I'm still working on that." Saylor laughed a little. "But I can tell you that a big reason Jameson and I broke up is because I'm a lesbian."

Silence reverberated through the phone. Callie didn't look surprised, but she also didn't look ecstatic either. Saylor wasn't sure what she'd expected. She hadn't said those words to anyone who didn't need to hear them, and primarily herself.

"You went to Seattle and they made you a lesbian?"

"Okay. Not how it works." Saylor sat up, pressing her heels

into the bed frame to keep herself steady. "But being here and meeting some people opened my eyes to what I'd been missing for a really long time. And as much as I love Jameson and who he is, though I'm a little annoyed he's still talking to you, sexually it just wasn't there."

"And it is with someone else?" Callie raised an eyebrow.

Jameson clearly hadn't told Callie much. Perhaps that was because he'd thought Saylor would have been talking to her the entire time, that she would be in the know and he wouldn't have had to. Perhaps when he'd realized Callie had been ignorant, he'd pulled back because it wasn't his place.

"Yes." Saylor bit her lip hard.

"Oh my God! You're seeing someone else?"

It was more than just dating, but Saylor wasn't sure she was ready to disclose all of that information to Callie yet. Then again, who the hell was she kidding? She wanted to be able to talk to someone about it.

"My dance instructor."

"What!?" Callie squeaked.

"Yeah. I um... I ended up cheating on Jameson. I thought it was just exploring who I was, but it was so much more than that. And I told him, and that was the final break to our relationship. It's not that I don't love him, but I can't be who he wants me to be either." It was getting easier to explain that every time she had to say it. Then again, the *cheating* word still clogged up her throat.

"You cheat? I can't imagine that." Callie frowned.

"I did." Saylor sighed. "And I'm not proud of it, either. I hurt a lot of people in the process."

"I imagine. But you're staying out there?"

"Yeah. Tia and I are exploring what it means to be together as a couple. She hasn't dated anyone, really like ever, so it's new to both of us."

"Oh, I sense a good story there." Callie chuckled and shook her head. "I miss you so much."

"I miss you too. But I'll see you soon. I promise." Saylor glanced at the time on her phone and froze. "Oh. I need to get going."

"To dance class?"

"Kind of!" Saylor stood up and settled the phone on the nightstand. She grabbed a change of clothes and moved off into the corner to change into them. "It's improv night. Tia's been asking me to go since I started at the studio, but I've never had the courage."

"And you do now?"

"I do." Saylor popped her head back into view of the camera frame as she finished pulling her shirt down her stomach. "Because I want to do something for her."

"Like dance with her?" Callie looked skeptical.

"Yes!" Saylor answered with a light laugh. "I do. I want to make sure that she knows I'll take risks for her, and I'm more comfortable there now than I was before."

"Because you have her."

"That and more." Saylor smoothed her hands down her sides. She'd specifically chosen a tighter-than-normal outfit, because she had plans for tonight. Plans that were hopefully going to out them to everyone. At least those who were paying attention. "I'm finding myself for the first time ever, Callie. I feel like I know who I am."

"Then keep on learning, babe." Callie grinned. "I wouldn't ever want to stop that."

"Thanks. I've got to run!"

"I better get videos from tonight."

"Damn straight." Saylor laughed as she ended the call.

Racing out of the apartment, Saylor made her way to the studio. Jericho was already there—she'd promised she would be because Saylor wasn't sure she could do this without some prompting. The studio was packed with people, all of them pushed to the outside walls of the dance room. Tia stood around, her long hair in two braids down the sides of her head and down her back. The blue color she wore that day offset her coloring perfectly.

Saylor's heart raced.

Was she really doing this?

Yes. She had to now. She didn't want to hide anymore.

Saylor settled into a space on the edge of the crowd. She hadn't realized how popular these nights were. Tia caught her eye and winked in her direction, a smile playing at her lips as she garnered everyone's attention and explained how the night was going to go. It was well-practiced—Saylor could tell she'd done this explanation a million times over.

Random couples moved onto the dance floor together. Saylor watched with rapt attention, trying to figure out exactly what was happening and how she could work her plan in. Jericho would probably need to help. Dancers moved, people clapped, and the entire studio was alive with energy. This was probably one of the best sessions Saylor had ever been to. It was just flat out fun.

Snagging Jericho's arm, Saylor whispered to her, "I need your help with something."

The hour and a half of improv was almost up. Saylor had to make her move.

"Sure. What's up?"

Saylor handed her phone over. "The song is loaded. I need you to play this specific one."

Jericho frowned at the phone, reading the title of the song and then glancing up at Saylor. "Who are you dancing with?"

"You remember when I told you there was someone new?"

"The person you cheated on Jameson with?"

"Uh... yeah. That person."

"She's here?" Jericho's eyebrows disappeared into her hairline.

Saylor just gave her a grin as she backed away. "Play the damn song, Jericho."

When the song that had been playing ended, Saylor moved

quickly. She couldn't miss her chance this time. She snagged Tia's hand and pulled her toward the middle of the dance floor. Saylor didn't hesitate as she stopped, turned, and stared directly into Tia's eyes.

"What are we doing?" Tia asked, her lips in a smile that didn't reach her eyes as curiosity hit her.

"I thought this was improv night," Saylor whispered.

"Somehow, I don't think you improvised this."

Laughing, Saylor stepped in closer so no one else could hear her. "You know me too well."

The first notes of the song hit the studio. Tia looked even more confused now as the obvious club-music beat through the room, but Saylor hadn't been able to find a better song for them in the two hours she'd searched. The idea had been a last-minute one, but like Tia had said, this wasn't total improvisation on her part.

Holding out her hand, Saylor raised an eyebrow as she waited.

It was Tia's turn to act now.

Once the first lines of *I like the way you kiss me* echoed through the room, Tia's cheeks turned bright red.

"You didn't!" She accused Saylor right out.

"Oh, I did." Saylor held out her hand, waiting for Tia to take it. In seconds, Tia laughed, her blush turning into a nice rosy color. She placed her hand in Saylor's and all bets were off.

Saylor pulled Tia to her, and Tia spun, landing her ass right against Saylor's front. Saylor leaned in and murmured, "Perfect," against Tia's ear before spinning her back out. Saylor rocked her hips when the words *hits, hits, hits,* landed in perfect rhythm.

Laughing, Tia took control of her own part of the dance, moving her arms and legs to the beat before she touched Saylor's arm and walked around her in a purposeful circle. Saylor watched Tia move, the sway of her hips, the confidence in each step she took. Tia's grin blossomed into something completely different than it had ever been before.

Saylor grabbed Tia's waist and pushed her backward. They

took careful steps, one right inside the other as they moved. Tia shook her head, but let Saylor lead every part of the dance. Saylor spun Tia around, once again pressing Tia's back to her front. She bent forward, still gripping Tia's hips. Tia pushed her arms out like she was reaching for something before Saylor dragged her backward and spun her around so they were pressed chest to chest.

With a satisfied smirk on her lips, Saylor started a quick two-step in several circles on the open part of the dance floor. Tia held her hands perfectly on Saylor's shoulders as they spun and spun. Winking, Saylor stopped them as soon as they got to the chorus again. She did huge fake kisses to each side of Tia's cheeks, missing her by a mile on purpose.

Tia looked moderately annoyed that she hadn't gotten a real kiss. Saylor walked away from Tia, moving her hands out to the sides as she turned her back. She glanced in the mirror to see what Tia was doing, the moves she was making, the dance she was continuing.

Had their whole time together been some sort of dance?

Saylor snorted that idea away. She had to get her mind out of the romance and back to the reality of who they were together. Then again, maybe she wasn't so far off with that assessment. They hadn't started in hot and heavy when they'd met. It had been a slow waltz of learning who the other person was, getting to know each other, becoming friends. The intensity had built up over time.

Stopping suddenly, Saylor lost her step. When had love become such a thing in their world? It didn't feel new. It was familiar, comforting, and peaceful. Saylor turned around, crooking her finger at Tia and beckoning her to make the next move.

This was them to a T. Always taking turns on who was leading, who was pushing and who was retreating. It wasn't that unlike a dance at all. Laughing, Saylor grabbed hold of Tia's hands and moved in a circle like a child, joy erupting in her chest and overflowing between them. Tia joined in her laughter, the pure bliss exchanged between them exactly what they needed in this moment.

The song was over, and Saylor hated for this moment to fade away. But the improv class was about done, and they'd need to clean up and kick everyone out. The beat kept on going. Saylor stumbled again, and Tia caught her. Letting out a sharp breath, Saylor tried to find her feet again, just as the last, *I like the way you kiss me* reverberated through the room.

Tia moved both her hands to the back of Saylor's neck and tugged her in, their mouths melding together. Saylor froze, her entire body stilled. Tia kept their lips together, mouths moving against each other as their chests heaved for air and Saylor's body came alive. She parted her lips and deepened the kiss.

Screw it.

People were there, and they would see.

She didn't care.

She just wanted Tia to know how much she loved her.

So much that she was willing to do this improv class.

So much that she'd picked a damn song for them.

So much that she'd willingly make out in front of fifty people.

A laugh bubbled in Saylor's chest, the giggles pushing out just as Tia pulled back and grinned broadly at her. When Saylor looked around, the entire room was cheering and whistling, clapping their hands. Jericho's jaw was dropped to the floor, but her look screamed excitement.

Were they all this happy for them?

Was it both of them or just Tia?

No, it had to be both of them.

No one had been this happy about Saylor and Jameson getting engaged, and Saylor's subsequent move here. No one had cheered them on. In fact, most had tried to convince her to stay. But this room was filled with people who would support them, no matter what. That's what family and friends looked like.

Tia wrapped an arm around Saylor's waist and tugged her in

slightly. Saylor was so out of breath, from the dance, from the kiss, from the rush of emotions. What was she supposed to do now?

"Thank you for coming out, everyone!"

Was that supposed to mean something else?

"We'll see you next week for the improv class!"

But no one really wanted to leave. They surrounded Saylor and Tia, congratulating them, asking for the full story. The amount of people was beyond overwhelming. But all Saylor had to do was reach for Tia and she was there, hands interlocked, and a comforting smile on her lips. This was who Saylor wanted to be —loved.

thirty-four

"Finally," Tia mumbled to herself, pushing the main lobby door closed and turning the lock. She pocketed the key and faced the studio. Saylor was in there, sweeping as usual. She hadn't expected tonight. Never in a million years.
    Saylor had been bold.
    Confident.
    So sure of what she wanted.
    And it was damn sexy.
    Tia had never wanted someone as much as she did right now. This was so much more than just sex, too. This was love. Taking her time, Tia walked slowly from the lobby into the studio. She made eye contact with Saylor and watched in silence as Saylor moved back and forth across the floor with the push broom.
    Tia wouldn't let her clean up much longer. She wanted as much time as possible with her tonight. Saylor paused as she set the push broom back in the small janitorial closet. She eyed Tia up and down, hands on her hips, a curious look gracing her features. "Why are you looking at me like that?"
    "Like what?" Tia asked innocently. She knew exactly what look she was giving.

She wanted to ravish Saylor.

Right here on the dance floor.

"Like you want to eat me alive." Saylor let out a chuckle, an undertone of nerves in it.

Tia shook her head. "I would love to do just that. The door's locked." She pointed over her shoulder toward the lobby.

"There are giant windows." Saylor pointed to the far wall, the one with two windows on it. They were anything but giant, but Tia got the hint.

"Tinted glass. No one can see in. But if you'd rather go upstairs..." Tia trailed that thought off. She was afraid if she stepped any closer to Saylor that she wouldn't give either one of them an option. She wanted Saylor that much in this moment. Tia wanted to hold her, dance with her, strip her down and never let her walk away again.

"What are you thinking now?" Saylor asked, stepping closer. Her hips moved saucily from one side to the other.

Did Saylor know what she was doing? Did she understand the amount of desperate arousal that coiled through Tia's body, ready to strike as soon as Saylor was close enough? "Do you really want to know?"

"Yes." Saylor's lips curled upward, and she was back to the confident woman from before.

"I have stared at you for hours in that mirror." Tia nodded her head toward the large, mirrored wall. "And I'm nowhere near done watching you move in it, writhe in it..." Her voice was filled with a breathy quality she hadn't expected. But Tia wasn't about to correct it either. "Tonight was electric."

"Electric?" Saylor took another step closer.

Tia could either back up now and save them both from what might happen in this room, or she could stay put and let Saylor make the decision on her own. "You outed yourself to an entire room tonight. You outed *us*."

"I did." Saylor pulled her lower lip between her teeth as her gaze roved all over Tia. "Was that wrong?"

"Fuck no." Tia laughed. "It was hot."

Saylor's lips quirked up. "If I can't be myself here, then where can I be?"

Tia took Saylor's hands in her own, staring at them. If she looked up into Saylor's eyes, she was worried how this would turn out. "I love you."

"And I love you." Saylor lifted her fingers to raise Tia's gaze. "And if you want to ravish me here, I'm all for it."

"What?" Tia's eyes widened.

"I want to be loved, Tia."

Tia's heart hammered, her chest tightening as she looked deep into Saylor's eyes. She could never get enough of this woman. Pulling Saylor closer, a hand at the back of Saylor's neck, Tia pressed their mouths together. Her eyes fluttered shut as she arched her back, tightening her grasp on Saylor's hand. This was perfect. This was wonderful. Even with their own oddities and their tumultuous pasts, they were able to come together and find each other.

Tia didn't ever want to let that go.

Saylor put her free hand on Tia's hip, turning her to the side. Then she walked. Tia stumbled at first, but their lips stayed touching as she got into the rhythm of moving backward until her shoulders hit the wall behind her. Saylor had her hands up and under Tia's shirt in an instant, cupping her breasts and rolling her thumb over Tia's nipples.

"Saylor, if you don't want..." Tia gasped when Saylor pinched her nipple. Laughing, she continued, "If you don't want to continue this here, then we need to go upstairs."

"Not a chance," Saylor murmured, pressing kisses down Tia's neck and to her shoulder.

"Then in that case..." Tia planted her foot on the outside of Saylor's. She used her hips to flip them, pushing Saylor hard against the mirror. She'd have to clean this in the morning, but it would be so worth it.

Tia slid her tongue against Saylor's, trailing her hands up and down Saylor's chest and hips. She teased, but she didn't push much further than that. She wanted to turn Saylor around. She wanted Saylor in front of her. Groaning in frustration, Tia stepped back. She took a sharp breath, clenching and unclenching her fingers several times before raising an eyebrow in Saylor's direction.

"Turn around. Hands on the wall."

"Okay?" Saylor's cheeks were flushed, that gentle pink solely from arousal and anticipation of more. Saylor did as she was told, turning her head to look at Tia over her shoulder.

With a quick breath, Tia stepped in closer. She started by brushing her palm over Saylor's ass, memorizing the curve as much as she could. She found the edge of Saylor's tight shirt and touched her fingers to the hot skin underneath.

"Fuck, you're amazing," Tia murmured. "How long did you take to pick out that song?"

"Too long," Saylor whispered back.

Tia pushed her hand up the front of Saylor's shirt and under her sports bra. "And what made you decide to wear this outfit tonight?"

"You," Saylor answered, pushing her butt into Tia's front as Tia teased her nipple.

"Seriously?"

"Yeah. I wanted you to be unable to avoid thinking about me."

Chuckling at the audacity, Tia agreed. "Well, it worked. So did that song. We should go clubbing more often."

"Is that going to include sex on the dance floor?" Tia moved her other hand down, under the edge of Saylor's leggings and underwear. She didn't hesitate as she immediately moved her fingers between Saylor's legs, finding her hot, wet, and swollen. "Because that night on the street..." Tia purposely pushed one finger in up until her first knuckle.

Saylor's fingers turned white against the mirror as she pushed hard into it. Her eyes fluttered shut, and Tia let her for now. This was about them. This was about finding each other in the most unexpected of ways, and then sticking it out through the rollercoaster in between.

Tia wetted her thumb from Saylor's juices and then spun a slow circle on her clit. Saylor grunted, pushing back into Tia again. Using her other hand, Tia cupped Saylor's breast, rolling her nipple in the opposite direction but with the same pace as she made circles on Saylor's clit.

"I think you like pushing the limits of decorum. I think you like being able to loudly say that we're together, without holding back," Tia confidently said.

"Of course I do." Saylor's voice was tight, as if she was working hard to control herself in the moment.

Tia added a second finger, deepening her hug around Saylor. Her own body was on fire, her underwear already damp, and her pussy tingling and begging for any kind of touch. But she could wait until they made their way upstairs.

"So why mention the windows?"

Saylor groaned. She moved her hips, rolling them into Tia's hand. Tia continued with the slow pattern she had created, stretching the tight circle cocooning her fingers. She pressed the pads of her fingers deep inside Saylor, as deep as she could make them go from this angle, and then released. Saylor breathed out before sucking in a rapid breath of air as Tia did it again.

"Because I would think that you rather like people watching." Tia added a kiss to Saylor's bare shoulder at the end. "Maybe I should strip you down completely naked so everyone can see you."

A flood of wet reached Tia's fingers. She scraped her teeth against Saylor's shoulder and down her back. Adding in a third finger, Tia pumped hard. Saylor's voice echoed through the studio, reverberating off the walls and coming back to reach their ears.

"I'd love..." Saylor had to catch her breath. "I'd love to grind on you until I come at a club."

Tia grinned broadly. "I thought so."

"Tia," Saylor started but stopped, as if she couldn't finish the thought or sentence.

"Just come," Tia ordered.

The moan that left Saylor's lips went straight between Tia's legs. She wished she could touch herself right now, relieve some of that pressure, but her priority was Saylor. They wouldn't be leaving each other's presence until the morning. Tia continued to pump her fingers, albeit much slower, as Saylor rutted against her and dragged out her orgasm for as long as she wanted.

Tia held her, touched her, kissed her. Saylor reached down and grabbed Tia's forearm, pulling her hand away.

"Too much."

Complying, Tia stepped back slightly to give Saylor more room to breathe and come back to herself. Saylor twisted around, putting her shoulders against the mirror and eyeing Tia with a hooded look and a satisfied smile on her lips. "Upstairs. Now."

"Yes, ma'am." Tia laughed.

She sashayed as she made her way to the office to grab her keys. Saylor stayed where she was until Tia reached the lobby again, her hand on the light switches. This was what she'd wanted, Saylor unhinged and both of them focused on nothing except each other for a few hours. Tia held her breath as Saylor stalked toward her.

Tia hit the lights and made sure the front door was shut and locked behind them. Saylor grabbed Tia's hand and moved swiftly up the stairs to Tia's apartment two floors up. Tia fumbled with the keys but finally managed to get the door open. She dragged Saylor inside and slammed the door shut behind them.

"Get this off." Tia pulled at Saylor's shirt, moving it up her body.

Saylor laughed as she helped pull it over her head, immediately moving in to steal a kiss. "Only if you take yours off."

"Well, that's the idea." Tia pushed Saylor backward toward the bedroom, pressing kisses to her lips and her neck and her chest as she went. She stopped when she kissed Saylor's hardened nipple, unable to resist the temptation to pull Saylor's nipple between her lips and twirl her tongue around it.

Saylor groaned, her fingers tangled in Tia's hair as she continued their movement toward the bedroom. Spinning them around, Saylor pushed Tia on the bed and immediately grabbed at her leggings, tugging them off and down to Tia's knees.

Tia tried to push her shoes off, but Saylor kept getting in the way and preventing it from happening. Tia leaned back slightly, waiting for the right moment, when Saylor pushed Tia's knees apart and planted her face right against Tia's pussy. Crying out, Tia arched her back and tilted her face toward the ceiling.

She hadn't expected that.

Saylor didn't hesitate. She immediately sucked on Tia's clit and slid two fingers inside her. Tia gripped onto the sheets on her messy bed and tried to hold herself upright, but it was impossible. She fell back onto the mattress and parted her legs as much as she could with her ankles still caught in her leggings.

She was so close to coming already. The entire situation that night had worked her up and kept her going. Tia scraped her dull nails across Saylor's scalp before brushing Saylor's hair to the side so she could see her face. She wanted nothing more than to watch Saylor make her fall apart.

Tia cried out and bucked her hips up as the final pull of her orgasm hit. She wasn't going to be able to let it go. She was going to careen over the edge of the cliff blissfully, and Saylor would catch her as soon as she fell.

Sure enough, Tia jerked with a start, her body reacting to every touch and lick from Saylor. She tightened, holding herself together as best as she could as Saylor continued to tease and pull pleasure from her. Tia didn't wait. She moved Saylor off her and shook her head as she caught her breath.

"Finish taking your clothes off."

"Okay." Saylor didn't hesitate as she stripped down, sitting on the edge of the mattress as she pulled her shoes off.

Tia took a couple extra seconds before she followed suit. She backed up on the bed and rested her head on the pillow as she waited for Saylor to come over to her. Tia's lips quirked up when Saylor canted her head to the side in curiosity.

"Turn around and straddle my face. We're doing this at the same time."

"The same...time?" Saylor seemed to gulp.

"Oh yeah."

Tia waited as Saylor got in position. She didn't hold back. She wanted to taste Saylor on her tongue. She wanted to make her burst with pleasure again and again. She never wanted nights like this to end. She wanted to stay wrapped in Saylor's arms for as long as possible.

Saylor settled on top of Tia, pressing gentle kisses to Tia's inner thighs before she planted a kiss right on top of Tia's swollen clit. Wriggling under Saylor's weight, Tia hyped herself up for when Saylor was finally going to start and not stop again. She wanted to be so spent by morning that she would regret everything about that night when she had to get up and go to work.

Then again, maybe Saylor would go with her.

Tia wrapped her arms around Saylor's hips and pulled her down so she sat more firmly against Tia's mouth and face. As she waited for Saylor to start, Tia gave everything she had. She wanted Saylor to come first. She wanted Saylor to fall apart on top of her, making Tia wet and satisfied to be able to bring Saylor to the pinnacle of orgasm again and again.

Focusing all her attention on Saylor, Tia did exactly that. She licked, she tasted, she focused. She moved as Saylor started to lose control. She kept as much touch against Saylor's body as possible until Saylor crashed again. Tia expected Saylor to move off her, to lie flat on her back on the bed next to her, but she didn't. She went right back to where she had left off. Tia held onto Saylor's legs as she concentrated on her own body and exactly where she was feeling pleasure. She chased it until it reached her clit, until every slip of Saylor's tongue and pull of her lips added to it.

Tia wiggled even more, waiting for the orgasm to wash through her, to pleasantly cover her entirely in its caress. She didn't want to let this go. And she wouldn't. She would work hard to keep Saylor with her, she would do her best to make this work between them. Because they'd been through so much already, and they deserved it.

"Saylor!" Tia cried out as her orgasm hit her hard and swift.

Saylor let up almost instantly, finally falling to the side. Tia lay on her back, staring up at the ceiling as she tried to catch her breath and come back to her body.

"I fucking love you," Tia said on a laugh. "So much."

Saylor chuckled. "That good, huh?"

"Amazing."

thirty-five

Saylor's phone buzzed in her pocket just as she stepped in the first doors of the studio's building. She'd already talked to Callie before she'd left, so it couldn't be Callie, and it wouldn't be Tia because that was where she was headed. Frowning, Saylor wiggled her phone from her back pocket and stared at the number across the screen.

It was a local number.

But it was also one she didn't recognize.

But the phone did say *Maybe: Savannah Logan*.

Saylor hesitated as she decided whether or not to answer. It could easily be a spam call, but something niggled in the pit of her belly and the back of her mind, telling her to see who was calling.

"Uh...hello?" Saylor's voice echoed in the hallway. She winced at how loud it was. Instead of walking in the studio doors, Saylor made her way to the stairs and started up toward Tia's apartment.

"Hi. My name is Savannah Logan. I met you and your lovely fiancée at the ice rink a few weeks back."

"Oh." Saylor paused in her ascent to Tia's apartment. Why was the weird picture woman calling her? Saylor tensed. Maybe it had been a really bad idea to answer. Was she tracking Saylor's phone? Was she stalking her?

"Sorry to call so abruptly, but when we met the other week, I thought I recognized your name but then I thought I was just going crazy."

"My name?" Saylor tried to pull herself back to the moment. This woman was confusing her. The entire phone call was confusing her.

"Yes, and then by the time I remembered and looked it up, you were already back on the rink, and I didn't want to spoil anything else on your engagement night."

When was Saylor supposed to tell her that they hadn't gotten engaged? That, in fact, they'd only been on their first date? She shuddered and walked up the next flight of stairs to Tia's apartment, pulling out the key Tia had given her and sliding it into the lock.

"Anyway," Savannah continued to ramble as Saylor stayed silent. "I work for Elite Skate."

Saylor froze. *Elite Skate?* They trained some of the best coaches out there, the ones who would work with champions. Saylor had never done that kind of coaching before, although she'd never been opposed to it either. But why would they be calling her? Surely it wasn't because they wanted to match her with a coach. She was done with the competitive world. She was too old for it now.

"I made a few calls after I met you, and checked you out."

"I'm sorry." Saylor sat heavily on Tia's couch. "You're going to have to start at the beginning."

Savannah chuckled. "I know I'm throwing a lot of random information at you. I'm sorry. Stop me if you need me to start again or answer something I missed." Savannah sounded chipper but confident. Truly happy to be in this position. "I contacted a few of your old coaches and a couple of the rinks that you used to work with in Denver. I hadn't realized you'd moved to Seattle, otherwise I probably would have contacted you sooner."

"Contacted me sooner?" Saylor glanced at the clock on the wall. The time ticked over to the start of the dance class. Tia would be worried about where she was because she hadn't shown up yet, but there wasn't anything Saylor could do about that now.

"Yes. We're looking for a few new coaches in the upcoming years as we anticipate some growth in our company. So I'd like to offer you a job coaching, and then training you for elite coaching."

Saylor was speechless. No matter how many times she tried to form words, she couldn't. She just sat on Tia's couch, her jaw dropped to the floor, with no clue what to say.

"Like I said, I talked with your coaches and a couple of the rinks you've worked with in the past, and I think you'd be a good fit for Elite."

"You already checked my references?" The disbelief in her tone was evident. Saylor hadn't thought she'd go back into figure skating of any kind after moving out here. She'd figured that part of her life had run its course and it was time for her to grow up and get a real job. Wasn't that what Jameson and her parents had always told her?

But to coach Olympians? Because that's what Savannah was talking about. At least the possibility to do that in the future if she could prove herself. She'd at least be training the young kids who might be headed in that direction. And it was a job.

Fuck.

A job.

Saylor bit her lip. She should jump at the opportunity no matter what, shouldn't she? Because she'd been searching for a job for months and had gotten nowhere. With no experience in anything other than skating and coaching, it had been insanely hard to find anyone who was willing to hire her for anything.

"I did." Savannah chuckled lightly. "I hope you don't mind, but I have contacts all over. It was easier to call them and talk with them than you might think."

"Oh, yeah, I get it." Saylor rubbed her palms against her thighs, removing the sweat that had instantly appeared. "Do you pay during training?"

"Yes, and we expect you to have your own private clients during that time as well. We'll work with you to find some, and it'll take a bit to build up your list, but we'll get you there. We don't leave you to hang out to dry."

"I'm sorry. This is all so unexpected."

"I know." Savannah sounded sad for a minute, but then she switched back to her professional voice. "How about I send you an email with the information packet, you can look it over, and then we can schedule another phone call to hash out some more of the details. The packet is our new-hire packet, so you'll be getting all the information that everyone else does when they accept."

"Okay." Saylor's eyebrows raised into her hairline. "But I'll be honest, aside from the other week, I haven't skated in months. I'm out of shape and out of practice."

Savannah clucked her tongue. "I'm not convinced of that. But we can try it out when we meet up again."

So they were meeting in person now? Saylor swallowed the lump in her throat. Savannah seemed pushy at best, and that wasn't going to work well with Saylor's temperament if she couldn't find some way to make her voice heard through the noise.

"Oh, and whenever you and your lovely fiancée set a date, you can let us know and we'll give you as much time off as you want for the wedding and honeymoon."

Saylor's stomach clenched hard. That little lie was now coming back to bite her in the ass hard. "That's an amazing offer. You should know..." Saylor sucked in a sharp breath. She couldn't let this lie continue. "...Tia and I aren't engaged. In fact, that was our first official date that night, though we did really appreciate the pictures."

"Oh." Savannah's voice dropped off instantly. "Really?"

"Yes."

"You two just seemed like you'd been together a while."

"No, no we haven't." Saylor nervously ran her hand through her hair before dropping it to her side and clenching and unclenching her fist. "But I'm glad to know that if we ever do end up engaged that taking time off for a wedding won't be an issue."

"Right. It won't." Savannah sounded as if she was thrown off her game.

Saylor hated that. She winced and glanced at the clock again. How had twenty minutes nearly passed already? Tia was bound to be worried for sure. Then again, maybe she wasn't. Tia didn't suffer from anxiety like Saylor did.

"Let me know what other questions you have. This is my cell phone number, so feel free to text or call it if you want to talk more before making a decision. The email will have the compensation package listed in it, and that of course doesn't include any private lessons you teach while working for us. That'll be all yours, and we'll help set you up with clients and rinks."

"This is a lot of information." Saylor sighed heavily. "I'll have to think about it, but my inclination is to agree. I've heard of Elite before, but I never thought—" Saylor stopped herself. *Confident.* She needed to act way more confident than she was. "I never thought the opportunity would present itself."

Much better than saying she didn't think she was good enough to work for them.

Saylor continued, "I'll look over the material that you'll be sending and get back to you in the next few days with questions and most likely a decision."

"Excellent." Savannah sounded all kinds of pleased now. "I look forward to our call and meeting you again, properly this time."

"Yes. For sure." Saylor swallowed the lump in her throat. She couldn't believe this was happening. "Talk to you soon."

When she settled her phone onto the coffee table, Saylor

winced. She couldn't have sounded more like an idiot on that call. Now that she was off the phone, everything she knew about Elite Skate was coming back to her brain. She'd be able to form functional sentences now if Savannah called back. Or rather, she probably wouldn't be able to. But it would be her nerves talking, not because she was struck silent by them. She'd still sound like an idiot, of course.

But a job!

And not only a job that would pay the bills—hopefully. She hadn't actually seen any numbers yet—but a job doing something she loved. Saylor blew out a breath, her lips curling upward into a big grin. Was she being serious right now? Was this actually happening?

She wanted nothing more than to run downstairs and tell Tia, but she couldn't do that. Interrupting class would be awful. Instead, Saylor sent Tia a text message telling her that she was upstairs and would talk to her when classes were done for the night. Because there was no way she could go to class now and focus on anything.

She was too ramped up.

As if on cue, a text message came in from Savannah asking for her email address. Within twenty minutes, Saylor had the email pulled up and was reading through every line of the information that Savannah had sent by squinting at the small screen on her phone.

This was a dream.

Absolute dream come true.

She'd be working weird hours while she was in her own classes and teaching at the same time, but the example schedules didn't seem unreasonable. This was entirely possible. She could actually do this. She could still be in figure skating even if she wasn't competing anymore. No one had ever thought that was a possibility. Her parents had told her for years to focus on schoolwork so she could get a real job when she'd ruined her body, and well, here she was. Ready to be a professional coach, with an actual salary.

Saylor sent off a reply to Savannah asking to meet with her in person. She would prepare for that meeting like it was her SAT exam. And she would nail it, even if she did basically already have an offer on the table. She needed to prove that she could be professional too.

She set up for dinner, pulling out some of the food Tia had in the fridge and starting cooking. It wasn't much longer before Tia stepped through the doorway, her skin glowing with a sheen of sweat and her hair loose around her shoulders and down her back.

"Hey?" Tia asked, curiously. "I didn't anticipate you'd cook me dinner when I gave you the key."

"I umm... needed to keep my hands busy." Saylor bit her lip, looking Tia over and trying to resist the urge to jump her in her own excitement. She had to tell Tia what happened first.

"I can think of much better ways to do that. The bottom of that list includes showing up for class."

Saylor snorted. "Yes, ma'am. I'll remember that next time."

Tia smiled fully as she dropped her keys on the counter and moved closer to Saylor, wrapping her arms around Saylor's back and pulling her in for a kiss. "You better have a really good excuse for missing class today."

"I promise you, it's a good excuse, and it involves way more than just cooking dinner."

Saylor moved in and pressed their mouths together. She pulled away and then rethought that move and slid back in. She wanted to deepen the kiss. They hadn't seen each other in two days, and she needed that comfort with Tia, the familiarity and ease that always came with her. Saylor slid her tongue along Tia's lip, asking for more, and Tia permitted.

The kiss was slow, long, deep, and everything Saylor wanted it to be. When she finally ended it with a smile on her lips, Saylor turned back to the stove. "Do you remember the weird lady at the ice rink? The one who took pictures of us?"

"The one who assumed we were engaged?" Tia snagged a piece of sautéed carrot and slid it between her lips.

"Yeah, that one."

"She was an odd duck."

"I think her purpose for taking pictures was twofold."

"Oh, don't tell me she's a creep."

"No, she's not. At least... no, she's not," Saylor corrected. She turned the heat off on the stove and started to plate up food for them both to sit down and eat. "She called me right when I was coming in for class."

"Called you?" Tia looked skeptical. "I thought you said she wasn't creepy."

"She works for Elite Skate." At Tia's blank stare, Saylor explained. "It's a company that trains coaches for figure skating. They were originally based in Chicago, but they have a branch in Seattle and in Texas."

"They train coaches?"

"Yeah." Saylor sat at the table and waited for Tia to join her. "She offered me a job."

"A job coaching?"

"Yes, while they train me to be an Elite coach, someone who coaches people who compete professionally."

"Like you used to do?" Tia stabbed another carrot with her fork.

"Yeah, like I used to, and beyond what I used to do."

Tia's fork dropped. Saylor jerked with a start and looked up into Tia's wide eyes. "That's amazing."

"Really?"

"Why wouldn't it be?"

"Because I'd be traveling a lot." That's what had bothered her. And it wasn't until this moment that Saylor had been able to put into words exactly what about the entire situation was irking her.

"I'd have to go all over the world for competitions, and I wouldn't be here as much."

"I also travel for competitions, Saylor." Tia rolled her eyes. "Not all over the world, but I do travel for them."

Saylor sucked in a sharp breath. It was clear that she was going to have to make it obvious for Tia to understand what the issue was. "Yeah, but I'd be putting us in the same situation I just left."

Tia narrowed her eyes, looking at Saylor directly. "We're not you and Jameson."

"I know that." And she did, but it was still ridiculously hard not to compare some days to the only serious relationship that Saylor had known. "But I also want to make sure that it doesn't become that."

"Then we'll work to make sure that doesn't happen."

"Are you sure?"

"Yes." Tia reached for Saylor's hand and squeezed. "You need to do this."

"I really do."

Tia laughed lightly. "I guess that means no reprise competition for you and me, then."

"Oh, you never know. I might find time for that." Saylor lifted Tia's hand and kissed her knuckles. "Dancing with you is sexy as hell."

Tia let out a light moan, as if she was thinking of the same thing Saylor was. Not the dance so much as the night after the dance. The very long night when Saylor had to convince herself to stop touching and inciting pleasure.

"Keep that up and this dinner is going to get cold."

"You do have a microwave," Saylor murmured.

Tia's lips parted in surprise, but then she shook her head. "Sustenance first. Then I need a quick shower. Then you're mine. All night."

"Yes, ma'am."

"You're going to need the energy, so eat up." Tia pointed at Saylor's still untouched plate. "Because I'm going to ravish you."

Laughing, Saylor shook her head. Whatever had she done to find someone like Tia? She was so glad she'd taken the risk that first night, taken the chance that perhaps she could trust her instincts. Perhaps she could find love.

epilogue

About a year later...

The lights were dim in the club. This wasn't like any club Tia had brought Saylor to before. This one was meant for ballroom dancing, not modern hip-hop or improv, and definitely not for grinding orgasms either. Tia's heart was in her throat. She wasn't prepared for this. The dance was nothing, that wasn't what she was worried about. It was what was going to happen by the time the music faded.

"I've got everything you need," Jericho said quietly, winking in Tia's direction.

"Thanks," Tia answered, not giving any more information than what was already said. She didn't need Saylor catching on.

"I hope this video goes viral. Do you know what it could do for the school if it did?"

"Make my life a living hell." Tia gave her a fake grin before she laughed. "Seriously, it would be a good thing, but that's not the point of tonight, is it?"

"No. No, it's not." Jericho winked again.

Jesus. If she kept that up, then Saylor was definitely going to know something was going on. Tia couldn't have that happening. She needed this to go as planned because Saylor's anxiety would shoot through the roof if it didn't. It might already be awful with everything that was going on.

"You're going to record it, right?"

"All of it, for sentimental purposes and for viral purposes and for improvement purposes."

"Always the smart-ass." Tia chuckled as she walked toward Saylor who was finishing up her stretches. "Are you ready for the dry run?"

"I don't think anything is ever *dry* between us."

Tia snorted a laugh. "This is why I love you."

"I love you too." Saylor smiled and leaned in for a kiss. "But yes, I'm ready."

"We're next."

They waited together as the song ended and the couple that was dancing ahead of them finished and bowed. They had already been waiting there for an hour, and with each passing minute, Tia got more and more nervous. It was ridiculous. She shouldn't be. But she'd never done this before.

Taking a sharp breath, Tia took Saylor's hand and led her out onto the dance floor. A year together, and Tia had never been more sure about a relationship before. Jericho nodded to her from the corner, phone in front of her face as the music picked up. Tia made eye contact with Saylor and nodded sharply.

Tia was sure.

Saylor was sure.

They were in this together.

Saylor's lips curled upward, that beautiful smile Tia hadn't been able to get out of her mind since the first time she saw it. She wanted to make Saylor smile every time they were together, and in between. She'd turned into an all-out romantic since they'd met.

The music started, and Tia didn't have any more time. She steadied her breathing and held her hands in the perfect position.

EPILOGUE

She and Saylor had practiced this dance for the last six months, preparing it for a competition next week, but Tia had told Saylor she wanted to test it out first. Smiling at Saylor, Tia spun her in the first circle.

The music dipped low, and Tia dropped her hand down Saylor's back in a saucy move, resting her fingers right on the top curve of Saylor's ass. Saylor swayed gently like she was supposed to, and then curled her body around Tia's, her leg locked around Tia's hip before Tia cupped her thigh and held her firmly, walking backward.

Tia glanced toward Jericho who gave her a huge thumbs-up and a grin. Tia's heart hammered hard. They still had two minutes of song to get through, and she wasn't sure she could make it to the end. They hadn't planned on this exact scenario. Everything had been discussed and decided already, but Tia wanted to make it special, have some date in mind to commemorate.

Looking intensely into Saylor's eyes, Tia led the dance. She walked toward Saylor, pushing her back before spinning her around and catching her. She was so distracted that it was hard to concentrate, and when her foot hit Saylor's unexpectedly, she nearly tripped and fell down.

Saylor, however, caught her. Her brows pulled together in confusion and worry. Tia couldn't have that, so she pressed onward. She pulled Saylor tight to her chest, their breasts pushing against each other through the outfits. With a full breath, Tia turned them in a tight circle. On cue, Saylor pushed her away, completely breaking contact.

They had eight beats before they would be back together again, and those eight beats were going to feel like a lifetime. But it did mark the halfway point in the song. Tia risked a glance toward Jericho, just behind Saylor, who grinned like an idiot at Tia and waved.

It was a good thing they were dancing, because Saylor would definitely know something was up if she saw that. Tia nearly missed the next cue, but Saylor was walking back to her, her hips moving saucily as the tempo picked up pace. This was where they switched. Saylor would lead the rest of the song until eighteen seconds before the end when they both took one half of the responsibility.

When they'd discussed the routine, they'd thought it was fitting. Neither one of them led their lives. They worked together to pave their own path as a couple, something they'd spent the last year building together. Tia grabbed hold of Saylor's hands and relaxed into her new position. It was odd to switch halfway through, after years of always doing one or the other, but with Saylor in her arms it was perfect.

Saylor twirled them in three very tight, very quick circles, one right after the other. Tia kept her gaze on Saylor's, locking her point of reference so she wouldn't get dizzy as they moved. It was their first time competing since Portland, and Tia was loving this moment. They hadn't had a lot of time together since Saylor's coaching had gotten underway, but they'd made as much time as they possibly could. Jericho had been essential to that. Controlling her breathing, Tia moved along with Saylor's gentle promptings.

The music lifted to its final few notes. Tia readied herself for the last switch. Saylor turned her back to Tia, and Tia dragged her hands from Saylor's shoulders to her hands and down her thighs to her knees before stepping back and away. Saylor gave her a cute look over her shoulder and then shook her head before grabbing Tia and pulling her back.

Tia had one hand on Saylor's shoulder and one on her waist while Saylor did the same. They moved together, well-practiced and perfect. Tia's stomach wouldn't stop flip-flopping. The song was ending, and she had no other choice. It was now or never.

They held their places as the final note rang through the room. Instead of turning to see Saylor, Tia looked for Jericho. She stopped short when Jericho handed Steven the phone and raced toward them, giddy and excited.

EPILOGUE

"Tia?" Saylor asked, but Tia didn't respond. She wasn't even sure she had the right words for what she was about to say, but she had to find them.

Jericho handed the small box to Tia and then faced Saylor, handing over a similar box. Tia frowned at it. She flicked her gaze from Saylor's hand to Saylor's eyes, her lips parted in surprise as she pointed at the box.

"You didn't," Tia said.

"I did." Saylor laughed, her eyes crinkling in the corners. "So did you, apparently."

"Yeah."

Tia didn't even bother to open the ring box. She wrapped her arms around Saylor's neck and tugged her in hard. Their lips melded together. Tia ran her fingers up into the back of Saylor's hair, tangling her fingers in the locks and pulling hard. Elation hit her first after the surprise wore off. She pulled back laughing and shook her head.

"But who will ask first?" Tia asked.

"Didn't we sort of already figure this out?" Saylor opened her ring box and held it out for Tia to look. A beautiful ruby stone sat in the center, surrounded by a halo of small diamonds.

"Oh my God." Tia's heart thumped. "It's gorgeous."

"So are you."

Tia moved in to kiss Saylor again. "I love you."

"I love you, too."

Saylor moved away on a laugh and took Tia's left hand. She pulled the ring out and slid it on before pulling her hand up to kiss her knuckles. It was hands down one of the most romantic things Tia had ever experienced in her life.

Cheers echoed around the room, blocking out any other noise. Tia was pretty sure her face was going to break from smiling so much. She took the box in her hand and opened it up to show Saylor.

"I told you that night in Portland that I wanted to find out who we could be together." Tia couldn't stop grinning. "I like the life we're weaving. Marry me?"

"I never thought I would get the chance to marry my best friend." Saylor cupped Tia's cheek. "So yeah, I'll marry you."

Tia pulled out the ring, the one that was a thin band of diamonds in a circle. She hadn't wanted it to be gaudy, so that Saylor could still wear it while skating and coaching, but she had wanted the bling. Tia slipped it onto Saylor's finger and kissed her again. "The only thing we didn't talk about is when."

"Yes." Saylor stepped in closer. "When are we getting married?"

"Since neither of us wants a big wedding..." Tia leaned in to whisper into Saylor's ear. "Courthouse. Next week."

"Deal."

Tia kissed Saylor again, hard and quick.

Jericho squealed loudly when they finally turned to face their friends. Steven was clapping hard, giving one loud whoop into the room. The score for their dance was already on the screen, but no one was paying attention. Tia glanced at it, but then faced Saylor again. She'd never thought she'd fall in love after all this time, that there could be someone out there who could make her swoon.

But they'd found each other.

Finally.

Tia laced her fingers with Saylor's and raised them up over their heads. Then unexpectedly, she swung Saylor around and started a quick dance with her on the floor in front of everyone. She had so many things she wanted to tell Saylor, so many compliments and loving words she wanted to rain down on Saylor. But for now, a dance would have to do.

"It's going viral!" Jericho shouted across the room.

Tia's cheeks burned.

Fuck—her life was about to change forever.

"What's going viral?" Saylor asked.

"Jericho apparently live streamed the whole dance." Tia kissed

Saylor's cheek, holding her breath for the reaction. Saylor's nerves could kick in triple time and she could hate the idea, or she would love it. It could help both their careers potentially. "I thought we'd like a video of the dance so we could sort out improvements, but I also just wanted a video of proposing."

"And you said you weren't a romantic." Saylor laughed and kissed Tia's lips. "You do think of everything, don't you?"

"I try to." Tia tightened her grip on Saylor's hand. "You ready for the crowd and congratulations?"

Saylor shook her head. "I'll never be ready for that. But I think I can handle it with you by my side."

"Good." Tia paused their dance. She purposely took a deep breath. "Because it's time."

"I'll follow your lead."

about the author

Adrian J. Smith has been publishing since 2013 but has been writing nearly her entire life. With a focus on women loving women fiction, AJ jumps genres from action-packed police procedurals to the seedier life of vampires and witches to sweet romances with an age gap twist. She loves writing and reading about women in the midst of the ordinariness of life.

AJ currently lives in Cheyenne, WY, although she moves often and has lived all over the United States. She loves to travel to different countries and places. She currently plays the roles of author, wife, and mother to two rambunctious youngsters, occasional handywoman. Connect with her on Facebook, Instagram, or Ream.

my boss's stalker: spoiler it's not me

An unrequited crush. A stalker on the loose. Will she be able to save her boss?

Zoe's boss is a force to be reckoned with. And Zoe has had a crush on Gwen Fudala for the last three years. In a twist of events, Zoe drunkenly ends up on the phone with Gwen while in a compromising position. But it sparks a wildfire that neither can put out.

Still, something isn't right.

Gwen is being stalked. Vowing to let nothing happen to her boss, Zoe winds up tangled in the stalker's game. Unable to see which way is out and loyal to a fault, Zoe sticks by Gwen's side through thick and thin.

Can they navigate a relationship under the watchful eye of a perpetrator?

Or does the stalker have a new target?

My Boss's Stalker is a steamy age gap sapphic romantic suspense. Follow these two as they navigate complicated relationships, fear, and unexpected serenity.

Read it today

shameless expectations

Escaping the past is hard. Living in the present is harder.

Monti Schroeder is on a quest for peace. She has been since the moment she was born, but peace has remained elusive. Living as a nomad, she takes work where she can get it. When her sister calls with a favor for her neurotic boss, Monti agrees for a few extra bucks. What Monti finds when she arrives is a woman just as broken as she is. And no matter what, she can't leave Athena to flounder on her own.

Athena Pruitt has made it through the last twenty-two years with one rule. Avoid everything uncomfortable. Her house has become her prison, and she is desperate for respite. Unable to handle physical touch, she's wary when her personal assistant hires a "special" masseuse who can help. But Monti isn't a typical massage therapist.

Each day, each massage, each moment Monti and Athena spend together they unravel just a little more. With wells of trauma and pain filling both to the brim, just what will happen when their vessels break?

Will Monti find peace? Will Athena learn to live without shame? Will they both mend their brokenness beyond repair?

Shameless Expectations is a book that crosses boundaries to find healing. An age gap, sapphic novel that explores deep trauma and the potential for healing decades later. If you're looking for a book that touches on hope and explores PTSD through the lens of a romance, this is the book for you. Read it today.

Printed in Great Britain
by Amazon